MICHELLE VERNAL LOVES a happy ending. She lives with her husband and their two boys in the beautiful and resilient city of Christchurch, New Zealand. She's partial to a glass of wine, loves a cheese scone, and has recently taken up yoga—a sight to behold indeed. As well as The Promise, Michelle's written eight novels including the sequel to The Promise, The Dancer. This is available to order through Amazon

Michelle also writes a series, The Guesthouse on the Green — the books are all written with humour and warmth and she hopes you enjoy reading them. If you enjoy The Promise then taking the time to say so by leaving a review would be wonderful. A book review is the best present you can give an author. If you'd like to hear about Michelle's new releases, you can subscribe to her Newsletter via her website: www.michellevernalbooks.com

D0058844

Also by Michelle Vernal
The Cooking School on the Bay
Second-hand Jane
Staying at Eleni's
The Traveller's Daughter
Sweet Home Summer
When We Say Goodbye
The Dancer
And...
Introducing: The Guesthouse on the Green
Book 1 - O'Mara's
Book 2 – Moira Lisa Smile
Book 3- What Goes on Tour
Book 4 – Rosi's Regrets
Book 5 – Christmas at O'Mara's
Book 6 - A Wedding at O'Mara's
Book 7 – Maureen's Song
Book 8 – coming soon, The O'Mara's in LaLa Land
Available on Amazon

The
Promise
Michelle Vernal

For Julie

The Beginning

Isabel's heart felt as though it would jump right out of her T-shirt as she crouched down beside the mangled car—later she would realise it was down to adrenalin. Now though she leaned in through the window and managed to cradle the elderly woman's head with her left hand leaving her right hand free to stroke the sparse floss of hair. She was careful to avoid the gaping wound from where the blood ran free. The woman's breath was faint and jagged, while Isabel's came in short puffs. She felt as though she'd fallen into a nightmare.

Less than a minute ago she'd been staring out the passenger window of the two-berth Jucy van she was sharing with her friend and travelling companion, Helena. Her mind absorbing and trying to imprint the beauty of the backdrop the Southern Alps provided against the rushing waters of the turquoise river they were crossing.

New Zealand had lived up to its hype, she'd been thinking, spotting the now familiar sight of a hawk soaring low in search of something to eat. It was amazing how much diverse scenery could be packaged up inside such a small country. In just four weeks, they'd seen volcanos, boiling mud geysers, rainforests, a glacier, fjords, mountains, rivers, and beaches to die for but the highlight for Isabel had been the sperm whale in Kaikoura. It had risen out of the water as though to say hello as she leaned over the railing of the whale watch boat, she'd been blown away by its size and grace. That moment was one she would never forget.

Yes, she was so pleased that she hadn't flown straight home from Australia when her work visa was up like so many of her fellow Brits. They were missing out by not coming here she'd mused as the hawk swooped.

She'd met Helena who hailed from Freyburg in Germany through the pub where she was working in Melbourne's hot spot of St Kilda. It had been while clearing tables and tallying up tips that the two girls had hatched the plan to spend a month traversing New Zealand before heading back to their respective countries. What a trip it had been, she'd thought rubbing her temples which were tender after last night's efforts at Pog Mahone's in Queenstown. Helena might have looked like butter wouldn't melt with her big brown eyes and sensible short haircut but she was naughty, and they'd had a right laugh together. They'd not had a moment's snippiness either, which was quite amazing given their close living quarters.

Imagine Dragons was playing on the stereo and Isabel's fingers had been tapping out the tune to "Radioactive" on her thighs. It was hard to imagine that in just over a fortnight she'd be back home in Southampton. Mind you it would be nice to have Mum fussing over her. She couldn't wait to have a hug and catch up on all the news properly. There was something about Skype that made her mum behave like a giggly teenager. It was the way she twiddled with her hair and her eyes kept flitting to her image in the corner. Her dad said she'd never been any different—a show-off in front of a camera who was born before her time. In the age of the selfie, she'd have been up there with the Kardashian clan.

Ahead, the road was a black twisty snake beneath the bright blue South Island sky. There was such a sense of freedom doing a roadie she'd thought, as Helena handled the camper around the corner with the expertise of someone who'd been driving it for the best part of the last month. She was thinking that one day she'd like to do a trip like this down Route 66 in the States, and that was when Isabel spied the car. It was still too far away to register what had happened, but she understood instantly that it was not good.

As Helena slowed and they drew closer, she saw the little hatchback had folded itself around a telegraph pole. The crumpled bonnet was still steaming like an alien ship that had crash landed.

'Shit!' It had obviously just happened, and Isabel wasn't sure if she'd sworn out loud or if it had been Helena.

Her friend braked and veered the camper over to the grass verge.

Isabel's hand hovered over the handle in readiness for the van to stop. 'You ring 111 and get help. I'll see what I can do.' She jumped down from the camper van, racing over to the car hoping for the best but petrified of what she might find.

Now, here she was, willing this poor old woman to be all right. She should not die like this; it would not be fair! To have lived this long and to die in the arms of a stranger on the side of an open road in the middle of nowhere was not how it should end. Isabel was no doctor, but it was obvious the woman was too old to survive the shock let alone her injuries. She watched as the woman's eyes, weighted down by crepe paper lids, fluttered before drifting and locking on hers. That her irises were the same piercing blue as the sky Isabel had been admiring only moments ago, she vaguely acknowledged as she continued to whisper her soothing platitudes.

The woman was trying to summon the strength to speak, a herculean task given the twisted groaning metal wedged against her chest from the impact.

'Shush now, you'll be fine. Help's on its way.'

'Wanted to go back to the Isle of Wight—Tell Constance I'm sorry. Was wrong—should never have left—too late, too late. Tell her for me—'

Her voice held the traces of an accent, almost forgotten it had lived elsewhere so long, but it was one which Isabel recognised as being from her part of the world. The woman's eyes fought to hold on to hers. She knew that she would not let go until she answered her and so she found herself nodding. 'I will; I'll tell Constance.'

'Promise.' The lips formed the words, but the breath behind them was faint.

'I promise.'

A smile flickered then the light behind those bright blue eyes clouded over, and then she was gone.

PART ONE

Verbena officinalis–Blue vervain/Common vervain

From Celtic/Druid culture and Ancient Roman herbalism–a sacred herb associated with magic and sorcery. Means 'to drive away a stone' and was said to remove urinary stones during those times. Used to purify homes and temples and to ward off the plague. Contribute to love potions and can be used as an aphrodisiac.

Used to ease nerves, stress, and depression.
To clear airways and expel mucous.
To aid in sleeplessness, nervousness, obstructed menstruation,
and weak digestion.

Using the dark green leaf of the plant, wash thoroughly and dry. Place leaves on baking paper and allow to dry naturally in an open space out of direct sunlight for several days. Turn the leaves occasionally ensuring there isn't any moisture present. Once dried out the leaves can be used for tea or placed in bathwater for a soothing effect while bathing. The vervain seeds can also be roasted and eaten.

Isabel

Chapter 1

Isabel looked around the crowded church hall as she waited behind a gentleman with a thick thatch of white hair many a younger man would be envious of. She was in the line for the tea and coffee although having held back from the initial rush it had thinned out considerably. In the middle of the room were three trestle tables bowed with the weight of the plates of food set out upon them. Seats had been lined up against the wall opposite the entrance from the main building, she noted, and all were taken. It was a good turn-out. People were milling about, some with cup and saucer in hand talking in low murmurs, and they were all strangers to her, every single one of them.

'What would you like, dear?' asked a woman who made Isabel think of apple pie for no reason other than she had a round face with rosy cheeks and a kind smile.

'Oh, um, coffee, please.'

'Coffee it is. My goodness that's an unusual hair colour,' she said looking properly at Isabel before lifting the coffee pot.

'Mmm.' The green colour she'd chosen on her last visit to the hairdressers always garnered second glances, which she didn't mind. She wouldn't have opted for such an unusual shade if she did. It was her way of standing out from the crowd. A crowd in which she was never very confident of where she fitted. She was never sure how she should reply though when someone actually commented. To launch into her reasons for wanting to set herself apart a little seemed far too long-winded for such a straightforward comment.

'And how did you know our Ginny then?' the woman asked, pouring the hot liquid into one of the cups set out on the table.

Isabel didn't want to blurt out the truth, so she said the first thing that sprang to mind. 'I only met her the once, but she made an impression on me, and well, I just wanted to come today.'

The woman was only half listening as she weighed up whether to signal to her catering side-kick, who was beavering away in the kitchen, that she needed another pot of coffee. 'That's nice, dear.' She decided she'd get away with what was left in the pot as she handed Isabel her drink. 'I have to say Father Joyce did her proud; it was a lovely service. Help yourself to milk and sugar.' She gestured to her right. 'And don't be shy with the food; it's there to be eaten.' She eyed Isabel's petite frame thinking she was a girl who could do with a sausage roll or two before turning her gaze to the next person in line.

'Thank you.' Isabel moved over to the tray she'd been directed to, and as she finished stirring the milk and a heaped teaspoon of sugar into her coffee, she wondered where she should stand. She spied a quiet corner near the entrance and opting for that weaved her way through the gathering being careful not to get knocked. If anyone was likely to send her cup of coffee flying, it was her!

Isabel hadn't been sure if she should have come today, but she'd been certain it was something she had to do. It might sound clichéd, but she was seeking closure. She hoped that by attending the funeral of Virginia May Havelock, the woman who'd died in her arms not quite a week and a half ago, closure was what she'd get. They didn't mess around in New Zealand, she thought, taking a sip of her drink and trying not to make eye contact with anyone because she did not want to have to get into a conversation on how she'd met Ginny.

The coffee was weak and flavourless the way coffee always is at weddings and funerals, and she wished she'd asked for tea. It was very different to her limited experience of a funeral in the United Kingdom where more often than not the congregation was mostly made up of family and close friends. Today, it looked as though the whole town had turned out.

She would have felt less out of place if she'd had Helena with her, but she'd left for Thailand four days ago. There was no way her friend was going to miss the Full Moon Party on the beaches of Koh Pha onlngan before heading home to Freyburg. One last rave-up before she got back to the serious business of real life. Isabel had planned ongoing with her, but everything had changed the afternoon they'd stumbled across the accident. It was awful, but in some respects, she wished she could rewind to the moment she and Helena had spotted the mangled hatchback. She wished it had been her no-nonsense German friend who'd gotten from the camper van to see if she could help. She would have been able to put the elderly woman's death into perspective and move on.

Isabel, however, couldn't which was why she'd changed her flight and was now heading home via a direct flight to the UK tomorrow instead. There was only one full moon a month, and it had been and gone. Helena had partied hard and staggered on board her Lufthansa flight the following day, texting Isabel to tell her she'd missed a fantastic night. She'd been unable to understand why her British friend wouldn't leave New Zealand before the funeral. 'You don't owe the woman anything. She was a stranger.'

'But I was there when she *died*, Helena. I saw the life go from her eyes. And I made her a promise before it did.'

'Yes, yes, it is very sad, but she was not young, and there was no one else involved, Isabel. People live, and people die, and at least she did not die alone. As for this promise, she is dead—like I said you owe her nothing,' she'd said in her clipped tones.

The thing Helena didn't get was that from the moment the police officer who'd arrived at the scene with an entourage of an ambulance and a fire truck told Isabel the woman's name was Ginny she'd become a real person. She was ninety-one according to her driver's license which had expired five years earlier, he'd gone on to tell her with a sage shake of his head. Ginny was a person who'd had a life and a family and who, thanks to a moment's misjudgment, was now gone. She was also a person to whom Isabel had made a promise. It was that promise that was haunting her no matter what Helena said.

She'd continued to tell her to put it behind her, as she set about making the most of her last couple of days in Christchurch. But Isabel couldn't. Instead of heading out to admire the street art the city was becoming renowned for post-earthquake, her hungry eyes had scanned the paper the hostel supplied in the foyer each morning for the next few days, until the obituary appeared. She'd torn it carefully from the page and had read it so many times over the last week that she knew it by heart.

HAVELOCK Virginia May (nee Moore)

In loving memory of Ginny who passed away suddenly on Wednesday afternoon aged 91 years. Dearly beloved wife of the late Neville, much-loved mother and mother-in-law of Edward Henry and Olga Havelock. Cherished grandmother of Tatiana. The family would like to acknowledge the support of Father Christopher Joyce of St Aidan's, Timaru who looked after their beloved Ginny in life and in death.

A celebration of Ginny's life will be held at St Aidan's, 160 Mountain View Road, Timaru on Saturday 15 April at 11 am. In lieu of flowers donations to St Vincent de Paul Society, Timaru may be placed in the church foyer.

Isabel's hand shook as she raised her cup to her mouth and a little coffee slopped over the side and down her front. She glanced down at her plain black shift dress bought specially for the occasion. The wearing of black was as foreign to her as was attending the funeral of someone she didn't know. She was a girl who loved colour, and the brighter the better. That was another anomaly about a Kiwi funeral, she thought, wiping off the liquid. Not everyone was dressed in formal black. Satisfied no one would see her mishap she looked up and spied Father Joyce making his way toward her. He wore the white robes of an Anglican priest, and despite his attire swamping him like a tent, it did little to hide his rotund frame. His wispy grey hair floated up with each purposeful step, and he had a serviette in one hand, cakes, a savoury and club sandwiches on a plate in the other.

'The parish ladies have outdone themselves,' he declared upon reaching her. The smear of cream on the top of his lip gave away the fact he was on second helpings. 'It's a spread our Ginny would have approved of. Have you partaken, my dear?'

'Erm no, I haven't had much of an appetite of late.' It was true, Isabel had not been sleeping well and not just because of the comings and goings at all hours in the hostel dormitory. She'd been running on empty for the past week.

Father Joyce nibbled on his club sandwich, declaring ham and egg to be his favourite combination and that she really should try them.

Isabel smiled politely as he dabbed at his mouth with the serviette. She was pleased to see the cream was gone because she'd been afraid her gaze would have kept slipping toward it the same way it would a large pimple or such like. The more you tried to pretend it wasn't there the more you stared.

'I don't believe we've met. In fact, I know we haven't met. I'd remember meeting a young lady with green hair.' He chortled. 'Are you a relative of Ginny's?'

'No.' Isabel's hand had automatically moved to her hair which she tucked behind her ears, a nervous habit. She hesitated and then decided to come clean. She couldn't tell a lie to a man of the cloth not even the teensiest of white ones. 'I'm Isabel Stark. I'm here on holiday from the UK, and my friend and I came across Ginny's accident just after it happened. I tried to help—but it was too late for that, so I held her head in my hands while my friend rang for help. I tried to soothe her before she uh—' Her voice caught in her throat as it closed over at the reliving of such a raw memory.

'Oh my, my.' Father Joyce reached out and rested his hand on Isabel's upper arm. From anyone else she'd only just met she would have flinched away from the gesture finding it intrusive, but from this man with his kindly buttonlike eyes, it was comforting. 'To witness the passing of a person in the circumstances such as you did must be terribly traumatic. But how very wonderful you were there, Isabel, for Ginny, to ease her passing.'

Isabel bit her bottom lip; she hadn't thought about it like that. She hoped her being there had helped in some small way.

'She'll be greatly missed you know. She was a force of nature our Ginny. You'd never have believed she was over ninety. I don't think she believed she was over ninety!' He gave a little snort. 'She was always happy to bake for the new mum's in the church or to pop a meal around if she heard someone was poorly. She kept herself busy too by volunteering in our local St Vincent de Paul second-hand shop here in Timaru.'

'She sounds like she was a wonderful person, and your eulogy was lovely by the way.'

His eyes twinkled. 'Ah. Now you see what I didn't say was Ginny was a woman who in later years, did not suffer fools gladly, and whose tongue could be more acerbic than a sharp lemon vinaigrette at times. But you don't say those sorts of things now do you. None of us is perfect, and she was no exception, but she was also incredibly generous of spirit with a heart as wide as the Clutha River, where I hail from.'

Isabel smiled. 'She was human then.'

'She was human, and we all have our foibles.'

'You said you met twenty years ago when you spoke about your friendship with her during the service.'

'Oh yes, it was when she brought a cake, carrot cake it was with proper cream cheese icing, to the manse not long after I took over the parish after Father Samuel retired. She'd clashed once or twice with him, something to do with the flower arrangements, I think. I never did get the full story, but she was hoping to get off on a better foot with myself. Father Samuel didn't have a sweet tooth like me.' He patted his girth, resplendent over the purple belt. 'Carrot cake with cream cheese icing is the fastest way to my heart.' His laugh was low and rumbly like an engine starting, and Isabel couldn't help but smile.

'We two sat together and put the world to rights over a cup of tea and many a generous slice of her cake over the years. I know she missed her son, Teddy, dreadfully I'm afraid; he was her only child which made it worse. I know she would have liked more, but it wasn't meant to be. I used to tell her, "Your children are only on loan, Ginny, they're not yours to keep." He spoke very well today, Teddy I mean, don't you think?' He cast his gaze around the room as though seeking him out.

'Yes, he did. I liked the story he told about the height of his mum's pavlovas and how she lost the title of being a ten-pound pom.'

'Having earned the respect of the local farmers' wives by winning the Biggest Pavlova competition at the annual country fete,' Father Joyce finished for her, chuckling at the tale before snaffling his slice of banana cake.

Teddy's hair, Isabel had noticed as he spoke, still whispered of the ginger, sandy colour of his youth, despite his years. The only clue to his age was in the wrinkles fanning out around his hazel eyes when he smiled and the way his hair had receded ever so slightly. There was a greying too around his temples. He was a tall man but lean and obviously kept himself in shape. There was a gentleness to his features, and he looked she decided, her inventory not quite done, like a nice man.

His suit even to Isabel's untrained eye was obviously tailor-made. It was clear by his confident manner that he was used to public speaking and he'd peppered his eulogy about his mother in a way that had managed to be humorous and eloquent at the same time. Isabel had been rather taken aback at the sight of his wife as he sat back down though. She'd leaned in and kissed him on the cheek, a glamorous vision who was at least half his age. A young girl sat by her side.

Isabel had passed by them as the congregation trailed from the church into the hall and the family of three stood at the entrance of the hall shaking hands, accepting condolences, and thanking people for coming. She hadn't the heart to say who she was and how she'd encountered Ginny and so she'd simply said, 'I'm sorry for your loss,' to which she'd received a sad smile and nod.

'I'll miss Ginny's pavlova almost as much as her carrot cake, and I think it's always a good thing to laugh at a funeral. A person's life should be celebrated.' Father Joyce said, finishing his sarnie. 'Yes really, rather good,' he mumbled, despite his mouthful.

Isabel was unsure if he meant laughing at a funeral, or if he was referring to the sandwich once more. She saw his eyes flit in the direction of the trestle tables where the plates of food were slowly being depleted.

'I rather fancy one of those ginger gems before they all go,' he said.

'Is a ginger gem like gingerbread?'

'They're a little crustier on the outside than gingerbread, but they melt in your mouth on the inside.'

'Sounds rather delicious.'

'Are you tempted, my dear, because if you do, then I can. Raewyn Morris, she's my secretary, has been keeping an eye on the afternoon tea proceedings, and she'll slap my hand if she sees me going back for thirds. I'm supposed to be trying to lose a few pounds.'

'I am partial to all things ginger.'

'Oh go on, Isabel,' he urged conspiratorially.

There was nothing else for it. Who was she to deprive Father Joyce of a ginger gem? Isabel returned after nearly sending the contents of her plate flying, thanks to the stray foot she tripped over on her journey back from the trestle table. Thankfully she was righted by the owner of the stray foot's helpful hand and returned with the two ginger treats intact.

'You almost lost those,' Father Joyce said in a tone that implied that would have been sacrilege indeed as he helped himself to one of the gems.

'I'm a proper klutz—always have been,' Isabel said as he looked furtively over at an angular woman standing near the cheese roll-ups. Her hawkish gaze was elsewhere.

In two bites his little cake was gone. Father Joyce wiped the crumbs from his robe and Isabel listened to him describe the woman whose gaze she had held until she passed while she ate hers at a much slower pace than the priest.

Chapter 2

'I rather think Ginny looked upon me as a stand-in for Teddy given we're of a similar age. He's a mover and shaker in the world of finance; does something or other in banking and lives in Hong Kong. I must say he strikes me as one of those men for whom retirement is a foreign word.'

It was a bit pot calling the kettle black Isabel thought, given the priest must be somewhere in his early seventies himself.

'His wife, Olga, is Russian, and they have a daughter, Tatiana, who's about to turn fourteen. I had the most heart-warming chat with her before the service; she's a charming young lady you know. A credit to her parents.' Father Joyce looked around making sure none of his parishioners were within earshot, but crowd in the hall as the afternoon wore on was slowly thinning. Nevertheless, he leaned in closer to Isabel and said, 'Between you and me it was a cause of consternation for Ginny when her son married Olga. That he should marry a woman he not only met on the Internet but who was half his age and so late in life too. Well,' he tapped the side of his nose, 'let's just say Ginny had rather a lot to say on the subject. I told her she should be happy he'd found love. Not everybody gets a second shot at it.'

'Had he been married before then?'

'Yes, his first wife passed away from a prolonged illness ten years after they were married and there were no children. He, as I understand it, threw himself wholeheartedly into his finance career and did not come to terms with his grief for a long time. On the occasions I've met with him over the years when he's been home visiting his mother, it was clear to me he's devoted to Olga and Tatiana. They both gave him a new lease of life.'

'She's very beautiful,' Isabel said spotting Olga, a willowy brunette, across the room in conversation with a woman who looked very staid by comparison in her tunic top and leggings.

'Yes, she's a beauty all right. That didn't impress Ginny though. She felt that at his age he should be retiring and spending his time on a golf course, a golf course preferably somewhere in the South Island of New Zealand near his mother. She didn't approve of him embarking on fatherhood along with the trials and tribulations of keeping a younger woman happy when he was of pensionable age. She was heard to mutter more than once, "Who did he think he was—Donald Trump?"'

Isabel suppressed a smile. Melania and Donald *had* sprung to mind when she initially saw them together.

Father Joyce finished his remaining savoury before continuing. 'Do you know Ginny remarked to me the last time Teddy, Olga, and Tatiana had been to visit that she didn't fancy Tatiana's chances of becoming the prima ballerina her mother seemed to have her heart set on. In her words, the poor sod who had to perform the pas de deux with her granddaughter would surely be left bowlegged were he to attempt a lift! A little unkind but humourous nonetheless, and I knew that at the crux of the comment was a wish for what was best for Tatiana.'

Isabel looked around until she spied Teddy. By his side was a solidly built young girl standing with the awkwardness of an adolescent who doesn't yet know where she fits in the world. Isabel knew that feeling well, except she no longer had the umbrella of her teenage years to hide under. The young teen standing next to her father looked like she'd be much more at home in a pair of jeans than the frilly ensemble she was currently decked out in. Isabel watched her as she tugged at her skirt with obvious irritation. It was hard to imagine the poor girl in a tutu.

'Ginny felt her daughter-in-law was trying to relive her childhood dreams through her daughter and that it was ludicrous to push a style of dance on poor Tatiana that required one to be sylphlike. She wondered whether perhaps with her granddaughter's sturdy frame, she might be better suited to women's rugby. "The New Zealand Black Ferns were doing ever so well on the world stage," she was fond of saying. Ginny loved her rugby; she felt it made her a proper Kiwi when she wrapped her All Blacks scarf around her neck and cheered the boys on.' Father Joyce looked off into the distance lost in his memories for a moment before lamenting, 'Funny that she should feel the need to be a 'proper' Kiwi given she spent more of her life here than in your part of the world.'

'Do you know where she hailed from in the UK?' Isabel recalled the traces of an accent, the slight rolling of an 'r' dropping of an 'h' she'd picked up as Ginny spoke her last words.

'Southampton originally.'

Goosebumps prickled her arms; she wasn't surprised she was from the South East she had managed to say that she wanted to go back to the Isle of Wight, but the same city as her? The coincidence sent a shiver coursing through her. 'I'm from Southampton.'

Father Joyce sensing he had a captive audience was only too happy to continue with his musings. 'Well now isn't that a coincidence, and it was definitely Southampton because I remember she mentioned it in conjunction with her being from the city from which the Titanic sailed forth. She didn't talk much about her life before coming to New Zealand. Although we got onto the subject of the war one day and she did remark that she'd gone to live in the town of Ryde on the Isle of Wight at the outbreak of World War Two. Ginny said it was deemed safer than the port city, and she married a local lad while she was there on the island.'

If Isabel had had antennae, they would have been quivering. Here was the connection Ginny had to the Isle of Wight.

'She never told me his name, but she did tell me she was pregnant when the news arrived that her husband had been killed in battle. The poor fellow, like so many other young men of the time, didn't get to celebrate his twentieth birthday or the birth of his son.' He shook his head, and the wisps of hair floated up briefly before settling back down on his scalp with a silent sigh. 'After his death, she felt she couldn't stay on the island with all its ghosts of what might have been, so she returned to the mainland with her son. It was there she met Neville who adopted Teddy. He was still a wee babe, and the three of them immigrated to New Zealand in the mid-forties along with the rest of the ten-pound poms wanting to put the war years behind them.

'They bought land upon arriving here and farmed it until Neville died. It wasn't an easy life she was always quick to mention, but it was a good life. She tried to run the farm on her own for a while after Neville passed but it was too much, and she sold up. I think it always saddened her that Teddy didn't come home and step in where his father left off, but he had a different path to follow. She'd downsized and moved into Timaru shortly before I arrived in town.'

Isabel seized the break in his story. 'Father Joyce, just before she passed she asked me to promise her something.'

He peered closely at her. 'I can see whatever it was she asked of you is weighing heavily on your mind, Isabel.' Then he did a little jiggle ridding himself of the crumbs that had settled on the front of his robe before turning his attention back to Isabel. 'You're welcome to share that promise with me if you think it might help.'

'She asked me to find someone called Constance and to tell her she was sorry—she should never have left. Those were pretty much her words, and the only clue she gave me was that she'd wanted to go back to the Isle of Wight herself to say sorry.'

'Now that is interesting,' he rubbed his chin, 'because there *was* something on Ginny's mind of late. She wouldn't allude to what it was other than to say she needed to go back to Ryde—there was someone she had to see. She must have been referring to this Constance she mentioned to you. She wouldn't tell me why she wanted to go back, but there was a desperation about her this last while which I can only put down to her age and the realisation that nobody lives forever. In fact, the day she died a suitcase was in the car as well as a return ticket to the United Kingdom. Did you know that?'

Isabel shook her head; she'd been in too much shock at the time to pay attention to anything other than Ginny.

'No, why would you? Teddy, told me he was most perturbed by this as he knew nothing of her plans.' Father Joyce laid a hand on her arm once more. 'Isabel, Ginny, for all her endearing attributes was also a woman with a stubborn streak. I believe it was this unwillingness of hers to listen to those who knew better that saw her continue to get behind the wheel. This was despite being told she was endangering others each time she did so. It's a blessing that nobody else was hurt in the accident as she wouldn't have been able to rest in peace had there been.' He nodded and raised his hand in a wave to signal goodbye to one of his parishioners who'd paused as though wanting to interrupt but had thought better of it. 'Mrs Mercer, a gossip of the highest order if you give her an in,' he mumbled out the corner of his mouth.

Isabel watched in amusement as the older woman, in a pair of black trousers that fitted a tad too snuggly—and would cause concern were she to attempt to bend over—scuttled over to join a small party also making their way toward the exit.

'You do realise you're in no way obligated to fulfill your promise to Ginny, don't you, my dear?'

Her attention turned to Father Joyce once more.

'You did more than enough by being there and offering comfort in her final moments, and it was very good of you to come today.'

'It wasn't, really; I think my reasons might be rather selfish. I was hoping by coming that I'd be able to move forward from what happened that afternoon. I haven't been sleeping well, you see.'

'Oh, dear, dear. Nightmares?'

'No, I thought I might have bad dreams, but I feel like I haven't been dreaming at all. It just takes me forever to drift off because my mind keeps replaying Ginny's last moments over and over.'

He patted her arm. 'It will get better. It might just take a bit of time. Do you think coming to the funeral today has helped?'

'I don't know, Father Joyce. I really just don't know.'

Chapter 3

Isabel poked her head out from under the duvet like a turtle stretching its neck from its shell before rubbing at her eyes; they felt puffy and gritty. It was a sure sign she'd slept heavily, oh, and the spot behind her knees was driving her mad. She reached down and scratched it, knowing it would make it worse but unable to resist the burning itch any longer. It had taken her forever to get to sleep—something she was getting used to, but it didn't help that her body clock was up the wop, and it had felt like the bed was rolling thanks to the thirty-plus hours flight home she'd stepped off yesterday.

She looked blankly around at her surroundings. Unfamiliar plush claret curtains with gold tassel tie-backs, and a faux Louis-whatever-he-was chair in the corner of the room with yesterday's clothes draped over its seat. The striped wine and gold duvet she was wrapped up in was not one she'd seen before either.

It took a few seconds for her to register that she was home in her old bedroom. Gone was the pink everything and white princess dressing table that had lived here for as long as she could remember. It was the framed artsy black and white print of Princess Diana on the wall opposite her that gave the game away. Her mum's attempt to make her only child's room look like the guest room she'd hankered after most of her married life. The two-up two-down where Isabel had grown up did not allow for an attic extension even if the finances had, so her daughter's empty bedroom was the next best thing! Her parents had worked hard all their married life, and she'd never gone without a thing, but her mum had, and a guest room at long last was the silver lining in Isabel packing her bags and leaving home.

Barbara Stark or Babs as she liked to be called, was a staunch royalist. Isabel had only been five when the Princess of Wales had died, but she could still recall the histrionics and her mum's insistence on wearing black for the best part of a month. These days she was a regular commentator on Kate

Middleton's latest look, and the birth of George and Charlotte had been akin to the arrival of her own grandchildren. The breaking news of a new baby had warranted an urgent, middle of the night in Australia, Skype call. For her part, Isabel was grateful to the young royals. She'd sent a silent thank you to Wills and Kate for taking the pressure off her to settle down and provide her parents with a grandchild as she flitted around the other side of the world in search of adventure.

Well, she was back now, and she'd told Mum the print had to go as she dropped her pack on the bedroom floor yesterday afternoon. Her mum's face took on the pained expression that Isabel knew meant she'd already lost the argument. She'd then insisted it was a well-known fact that to remove a photograph of royalty from one's home was bad luck—especially a late member. Oh yes, Babs had stated knowingly, patting her freshly blow-waved hair the trip to Heathrow Airport had warranted, to do so would invoke the ancient curse of the House of Windsor.

She'd gone on to play the, *and you had left home* card saying that she didn't need to invoke any curses given her age. Isabel had eyed her suspiciously. She was fairly sure she'd made the whole curse thing up, and her mum was only nudging sixty. Nevertheless, she dropped her case on the grounds of knowing it was pointless to protest. Hence the beaming Diana that was here to greet her the moment she opened her eyes.

She yawned and stretched not knowing what time it was, but the dull light peeping through the gap where the drapes didn't quite meet signalled morning had broken. She heard the drone of the radio in the kitchen beneath and guessed her mum would be going about her morning routines before heading off to her part-time job at the Asda Superstore. If that were the case, then it would be around 8 am which meant she'd slept for twelve hours solid. She wondered if her dad had already left for work. The temptation to snuggle back down to sleep tugged at her, but she fought off the urge and pulled herself upright. The sooner she got herself back into a routine the better. Her hand fluttered up to her hair. Yes, as she'd suspected her curls were matted. She probably looked, given its current colour, as though she had a laurel wreath atop her head.

'I bet you never woke up looking anything but gorgeous, and I guarantee you brushed your teeth before bed each night,' she muttered to Princess Di.

She was normally diligent on that front, but from the sour taste in mouth, she guessed she'd missed last night's session. Jet lag, that was her excuse, and she was running with it. That was when the events of that afternoon on the back roads of New Zealand's South Island came flooding back, as they had each morning since it had happened. She whimpered and dived back down under the duvet cover pulling it tightly over her head. How she wished it had all been one of those horribly real nightmares; she wished she *was* a turtle with a hard shell who could hide away forever inside it.

Her breath was hot under the weight of the bedding as she wondered again why it was her that had been the one to make Ginny Havelock a promise she wasn't sure she could keep. It was a question she'd asked herself on the plane. What had kept nagging at her as the hours between meals ticked away in economy class was Ginny's connection with the Isle of Wight—an island that was now just a ferry ride away. Her thoughts were interrupted by a tapping on her door. It was followed by, 'Yoo-hoo, Dizzy Izzy. Are you awake?'

'No. Go away, Mum, I'm still asleep.' Isabel heard a snuffling, and a whimper as the door creaked open. 'Don't let that bloody dog near me. I'm not in the mood for fending him off.'

'Don't shout, Isabel. You know he doesn't like it. Come on, out you go, Prince Charles,' Babs cooed.

She heard her mum step into the room, and even under her covers could smell the floral notes of her favourite perfume, Yves Saint Laurent's Paris. Isabel's dad, Gary or Gaz as he was called more often than not, bought his wife a bottle each birthday. With the knowledge her supply would be topped up annually, she sprayed each morning liberally. A split second later a dragging, scuffling commotion sounded, signalling Babs was dragging her beloved corgi from the room. The door clicked shut, and a mournful howling erupted from the hallway.

'He's just happy to have you home,' Babs said.

By the proximity of her voice, Isabel knew she was standing beside the bed. At least, Prince Charles had been banished. Life was bad enough without that bloody corgi making advances. From the time he was a pup he'd decided the one true love of his life was Isabel.

'Come on now, Izzy. Out from under there. I've got to head off in a minute, but I wanted to see my girl before I go.' There was a gentle tug on the duvet. 'I've brought you a cup of tea. I bet you've missed good old English tea. I made it extra strong and put sugar in it; there's a plate of marmalade toast too. Dad's already left for work, but he'll skip footie practice tonight to be home for a proper family tea. Your favourite, pie, proper mushy peas, and mash.'

Isabel emerged from the duvet like a crumpled butterfly from its cocoon and pulled herself up to a sitting position. She'd been astounded when her dad, a self-declared couch potato and borderline obsessive Saints fan, had taken up football once more after a forty-year hiatus.

'You'll have to do something about that hair if you want to find yourself a job, young lady.' Babs eyed her daughter's hair with a frown and Isabel knew she was envisaging her with the softly waving brown locks of the Duchess of Cambridge. 'That colour reminds me of flipping mushy peas. It's the worst I've seen you with yet. Whatever possessed you to dye your hair green?'

'I like it. It's different.'

'There's nothing wrong with being normal, you know, Isabel.'

'How's Dad getting on with his late-life crisis?' Distraction was the best course of action, Isabel decided, and personally, she *loved* mushy peas.

It worked. Bab's sigh was as weighty as Isabel's duvet as she shoved her hands into the pockets of her Asda-issue black pants. 'Honestly, Izzy. That man of mine—your father. He's doing my head in and all. Truly, as much as I love him, he comes home every Saturday afternoon moaning and groaning. He's got a perpetual limp because he's pulled his ruddy groin muscle or some other body part he'd forgotten he had. I tell you what though, I'm not going to rub him down with that smelly wintergreen anti-inflammatory stuff anymore. I've had it. I'm officially on strike. He can do it himself from now on, and I hope he forgets to wash his hands before he piddles.'

'Mum!' Isabel snorted.

'Well, I mean come on, he does nothing physical for nearly fifteen years aside from lifting a few boxes at work and then decides to go and run around a muddy field, kicking a ball with a bunch of other old farts who all think they're teenagers. It wouldn't have crossed his mind to go and do Latin

American dance classes with his wife if he felt the sudden urge to get off the settee now, would it?'

'Ah, Mum, you know he's got two left feet when it comes to dancing, and it could be worse. He could've taken up with a nubile twenty-something or gone out and put a Porsche on credit.'

'He'd never get out of a Porsche. Too low to the ground and the twenty-something wouldn't stick around for long, not with his recurring groin injury,' Babs muttered.

'Too much information.' Isabel reached over and took a sip from the mug. The tea was strong and sweet, just how she liked it.

Her mum's eyes narrowed as they focussed on the patch of skin on the inside of Isabel's elbow. 'Your eczema's playing up I see. I hope you haven't been scratching at it. You know it only makes it worse.'

'I know, and I haven't,' Isabel lied.

'I have a pot of your cream still in the bathroom.' She got up and resembling the Green Lantern in her uniform whirled out of the room, reappearing a second later brandishing a tub of ointment. 'There you go pop that on it, nice and thick. Now, I'd better make tracks. I'll be home around two-ish, and I expect to find you showered and dressed with some good news to report.'

'Ah come on, Mum, I only got back yesterday. You can't expect me to go to the job centre.'

'Oh yes, I can. You had all of yesterday afternoon and last night to recuperate. There's no time like the present, Isabel. Strike while the iron is hot.' Her mum's gaze flickered to the tea and toast as she tapped her foot.

'Thanks for breakfast.'

'I'm glad you didn't leave your manners behind in Australia.' She hovered in the doorway for a moment. 'Ah, but it's lovely to have you home, Izzy. We've missed you, and as for Prince Charles, well, he's been a lost lamb this last year.' The bedroom door clicked shut behind her.

Lost lamb! What a load of rubbish. Isabel snorted silently. She'd seen him cavorting with his bone in the background when her mum and dad Skyped. She glanced at her tea and the plate of buttery marmalade toast; it was lovely to be home though. It had been forever since someone had brought her breakfast in bed. She opened the pot her mum had just handed to her and rubbed the greasy salve into the crook of her arm. The relief from the burning itch was instant, and she reached under the covers to deal with the patch behind her knees. It wouldn't clear eczema up, but it would stop her scratching for a bit and running the risk of getting it infected.

She put the pot back on the bedside table and rested her head back against the pillows. She'd get up in a little while. As for the job centre, she shuddered; she couldn't face it. Babs had never sat on a plane longer than the two-and-a-half hours it took to get from London to Benidorm. She'd give herself today to get over the seemingly endless flight home; she decided to add the job centre to her mental "I'll do it tomorrow" list.

Chapter 4

I sabel pulled her curtains back and looked at the overcast sky outside. She'd been home two days, and it had been gloomy both of them. Might as well go for the trifecta, she thought. It didn't matter, anyway. It wasn't like she had plans for the beach or anything. No, today was the day she would find gainful employment. She'd visited the job centre yesterday and hadn't had any luck. Admittedly, she'd turned her nose up at the McDonald's job, but beggars couldn't be choosers, and she did enjoy the odd Big Mac she told herself, trying to put a positive spin on things. If the job was still going, she'd put herself forward for it.

She set about making her bed, and as she puffed the pillows to avoid another live demonstration on pillow puffing from Babs, she recalled how she'd bumped into her old friend, Charity, yesterday. She'd been feeling flat and deflated as she left the grim, box-like building with its myriad windows when Charity had called out to her. Catching her up on a pair of heels that beggared belief, she'd hugged Isabel and said she'd heard she was back in town and had meant to text. The irony of the flippancy of a text didn't escape Isabel; there was a time she and Charity had been inseparable.

Charity was on her lunch break, and after Isabel had admired the sparkly diamond on her friend's finger, they'd had a somewhat awkward catch up over coffee. Now that she thought about it, Charity had monopolised the conversation. She'd been so full of the news of her engagement to a chap Isabel vaguely recalled her dragging her home from the pub the night of her going away do, to bother asking Isabel what her plans were now she was back. Still, Isabel figured it was fairly obvious she didn't have a lot going on given she'd spotted her leaving the job centre. She wished she hadn't agreed to meeting up for lunch today with her though. She'd never been very good at saying no. Charity hadn't come up for air long enough to ask if she'd seen

Ashley or Connor since she got back, but Isabel didn't fancy her chances of avoiding that particular topic of conversation a second time.

The thing with having been away for a reasonable spell was that life carried on with the same day-to-day rhythms for those at home. She'd held off contacting any of her old crowd—she didn't know where she slotted in with them anymore since she and Connor had split up. Besides which, they were all busy doing the same stuff they'd been doing before she left for Australia from what she'd seen on Instagram. She didn't feel like the same girl she'd been a year ago and thank God for that because she'd been a bit of a mess.

Isabel couldn't just pick up where she'd left off; she'd changed. Oh, she knew she should make an effort and organise a night out, and it would be good to have time out from her dad's endless supply of Shrek and Kermit jokes where her hair was concerned. It wasn't as if he was in a position to pass remark on her hair anyway, not with the state of his geriatric boy band do. The problem was she didn't have the cash to splash on a night on the town.

The thing was with everything going around in her head the way it was at the moment she couldn't face trying to be the life and soul of the party. Yes, she was over Connor—the time away had seen to that, and it would be satisfying to prove to her old crowd that she'd moved on. That didn't mean she was ready to see Connor and Ashley because while her heart might have mended, they'd shattered her trust and humiliated her. She doubted she'd ever forget what had happened.

Isabel chewed her bottom lip feeling a pang for the wide, blue skies of Australia; she'd had such a good time putting her last few months in Southampton behind her and tripping about this last year. It had been marvellous to push stop on her real life, bundle all the crappy Connor and Ashley stuff up and shove it behind her as she flitted off to the sunshine. The feeling of liberation, of not having to make any serious decisions about anything other than where she'd like to swan off to next was one she'd relished.

For one whole blissful year, Isabel had not had to question what she wanted to do with her life or where she wanted to be. The unsettling feeling of not quite fitting into the hole she found herself in had vanished. It had returned with a vengeance now though as had the big grey cloud that had settled on top of her since making her promise to Ginny.

A hot shower would fix her, she told herself, tripping over Prince Charles who'd taken up residence on the floor outside her bedroom door. He was nonplussed as she lay sprawled in front of him on the carpet and despite her expletives, his tail thumped at the sight of her. He roused his head from where it had been resting on his front paws, and his tongue lolled forth in anticipation of a tummy scratch or at the very least a pat from the light of his life. 'You don't deserve it; I could have broken my flipping neck.' Isabel stated as she gave him a fuss. His little woof signalled he was listening, but if he was true to form, he'd pay no attention whatsoever to what she'd just said.

'Right, I've got to have a shower. I can't be tickling you on the tum all day.' She got to her feet ignoring his plaintive whine as she headed into the bathroom. A few moments later she stood under the hot water. It stung the raw patches of skin, but it was having a restorative effect on her mind. As the minutes ticked by, she was glad her dad was at work otherwise he'd be hammering on the door. Her lengthy showers had always managed to rouse him from the couch. He'd launch himself up the stairs at a surprising rate of knots for someone who liked to profess his golden years were within his line of sight. As such he'd tell Isabel, he should be able to enjoy them without his only child giving him grief.

Watching the water swirl down the drain, Isabel pondered her lot. She'd hoped that after her year of picking up work here and there in Australia, she might be closer to figuring out what she wanted to do with herself once she got home, but she wasn't. And, now here she was trying to find work that was simply a means to an end once more. She felt as though she'd gone around in a great big circle as she squeezed a dollop of shampoo into her palm, lathering it up in her hair.

She was officially over a quarter of a century, twenty-six years old and life was bloody complicated. When she was little, everything had seemed so simple. 'I'm going to be a singer when I grow up, Mum,' she'd state, and hairbrush in hand, pretending it was a microphone, she'd sing along to the hit parade. Back then she'd believed that anything was possible. She'd had so much confidence as a child, but as she'd entered her teens, she'd developed an awkwardness and shyness that had stomped all over that belief in her abilities.

Oh, she could sing, she knew that, but it wasn't enough, not in this digital age where anybody could be famous so long as they had the self-assurance to put themselves out there. Isabel did not like to be centre stage; she liked to fly under the radar. Singing anywhere other than the shower was not for her. Her form mistress at school had summed her up in her leaving report.

Isabel is a quiet girl, with a very sensitive nature. She shows promise but needs to learn to put herself forward.

It was a nice way of saying she was one of life's worriers and a wallflower. Her response to this had been to colour her hair. It was the most startling thing about her. The colours she chose were a point of difference that allowed her to stand out in her quiet way.

She began rinsing the shampoo out squeezing her eyes shut to avoid the suds. The problem was she'd never had a Plan B; she was going to be a famous singer, and that was that. Thus she'd spent her working career to date picking up a series of jobs, which did not offer much in the way of prospects.

It wasn't just knowing what direction she wanted to take that had her feeling edgy though. It was that bloody promise to Ginny; she couldn't focus on anything else. She knew she needed to find work. That was today's plan after all, but shouldn't she at least try to find this Constance woman? Didn't she owe Ginny that much at least?

She wiped the water from her eyes and turned the handle around to "off". She had a basket full of dirty laundry to tackle before she went anywhere and stepping out of the shower, she dried herself off. She'd spruce herself up later because first things first, she thought slipping into slouch pants and a sweatshirt she'd make the most of the house being empty and put her favourite Andrea Bocelli CD on.

That Isabel loved opera was an enigma to her parents who had every record Bruce Springsteen ever made. She liked other more dancey stuff too, but there was something magical about opera. The power in the singers' voices never ceased to amaze her. Andrea was her favourite and had been since she was seventeen when she'd seen a Christmas concert special he'd recorded. Being a huge fan was not something she owned up to often, and her dad liked to tease her by following her about the house pretending to be Pavarotti.

Both parents used to drive her mad on a Friday night when under the influence of lager and Babycham they'd dig out their old Springsteen albums. Dad would don a red bandana and an air guitar while Mum would pretend to be Patti Scialfa. As a teenager, to watch her parents carry on had been cringeworthy, but now the memory made her smile and grinning she hit "play".

"Time to Say Goodbye" filled the house as she set about making herself some breakfast.

The morning had disappeared by the time Isabel had sorted out her washing and, sitting down at the kitchen table, she opened her laptop. It wouldn't do any harm to check out the ferry timetable and fares to the Isle of Wight; she'd tidy herself up in a minute.

'Ooh, my feet are bloody well killing me. What are you looking at, Izzy?' Babs Stark asked from the kitchen doorway. She was knackered having done the weekly shop at the end of her shift, and she was eager for the good news that her daughter had, in the ensuing hours since she'd left for work, found herself gainful employment. She dumped the two bags full of groceries down on the floor and shooed the hopeful Prince Charles away. 'Get your nose out; there's nothing in there for you. He'd live on fillet steak that one, given half a chance.'

At the sound of her mum's voice, Isabel jumped and snapped shut the cover of her laptop. She hadn't heard the front door. She swung around to face the Southampton Inquisition she knew she was in for.

'What are you up to, Isabel Stark?' Her mum's eyes narrowed. 'Gemma from work says she can always tell if her fella's looking at things he shouldn't be on the computer by the way he slams the lid shut whenever she walks in the room.' She nudged the persistent Prince Charles away from the shopping bags with her foot. 'At least I don't have to worry about your father getting up to no good; he doesn't even know how to switch the bloody thing on.' She gazed hard at her daughter. 'You've got a guilty look on your face. Is it boy trouble?'

Isabel snorted. 'Mum, I'm twenty-six not fourteen and no it's not.'

'Isabel when you have children of your own, and that is a big when, you will understand that your baby is always your baby. So, come on then spill, what is it?'

Isabel took a deep breath and fought the urge not to scratch at her arm. She knew stress was exacerbating the problem. The only people who knew about the awful afternoon on the outskirts of that South Island town were those that were there and Father Joyce. It was all bubbling up inside her again now though. She needed to talk to someone and Helena had not mentioned the accident since she'd arrived home; her Facebook messages were filled with fun times being had at home in Freyburg catching up with friends and family. Isabel had not wanted to put a dampener on her homecoming by telling her friend that she simply could not put the accident behind her.

'Right, I'll put the kettle on and you, young lady, had better spill the beans as to what is going on.'

It was all the prompting needed. In one big burst, while her mum busied herself making a brew and cutting generous slices from her homemade fruit loaf she was convinced fixed everything, Isabel told her all about how she'd given her word to the dying Ginny. When she'd finished, Babs brought two steaming mugs over to the table and a plate of the buttered loaf. She put them down and held out her arms to wrap Isabel up in a cuddle that smelt faintly of her morning dousing of Paris and the baking counter behind which she worked. Isabel inhaled deeply feeling like she had when she was a little girl and a cuddle from her mum had meant that everything would be okay.

'Right then, my girl, you need to decide what you're going to do,' Babs said, giving her daughter's back a rub. 'The way I see it is you've two choices. You can put what happened behind you and move on, starting by finding yourself some work because you know what I always say, a busy mind is a healthy mind. Or, you can try to set about finding Constance, whoever she may be, if she's still alive. You said this Ginny woman was ninety-something, Iz, it's not all that likely.'

Isabel's voice was muffled against her mum's chest. 'I want to go to the Isle of Wight and see if I can find her and if she's still alive, which I know given Ginny left the island in the late forties is unlikely, I can pass her message on. And if she's dead, well, at least I tried. Mum, you and dad always taught me that a promise is a promise.' She hadn't known for certain that this was what she wanted to do until the words popped out of her mouth but as she'd just told her mum a promise was a promise.

'Oh, Izzy, I had a feeling that's what you'd say.' Babs disentangled herself from her daughter and scanning the plate, she picked up the thickest slice of fruit slice.

Chapter 5

'I think it's nice you're off out to catch up with your old friends for lunch today, Izzy. Although how you can afford to, given your current employment status, I don't know,' Babs said, pouring herself a second cup of tea from the pot sitting between her and Isabel.

'I'm only meeting Charity, Mum, not half of Southampton, and it won't be anywhere fancy.' Isabel, still in her nightie, didn't want to get into a discussion about the state of her finances at this time of the morning—any time of the day come to that.

Bab's shot her a pursed lip look over the top of her teacup. 'Dad and I had a good chat last night about this Isle of Wight business.'

'Oh yes, and what did Dad say?' Isabel squinted across the table at her mum. The sun had decided to come out and cheerful rays of sunshine streamed into the kitchen. An excitable woof sounded from the back garden where Prince Charles was frolicking.

'Well, once he'd finished moaning on about how he thinks he's pulled his calf muscle after Monday night practice he said that you're bonkers.'

'Sounds about right.'

'I told him, "Be that as it may, you're an adult and as such you can make your own mind up."'

'And what did he say to that?'

'That he still thinks you're bonkers. I'm having another round of toast, would you like a piece?'

'Yes, please.'

Babs got up and popped a couple of slices of bread in the toaster. 'I always liked Charity you know, even if she was a bit too heavy handed with the slap in my opinion.'

It was true, Isabel mused, stuffing in the last of her toast. Her old school friend was a beautician and as such had always been a dedicated follower of the latest trends and was forever watching YouTube make-up tutorials. 'Charity calls her look "photo ready".'

'I call it tarty. Did I hear through the grapevine that she's engaged?'

'Mmm, I don't know him, they met at the pub the night of my leaving drinks.'

'Ooh, you might get to be a bridesmaid. Then you *would* have to do something about that hair,' Babs said as two pieces of toast popped up.

Isabel doubted it. For one thing, it would place Charity in an awkward position having to choose between her two friends and Isabel was the one who'd been away not Ashley.

'You know, Izzy,' Babs said pausing mid buttering of the toast, 'it wasn't just you I missed when you went away. I missed your friends bowling in and out of the house too.'

Babs and Gaz had always had an open home policy when it came to Isabel's friends. Her mum would have home baking on hand to offer around, and her dad never said no when it came to ferrying them all about. It made Isabel feel a bit sad sometimes because she could see how well-suited her parents would have been to a large, noisy family but fate had dealt them a different hand.

Charity had spent so much time at their house over the years that it was like having a sister. It was Charity who first met Ashley when they both started work at the same beauty salon. The three of them soon became firm friends. Ashley with her natural good looks was the confident one, Charity the naughty one, and Isabel, well she made them both laugh and she was the one they turned to when they needed to talk. 'You're a faithful friend, Izzy,' Babs would often say.

The girls enjoyed countless Friday and Saturday nights dancing around their handbags and shared annual holidays in Ibiza. They'd been there with wine and chocolate when there were boyfriend dramas, and they'd promised each other that one day when they finally found Mr Right, they'd be one another's bridesmaids. Then, after what happened with Connor all those years of friendship had gone sour.

Isabel had met Connor when she was working for the mobile phone company. He'd come in to upgrade his plan, signing himself up for another two years. Before he left, he'd looked at her from under his heavy sweep of dark fringe and asked if she'd like to meet him for a drink after work. By the end of their first date, she was smitten. Connor ticked every box: funny, smart, kind, gorgeous but what she'd loved most about him was the way he always made her feel like she was the most interesting girl in the world. Okay, so his inability to put the loo seat down wasn't all that endearing. Neither was the way he'd just kick off his smelly socks leaving them to lie about on the floor of his bedroom until he ran out of them and had to go to the laundromat. Worst of all though, was his channel-surfing habit—it drove her nuts and thanks to him she'd missed some of the most crucial moments on *Downton Abbey*! But nobody's perfect, and she'd loved him even if he did hate opera.

'How's that other one these days?' Babs' lip curled, interrupting Isabel's reverie. 'The one with the look of a weasel about her. Is she still with Connor?' Connor's name was said with appropriate vehemence.

Ashley looked nothing like a weasel; she was blonde and beautiful, but her mum was loyal. 'Ashley?'

'Yes her, with the squinty, mean eyes. She always did remind me of a ferret.'

'I wouldn't know, Mum. Aren't you supposed to be at work soon?' It was after eight thirty; her mum was due behind the bakery counter in half an hour.

'Oh, bloody hell!' Babs dropped the buttery knife, 'You'll have to put the jam on yourself.'

Isabel got up from the table and hearing her mum thundering up the stairs, picked up the two pieces of toast, and dropped them in the bin. She'd lost her appetite.~

Charity forked up her salad and gazed wistfully across the table at Isabel's bowl of nachos. The corn chips were draped thickly with melted cheese and Isabel, hungry after her light breakfast, piled a chip high with mince, avocado, and salsa. The pub they'd met in was new, it didn't have the cosy ambiance Isabel liked. It was obviously a place to be seen, she thought, her eyes sweeping past the well-heeled lunchtime patrons all trying to outdo one another on their cell phones.

'Do you want one?' She pushed the bowl toward Charity. 'I won't be able to eat all of it.' It was a lie; she knew she was quite capable of chomping through the lot.

Indecision flitted across Charity's face before she shoved the salad into her mouth and mumbled, 'No I'm trying to lose a few pounds before the wedding. I like your hair by the way. Very early Katy Perry.'

Isabel wasn't sure if that was a compliment or not. Still, it was a break from the topic of her upcoming wedding, which was all Charity had talked about since they'd sat down. Her dress, the venue, the menu, the music, the cake, but the one thing she had not touched upon over the last thirty minutes was who was in her bridal party. Given the fact the wedding was in less than two months, Isabel was fairly certain she was not. It made her sad because they'd discussed the finer details of their imaginary weddings so many times over the years. Charity was always Isabel's chief bridesmaid, and her dress would be mint green while Isabel was always Charity's and her dress would be a pale lemon. Sitting here now, she found it hard to believe that the two of them had once confided everything to each other.

'Iz, the reason I suggested we meet today...' Charity squirmed in her seat. 'This is awkward, so I'm just going to come out with it.'

Isabel did not say a word; she wasn't going to help her out.

'Look, Iz, I would have loved for you to be my bridesmaid, but you haven't met Sam, not properly anyway and well Ashley was here, and you weren't, and I can't very well have both of you, can I? Not with how it stands between you two. Unless you want to try to patch things up with her?' Her eyes, sandwiched between a thick layer of top and bottom mascaraed lashes, were hopeful.

Isabel thought she might choke on her corn chip and she took a sip of water before trusting herself to be able to speak. 'Charity, you know why I wasn't here. I went to Australia because Ashley stole my boyfriend, which left me a bit of a wreck and I needed to get away.'

Charity speared a tomato defensively. 'Yes, I know that, and I'll admit it wasn't handled very well by Connor or Ashley. Ashley knows that too, and she's prepared to meet you halfway.' Seeing her friends stony gaze she added, 'Ah come on, Iz, it's not as if you and Connor were ever *that* serious. It's not like you were engaged or anything.' Her eyes flitted to the shiny bauble on her finger and a self-satisfied smile danced across her lips. 'It's ancient history. Ashley and Connor are made for each other, and you'll meet Mr Right too, that's if you haven't already. Tell me do the men in Australia all look like the Hemsworth brothers?' She giggled. 'I bet you had a blast checking them all out.'

Isabel felt like kicking Charity, really, really hard under the table. Had she always been this much of a self-absorbed, insensitive bitch? And if so, how come she'd never noticed it before? That she and Connor had never been serious was breaking news to her. She'd been very serious about Connor; he'd said he was serious about her too, and then he'd gone and slept with Ashley.

She'd walked in on them when she let herself into Connor's flat one evening when he thought she'd gone to the cinema with Charity. Her friend had cancelled at the last minute, and Isabel hadn't fancied spending the evening at home, so she thought she'd surprise her boyfriend. It was her that had gotten the surprise, and the sight of her so-called good friend and Connor—bare bum in the air going for gold with Ashley's fingernails digging into his back was one she didn't think she'd ever forget. She hadn't stuck around to hear what they had to say and two weeks later she was on her way to Australia.

'You know, if I hadn't made you have leaving drinks at the Fox 'n' Hound, I might never have met Sam. How weird is that?'

Isabel was filled with a sudden urge to run away once more, but this time it would not be to the other side of the world. This time it would be to the Isle of Wight. It didn't matter that it was only for a night or two it would give her some breathing space from the likes of Bridezilla sitting across the table from her.

'Oh, crap. Is that the time?' Isabel exclaimed. 'I've got to run. I'm interviewing for the manageress position at Coast over in West Quay—the in-store clothes discount is supposed to be fab!'

It was a lie, but the look on Charity's face was worth it.

'Go on, you finish them.' She pushed the barely touched bowl of corn chips toward Charity. *I hope you split your bloody dress.*

Isabel would have made quite the grand exit if she hadn't marched out of the pub with a serviette stuck to the heel of her shoe.

Chapter 6

Isabel stood by the railings down the back of the Red Funnel ferry enjoying the sting of salty spray hitting her face. Her backpack leaned against her legs. It was going to be a bumpy crossing she thought, as strands of her green hair were whipped into a tangle. She threw her head down and wound it into a loose topknot, securing it with the bobble she kept on her wrist for moments like this. Southampton began to dissipate like fog, and the doll-like waving figures of her parents, who'd driven her to the terminal, got smaller and smaller.

Two days had passed since she'd made her mind up to cross over to the Isle of Wight to see if she could find Constance. It was crazy given her recent adventures on the other side of the world, but today she felt like she was heading off on an epic voyage into the unknown, not the hour-long ferry crossing to East Cowes. She had a plan of sorts; she would get the bus to Ryde and, well that was as far as she'd gotten. She'd fibbed to her mum when asked as to how she was off for money.

'I've enough put by to find somewhere nice to stay for a few nights, Mum,' she'd said, waiting to board the ferry. The truth of the matter was she had enough for her ferry fare, and one night's accommodation so long as it was budget and she didn't stretch to more than a bag of hot chips for her dinner. Isabel had never mastered the art of saving.

Her mum had been appeased, but her dad wasn't fooled. He knew his daughter only too well, and he'd pressed a handful of crumpled twenty-pound notes into her hand when her mum was side-tracked having spotted one of the girls from work in the queue. She'd decided to forgive him for last night's leprechaun joke as she gave him a big hug. He told her to watch his latest football injury, a sore rib, before adding, 'Mind how you go, eh, love?'

'I'll only be gone a few days, Dad,' she said, noticing he had a hole in the shoulder of his Saints shirt. It wasn't surprising given how often he wore it. He was off down to the pub later to watch the game with the lads, as he called them, or, as her mum liked to refer to them, "the long in the tooth louts".

'And when you've got this out of your system—' Babs said, turning her attention back to her family.

'I will find a job. I promise, Mum!'

'And promise me you'll do something about that hair.'

~

Isabel spotted the two-tone green double-decker bus that would take her to Ryde outside the Waitrose supermarket and clambered aboard. She ignored the young lad who was pushing past her to get off as he remarked loudly, 'Oi, mate, the bus matches her hair. She should get free fare for that.' The driver glared at him muttering something about the youth of today before taking Isabel's money.

He paused before handing her her change and stared at her hair, 'He's right you know; it is the same colour.'

Obviously not right about the free fare, though, she thought, glaring at him. She snatched her ticket and marched down the aisle managing to smack an unsuspecting passenger with her backpack. 'Ooh, sorry,' she mumbled, only just managing to sit down before the bus juddered off once more. Through the smudged window she could see the landscape unfurling exactly how she remembered it from childhood jaunts to the island with her parents.

The bus stopped and started its way through Whippingham, Wootton, and the small village of Fishbourne where the car ferry from Portsmouth docked. As they passed through pretty wee Binstead with its post office that also served as the village's general store, Isabel felt a frisson of excitement. Next stop, Ryde! Who knew what she would discover? She felt at that moment like she was starring in her very own mystery TV show and titles for the imaginary show whirled about her head. *Isabel Stark Investigates* or *Chasing Constance, perhaps.* She decided she'd run with *The Promise*; it sounded edgy.

Ryde Pier was Isabel's stop, and after the bus had nosed its way into the interchange, she hopped off, calling out a curt thank you to the driver. She was glad of her choice of jumper and jeans because the breeze off the water was bracing and the sky ominous. Isabel shivered despite her warm clothes and swinging her pack onto her back she set off down the Esplanade. It had been years since she'd been here and she decided to have a wander about and get a feel for the place. She'd see what was about in the way of accommodation too and if nothing leaped out at her, she could always search for a room on her phone.

She turned left at the lights and began the gentle climb away from the seafront. A short distance ahead she saw a middle-aged couple blowing clouds of smoke into the air outside a lime washed pub. Above their head was a sign for the Rum Den. She was thirsty and it looked as good a place as any for a pit stop. She pushed open the door and stepped inside, surprised at how busy it was for a Saturday afternoon thanks to a pub quiz that was underway. A chap with a top hat stood on the small stage in the corner of the low beamed space. He was holding a microphone in one hand and reading a question off the card he held in his other.

Isabel's gaze moved over to the bar as she sensed she was being stared at. A woman stood behind it, eyeing her curiously. She had jet black, teased hair and tapped her long fingernails, inset with sparkly jewels, on the expansive timber splayed out before her as she waited, Isabel presumed, for her to place her order. 'Alright, luv,' came a decidedly Cockney voice as she raised a pencilled-in eyebrow. 'What can I get you then?'

Isabel stopped hovering in the doorway, took a deep breath and smiled as she put her best foot forward. 'Hi, um, I'll just have a lemonade please.' She took her pack off and leaned it up against the bar before perching on a stool.

'That'll be one pound sixty, ta, and it's Rod Stewart,' the publican said sliding Isabel's glass of lemonade toward her. She leaned across the bar and whispered conspiratorially. 'Rocking Rod rocks my world. I almost considered dying my hair blonde for him back in my day.' Her eyes flicked over Isabel's hair. 'What colour do you call that then?'

'Erm, green.' Isabel fished the money from her purse wondering why on earth the woman was on about Rod Stewart?

'You, young ones always think you're the first to do everything; you know David Bowie was doing his orange before you were even a twinkle in your father's eye.'

'I'll repeat that,' the quizmaster said into his microphone distracting them both. 'Which famous singer was an apprentice for the then third division Brentford Town Football Club?'

Isabel twigged, the answer was Rod Stewart. The publican wasn't a complete nutter then. 'My dad's a big Rod fan, although Bruce Springsteen is his all-time favourite. I'm more into classical music. I love opera.' She didn't often confide that she loved the genre, and she certainly never told anyone about her dream of seeing Andrea Bocelli sing at Teatro del Silenzio near the tenor's home in Tuscany. It all seemed a little too highfalutin for an unemployed twenty-six-year-old from Southampton. There was something about this woman's forthright manner that invited her to share though.

'We don't have much call for opera and the like around these parts.'

'Ooh, ooh, I know this one, I know it.' A woman's voice carried across the array of glasses on her table closest to the stage. Isabel glanced over to see her jiggling about in her seat.

'That's one of the regulars, Linda, and she'll wet herself if she's not careful. I'm Brenda by the way.'

'Isabel,' she replied with a smile before taking a sip of her drink. It was cold and sweet, just what she needed.

'Where are you from then, Isabel who loves opera, and what brings you to the island?'

'I'm from Southampton, but I've just returned from a working holiday in Australia and, well I just fancied a few days break on the island before I settle back down.'

'And what did you do for a crust in Australia then?'

'Bar work mostly,' Isabel replied, putting her glass down.

'So, you're in between jobs at the mo?'

'I suppose so, yes.' Applying for the McDonald's job had been put on hold, for a few days at least.

'And where are you planning on staying while you're here?' Brenda eyed Isabel's pack.

'I haven't sorted anywhere out yet; I thought I'd have a wander around and see what was about.'

'There's a room you can doss down in tonight upstairs if you like. Me lodger's away.'

'Oh.' Isabel was taken aback.

'I won't charge you board neither if you give us a hand behind the bar. I've been run off me feet since Patsy up and left.'

Isabel necked her lemonade, startled by what had just transpired—a few hours work in exchange for a night's lodging—she would not look a gift horse, so to speak, in the mouth.

'That would be great, thank you.'

Brenda waved her thanks aside. 'Right then. Let's see if you can handle this lot when they break in ten minutes. You can stick your pack out the back for now.' She lifted the flip top of the bar and beckoned her over to the other side.

~

The quizmaster put down his microphone, having just told his contestants he was taking a short break. This news was followed by a mass scraping of chairs as a tidal wave of thirsty punters surged toward the bar. Isabel felt like her feet were frozen to the floor in the path of the migrating wildebeest on a prairie plain. Bloody hell! Talk about being thrown in at the deep end, she thought as the patch of skin that had flared up on her neck began to burn with intensity. Come on, Isabel, you can do this. She took a deep breath and followed Brenda's cue, watching the maestro at work before launching into action herself.

It was like getting back on a bicycle after she'd fallen off it. The drinks were slightly different, and it was pounds not Australian dollars, that was all. 'Hi, everyone. If you could just bear with me while I find my way around this bar, I'll get to you all in just a moment.' She smiled at a man with a paunch pushing his glass toward her. 'Right then, sir, what can I get you?'

'Half a pint of bitter, love. Where've you popped up from then?'

'I called in for a drink and when Brenda heard I'd worked in pubs before she asked me to give her a hand,' Isabel said, going on to give him an abbreviated backstory of having just come home from overseas and fancying a few days on the island.

'I didn't think she was a caulkhead, not with that hair,' a woman who looked to be a hardy seafaring type said, eyeing her suspiciously over the top of her lemon and bitters.

The word she'd used, caulkhead, tickled at the back of Isabel's mind, but she couldn't remember what it meant.

'It means islander. That sort of thing matters to this lot, but if they like you, they'll treat you like family,' Brenda whispered out the corner of her mouth spying Isabel's puzzled expression as she reached for a packet of pork scratchings. 'I'm a cockney, and they never let me forget it, but when my husband left, they rallied around me, so I stayed.'

The last of the customers carried her gin and tonic back to the table to join her team who were waiting, with their pencils poised, for the quizmaster to launch into his spiel. The topic was sports. She'd be no help to them Isabel thought, breathing out a sigh of relief as she looked at the empty bar area and the tables full of happy customers.

'I don't know what you're standing there grinning about; you should be cracking on with this lot,' Brenda said, pulling open the dishwasher tucked away under the bar. A gush of steam burst forth. It was full of glasses and Isabel set about emptying it.

~

The pub doors closed at four thirty, reopening for the evening at six o'clock. Isabel began clearing the glasses. 'So you're a cockney, Brenda.'

'Born and bred. I've two sons, in their thirties they are, still living in the East End.'

Isabel instantly pictured the Mitchell brothers from EastEnders.

'What brought you to the Isle of Wight then?' They had plenty of pubs in the East End so far as Isabel knew.

'The old man wanted a lifestyle change, so we bought the pub here. Six months down the line he left me for the twenty-one-year-old tart we took on behind the bar. Last I heard they're back in the East End running a pub there. I don't ask, and me boys don't tell me.' She shrugged. 'I stayed on here, cos like I said, the locals looked after me. That was five years ago now.'

'Oh.' Isabel couldn't think of much else to say to that.

'What's your story then, miss? What is it that brings you to Ryde other than putting off settling back down in Southampton?'

Isabel hesitated. 'Well, it's pretty much what I said before. I've been overseas for a year, and I'm just here for a bit of a break before I crack on with finding fulltime work back in Southampton.'

Brenda paused mid table wipe and eyed her speculatively through mascara rimmed eyes. 'In my experience, most people your age don't come over here on their own for a bit of a break and especially not without booking somewhere to stay first.'

Isabel didn't meet her gaze as she carried the glasses she'd collected over to the bar.

'So, come on then, they don't call me Brenda the Bloodhound for nuffink. What's your real story? I'm not buying this *just here for a bit of a break* malarkey.'

'Do you really get called that?'

'No, but I'm not letting it go.'

Isabel pursed her lips; she could see she wasn't going to get out of this one, she might as well come clean. And so as she set about loading the dishwasher, she told Brenda about what had transpired at the end of her trip around New Zealand.

Brenda had stopped wiping the tables, engrossed in listening to Isabel's story. 'Well, I can see how you'd feel obliged to try to keep your word to the old gal what with her dying on you and all.' Her brow furrowed giving her a perplexed poodle look. 'You know, thinking about it, Constance ain't that common a name, and there was a Constance who was quite well known around these parts. Bit of a character she was, ran a herbal medicine shop down on the Esplanade for years. I fink it's an art gallery or summink now. The last I 'eard she'd gone into a retirement home. There's three I know of here in Ryde; chances are you'll find her in one of those if you go door knocking. She could well be the woman you're looking for.'

Isabel felt a frisson of excitement. It felt like too much of a coincidence for her not to be Ginny's Constance and she was still alive! She'd just been given her first clue on her journey to fulfilling her promise, and she'd gone no further than the first pub she'd stumbled across!

'Mind, with all them privacy laws now, it might pay to pretend you're long lost family or summink.'

Brenda was right, Isabel realised. 'I could say Constance is my great aunt, and—' Isabel thought for a second and then had a brainwave. 'She fell out with my nan; they lost touch and nan made me promise before she passed on that I'd find her and say she was sorry about everything that had happened.'

'A half-truth.'

'Exactly.'

Brenda winked at her; they were co-conspirators.

'Right then, that's sorted. Now it seems to me that you might need to earn a few pounds to keep yourself going while you're 'ere. And seeing as I need a barmaid, you've got yourself some hours for as long as you need them. If you want them like?'

Isabel nodded so hard she jarred her neck. She didn't quite believe her luck.

Brenda grinned, revealing teeth that reminded Isabel of a pony with a somewhat vicious streak she'd once ridden at a fair as a child. She rubbed her neck while Brenda got down to business.

'The going rate's five pounds fifty pence. I'd expect you on board from midday with a tea break from four thirty to six, Friday to Sunday, then it's all hands on deck until eleven o'clock closing. Monday's your day off and Tuesday, Wednesday, and Thursday, I need you here for the evening shift only.' She stalked over to the door behind the bar, her hand resting on the knob as she winced, 'Me bloody bunions are killing me. So what do you say?'

Pub work would be marginally better for her figure than working at a fast-food joint, and it meant she wouldn't have to listen to her dad's endless supply of leprechaun jokes for a bit Isabel thought. She glanced down at her new boss's black stilettos; she wasn't surprised her feet were sore.

'Well then?' Brenda tapped her foot and then thought better of it.

'Oh, sorry. It sounds brilliant, Brenda, thank you.' Wait until she told her mum she'd scored a job and she hadn't had to do a thing to her hair!

'Right, sorted. Come on then, I need to get off my feet for half an hour. I'll show you where you can kip down tonight. Like I said, Terry me lodger's away for a couple of nights, and he won't mind you 'aving his room. You can sort yourself out something more permanent over the next day or two. It's good timing you showing up like this what with me barmaid Patsy leaving me last week. She wanted more time to help look after her daughter's little 'un, but she didn't half leave me in the lurch.'

Isabel shook her head in wonderment at how the day was unfolding before following Brenda up the narrow stairs, being careful not to scrape her backpack against the old floral wallpaper on either side of her. It was already beginning to peel in places and didn't need a helping hand from her. She could see a small lounge at the top of the landing which looked homely and lived-in, but Brenda turned to the right. 'Bathroom's in there,' she said, opening a door and gesturing to the bath with a blue shower curtain, but not slowing down. 'And this 'ere is where you are.' The room was spartan but clean with a small double bed, and a window open just a crack to allow the salted air to waft in. 'I'll get you some fresh sheets, and you can make the bed up while I heat us up the shepherd's pie I made earlier for our dinner.'

Isabel leaned her pack up against the wardrobe and sat down on the end of the bed feeling bewildered by the pace at which she'd found both work and accommodation for the night. It seemed she just might stay here on the island longer than she'd thought.

Chapter 7

Isabel woke smartly thanks to a particularly noisy bird full of the joys of spring outside the window, but despite not getting her full eight hours, she felt strangely energised. This was not the norm. She could never be accused of being a morning person and had spent most of her teen years being woken by her mum ripping open her curtains. This was followed by her announcing that Isabel was sleeping her life away before, her grand finale, yanking the covers off her.

Despite the strange surroundings, she'd gone out like a light last night only waking once for the loo. She'd been shattered by her unexpected shift downstairs at the Rum Den the day before.

Her hair was still in the messy topknot she'd tied it into on the boat yesterday. She threw a sweater over the top of her pyjamas and wondered if Brenda was up and about as she mooched forth. The barefaced publican was reading the paper at the table with an empty plate and mug beside her. She looked at Isabel over the top of her reading glasses. 'Ere she is then, Sleeping Beauty, or is it Shrek? You obviously slept well. Knock yourself out did yer?'

Isabel flushed. 'Sorry about the noise, Brenda. I should've put the bedroom light on when I got up for the toilet. I tripped over my shoes.' Her knees were a bit tender she realised, recalling how she'd gone flying. A mental image of her mother shaking her head popped up in front of her, and she could hear her saying, 'For the hundredth time, Isabel, watch where you're going! You'll come a proper cropper one of these days, my girl.'

'Ah well, no harm done. Help yourself to coffee and toast. Paper's yours too if you want a read.' She folded it up noisily before gesturing to the bench where the kettle sat waiting alongside the toaster. 'I'm off to put me face on.' A frown settled between her non-existent brows as she peered at Isabel's neck. 'That looks nasty. Have you got summit you can put on it?'

Isabel's hand flew to the spot behind her ear; it was hot and sore to the touch, which she hoped didn't mean she was starting with an infection. She must have been scratching at it in her sleep. 'My eczema's been playing up since I got back to the UK. I've got some stuff in my pack that helps a bit. Hopefully, it will settle down, and I won't have to go to the doctor for a steroid prescription.'

'We've all got our crosses to bear,' Brenda tutted and, watching her hobble off to the bathroom, Isabel assumed she was talking about her bunions. She shook her head at the memory of the heels Brenda wore for the duration of her shift. No wonder her feet were crippling her! There was no time to sit around lamenting Brenda's bunions though she thought, galvanising herself into action. She set about making coffee and toast and then, in between sips and bites, wrote down the names of all the local retirement homes both in and around Ryde. There were seven worth calling on. By the time she'd showered and dressed, and the checklist of homes to call in on was tucked away safely in her bag, she felt ready to take on the day.

'I'll be back at twelve, Brenda. Thanks so much for letting me stay last night and for the shifts.'

Brenda, looking much more like the same woman she'd met yesterday now her eyebrows were back in place, and her lips a shade of red no other woman would get away with at this hour of the day, shooed her on her way.

Isabel began her search for Constance by ticking off the furthermost care home on the list she'd compiled. It was a short bus ride over to Wootton Bridge and the home she saw, making her way to the entrance, sat in impressive leafy grounds near the sea. The staff looked at her curiously, and whether it was because of her inquiry or her hair, she wasn't sure. Either way, there was no Constance currently residing with them, they'd assured her. Oh well, she thought, as she waited for the bus to take her back to the centre of Ryde. It would have been far too easy had she found Constance in the very first place she called at. Besides, it was only just after nine. The morning stretched long; she had plenty of time.

However, by the time she found herself walking away from her third port of call, a beautifully restored Victorian residence on Queens Road, her earlier positivity was beginning to waver. The phrase, a needle in a haystack, sprang to mind and given it was now approaching ten am, she needed a mid-morning caffeine hit. She supposed she should do something about sorting out a place to stay too.

As she turned right, the Esplanade had a steady flow of people going about their day and making the most of the blue sky on offer. She caught a whiff of brewing coffee on the breeze and was following the direction of her twitching nose when a sign in the window of a gallery caught her eye. She would have missed it if it wasn't for the bold beach scene canvas displayed on an easel that had initially grabbed her attention. The handwritten sign next to the artwork said "Room to Let Enquire Within". It was worth checking out, she thought, as something tickled at the back of her brain, something Brenda had said. What was it? It was no good; it would come back to her when it was good and ready.

The gallery, she noted, taking a step back for a better look, was called A Leap of Faith–Art and Sculpture, and the flat above the yellow and white striped awning was two storeys with two sets of large Victorian sash windows on each floor. The establishment looked perfectly presentable from the outside she decided, pressing her nose to the window pane to see further inside.

She jumped back from the glass, narrowly missing colliding with an older woman walking her dog, as a man appeared from behind the canvas. He was smiling at her, and her hand flew to her chest. He'd given her a proper fright and she waited for her heart to return to its normal number of beats per minute. She turned back toward the window, but he'd disappeared, and she stood there feeling rather foolish at having been caught out like some peeping Tom. She tossed up whether she should go inside and see how the land lay. What did she have to lose? Isabel decided, pulling the door open with gusto and smacking straight into the solid frame of the man she'd seen a second or two earlier.

She had to wait to get her breath back before replying to his concerned questioning that yes, she was okay. His voice was rich and melodious with the almost incoherent musical quality of a thick Welsh accent. 'I'm sorry about that. I'm Rhodri Rees, the proprietor. Now then, was it the canvas in the window you were interested in?'

'What?' Isabel felt wrong-footed and unsure of herself as she gazed up at his welcoming face.

'I asked if it was—'

'No, no, that's not why I'm here.' She gathered herself. Good grief. Did she look as though she could afford expensive pieces of artwork? 'Not that the painting isn't lovely—I wondered about the room you have to let. My name's Isabel Stark, and I'm over from Southampton, but I've found some work at the Rum Den up the road, and well, it looks like I'll be staying here longer than I initially thought.' She stopped to draw breath.

Rhodri looked amused. 'I quite often pop in the Rum Den for a pint. It's a lovely old pub.'

Good for you, Isabel thought, annoyed by his twitching mouth. 'So, are you letting a room or not?'

'I most certainly am. Would you like to have a look upstairs?'

Isabel hesitated. She did want to have a look, but it wouldn't be the smartest of moves going to view a stranger's flat when nobody knew where she was. Her mum's voice rang in her ears, for the second time that morning. 'Stranger danger, Isabel.'

'If you don't have time now—'

'No, it's fine.' She fished her phone out having had a bright idea. 'My friend's waiting for me in the coffee shop a few doors down. I'll just flick her a quick text and tell her not to order my latte just yet.'

He smiled. 'Good idea. Nothing worse than cold coffee.' He busied himself straightening up a rack of postcard-size prints while Isabel texted her pretend friend.

'Right, all sorted. I told her I'd be about ten minutes or so.' She put her phone back in her bag.

'We'd better go on up then. I'm glad I cleared the breakfast things away.' He laughed.

The Welsh accent, when thick, could sound like a very beautiful form of flowing gibberish, Isabel thought, watching as he hung a "Back in five minutes" sign in the door before locking it. Her eyes narrowed. He didn't look like a nutcase. In fact, he was quite good looking in a dark and brooding way. He'd most likely have a girlfriend called Myfanwy or something like that, she reassured herself. Besides it was too late to change her mind now and, crossing her fingers behind her back, she followed his long-legged stride the length of the gallery to a door behind the counter.

On the other side of the door was a corridor of sorts. A steep set of stairs ran up to the first floor and at the end of the corridor was a door which she guessed led to the back-garden area. Rhodri took the stairs two at a time calling back over his shoulder that it was great exercise. She'd take his word for it, she thought, holding onto the railing with no intention of picking up her pace.

The living room space, she saw reaching the top, was surprisingly light and airy thanks to those windows she'd spied from the street. The kitchen was at the opposite end and she guessed a wall had been knocked through at some point to make the two spaces open-plan. The furnishings were smart but plain and functional; they smacked of a man living alone.

'It's fairly self–explanatory.' Rhodri waved his arm around and Isabel nodded.

'It's nice.'

'Ah, it's a bit clinical. I've been busy getting the gallery up and running. I haven't had much time to put my stamp on the living quarters yet, but it's functional.'

'Do you own the building then?'

'I do, yes. I bought it last year from a lovely old lady, Miss Downer, who'd lived here her whole life. I wanted a sea change from London, and this place was perfect. Come on, I'll show you your room if you decide to take it.'

They carried on up the stairs to where there were three bedrooms, the smaller one of which was being used as a study. The bathroom was at the end of the hall. He gestured to a door, open just enough for her to see a neatly made bed. He was obviously a tidy sort of person, Isabel thought, and she could be too when she put her mind to it.

'Here you go,' he said, pushing open the door to a perfectly acceptable room with a faintly nautical feel about it thanks to the blue curtains and blue and white duvet on the small double bed. There was a dressing table against the wall and a freestanding wardrobe. A small set of drawers were beside the bed with a lamp on top of it.

It would do nicely, Isabel thought, providing the price was right. 'Erm, so how much are you looking for?'

'Eighty pounds a week. It's the going rate around here.'

Isabel worked out what she could expect to earn a week from the Rum Den; it was doable.

'Do you cook?' Rhodri asked.

'Not if I can help it.'

He laughed.

Even his laugh had a musical quality Isabel thought, wondering if she'd just sabotaged her chances.

'That's alright then because I'll do you a deal. I love cooking. It's my way of unwinding at the end of the day, so if you're happy to do the washing up—'

'Would we split the food bill and the amenities?' Isabel interrupted, liking the sound of this arrangement.

'We would. What do you reckon then?'

'I'd like to take it, thanks.'

'Great.' Rhodri held out his hand, and she shook it feeling very pleased with the way her morning had panned out even if she hadn't had any luck locating Constance as yet. 'Welcome to Pier View House, Isabel.'

'Ooh, a house with a name. I've never lived in one of those before. Wait until I tell my mum, she'll be well impressed. She always wanted to call our house Maybush Mews, but Dad wouldn't have a bar of it.'

Rhodri grinned and she was reminded of someone. It took her a second, but it came to her—Ben Affleck that was it.

Oblivious to the fact he'd just been likened to a Hollywood actor, Rhodri chatted on, 'Miss Downer shared a bit of Pier View House's history with me before she moved to Sea Vistas—it's a retirement home just down the road. The gallery downstairs used to be the Downer family's haberdashery shop. It opened just after World War One and survived World War Two. Miss Downer never married, and she helped run the business until her parents passed away. She told me there wasn't much call for haberdashery once the big supermarkets began opening on the island and that she had to think outside the box if she was going to stay in business. Apparently, she is a firm believer in the power of herbs to heal, so she began selling natural remedies which were very popular with locals and tourist alike. There was talk amongst the locals of her being a witch, and that of course added to her allure. She's a bit of a marvel really because she ran Constance's Cure-alls until she was well into her eighties and was quite the fixture around these parts. People are always popping in to ask after her.'

Isabel's mouth fell open. That was what had been tickling at the back of her mind. Brenda had mentioned Constance had owned a herbal shop that was now an art gallery. She felt a surge of excitement. 'What did you say the name of the retirement home Constance moved into was?'

Chapter 8

I didn't ring to talk to the dog, Mum,' Isabel shouted down her mobile hoping her mum would hear her and remove the mouthpiece from the vicinity of Prince Charles. The dog's howl was both deafening and mournful. She was standing outside A Leap of Faith. There was no time to call in on Constance today to see if she was the one and same woman that Ginny had asked her to find. It would have to wait until first thing tomorrow. She only had ten minutes before she was due back at the Rum Den.

Her shouting had the desired effect, and Babs Stark cheerily stated, 'Ah, he misses you, Bel. I'm telling you it's pathetic to see him like this. He's pining. You'd only just got home and you were off again. I've had to buy him doggy treats to try to cheer him up. He'll send your father and I broke with all the Tasty Tidbits he's chomping through even with my in-store discount.'

'It's only been a day, Mum, and he's spoilt, that's the problem. He's the second child you never got to have.' She studied her thumbnail. Biting her nails was a habit she'd never been able to break. She'd have loved a brother or a sister growing up, someone to take the focus off her, someone to boss about, and someone to play with. Instead, she'd gotten Prince Charles, a neurotic corgi.

She'd pestered her parents about fostering for a while when she was too young to understand what that would entail. It hadn't been on the cards though, her mum telling her that they wouldn't be able to cope with not being able to keep the child. Her parents had told her often enough the adoption process had been hard emotionally and that they'd all but jumped through hoops to get her. The waiting list had been so long they'd thought it would never happen, but by some small miracle, one day they picked up the telephone to find out it had.

Her mum reckoned from the very first moment she'd held her in her arms she'd been theirs. She told a story of how when they'd left the Barnardo's

Agency in London, she was holding Isabel tightly in her arms when the woman who'd been looking after their case file came running out after them. Babs had thought she was going to tell them it had all been a misunderstanding and that baby, Isabel, wasn't theirs after all, so she'd started running off down the street. Now that she had her baby, she wasn't giving her back! It turned out the woman only wanted to give her handbag back, which she'd left sitting on the office floor in her haste to leave. She'd laugh and finish her tale by saying, she and Dad had been blessed.

Isabel had reminded them they were blessed more than once when they weren't feeling particularly so, thanks to some teenage misdemeanour of hers. She couldn't remember a time when she hadn't known she was adopted either. The book *Yours by Choice* had always sat on the bookshelf. It was there if she wanted to look at it, but she'd never felt the need. Her mum and dad were her mum and dad, and that was that, no big deal. It was other people who saw it as being different, but for the Starks, it was just their little family.

It was strange though because a small part of her was always aware of how old her birth mother would be now—forty-two. And she had, when she was younger, wondered whether she had any siblings, but it wasn't something she'd dwell on for long. She'd once tried to write a speech about being adopted, for a school project when she was ten, after a snotty little madam had teased her about her mum and dad not being her *real* mum and dad. Her dad had offered to sit and help her with it. This was an unusual and generous offer given the football world cup had been on at the time, but for some reason just talking about it with him made her well up. In the end, she'd decided to do it on something else; she couldn't remember what now.

There was the time too when she'd had her first ever sleepover and had woken in a panic having dreamed her birth mother had arrived at her friend's house to take her back. A faceless person in her dream as her adoption was a closed one, and all she knew about the woman who'd given birth to her was she wasn't a woman at all; she was a girl, and her name was Veronica. She was just fifteen when she'd had her and had decided adoption was the best thing all round; she'd been the one to call her Isabel. Isabel was grateful her parents hadn't changed her name. If Babs had been inclined to do so, it would have been more than likely she'd have been christened, Diana or if she'd had particularly lofty aspirations for her new daughter, Elizabeth.

She didn't know where those feelings of fear at losing everything familiar to her had come from the night she'd stayed away from home for the first time. Wherever they'd welled up from, they'd stayed with her for a long time afterward. She'd been told she was an overly sensitive girl more than once during her twenty-six years, but to Isabel's mind it was a fine line between sensitivity and anxiety. She gave her thumbnail a look of disgust and felt her neck burning once more.

Babs broke her train of thought. 'Hang on will you, Isabel? I'll put Prince Charles outside or I won't be able to hear a thing you're saying.'

'Right-oh.' Isabel leaned back against the rails, her back to the pier as she chewed on a strand of muted green hair.

'Oh dear, that was worse than your dad's attitude when I make fish pie for tea.'

Isabel laughed, having borne witness to this, although she couldn't quite understand his aversion to the humble fish pie; she was quite partial to it, and her tummy rumbled at the thought of a serving. Despite her husband's dislike of the dish, Babs insisted on making it arguing that it was brain food and if it was good enough for the queen, then it was good enough for the Stark family. She'd once read that the people of Gloucester make a fish pie for the queen each jubilee and coronation. Dad would mutter in reply to this that he'd gladly drop his serving up at Buckingham Palace.

Her mum diverted her thoughts. 'So, now tell me, how is your search going?'

'Mum, coming here is working out a bit differently to how I thought it would.' She filled her in on all that had transpired since she'd arrived in Ryde yesterday.

Once Bab's had gotten over her disbelief and excitement at the possibility of Isabel having located Constance, she moved on to her daughter's new landlord. 'Rhodri? He sounds like a Cornish historical romance hero.'

'You watch way too much Poldark, Mum, and he's Welsh by the way, not Cornish.'

'Is he a nice young man though? He doesn't have any peculiar habits like—'

Isabel cut her off. 'Yes, Mum, he seems perfectly nice and normal.' Isabel scratched at her neck.

'Stop scratching, Bel.'

She had hearing like that ruddy corgi! Isabel grumped but did as she was told.

'Well, Dad and I are only a phone call away if you need us. I suppose I should count my blessings that you've found yourself some work to tide you over. It's a shame you couldn't find something this side of the water though, what with you only just getting home. Still, it's only a ferry ride away. Make sure you ring me as soon as you've been to see your Constance tomorrow and let me know how it goes. I won't sleep a wink tonight for wondering what Ginny was sorry for. I hope she tells you. Oh, bugger it!'

'What?'

'The white sauce is all lumpy. That'll teach me for multitasking.'

'What are you having for dinner?' Isabel's tummy rumbled with more ferocity this time; she'd not gotten her morning coffee in because, by the time she'd finished grilling Rhodri about his connection with Constance, there'd been no time for sitting in cafes sipping coffee and nibbling on cake. She might just have enough time to snaffle down a sandwich if she got her A into G though.

'Fish pie,' her mum replied.

Isabel laughed. 'Not Dad's lucky night then.'

~

Isabel dodged the merry punters as she pushed her way back to the bar and dumped the collection of glasses she'd just cleared down on the bar top. The pub was jumping tonight; there'd be a few sore heads on Monday morning, she thought, glancing around. It was eight pm, another three hours to go, and she was eager for tonight to be over and for tomorrow morning to roll around. She'd taken her pack down to Pier View House and deposited it in her new room on her dinner break, handing Rhodri a fistful of crumpled notes, her week's rent in advance. He'd been about to head out to a pottery class; he informed her taking a key from his key ring and passing it to her.

'It's for the door to the gallery. I don't use the back door,' Rhodri said, grabbing his jacket before telling her he might pop down to the Rum Den after his class for a pint.

Isabel hadn't stayed in the empty flat long. Brenda had a bowl of mac 'n' cheese waiting for her when she got back.

Now, she lifted the flip top and scooted around to the business side of the bar. The dishwasher needed loading, and she grimaced at the tackiness of the bar top beneath the glasses she'd just lined up. There'd been a spillage, and she'd clean it up in a jiffy. First things first though, she thought, eyeing the glasses, she'd clear this lot away.

Brenda was down the other end of the bar taking orders from a group of lads who looked a motley crew. They'd come in off the street yahooing, and the young fellow with an earring in his nose and a pink veil atop his head gave the game away. They were on a stag's night, over from the mainland for a long weekend and determined to rave-up to the best of their ability. It was obvious they were already three sheets to the wind.

Isabel began stacking the dishwasher and, the next time she glanced over, the groom was tossing a nip down his throat while Brenda was busy pulling pints for his mates. The group of larrikins were jostling one another loudly, and she debated offering a helping hand but knew she'd be called over if need be. She was better served up her end of the bar and in keeping the tables cleared and wiped. Besides, Brenda was more than capable of handling a bunch of lager louts in their boxers and boots and, closing the dishwasher door; she set it to run before grabbing a cloth.

The stag's-do lads were now clutching their pint glasses and attempting to weave their way over to a table another group had just exited. Isabel sighed. She'd best go and clear it and, cloth in hand, she lifted the flip top once more, pushing through the crowded space. Fellow drinkers raised their glasses as the boys camped it up, enjoying the attention their semi-nude state was garnering. There were shouted congratulations to the groom-to-be and remarks about life sentences and such over the thud of the jukebox. Isabel had seen it all before. Hilarious, she thought, sighing again. It was going to be a long night.

'Sorry, boys,' she said a moment later. 'Just let me squeeze in, and I'll get rid of these glasses for you.' She bent over and scooped up the glasses with a now well-practiced hand. 'Oi!' A glass slipped from her hand as she felt a sharp pinch on her bottom. It smashed, splintering as it caught the edge of the table and she heard laughter. Her blood boiled. 'Hey, not funny! Keep your hands to yourself and stay away from that mess,' Isabel sniped, annoyed at their childish behaviour. She'd have to go and get a dustpan and brush to clear up the broken glass pronto before one of these plonkers cut themselves.

'Ooh, Katy's angry.'

She assumed they meant Katy Perry. It wasn't the first time she'd been likened to the singer with her whacky choice of hair colours. Charity's comment of the other day sprang to mind. Ignoring them, she moved off with a tight grip on the rest of the glasses, only to feel a hand grab and squeeze her backside this time. Okay, a joke was a joke, she thought, but that was plain offensive. She turned around ready to let rip, and the words died in her throat. Rhodri was pushing his way toward the cluster of clowns who were all bent over laughing as they passed the blame from one to the other. His expression said he meant business.

'Hey, mate,' Rhodri shouted over the pulsating beat. 'I think you owe the lady here an apology.' He glowered over the culprit, a spotty chap who barely filled his boxers. He looked young, Isabel thought—barely legal, and if she hadn't been so aggrieved, she'd have found the multiple emotions crossing his face as he weighed up his options amusing. It was like reading a book, watching him toss up on whether he should tough it out to look big in front of his mates. He was tempted to puff up and prod the big Welshman back but knew he'd likely wind up with a fat lip. He'd get a slap around the head too when he got home and was forced to own up to his mum as to what he'd been up to on his weekend away. He hesitated, or, he could do the right thing and say sorry. He took the latter option, and Isabel accepted his apology, eager to put a halt to any further altercation.

'Thanks,' she mouthed to Rhodri, before shoving her way back to the bar to dig out the dustpan and brush; she didn't want any injuries on her watch. Rhodri hadn't finished though. When she returned, he took the cleaning apparatus from her and shoved it toward the puny-chested punter. 'Here you go, son. It's time you put that hand of yours to some good use. Clean that mess up.'

'All right, mate. We're out for a good night, not a fight night,' he muttered, not keen to argue with the Welshman. He took the pan and brush and set about clearing up the shards of glass while his mates made a few half-hearted jests at his expense. They were a few degrees less boisterous and Isabel guessed they'd clean their drinks up and that would be the last they'd see of that little drunken group of yobs for the night. They were already edging their way towards the door. She smiled her gratefulness at Rhodri.

'Come on. I think you just earned yourself a pint on the house.'

Chapter 9

The next morning, Isabel hung up the last of her clothes and shut the door on the wardrobe, catching sight of herself in the mirrored panels as she did so. She'd dressed in jeans, boots, and her favourite pink T-shirt with its yellow Hard Rock Cafe logo, bought on a particularly memorable night out on the Gold Coast. She had an aqua coloured cardigan she could shove in her bag if it got nippy too. She scooped her hair back into a ponytail, securing it with the band on her wrist and eyed the sore, weepy patch on her neck, covered in greasy salve, with distaste. A scarf day, she decided fishing it out of her bag.

It was yellow silk, and the flecks of bluish green in it, she liked to think matched her eyes. If not her eyes then her hair, and definitely her cardi, she thought, tying it at a jaunty angle. That was better, and the silk was gentle against her irritated skin. She stood in front of the wardrobe mirror giving herself a final once over—she'd do. It was Monday morning and today was the day she would go to see Constance at Sea Vistas. Would she be Ginny's Constance? A shiver coursed through her. It was still too early to call on her, but in the meantime, a cup of tea would go down a treat. *Hmm, so would something to eat.* Perhaps she'd make a brew and take a cuppa down to Rhodri; he'd said to make herself at home, but did that include helping herself to his milk and teabags? It was all very murky waters this business of flat sharing, she thought, chewing on her nails before deciding to make the tea.

He was very neat; her first impressions yesterday were reconfirmed as she opened the overhead cupboards and peered inside in search of teabags. She hoped he didn't have OCD. The contents of the cupboard, however, were well ordered but not in perfect alignment, so she breathed easier locating the teabags. She filled the kettle and flicked it on, wondering if he was a bit of a health nut as she waited for it to boil. That she knew nothing about him was clear, but seedy, nutty things had been abundant in the cupboard.

Would he have sugar given all those healthy seedy things? Probably not she decided, taking a risk and adding milk to his mug, hoping he wasn't the type to have a squeeze of lemon in his tea. She picked up the two steaming brews and carried them downstairs being careful not to spill any.

'Knock, knock,' Isabel said, raising the two mugs she was carrying as he looked up from where he was sitting at the counter staring at his open laptop.

'You read my mind; I was just thinking it was time for a cuppa. Cheers.' He took the proffered mug from her, and she placed her tea down on the counter. 'Did you sleep all right?'

'Yes, it's a comfy bed. Um, I wasn't sure if you took milk or not, so I took a gamble.'

'You hit the jackpot. Jaffa Cake, or is it too early?' He smiled and went up in her estimation as he produced a packet of the chocolate treats from the drawer beneath the counter. Not too much of a health nut then!

'It's never too early for Jaffa Cakes.' Isabel took one and munched it down, glancing around the gallery. It was busy given the early hour but then if the blue skies she'd spied outside her bedroom window were anything to go by the day was going to be a corker. Holidaymakers would be out and about wanting to make the most of it. She rubbed at the crook of her arm, perhaps the sun and salt air would work some magic on her eczema. She distracted herself by checking out the customers wandering around the gallery. She'd always enjoyed people watching.

'Honeymooners,' she whispered out the corner of her mouth, her gaze indicating the young couple rifling through the postcard prints near the door.'

'How do you know? 'Rhodri looked bemused.

'Sappy expressions on their faces.'

He laughed. 'You're right, I reckon. Him?' Rhodri asked playing the game as he nodded toward a middle-aged man with a T-shirt stretched tight over his belly. He was trailing behind a woman, his wife presumably, and looked like he would rather be somewhere else.

Isabel grinned and whispered. 'She's got him on a strict diet, and all he can think about is how he is going to sneak away and hit the Mr Whippy parked along the waterfront.'

Rhodri laughed loudly this time, causing the honeymooners to look over at him disconcerted. 'You're good.'

Isabel spotted a big man, clad in the casual and unmistakable clobber of a tourist, gazing up at a framed painting of a white-sailed ship in a harbour. He had a camera slung around his neck, but it was the cap on his head with Florida in white stitching that gave the game away, really. Indecision was written all over his face.

'A sale?' Isabel mouthed at Rhodri who mouthed back. 'I hope so.'

She couldn't help herself; she'd done a one-day sales-maker course when she'd had a brief stint selling mobile phones before she left for Australia. You had to overcome your natural hesitation at talking to a stranger and put your friendliest foot forward. There was no room for being shy when it came to closing a deal, and Isabel had developed a knack of stepping a little outside of herself when it came to dealing with the public. It served her well pulling pints too, and instead of clumsy, anxious Isabel, she became confident, chatty Isabel. It felt like that was who she was supposed to be all the time, but she didn't know how to be that girl when she didn't have a role to hide behind.

This was no good though, Rhodri couldn't just sit here sipping tea, she thought. He needed to *sell* the painting to the customer. A bit of sales patter was what was needed she decided, making up her mind. She put her tea down and leaving a bemused Rhodri, she moseyed up alongside the customer. 'Hello there,' she beamed, startling him out of his reverie.

The tourist looked bemusedly at the young woman with strange coloured hair who'd appeared next to him before replying. 'Hi there.'

Yes, indeed, thought Isabel; an American twang. She peered at the card under the canvas. 'I see you're admiring, *Tidal Goodbye*. Do you know Cowes, sir?'

'We visited it yesterday. It sure was a pretty spot.'

'You're here on holiday?' She stated the obvious.

'Sure am. I'm with my wife, but she's around the corner looking for presents to take home for the grandkiddies. We're following in my ancestors' footsteps. Hale's the family name.'

He looked at her as if expecting her to know all members of the Hale family from the Isle of Wight personally before continuing. 'Yep, we sailed from Cowes on the *Hercules of Rye* to Virginia in 1610.' He announced this loudly and proudly, another clue as to where he hailed from. 'Of course, we spread ourselves far and wide; I live in Florida these days. The Sunshine State.'

'Ah, but if your family comes from the island originally, then that means you're practically local!' Isabel beamed. 'And this beautiful artwork would be a reminder of your brave ancestors sailing forth to embrace a new life in a new world. A permanent visual treat to hang on your wall at home to hark back to your roots.' She chewed her bottom lip hoping she hadn't overdone it. The man turned his attention back to the painting. Only now, Isabel hoped he wasn't admiring it because of its moody hues and delicate brush strokes. No, now he saw the Hale family sailing forth leaving their home for adventures in a new frontier. In fact, that could be the same *Hercules of Rye* leaving the shores of the Isle of Wight for all he knew, dang it, that could be his great-granddaddy six times removed up on the prow there.

'Hey there,' he called over to Rhodri, 'this here young lady has sold me on this fine piece of art. It's part of my heritage, a conversational piece, that's what it is. So how're we going to set about getting it back home to the U–nited States?'

~

Rhodri saw the American to the door, a satisfied customer whose artwork would be couriered to his home address in Florida. Isabel was hoping his wife managed to see her husband's ancestors on the ship, too and not the hefty price tag attached.

'Well, you sure earned your keep. That was impressive sales work,' he said to Isabel, sitting back down and picking up the Jaffa Cakes. 'Here have another. Sod it, have the whole pack!'

Isabel grinned and helped herself, she shouldn't really, but she was a sucker for the sweet treats. The day was off to a good start. She sipped her tea and shot a sideways glance at Rhodri. She knew nothing about him other than that he had fancied a change of scene from his life in London and Pier View House had been a prime opportunity for him. Well, there was no time like the present she decided, still feeling rather bold after her painting sale. 'So then, Rhodri, tell me a bit about yourself.'

He snorted. 'You might as well have said, "so, do you come here often?"'

She blushed. He was right it had sounded like a corny pickup line. 'Sorry, it came out wrong. What I meant to say was given our living circumstances it would be nice to know a bit more about your life before you came here.' She tripped over the words.

'Ah, well, so long as you weren't trying to chat me up, that's all right then.'

She stared at him hard; it was difficult to tell if he was having her on or not. His expression as he sipped at the contents of his mug gave nothing away.

'I grew up in Pontypridd in Wales.'

Isabel had only been to Wales once, and that was on a school trip to Cardiff. 'And were you always interested in art?'

'Always. My finger painting when I was in the Pontypridd infants was far and away the most superior of all the other five-year-olds.'

'Really?'

'No, I'm teasing you, but yes, I always loved art. Painting was a passion right from when I was a lad in short pants. I was, my mam used to say, a sensitive boy, and it was my saving grace where Dad was concerned that I also liked rugby. Mam and Dad weren't best keen when I said I wanted to make a career in art, they'd have preferred a doctor or a lawyer, but they got over it okay in the end.'

Isabel nodded. Her parents had held hopes of a university education for her until they'd seen her leaving results. She'd only ever wanted to sing though, and she was not one of life's academics. So, instead of university, she'd embarked on a wide and varied career in drifting.

'I did an art history degree at college in Cardiff, and I was fortunate enough to receive an apprenticeship at Christie's in London. I learned the art auction trade from the bottom up before branching out into opening my gallery and becoming a dealer.'

'What about your painting though?'

He shrugged. 'I got a taste of the high life. I liked living a certain way and painting wasn't going to provide me with the money I needed to fund that lifestyle. Besides which, I'd seen first-hand how cutthroat the art world is. It can be brutal, and I suppose I lacked the courage to put my work out there. A classic case of fear of failure. Until one day I took my blinkers off or rather had them taken off for me, a messy break-up, and concluded I wasn't that twenty-one-year-old living it up in London anymore. That life had long since gotten stale; it was time to get back to what I wanted to do in the first place which was appreciate art, paint, and make a living at the same time. Fortunately, I was lucky enough to be in a position this time around to take a gamble.'

'So you took a leap of faith and came to the Isle of Wight.' She smiled, feeling clever at her play on the gallery's name.

'Exactly.' He looked away, and Isabel sensed there was more to his story than he was saying, but she could tell by the closed expression on his face that he'd told her all he was going to. It was time to move on.

'Well, I think it's probably a respectable time of the day now for me to call in at Sea Vistas. Wish me luck.' She felt a nervous kind of excitement at what lay ahead.

The shadow lifted from Rhodri's face. 'Good luck. I can't wait to hear if my Constance is the woman you're looking for.'

.. ✿ ..

ISABEL INHALED THE seaside smells as she weaved her way down the Esplanade passing locals going about their daily business, and the clusters of visitors. It was easy to spot the early holidaymakers who had a certain dawdling demeanour that instantly gave them away. They were here for a shoulder season cheaper break and to beat the crowds that descended in the manic summer months.

She sidestepped a melting blob of ice cream and pictured a small child wailing at such a catastrophic loss. As she rounded the bend in the waterfront, past the shops, the grand building that was Sea Vistas Retirement Home swept into view. She admired the old girl's beautiful stonework; her soaring chimneys looked as though they were grazing the sky. Sea Vistas' architecture spoke of bygone days. She drew closer and saw that the grounds too were expansive and well-manicured.

The flowerbeds would soon be a mass of spring flowers, she thought, pausing to soak up the scene. She couldn't stand here waxing lyrical all day like Alan Titchmarsh she decided, carrying on down the footpath. Her

tummy reminded her she was anxious for the woman she hoped she was
about to meet to be her Constance as she'd come to think of her.

PART TWO

Humulus lupulus/Wild hops
Mostly used for its sedative like effect, therefore, aiding sleeplessness and restlessness.
Improves appetite.
Antibacterial and antifungal.
Ingested it is said to benefit menstruation/menopausal symptoms.
Can be made into an infusion tincture for a soothing effect or more commonly as a hop pillow.
For sleeplessness:

Harvest fresh hop bulbs and wash in a plastic colander. As a method of drying out the hops placing them in a microwave helps retain the essential oils and aroma. Set to fifty per cent power and check bulbs every three seconds to ensure even drying. After three minutes bulbs should be dry. Allow to cool and collect hops for preparation in a pillow. Dried lavender and chamomile can also be added for a stronger aroma. Place the mixture into a small canvas pocket or bag and tie or sew the end to seal shut. Place the bag under your pillow to aid sleep, or soothe an earache or toothache.

Constance
Chapter 10

Constance eased her stockinged feet into the shoes waiting on the floor beside her bed. Jill always placed them there for her each evening, lined up and ready for the morning. Such were the extra touches one received at Sea Vistas Residential Care Home. So far as rest homes on the island went, this one, Constance knew, was the crème de la crème. Jill knew her charge didn't feel dressed unless she had her shoes on. Constance drew the line at becoming one of the slipper shuffler residents. That was how she viewed any persons lurking about in the shadows of the care home, still in their dressing gowns and slippers, past ten am.

The shoes cost a bomb. Jill had organised their online purchase for her; her clothes too were bought online by Jill these days. She'd known Jill since she was a little girl who would enter her shop on a dare from her friends. That was how she still saw her when she looked at her, a little girl, freckles across her nose and two plaits framing her face as she looked around Constance's shop. Her eyes would be wide with wonder as they scanned the various potion laden shelves, trying to memorise their names to relay them back to her giggling friends outside—thus reinforcing their certainty that Constance was a real live witch.

It was somewhat surreal, Constance thought, that she'd lived long enough for that little girl now to be a woman in the latter stages of middle-age, and her nurse no less. It was strange too, to find herself on the outside looking in on a world she'd never have imagined. A world where one could purchase things from a computer! As for these ruddy shoes though, they still pinched despite their weighty price tag, and when had her ankles gotten so fat and puffy? She gazed at the flesh that seemed to spill over either side of the shoes. She'd always prided herself on her slim ankles. They'd been the only reliably slender part of her body, given her sweet tooth, for the best part of her adult life and now look at them, like pork sausages squeezed inside a sinuous skin.

That was another thing she could add to her list of annoying things about reaching the grand age of eighty-nine, the cost of her shoes had gone through the roof to accommodate her traitorous ankles. And they were boring. *Boring, boring, boring!* So too were her cardigan, skirt, and blouse ensemble. *It was the price you paid for so-called comfort, and an orthopedic sole,* she thought, her eyes glancing over her outfit and her soft black leather Mary Janes with distaste. She'd been a peacock in her day but now was reduced to being a plain old peahen.

Constance had once owned the most fabulous pair of pink satin shoes, bought by her parents for a special birthday. She'd looked at those shoes her mother had picked out for her and felt she was finally closing the door on the past. It wasn't just that the war was over, it was that she'd felt as if she were a butterfly unfurling its crumpled wings wearing those shoes. She'd felt trapped, entombed in a chrysalis of sadness after all that had transpired, for so long and as she slipped her foot inside that pretty pink satin, she'd caught glimpses of a brighter future.

Constance learned as the years trundled by though, that one never really escaped the past not even when dancing in pink satin shoes. It could be swept into the background with a swish of vibrant fabrics, but it was still there nipping at one's heels, be they clad in leather, satin, pigskin, or suede.

While others might lose themselves in the abuse of substances to escape their unhappiness, for Constance, her vice had been shoes, and she'd used the rich colours of her wardrobe as her coat of armour. Those satin party shoes of her eighteenth birthday had triggered a love affair. Stiletto, kitten, wedge, flat, so long as they were bright and beautiful, she had to have them. The Islanders had referred to her fondly in later years as the Imelda Marcos of the Isle of Wight, and then there was Lizzy Harris who worked in the tearooms on Union Street. She used to pop her head into Constance's emporium of cure-alls each morning on her way to work. Her sole purpose for doing so to see which shoes she'd chosen to wear that day, and to admire the brightness of her outfit after so many years shrouded in the sepia tones of war.

The pink of those satin shoes was the same shade as the petals of the roses dotted across the eiderdown draped over the bed she was perched upon now. It was in the stripes of the custom-made curtains that framed the large Georgian window too, and it had been picked out in the plumped cushion resting on the back of the armchair where she sat most days to admire the view. If she had to live anywhere other than Pier View House, then there'd been no choice but here. Sea Vistas echoed with ties to her past. Her room was pretty and plush, and it was that shade of pink that had drawn her to it, that and the view out to the sea, of course. She couldn't imagine not being able to see the sea each day. It would be akin to a farmer upping sticks from acreage to an urban outlook of chimney pots.

Sea Vistas Residential Care sat at the furthermost end of the Esplanade, past the working buildings of the pier, standing sentry, as it had for as long as Constance could remember, on a lonely patch of the greenbelt. It had lived many lives since its story began with Sir Albert Whitely building a magnificent baroque-style house known as Whitely Manor. That had been back in the late 1800s. Constance knew this because she'd looked up the house's story at the Museum of Island History in Newport once.

It had stayed in the Whitely family until the 1920s when it was sold off to pay their debts. Then it became a holiday home for a wealthy lot from Bournemouth and the name was changed to Darlinghurst House. The new owners would descend during the summer months, hangers-on in tow, with shouts of, 'I say, is it Pimm's o'clock, old girl, and anyone for tennis?' Or at least that's what Constance fancied them as having said when she'd seen pictures of the bright young things gathered on the manor house's lawn in the museum's archives.

Troops were billeted to Darlinghurst during the First World War, and in the second it had served as a convalescence home for soldiers once they were deemed well enough to leave the Royal Isle of Wight County Hospital. Constance herself was a child when the Second World War began, but as it dragged on and on, she'd grown into a young woman. She'd been eager to volunteer along with her friend Norma to darn the socks of the poor wounded soldiers housed at Darlinghurst. She and Norma had pinched their cheeks and applied Vaseline to their lips, desperately wishing they looked like Rita Hayworth, before setting off to the big house as they sometimes referred to Darlinghurst, to collect the baskets full of holey socks that had been put aside for them.

If she hadn't trooped up that garden path, badly in need of weeding, things might have panned out so very differently but such was life. *She did* venture up the path with the formidably impressive stone masonry looming in front of her and *it did* open up an avenue for a conversation with a young man that might not otherwise have come about. C'est la vie.

The house was abandoned after the war, the gaping hole in the roof left as was, and the interiors removed and sold off. It had seemed symbolic to Constance. The island was notorious for its ghosts, and Darlinghurst's halls echoed with them, ghosts she was glad to embrace now, but ghosts that for so long had haunted her with her regrets.

The house was in far too prime a spot to just be allowed to crumble and the corporate owners of Sea Vistas had seen a business opportunity. They'd poured a small fortune into doing the old girl up and had relaunched her in her current guise as an upmarket care home.

Constance's experience of care homes was non-existent but Sea Vistas she imagined, given its hefty price tag, was as good as they got. She'd never had any intention of moving from Pier View House, but age had seen fit to make it impossible for her to stay. So here she was with her own, what did they call her? Key worker that was it, Jill, whose background was nursing in the public system, but who'd confided the money and hours were much better at Sea Vistas.

Constance's hand drifted over to the bag of Maltesers she always had on hand, her only vice these days, and she popped a chocolate ball in her mouth. As she sucked on the sweet chocolate, she raised her gaze to look out the window. The expanse of foam-tipped waves betrayed the direction of the wind. When the window was open, she could smell the salty coastline and liked to think she could hear the drift of happy seaside chatter; they were the scent and sounds of her life.

She startled at the knock on the door behind her. It was the second knock of the day, the first coming at seven. when Jill popped in to help her dress before carrying on with her rounds. The second knock signified that it was eight thirty already.

'Miss Downer, it's Jill again. Can I come in?' her familiar cheery voice called.

Constance frowned. For goodness sake, she couldn't understand why Jill felt the need to announce herself. She was a superb timekeeper; who else would it be knocking at her door this time of the morning?

The whole damned business of being old was exhausting and left her frustrated beyond belief. Still, at least Jill talked to her like she was an adult. Not like Monday's visitor, Adele Stanton.

Constance's foot had quavered inside her black slip-on shoe with the urge to boot Adele. She might have been thirty years younger than Constance, but her manner was that of a bossy mother hen as she filled her in with all the latest goings on in Fishbourne. Adele had sold the florist business she owned two doors down from Pier View House when her husband passed away a few years ago, and she'd retired to the small nearby village which, if Adele were to be believed, was a Sodom and Gomorrah hotbed of activity.

Constance had sat trapped in her armchair while she prattled on. It would seem Adele kept an ear to the ground in Fishbourne just as she'd done in Ryde. The woman was a gossip of the highest order, but she *had* remembered that Constance's favourite flower was the early purple orchid, bringing her a cutting. Jill had searched out a vase for it, and the orchid was a splash of fragrant colour on her bedside table. For Constance, the purple bloom signified spring, beginning to flower as it did on the island each April. This year, however, it was unseasonably early, given it was only halfway through March. Perhaps they were in for a long, hot summer.

Usually, the sight of the purple bloom cheered her, but this year her mind kept slipping back, reliving her younger days. That was another thing about one's golden years; you couldn't remember what you ate for lunch that day, but you could remember clear as a bell the events of over seventy years ago. It was a peculiar thing. As though to re-confirm this train of thought, Constance put the lid back on the box she'd been leafing through earlier.

It was a blue cardboard box, slightly faded by age with a yellow stripe around the lid, and it had once contained, amongst other things, those precious shoes of hers. Now, it was filled with a collection of memories, a lifetime's worth.

She registered another knock; it was a bit louder this time. She'd almost forgotten Jill was waiting to come in. She put the box back in the drawer where she kept it before opening her mouth to call out that yes, she could come in.

'Are you ready for me to take you down to breakfast then Miss D?' Jill asked upon opening the door.

Constance felt like screaming. Did Jill think she was starring in her very own American sitcom? *Caring for Miss D* or perhaps *Me 'n' Miss D*. All of this she kept to herself, however, as she nodded. She eased herself upright and allowed Jill to take her elbow to help her the short distance down the corridor to the lift although she was quite capable of walking the short distance on her own.

Her usual table beside the bay window looking out to sea would be set, the tea brewing in the pot for one. Her poached egg, done the way she liked it—dippy in the middle with toast soldiers to the side—would arrive with a flourish and a sprig of parsley as soon as she was seated. She would be sure to position herself in her seat, just so, to ensure nobody asked to join her. She couldn't be doing with idle chit-chat and especially not when she wanted to concentrate on the simple pleasure of dipping her toast into her egg. For the most part, she was left alone.

These days, she looked forward to her meals. They structured her day for one thing and for another, she was no longer in charge of their actual preparation—cooking had never been her forte. She handpicked her week's choice of breakfast—that never differed from the poached egg, lunch, and dinner from the menu provided on a Sunday morning. She could have wine with her evening meal if she wanted too. No cause for complaint on the dining front.

Mind you, she thought, nodding at Iris Marshall who was also waiting for the lift, some of them seemed to think being old gave them a license to complain; Iris being a prime example. Only last night, Constance had heard her trilling in a voice designed to carry through to the kitchen to her crony, Jean, that she reckoned it was cask wine, not bottle, being served with dinner. And that for the money they forked out to stay at Sea Vistas they shouldn't be fobbed off with cheap plonk! Didn't it all taste the same after the first glass? Constance had thought waving her glass for a refill and knowing that as she sipped its contents, she'd stop hearing the chatter combined with the chink of the residents' knives and forks. She'd gaze out the window seeing a different story in a different time unfolding.

The dining room was cast in the rosy glow of morning, and the unmistakable smell of bacon mingling with toast wafted forth as Jill, her arm linked firmly through Constance's, steered them toward her table. Constance nodded good morning at several of the diners before Jill saw her to her seat. The nurse glanced up at the time and announced she was due to see one of her ladies. Constance muttered her thanks and watched her sprightly form stride from the dining room, before unfolding her napkin. She smoothed it on her lap and sat waiting for her day to unfold just as it had yesterday, and the day before that, and well, every day since she'd moved to Sea Vistas.

Chapter 11

Constance had woken early. Far too early. She pulled herself up to a sitting position, her huffing sigh of exertion sounding loud in the surrounding space. Jill had plumped the pillows for her the way she liked them before she'd turned in the night before, but now they were squished at awkward angles beneath her back. It would require too much effort to rearrange them she decided, straining to hear the familiar routines of Sea Vistas outside her door.

It was silent in the hall, no rattle of trolleys signifying that morning was here. Her eyes felt gravelly, and the feeling reminded her of when she was a girl playing on the beach. The wind would whip up the sand near the Solent's edge and she'd blink against the sudden deluge of gritty, fine particles. Now, she squeezed her eyes shut once more. She'd passed a restless night, sleeping soundly for a few hours and then waking for no reason other than things were playing on her mind. It seemed that the past was always there these days lurking in the wings of her subconscious, waiting for her to drift off to accost her.

Constance let out another huff and plucked at the covers; it had always frustrated her so when she couldn't sleep. In bygone years it had been because there was so much living she wanted to cram into each day and energy was needed for that. It had been an obligation of sorts to those whose lives had been cut short or never even had the chance to begin. The war had done that. Now there wasn't much with which she was desperate to fill her day, but not sleeping still frustrated her, simply because it added unnecessary length to those long daylight hours of sameness looming ahead.

'Oh, stop it, Constance Downer, you old misery guts,' she murmured, unsure whether the words had been breathed aloud. It wasn't like her to be maudlin, her inherent nature was sunny, but this mood had settled on her while she tossed and turned through the long night. It would not be banished lightly she knew, recalling how the memories had come in thick, fast drifts like snow.

Constance opened her eyes and turned her gaze toward the window. The only clue as to the advent of the morning was slanting in through the window, snaking in around the edges of the drapes. No dust motes were dancing in the shards of light as they'd done in the bedroom of her youth, though. You'd think not too, she thought, what with the exorbitant fees she paid for the privilege of being housed at Sea Vistas. She missed watching the dust motes though, convinced as she'd once been that they were the tiniest of fairies dancing just for her in the light. She sighed. Life had been simple back then when she'd believed in fairies and before the war crashed into their lives.

Constance took a little sip of water from the glass on her bedside table. Those despised black shoes she saw were on the floor beside the bed, and it made her think of when she was young. As a girl, she'd sneak a look at dad's feet in those sturdy polished black leather shoes of his sometimes. She'd wonder why it was his flat feet hadn't saved him from having to serve that first time around. She'd never asked, and so she'd never known, but she knew instinctively raising the subject would be rocking the boat and she'd never been one for that. Well, leastways not until she grew older because Constance knew her advancing age had brought an uncaring nonchalance for what others thought when it came to most things.

It was during those latter war years that she'd come to understand why their father had chosen never to speak of what he went through on those muddy, blood-soaked fields far from home during the Great War. He wasn't alone in this. She'd understood when the war that took Ted and so many others finally ended, why his lips had stayed sealed. Nobody wanted to speak of it not the soldiers, not the widows, not the mothers, no one. They were grateful for long-imagined peacetime and too frightened that talking about their experiences might somehow breathe life back into them once more. Awaken the nightmare once more.

Constance assumed it had been the same in 1918 when her father, Arthur Downer, barely twenty years of age had arrived home and got down on bended knee to ask his Eleanor to marry him. He'd decided to look to his future, not his past. It was the only way he could move forward and prove to himself that he had indeed lived through it. Those nightmares of his served to prove one could never outrun one's history, however.

People were different back then, she mused. They were stoic and private and oh so very proud. The adage of the British keeping a stiff upper lip was indeed the case. These days everything was plastered all over the Internet and talked about until it had been dissected into microscopic pieces. Dignity was a dying word in her opinion. She blamed a large portion of it on television chat shows. It was compulsive viewing watching others air their dirty laundry publicly.

There'd come a time, the same year the terrible news that Ted, her brother, had died reached them, when she too had tried to lock her experiences away. To pretend they'd never happened. But just like with her father they always crept back, beckoning to her in the darkness when her defenses were down. Her choices were taken away from her back then. She'd had no say in the way it all transpired. Things were different now; people's sense of morality was different. Her life could have been so very different had the lyrics played a different tune in a different time.

The feelings that had consumed her sixteen-year-old self, however, were too powerful to contain, they refused to be boxed away and seemed to intensify daily. There was nothing for it and nowhere to vent, and so she set about her mundane routine at the factory hoping to still her mind. These confusing and frustrating new emotions consumed her the first time she laid eyes on Henry.

'Henry,' she whispered to the empty room where she still couldn't quite believe she now lived. Her mouth forming the name she'd cherished so and her gaze settled on the framed certificate on the wall. It had been hung on the walls of the Downer family's old haberdashery shop on the ground floor of Pier View House to state her father's qualification as a tailor.

Pier View House had lived several lives since the days her parents had run A Stitch in Time in the ground floor space. These days it was a light and airy art gallery. Constance herself had converted it into an emporium of sorts a year or so after her parents passing. She had a talent; she'd discovered inadvertently one winter's afternoon when having sourced an armful of comfrey from the side of a boggy riverbed. She'd happened across old Mrs

Glyn, her headscarf knotted tightly under her chin to keep the biting wind off the Solent at bay.

Her varicose veins were playing merry hell with her she said after enquiring as to what Constance was up to with an armful of comfrey. 'It's no more than a weed,' she said, shaking her head with such vigour that the bread she'd just bought to make jam sandwiches for her and Mr Glyn's supper threatened to slip from the bag. She readjusted it in her arms while waiting for Constance to explain herself, giving her the once-over as she did so. What a woman pushing fifty was doing getting about in an ensemble so bright she could be stood on a rock at sea and used as a beacon for the passing ships was beyond her. She straightened her sedate tan coat. Mind, Connie Downer had always been a bit of an oddball.

'I make a poultice with it to ease the ache in my knee, Mrs Glyn. This cold weather's no good for it.' Mrs Glyn might have only been twenty years older than Constance but she'd known her since she was a little girl and as such had always addressed her by her formal title.

Mrs Glyn's eyes narrowed. 'A poultice you say? Would it help with my veins?'

'It may do, Mrs Glyn, but I can't make you any promises.'

'I'll try anything; the pain's driving me potty.'

Constance had trudged back home in her wellies making her way through the shop oblivious to the trail of mud she was leaving behind. The shelves of A Stitch in Time were still full of cotton reels, zippers, and buttons. They were items that for whatever reason—Constance suspected it could have something to do with the newly opened big supermarket—were rarely required by the general public since her parents passing. This was despite her valiant efforts to keep the business running. She passed through the door at the back of the shop and took the stairs gingerly, thanks to her aching knee. It dawned on her then as she placed the herbs on the kitchen bench that the absence of her parents, who'd gone within six months of each other, was not so sharp today.

The comfrey leaves needed to be chopped, and she set about doing this. The poultice she was going to prepare was a recipe from Molly's journal. It was for the relief of aches and pains. The knee Constance had twisted as a child, tripping down the stairs of the folly as she made to get away from the evil witch, still plagued her on occasion. The comfrey poultice always eased it.

Next, Constance added water to the chopped leaves and with her mortar and pestle bashed away until it was the consistency of an unappetising soup before tipping the green mess into a large bowl. She added a couple of handfuls of flour and mixed it with her hands until it had a gloopy texture. Once she was satisfied it was as it should be, she scrubbed her hands clean and retrieved the swathe of muslin cloth she kept in the cupboard before cutting it into two equal sizes. She split the comfrey poultice evenly between the two and wrapped them parcel-like before taking one around to Mrs Glyn's cottage down the way.

Constance fussed around the older woman, affixing the poultice into place over the bothersome vein for her. 'Have you a clean tea towel, Mrs Glyn?'

'Of course, me luvvie. In the bottom kitchen drawer.'

Constance reappeared a moment later and wrapped the tea towel around her leg before taking a piece of cord she'd cut from a reel in the shop and tying it into place. 'Now then, Mrs Glyn. You tell Mr Glyn to get his supper tonight while you keep that leg elevated this evening. If you do that, by tomorrow, hopefully, you'll be good as gold.'

Indeed, the following morning, Mrs Glyn appeared at A Stitch in Time and announced she felt sprightly enough to dance the cancan. She lifted her skirt as though to give an example before thinking better of it. Word of Constance's miraculous poultice spread, the way the word always spread on the island, and Constance rose from being an eccentric spinster to Constance Downer of Ryde; healer, and when she wasn't in earshot, it was whispered she was, in fact, a witch. Such was the demand for her services that she decided the time had come to reinvent A Stitch in Time. A sale was had, the shop cleared of all its stock and a new sign declared the premises to be Constance's Cure-alls. If you were an islander and if something was ailing you, then Constance's Cure-alls was your first port of call.

Of course, it was muttered behind her back that it was in her blood, by those who were old enough to remember the story. She was descended from Molly Downer now, wasn't she—the last witch on the Isle of Wight—so it should be no surprise...

Chapter 12

MOLLY DOWNER, THE WITCH OF BEMBRIDGE

How Molly left everything to the parson.

In Bembridge Town there lived a Dame,
Now Molly Downer was her name,
And she in story has her niche,
Because they say, she was a witch.
All by herself she did reside,
No friend or partner at her side,
In a snug cottage warmed with thatch,
And people called it Witches Hatch.
Miss Molly, who was ne'er a wife,
There lived a lonely life,
And in seclusion passed the hours,
For folk were frightened of her powers,
In fact her most strange husbandry
Truly frightened all and sundry.
She was I fear most happy when
She could bewitch the Customs Men,
Her guiles she used, with every ruse,
To bring in free trade brandy booze.
The Customs Men so runs the tale,
Would, at her name, turn deathly pale.
And should they be inclined to mock her,
She'd threaten Davey Jones' Locker,
Now parson, hearing of her way,
Betook upon himself to pray
That Moll should give up charm and spell,
In case she ended up in hell.

Our Molly, who was well past twenty,
Liked the parson good and plenty,
So she spoke the reverend fair,
Carefully dressing up her hair.
But of his words, she took no heed,
And altered neither word nor deed.
And so it was that in the end
He was poor Molly's only friend.
Now Molly one day feeling ill,
Decided she would make her Will,
And without waiting one more minute,
Bequeathed her house and all things in it.
And being of all kin bereft
Her fortune to her friend she left.
Then Molly dressed her in her best
And laid her down for her last rest.
Stiff on the kitchen table bare,
The parson found her lying there,
Dead as the Dodo, stark and cold,
And in her hand, her Will did hold.
So when he'd had sufficient toddy,
Sexton buried Molly's body,
Then parson, fearing witchcraft's seed,
The burning of her house decreed.
And so, as soon as she was buried,
To burn the house, the people hurried,
So that no feature should survive
To keep her charms and spells alive.
From miles around the people came.
The cottage roared with smoke and flame,
And as the night in blackness fell,
The fire had conquered every spell.
Though not yet quite as I shall tell,
For here and there, as timbers fell,
A useful piece some sinner took,

Or souvenir was pinched for luck.
Now in the churchyard, by her grave
Whom parson tried so hard to save,
They set a stone with Molly's date,
All wondering what would be her fate.
But Molly's art was not quite tamed.
Some witchcraft seemingly remained.
For if, when summer's sun is high,
This old churchyard you come by,
You'll find the stone, which was set there,
Has vanished, quite, into thin air.

–Ballads of the Wight
J.R. Brummell

~

Molly's leather-bound journal filled with herbal cure-alls lived in Constance's faded blue memory box. It had been pressed into her coltish twelve-year-old hands as she played with the neighbourhood children at Appley Folly by a local woman, Elsie Parker.

Elsie was a grandmother and thus far too old to be the main caregiver to an unruly tribe who terrorised the locals in Bembridge. Mrs Downer wouldn't let Constance or her older sister, Evelyn associate with the family, given their common status. Constance assumed Elsie had chosen her to approach to return the book as she was the youngest and therefore most malleable of the Downers. Mum could be quite formidable should the mood so take her and Evelyn, a known telltale tit. The animosity between Elsie Parker and Mrs Downer of A Stitch in Time stemmed from the trifling matter of an unpaid bill for mending services.

Elsie elaborated to a bewildered Constance that her late mother, God rest her soul, had snatched the book from Molly's cottage in the days following her death. The stone building had stood empty and alone, cooling its heels, unlike the local folk who were feeding their voracious superstitious appetites, until the only thing that could satiate it was the cottage being burned to the ground.

Elsie's mother had been not much more than a curious tot at the time and didn't know why she'd seen fit to pocket such an item. The only reasoning she could give was that there was nobody to stop her and it had felt very daring to do so. That the book was in her possession had remained her lifelong secret; she'd not known what to do with it once stolen and was frightened of the consequences should she disclose what she'd done. As she lay struggling, her breath coming in short gasping bursts in her last days, she'd urged her daughter to give it back to its rightful owners, the Downer family of Ryde. And Elsie, a superstitious woman herself, was doing so now by handing it to Constance.

This was the first Constance had heard of a Molly Downer, and Elsie was only too happy to relay the tale of how this long since passed relative of the Downer family was the last witch on the Isle of Wight. Constance's eyes grew wide, ignoring the other children calling her back to continue playing their game, as she listened enthralled with the tale.

'Of course, it depends on how you define witch,' Elsie stated. 'People were quick to point the finger at anyone who was a bit different back in those days.' She made a harrumphing sound. 'Still are in my opinion, but with Molly, well *there was* the unfortunate business of the curse. Poor love didn't have the most salubrious of starts neither what with her being born the illegitimate daughter of a reverend no less.'

'What does illegitimate mean?' Constance interrupted wondering as to Elsie's sudden plummy tone as she rolled the foreign word forth.

'Well, now you're old enough to know what a bastard is, i'nt ya?'

Constance flushed, she'd heard Elsie's grandchildren referenced as such.

'Well, there you go then. Molly's mother was known as a healer, and although her family wanted nothing to do with her once they found out she was to be an unwed mother, they gave her enough money to build a little cottage in Hillway. She grew up in that cottage, and she had a best friend for most of her young life. They were inseparable even when their heads began to be turned by the local boys. Molly was a pretty girl, and the fellows were sweet on her, but not everybody liked her.

'There was a girl of a similar age to her called Harriet, who took an instant dislike to Molly. It was jealousy on Harriet's part, and she made poor Molly's life a misery by teasing and taunting her. She'd developed a thick skin though, over the years, had to, didn't she? The stigma of being illegitimate had seen to that, and as she grew, she learned the healing skills of her mother. Sadly, Molly's mother grew ill and passed on when she was a teenager, as did her father. He never formally acknowledged her, and he left her a pittance to live on.

'It wasn't long after that life turned sour for Molly. She had a terrible falling out with her dear friend, and here's where it all gets a bit muddy. Some say the two friends fought because Molly was a God-fearing and chaste young woman and when she learned her friend was carrying on with a married man she let loose. Others say it was because her friend married and Molly felt she'd been abandoned after losing both parents as well. Whatever it was, it was around this time that she tripped up and sealed her fate by cursing Harriet. She was heard to say that should any good fortune fall upon her, she would die before possession.'

Constance gasped, and Elsie looked pleased with the reaction.

'Well, Harriet got sick, didn't she? The very same day she received a letter telling her she'd been bequeathed the sum of twenty pounds. Of course, Molly didn't help her cause by becoming a recluse who lived, by all accounts, in squalor. The local folk liked to talk of poppets and bottles of liquid hanging in her windows.'

'What's a poppet?'

'It's a little doll, i'nt it.'

Constance was picturing it all in her mind, but Elsie wasn't finished yet.

'Then there were the rumours of her being thick as thieves with the smugglers who used to roam our shores, but I'm not sure about all that. There were those who wanted to try her as a witch, but the trials had recently stopped. When she was found dead, it's said the villagers stripped her body and, after finding no mark of a witch, they ransacked her cottage before burning it to the ground.'

Constance exclaimed at the cruelty of it all.

'There's now't so cruel as folk,' Elsie said, nodding sagely. 'Now take that book and do what you will with it. It's yours by rights.'

Constance was unsure whether she should thank the woman or not, but Elsie had done what she'd come to do. She'd already turned away and begun to holler at the youngest of her grandchildren, who'd dropped her knickers to go for a wee on the grass verge of the Esplanade path, uncaring that several couples taking in the sea air were tutting their disapproval at such a carry-on.

Now, on this seemingly normal Tuesday morning, the shard of light sneaking into her room was gaining strength, and there were sounds of life in the corridor outside her room. Constance realised she was unsure of how much time had passed, she'd been so lost in her thoughts. She wasn't ready to clear them away for the day though, not just yet and her eyes flitted to the drawer in the bedside cabinet where she kept her old blue memory box. She retrieved it now, lifting the lid, her fingers touching the items hidden within it. She'd never told a soul about the book, waving Norma's nosy questions away at the folly that day with a vague reply that it was an old recipe book she was to pass on to her mother, that was all. It was Mrs Parker's way of making amends for her tardy bill paying, she'd fibbed. She'd taken the book home and hidden it under the loose floorboard beneath her bed. It was safe from Evelyn's all-seeing gaze there.

The hidey-hole was Constance's secret, and home to her most special things. She kept the rose her childhood friend, Jonathan, had given her, hidden between the pages of a notebook, dried and pressed. There were ticket stubs too, from films she'd seen, with glamorous women hinting at life beyond what she knew on the island. A programme for the circus Dad had taken her to see as a special treat in Portsmouth one Christmas was secreted away too.

Oh, what a wonderful treat that day at the circus was she recalled, even now so many years later. She'd been mesmerised by the beautiful tightrope artist and had spent weeks afterward unsuccessfully attempting to cross her skipping rope. Mum was not best pleased to find it tethered to the washing line and a drain pipe with her broom re-purposed as a balancing pole. Then, as the girl she'd been reached the cusp of womanhood the shells had been added to the box. Her pretty shells, whose watercolour patterns time had not seen fit to fade. One for each day of the week.

These saved trinkets and scraps of paper would mean nothing to a stranger, but Constance treasured them. Somehow during wartime, it had become vitally important to hold on to those things she held dear lest she blink and they were gone.

As a girl, she'd take the book out from time to time when the coast was clear. There she'd sit cross-legged on her bed, carefully turning the brittle, tannin pages hoping this time she'd find something to hold her interest. She was always left feeling disappointed by the time she'd turned to the last page. It was like biting into an apple that promised to be crisp and sweet only to find it floury. For all Mrs Parker's drama when she'd handed it to her, she'd have thought it would contain at least one recipe for eye of newt and toe of frog. A proper witch's brew.

Instead, the elaborately inked swirls were no more than wordy entries for simple herbal remedies. These were of little interest to Constance, and so she'd put the book back, unwilling for whatever reason she couldn't put her finger on, to share it with the rest of the family. She'd asked her mother once about Molly, but her tart expression brooked no further badgering on the subject, and she'd let it lie. Molly, she'd concluded was a skeleton in the Downer family cupboard. Sometimes she'd wondered as she prepared her tinctures, teas, and poultices what her mother would say if she'd known what trade her only surviving child had wound up plying on the ground floor of Pier View House, thanks to Molly's journal. It would have had her turning in her grave for sure, Constance thought.

Her fingers touched on the rippled surface of a shell. She took it from the box turning it over in her hand and admiring its deep pink tones. As she waited for Jill's soft knock to tell her it was time to get up, she held it to her ear and listening to the echo of the sea her mind once more wandered through the door that seemed to be opening wider each day into the past.

Chapter 13

1944

Constance sat down on the stone bench off to the side of Appley Tower. It was the start of the working week, and she'd not long got off the bus from Cowes. Her bones ached, and her fingers were stiff with the long shift just finished at the shipyard. Appley Bay she thought, gazing out in front of her, was a very different scene to the one of her childhood. Back then all she'd seen when she looked out to the water was the ferry plying its lazy way back and forth. That, and a smattering of fishing boats casting their nets wide as they bobbed atop the water.

Now, the sea was packed with ominous, hulking steel ships plotting their next move, poised in their strategic positions. Constance felt as though she could step from one of those great floating monoliths to the other and jump off once she reached Portsmouth. Something was coming; it was something big, everybody sensed it. It was in the air, being whispered about but never properly spoken of.

The folly, beside which she sat, was still standing sentry, miraculously unscathed. Constance had always loved it, having grown up thinking of it as her miniature castle with its turrets at the top. She smiled now, thinking back to all the games of princesses imprisoned by a nasty witch and being rescued by knights in shining armour that she and Norma had played here. Occasionally they'd managed to rope a real-life knight in, well that's if you counted Jonathan Martin with his knobbly knees. She smiled, recalling how those knees of Jonny's were always bruised or grazed from his many boyish adventures, and how his socks used to sit in a woolly puddle around his ankles.

Poor Jonathan. The Martins had moved inland feeling it would be safer when the bombs began to rain down on the island. A few short weeks after they moved, the cottage they'd relocated to suffered a direct hit from an incendiary as they slept. None of the Martins had survived. There'd been too much loss, Constance thought shuddering, far too much. Her brother Ted's recent death, just on two months ago, was so very raw and close to the surface.

Ted was in the Forty-Sixth Infantry Division and had been killed in battle at Monte Cassino in January. He'd only left home a month earlier. Poor Teddy had been waiting with bated breath to turn eighteen to enlist. He would have lied about his age and sailed away long before then too if it wasn't for Ginny. They'd been sweethearts since they were fourteen, having met when Ginny was sent from Southampton to Ryde at the start of the war to stay with an aunt and her family. Her father, a widower, was killed at the Portsmouth Dockyard soon after and so Ginny had stayed on the island.

It was with the knowledge he'd be leaving that Ginny and Ted had gotten married a month before Teddy's coming of age birthday. Ginny had made a beautiful bride although there were tense and tearful moments on her part in the prior weeks as to her dress. It was Constance's elder sister Evelyn who'd come to the rescue in the end. Her friend Margaret's cousin who'd gotten married before rationing had begun to bite had dug out her gown on the condition that Ginny pass it on to anyone else who should need it. Their mother, a seamstress, had altered it to fit her soon-to-be daughter-in-law's petite frame and the white satin had hung beautifully on her in time for her big day.

And what a day it was. The sun had beamed down on the Downer family despite it being mid-winter, and the promise of a bright future had been palpable. Ginny had moved into Pier View House after the wedding, squeezing in alongside the rest of them, and it was as though she'd always been there. Then, four short weeks later it was time for Teddy to go. Constance closed her eyes conjuring up her precious last images of her brother. She liked to take them out and examine them as though giving them an airing would allow her to hang onto him that little bit longer.

They'd all gone down to the pier to wave him off. Mum's hair, she'd noticed as they milled around waiting to say their goodbyes, had more daubs of grey in it these days than the vibrant auburn of her youth. She'd set it in careful pin curls and was dressed in her Sunday best. A freshly pressed handkerchief, now crumpled, clutched tightly in her hand as she dabbed at her eyes, all the while sniffing. Dad stood, stoic beside her. His hat was tilted at what he liked to think was a rakish angle. It was important to look the part in their line of business he'd tell them all as he fiddled with the arrangement of his hat in the mirror that hung over the sideboard. A peacock if ever there was, their dad! He'd maintained a stiff upper lip and a ramrod back that day, unlike his wife, as he gave his eldest child, and only son, a nod farewell.

Evelyn who was the middle child of the three Downer children had dressed for the occasion too. She'd been busy eyeing up the youngest Duff lad, whose birthday had fallen the day before Ted's. Constance was surprised to see how well he looked minus his butcher's apron. She looked at him from under her lashes while he marched proudly alongside Ted down the pier. Unlike her sister though she had the presence of mind to give no clues away as to where her mind might be wandering. Evelyn's sharp intake of breath at the sight of Robert Duff, a duffle bag slung over his shoulder, looking impossibly handsome in his uniform, earned her an elbow in the ribs from Mum.

Then there'd been Ginny. She'd put such a brave face on things for Ted's sake. She'd waved to him until Constance had thought her poor sister-in-law's arm would drop off, but when the Solent's horizon swallowed him up, she'd been inconsolable.

Constance opened her eyes, seeing but not seeing the hub of activity on the Solent in front of her as she carefully stored the memory of that final scene away for another day. She hadn't understood the gravitas of saying goodbye to Ted. The possibility that she might not see him again was not something she'd entertained. It was childish of her, she understood now. Dad, standing there squinting into the sun, would have known what his boy faced. He'd done his duty in the First World War and still cried out in his sleep from time to time all these years later.

It would have been cruel to share this knowledge with Ted, or any of them for that matter, because it wouldn't have changed things. What was to come was as inevitable as the tide that had been inching its way up the beach as they huddled together watching him leave. So it was, her brother had left them all with the excited gleam of an impending adventure in his eyes, sure that he'd be back to a hero's welcome before the year was out to live his life with his pretty, young wife.

The sounds of family life above the haberdashery shop on the ground floor of Pier View House, which her parents had run since they were first married, were different with Ted gone. It was the absence of his boisterous banter Constance would often think as she lay in bed fully dressed. That was the custom in case the need to troop down to the freezing Anderson Shelter at the bottom of the garden arose. It was funny how quickly one grew used to change no matter how hard one fought against it, and how she couldn't recall a time when they'd slept soundly and uninterrupted.

It had become increasingly clear as the fighting showed no signs of abating that the Nazis, nocturnal and efficient creatures that they were, had decided the Islanders should be the recipients of the bombs that didn't quite make it all the way to Southampton or Portsmouth. Their motto it would appear had been waste not, want not.

Ted being taken from them changed everything. The boy, far too young to be the bearer of such news, had delivered the telegram to the shop. His eyes, filled with feeling, too big in his sombre face as he handed Ginny the official envelope. It was those eyes of his that had given the game away from the instant he walked into the shop on a wild and windy day, '*It is with regret we inform you—*'

In the minutes before receiving this news, Evelyn, who'd not long tossed her coat over her father's stool, had been holding court. She had her hair tucked up in a turban and was clad in her overalls; the belt cinched so tightly at the waist that Constance had wondered how she could breathe let alone speak. Nevertheless, she could and had been spouting off about how she'd learned to milk a cow this week. Further evidence of this was the billy of milk she'd given their mum on this rare trip home from Norris Castle Farm. There was such a sense of friendship, and despite the hard work, fun amongst the Land Girls, Constance always thought with a touch of envy as she listened to her sister's stories of their shenanigans.

She was sure these tales Evelyn brought home with her were heavily censored for their parent's benefit. Her sister's backbreaking work was much sweetened, she knew, by its proximity to the castle. It had been converted to soldiers' barracks, hence the cinching of the belt. The girls at the shipyard factory in Cowes where she worked were, for the most part, a coarse bunch

who were there under sufferance. She'd have given anything to join Evelyn at
Norris Castle Farm but they were full, and she was needed elsewhere.

Dad was busy tuning Evelyn's chatter out as he sorted the pile of drab
olive coloured trousers that had been brought in for repair from the camp
at Puckpool Park. His wife, carrying out a meagre stock take thanks to
rationing and pondering whether to touch on making shorts from old
pillowcases or skirts from trousers at her 'make do and mend' class later that
week, rolled her eyes. She still found it hard to believe that Evelyn, who'd
always been hard pressed to help with so much as peeling the spuds, survived
the daily demands of the Land Army. It had been the making of her daughter
in her humble opinion.

As for Constance, she was home early from her loathed work riveting,
thanks to the air-raid siren having sounded a false alarm. She could have gone
with Lil and the others back to her house where they planned on practicing
the numbers they'd chosen for their upcoming performance at Darlinghurst
House. She'd begged off though, telling them she wasn't feeling the best. In
truth every time she thought about getting up in front of all those soldiers
and the nursing staff to sing, she really did feel sick. Their factory manager
thought it would be good form for some of his girls to entertain the poor lads
recuperating at Darlinghurst House with a bit of a sing-song.

Constance, who often sang as she sorted her rivets, was one of the first
to be put forward, and how could she say no? Although, when bossy Doris
Cosby, their pianist, suggested she sing Vera Lynn's "The White Cliffs of
Dover" solo she had been sorely tempted.

So instead of battling her nerves as she sang about the bluebirds over the
white cliffs of Dover, she'd been balanced on a stool behind the shop counter.
She didn't want to be on her own upstairs and was busying her hands by
unpicking a childhood jumper. It had seen better days and could be reused in
her and Norma's sock darning efforts for those same soldiers at Darlinghurst
House.

So, there they all were minus one. The Downer family gathered like the
cast of a play ready for the opening scene, and Constance could recall the
words that had run through her head upon Ginny tearing open the telegram
to confirm what they already knew. She had asked herself, how on earth
could anything bad happen on such an ordinary winter's day?

How could she have been thinking wistfully of shirking her chores, and wrapping up to go for a stroll along the seafront just a few minutes before her world, as she'd known it, tipped on its axis? And all the while her lovely, kind-hearted big brother had been dead.

That was when the reality of war had come crashing home for Constance. Until then she'd been rather removed from it. Her days before this news had felt as though she were play-acting in an exciting, albeit at times terrifying, drama. Oh, she didn't much like the role she'd been given, bussing down to Cowes each day to put in long hours at the shipyard factory to toil at a grimy mundane task. Needs must, though, and with rationing had come austerity. The meagre wages she pocketed weekly helped to put food on the table at home. Nevertheless, it was a drama, which although always just close enough to nip at her heels, had not yet gotten close enough to bite. That afternoon, however, she was wounded deeply.

Now as she sat on the bench beside the folly, Constance felt the cold of the stone slab beneath her begin to seep through to her underclothes. She flexed her fingers, scrunching them into fists before unfurling them and stretching them. They throbbed with the fiddly, dirty work of sorting through the rivets for the correct thickness and length needed, and she eyed her blackened nails with distaste. It kept her busy though, and when she was busy, her mind didn't dwell on Ted. At least she didn't have to heat the rivets in the furnace or hold on to them with the wretched dolly as they were pounded into place. The latter was mouthy Myrtle's job.

Myrtle had deemed her not strong enough for much, and so she'd been set the task of sorting. She took comfort from the fact she was doing her bit for the war effort. She could hold her head up high, knowing Ted would be proud of her, even if it wasn't where she'd seen herself when she'd been hunched over her school desk. It earned enough for her to pay her way at home too, and Mum's grateful expression when she handed her wage packet over told her that it was helping keep the family afloat. Rationing had hit their little shop hard.

She was supposed to go straight home after work. The air raid sirens regularly sounded these days and were coupled with the never-ending drone of doodlebugs too noisy to sneak their way across the night sky. She didn't want to go home, though, not just yet. It wasn't quite five o'clock, but the air was growing dense and moist with encroaching nightfall. Spring was a good month or so off yet, but despite the cold, she wanted to sit for a while. It had become her custom to perch here for ten or so minutes before venturing home.

It was her quiet time, a chance to unwind from the boisterous, and sometimes lewd chatter in the factory. It was a time in which to brace herself for the oppressive atmosphere grief had brought with it at home. She sighed heavily watching the fine mist escape her mouth like wisps of smoke, and the plumes of white reminded her of Evelyn who had taken the habit up in recent times. Her sister had it easy living up at Norris Castle Farm, she mused. Popping in on her family now and again with a pat of butter or a billy of milk and regaling them with her tall tales. Oh, she knew Evelyn was casting her life as a Land Girl in a positive light, it was Evelyn's way. She wouldn't let on that it was hard, back-breaking work but even knowing this, each time she left, Constance found herself restless, and a little resentful of her sister's freedom.

Now, she retrieved a hanky out of the pocket of the coat she wore over the top of her overall uniform. The coat had belonged to Evelyn, and the colour, a rather bland brown in Constance's opinion had served to warm her sister's amber features whereas it made Constance with her English rose complexion look insipid. *At least it kept the chill out*, she thought, shrinking down inside it. One day, she vowed, swiping at her face before inspecting the blackened smudges left behind on the hanky, when this blasted war was over, she'd have a rainbow wardrobe. She'd have dresses of pink and yellow, and a red coat and — 'Hello.' A melodious, and richly accented voice echoed behind her.

'Oh!' She startled, spinning around on the seat. A tall, young man in a uniform she recognised as being Air Force was standing on the path behind the folly.

Chapter 14

Constance had no idea how long the young man standing behind her had been there. The folly loomed large to his left, and the path to his right was deserted. He sensed her fright and held his hand up. 'Hey there, sorry I didn't mean to startle you.'

Her heart slowed back down to a regular beat; there was something about his smile that made her feel at ease. 'I was lost in my thoughts; I didn't hear you coming.' She picked his accent as belonging to the Canadian contingent that had been stationed on the island. As she looked at him properly, she had the strongest sense that they'd met before, but she couldn't think where.

'Penny for them. Isn't that what you British say?'

She raised a smile. 'It is, but I'm sad to say they weren't very deep thoughts.'

'It doesn't pay to think too deeply given the times we're living in.' He took his hat off, rubbing his fingers across a short buzz cut before nodding at her and taking a step forward. He had a limp she saw, by the awkward way he moved. 'I'm Henry Johnson by the way. It's a pleasure to meet you.' He thrust his hand out toward her.

'Constance Downer.' She forgot to be embarrassed by her work stained hands as she took his hand giving it a small shake in return. She snatched her hand back instinctively as a spark of unfamiliar feelings flared at his touch and was hopeful that the dimming light would hide her reddened cheeks. She waited a breath or two, composing herself before agreeing with his sentiment. 'You're right, it doesn't pay to dwell on things.' She decided to wade on in with the truth. 'I was imagining the technicolor wardrobe I'm going to have when this war finishes.' She flashed him a smile. 'See, I told you it wasn't deep; in fact, it's rather shallow.'

'Oh, I don't know about that.' He smiled, his hand dipping lazily into his trouser pocket and reappearing with a tobacco tin. 'A technicolor wardrobe you say?'

She liked the richness of his vowels, and she couldn't help but smile back at him. 'I do say, and one day I'm going to have dresses in every colour of the rainbow.'

The dimples on either side of his cheek gave him a schoolboyish charm, and she guessed he was around the same age as Teddy was the day he sailed away. She took advantage of the opportunity to stare as he deftly rolled a cigarette.

'Smoke?'

'No thank you.' She hoped she didn't sound prim and added hastily, 'But maybe a puff?'

He flashed her a grin, and she felt something soften and begin to melt inside her. A flame flared, and it illuminated him for a split second as he lowered his head and lit his smoke. As he raised his gaze Constance was struck by the colour of his eyes, neither brown nor green, somewhere in between, and the lashes framing them had a tinge of gold on their tips. She watched as he exhaled with languor, the pungent tang of tobacco drifting toward her. He held the cigarette out, and she reached for it holding it uncertainly between her fingers before putting it to her mouth and taking a small puff. She coughed as it burnt the back of her throat and her eyes watered. She passed it back, scalded.

He looked amused but not, she saw condescendingly so, and swallowing the burnt taste of ash away she cast around for something to say, not wanting their exchange to end just yet. 'You're from Canada?'

'Good guess. I don't like to be mistaken for a Yank. It's a bit like calling a Scotsman, English from what I gather. Vancouver's where I call home to be exact which is why I'm down here now. I needed to see the water and breathe in the sea air.'

'It's hard to make it out what with all those out there.' Constance pointed at the ships.

'It's enough to know it's there.'

'What's Vancouver like?' Her eyes lit up with the wanderlust of a young woman who'd been no further abroad than Portsmouth, and even that had been years ago now.

She listened raptly as he described his city's delights from the exotic sounding China Town to the Capilano Suspension Bridge that swung out over a deep canyon and was surrounded by totem poles. It was when he began talking about Stanley Park though—almost a thousand acres of it—that his face lit up. She watched his expression grow animated as he told her about the bald eagles that flew over it, the mute swans and the great blue herons.

'When I was a kid, I used to help out at a bird rescue sanctuary after school. That's what I want to do when this—' It was his turn to gesture to the naval boats consuming the Solent, '—is over. I'm leaving the air force, and I'm going to go back to school. I want to be a wildlife biologist.'

Constance had never heard of such thing but didn't like to show her naivety, and so she remained quiet.

'If I've learned anything since I've been away it's that you only get one life and you have to do everything you can to make it the best life it can be.' He looked a little surprised at his impassioned speech, but it was a sentiment that Constance agreed with wholeheartedly.

'You're right.' They exchanged a smile over the haze of drifting smoke.

'What about you, what do you do?'

Constance touched her hand to her face aware that her skin still bore the smudges of toiling at the factory, but it was too late to feel self-conscious now. 'I'm working in the shipyard at Cowes, riveting.' It was honest and necessary work, but she wished she'd been able to come up with something a little more glamorous to impress this handsome, young Canadian.

'That's not easy work I'd imagine, and when this is over?'

It surprised Constance that she didn't know, she'd never really thought that far ahead and besides, her path to date had been mapped out for her. She'd not had any say as to what she wanted to do, and she knew she was not unique in this, it was a side effect of the war. It had been a case of what was needed and therefore what she should do. She didn't mind—it was the way it was.

Looking at Henry, she gave a small shrug. 'My parents run a haberdashery shop opposite the pier.' She waved her arm down the Esplanade in the general direction of Ryde Pier. 'It's quiet now, but we scrape by with mine and my sister's wages—she's with the Land Girls. Business will pick up again when rationing finishes so I suppose I'll work in the shop until—' she'd been about to say until she got married, but the words died on her tongue. She didn't want to share this assumption with him, and she changed tack. 'I guess the island is pretty different to what you're used to.' She imagined they must seem like country bumpkins compared to the cosmopolitan and vibrant place he came from.

She didn't know much about Canada, even less about Vancouver, but she did know it was the country's third-largest city. She'd always paid attention when the teacher had turned to the topic of geography at school. It had fascinated her because the world she knew and occupied was such a small one compared to what lay beyond their island home.

'Yeah it is, but the people here are kind, real kind. It'll sound kind of weird but what I miss is the smell of the Douglas firs. They're sweet and fruity, and they just smell like home. Most of all, though, I miss my family.'

'Do you have a large family?' She pictured him as the middle son with a bossy older sister and a younger brother who was forever getting into trouble. He would be the peacemaker.

'No, it's just me, my mom and my baby sister. My dad died a couple of years back. He's why I joined the air force. I was born in Canada, but I'm half British. Dad was born in Kent. He was in the air force too. Flew a Handley Page during the Great War. I grew up hearing stories of his time in England, and I guess I wanted to see it for myself and follow in his footsteps. My mom's done it tough since he died, but we get by. It'll be hard putting myself through college when I get home, but I'll do it. We'll manage somehow, and hey it's gotta be easier than this.' His gaze drifted above her head out to sea, and something in those unusual eyes of his looked lost, a clue that he would have seen and done things that no young man should ever have to experience.

'I'm sorry about your father,' Constance said and then found herself telling him about Ted and how Ginny, his widow, lived with them. Henry's sympathy was genuine. He took one last drag of his smoke and had the good sense not to offer it to her again, sparing them both the embarrassment as he ground it out with his foot. She noticed the motion caused him to grimace. His leg obviously pained him. Constance felt rude for not patting the seat beside her and asking him to join her, but she wasn't sure that would have been right.

'So, where are you billeted?' She asked this with what she hoped was an air of nonchalance.

'I'm at Darlinghurst House just a ways down the road there.'

'Oh,' popped out of her mouth. That explained his limp, his injury must be recent. Darlinghurst House was where she and Norma had collected the basket full of socks in need of darning. They'd whiled away their Saturday nights this last month at the library, where Norma was on fire watch duty once a week, chatting over the fact that they were there knitting no less! And not at a dance flirting with handsome soldiers like Evelyn undoubtedly was. The most excitement offered to them on a Saturday night was giving their needles a rest as they headed outside to watch the dogfights in the skies over the Solent. That was another thing both girls had in common; parents who kept their youngest children on a tight leash since the war had escalated. Darlinghurst too was where her dreaded solo was to be sung in just over a week thanks to the powers that be at the shipping yard factory.

'I'll tell you a secret.' Henry interrupted her thoughts.

Her eyes widened, and she wished Norma could be a fly on the wall to this exchange as he gave her a cheeky grin. She would turn pea-green unable to believe her friend's luck in meeting a handsome Canadian at the old folly no less!

He bent down and tugged his trouser leg up. 'I've got you to thank for the fact my feet are warm and dry now because my socks don't have holes in them anymore.'

Constance clapped her hands. She remembered him now. It had been Henry who'd answered the door at the manor when she and Norma had come to return the pile of mended socks they'd laboured over. She recalled having winced at the sight of his battered face, his head had been swathed in bandages, but his eyes had held her attention and she'd thought them rather beautiful. He'd been on crutches, unable to take the basket she and Norma carried between them, and had called over his shoulder for help from the passing matron. She'd shooed him past where the two girls were poised on the doorstep to the expansive lawn outside to make the most of the sunshine, tsking about there being no better tonic for the soul than sunshine.

'It was you who opened the door when Norma and I returned the basket of mended socks!'

He grinned and said, 'I did indeed, and I don't mind telling you it was a tonic to see your pretty face standing there after some of those po-faced nurses that had been looking after me. More of a tonic than sitting on my own in the garden, sun or no sun.'

Constance giggled at the compliment. 'I've heard stories about there being weevils in the porridge at the hospital. Is it true?' Her pert nose wrinkled.

'It's true, but beggars can't be choosers.'

She shuddered at the thought of being hungry enough to eat the writhing oats. 'Are you better now? I mean you look well apart from—'

'My limp?'

She nodded.

'It's a lot better than it was, believe it or not. A piece of shrapnel decided to take up residence in my leg, but I'm nearly as good as new. I'll be back on duty at Puckpool before the week's done.'

Constance felt a stab of jealousy, Warners Holiday Camp at Puckpool Park here in Ryde had been commissioned as the naval branch of the Royal Air Force, and she knew it was home to the WRNS as well. Norma's cousin worked in the pay office there and was stepping out with one of the officers. It was the worst luck that of all the places she could have been sent to work, she'd wound up at the shipyard. She blinked as she registered what he'd gone on to say.

'That's where it happened, at the camp. There was an air raid, and I didn't get to the shelter in time. I don't remember it, but I'm told they found me under a pile of rubble. It coulda been a lot worse, and I got off lightly compared to some of the poor fellas I saw at the Royal.' He shrugged.

Constance nodded. He could have died. There were plenty of others that had. He was one of the lucky ones.

With a start, she became aware that time was marching on. It would be dark soon, and if she didn't want her dad to set out combing the streets for her, she'd best get herself off home. She stood up, smoothing down the bulk of her coat, stalling as she told Henry she had to be off.

'Could I walk you home?' he asked hopefully.

'I'd like that.' She smiled shyly, linking her arm through his as they set off down the Esplanade.

Constance felt as though she were walking a little taller as she meandered alongside the tall Canadian especially as Beryl Stubbs, a girl she'd never been particularly friendly with at school, hurried past on her way home. Her envious glance didn't escape her notice.

'So then, Constance Downer. What do you do for fun around here?'

Constance liked the way her name sounded when he said it. She thought for a moment; she wasn't about to tell him that knitting and listening to the wireless was a leisure time fixture! 'Well, there are dances, and we go to the pictures.'

'The pictures?'

'Oh, er, the cinema.'

'Ah, now I got you. What's your all-time favourite film?'

'Casablanca. I went to see it three times.'

'You're a Bogart fan?

'No—Ingrid Bergman, she's beautiful. What about you, what's your favourite film?'

'You'll laugh.'

Constance looked up at him. 'I won't.'

'You promise?'

'I promise.'

'The Wizard of Oz.'

Constance giggled, and they garnered strange looks from passers-by as the tall Canadian Air Force man, and young Connie Downer from A Stitch in Time began to sing at the top of their lungs. "Follow the Yellow Brick Road."

Chapter 15

'This is me,' Constance said as they reached Pier View House. The shop was deserted, and the closed sign hung in the window.

For the first time since they'd met the conversation dried up with neither of them wanting to say goodnight just yet but not knowing how to prolong things either. It was Henry who broke the silence. 'Constance, would you like to come out with me on Saturday night? Maybe we could have one of those fish suppers I hear are so good?'

Constance had been planning on pleading with her mum and dad to be allowed to go to a dance she knew was being held at the local school hall with Norma on Friday night, but this was an opportunity not to be missed. Norma could still go, if she was allowed, she could meet up with the rest of their crowd there. 'Oh, I'd like that, but I'd have to check with my parents first.'

'Well since I'm here maybe I could, you know, introduce myself to them.'

Constance smiled up at him and all the while her heart began to race. He wanted to meet her parents! 'Will you wait while I let them know you're here?'

'Sure.'

She left Henry standing on the footpath outside the haberdashery shop and set off down the side path that led around the back of Pier View House. Before she rounded the corner, she looked over her shoulder and saw him pacing with his hat held in his hands. He was so handsome; she could pinch herself because she must be dreaming!

'Mummy!' Constance called from the bottom of the stairs, flying up them and into the kitchen as though she had the hounds of the Baskervilles after her.

Ginny was setting the table, and her mother had her back to her at the cooker. She turned, spoon in hand, to see what had her daughter in such a flap. 'What is it, what's happened, Connie?'

Constance tried to catch her breath. 'There's someone who wants to meet you and Daddy. He's waiting outside on the street.'

Ginny watched on as Eleanor Downer's shoulders relaxed at the realisation that there was no bad news. 'Ginny, would you mind keeping an eye on this?' she asked, gesturing to the pan she'd been tending to on the stove before slipping her apron over her head and passing it to her daughter-in-law. 'And who is this someone?' she asked Constance, smoothing her skirt. She had an inkling, given the way her daughter's cheeks were flushed and her eyes were sparkling, that this someone was a 'he'.

'Mummy, his name's Henry Johnson, he's in the Royal Canadian Air Force, and he's recuperating from an injury at Darlinghurst House. He walked me home from the folly,' she blurted, eager to get it all out lest she get back downstairs only to find Henry had given up on her coming back to get him.

'What were you doing at the folly? You know you're supposed to come straight home.' Eleanor frowned.

'I just fancied sitting in the fresh air for a bit after being in the factory all day, that's all.' She didn't want her mother getting sidetracked, so she rushed on. 'He wants to take me for a fish supper on Friday night. Please say yes. Please, please, please!'

Amusement lit up Eleanor Downer's features as she forgot about the folly, focussing instead on her daughter's coltish excitement. She exchanged a glance with Ginny who was also smiling, a rare sight these days. 'Well then, Connie,' Eleanor said. 'Don't leave the lad hanging about on the street, best you tell him to come on up.'

~

Constance, her stomach flip-flopping, led Henry through to the sitting room. Her mother was standing by the fireplace alongside her father who until a moment ago, she knew would have been relaxing in his favourite chair listening to the wireless as was his custom at the end of the working day.

'Mr and Mrs Downer, it's a pleasure to meet you,' Henry said, stepping forward with his hand outstretched toward her father. The two men shook hands and Constance noticed the freckles scattered across the back of Henry's. He turned his attention to her mother. 'You're surely not Constance's mother? Her elder sister perhaps?'

Her mother giggled despite the cliché, and Constance knew he'd won her over. Eleanor Downer had not giggled in ever such a long time.

Ginny poked her head in through the door to say that dinner was ready before stepping shyly forth to be introduced to Henry. Even she seemed to blossom and shake off a little of the heavy weight she perpetually dragged around as he chatted amiably to her.

'Now tell me, Henry, what do they feed you at that camp of yours?' Eleanor interrupted, wary of the meal turning into a congealed mess if she didn't serve up shortly.

Henry took the bait. 'Well now, Mrs Downer, the cook does her best, but the food's not a patch on my mom's home cooking.'

'Then perhaps you'd like to join us for supper? It's nothing fancy but it is home cooking.'

'I'd like that very much. Thank you, Mrs Downer.'

An extra place was set and Constance could have hugged her mother for eking out the spam hash so that Henry had an ample serving on his plate. She looked at him across the table noting the almost gingery glint of his stubble in the light. His face was strong and chiselled, but it was softened by the dusting of freckles across his nose and the dimples that appeared each time he smiled. He seemed to fill a void, space where Ted had once sat, making them laugh with tales of his escapades. The sound of laughter shooed away the sombre atmosphere that had lingered since her brother's passing as Henry told them a story about a naughty black bear who'd got the family's trash can stuck on his head. The most they'd ever had to contend with was the odd fox! By the time they'd all cleaned their plates, their bellies were both full and aching from laughing. And nobody cared in the slightest that it was bread and butter pudding *again* for afters.

Henry joined her father for a snifter of sherry in the sitting room when the last of the pudding had been scraped from its bowl, leaving the three women to clear the dinner things away.

Ginny, wielding the tea towel, whispered in Constance's ear before setting about wiping the plates dry that Connie had found herself a fine young man and that Evie would turn pea-green when she heard. Constance grinned back at her. She could tell by the way her mother was humming as she tackled the pan with the wire brush that it was a sentiment she shared too.

'Connie, Henry's off now,' Arthur said, appearing in the kitchen a while later. It was her cue to walk him downstairs.

Henry stepped past him. 'Thank you so much for welcoming me into your home, Mr and Mrs Downer, Ginny.' He shook hands with Constance's father once more and nodded toward the two women. 'I'll be sure to write to my mom as soon as I get back to camp and tell her I just ate the best meal I've had since I left home.' Both Ginny and Eleanor preened. He turned his attention back to Constance's father. 'Before I go, sir, I was wondering if I could have your permission to take Constance out for a fish supper and a stroll along the waterfront this Friday night.'

Arthur Downer looked at his daughter whose eyes were wide with silent pleading, and a smile twitched at the corners of his mouth. His wife and daughter-in-law too were waiting for his answer with bated breath. He knew there was a likelihood of being lynched with a tea towel and a wire brush were he to say no. 'I think that would be fine, Henry. You'll call for her here, of course.'

'Of course, sir. Six thirty on the dot.'

'And home by nine.'

Nine! Constance was outraged. That was ridiculously early. She caught her mother's warning gaze and decided to keep her thoughts to herself.

'Yes, sir.'

'Friday it is then.'

Henry's smile was wide. 'Thanks again for your hospitality. It was real good to meet you all.

Goodnight then.'

'Goodnight, mind how you go.'

Constance led the way down the stairs and out the back door. It had grown dark in the interim, and she wrapped her arms around herself to ward off the chill air as she stood on the empty Esplanade.

'I'm really glad I met you, Constance.' Henry's face was earnest despite the dim light.

She smiled shyly up at him. 'Call me Connie, and I'll see you on Friday then?'

'Six thirty.' He smiled and for a moment as he hesitated, she thought he might lean down to kiss her goodnight, and she held her breath. Instead, he gave her one last wave, before crossing the deserted strip of road to follow the waterfront back to the camp.

Constance waited until he had disappeared into the inky night before turning and heading back inside with a sprightliness to her step. She had no idea how she was supposed to survive five whole days before she saw him again.

~

The bus chugged to a halt seeming to sigh with relief as its grumbling engine stilled. Constance, who had chosen to sit down the back as was her custom, was holding on for grim death as she was bounced along the craterous roads. She liked to keep an eye on the trailer hooked onto the back carrying the gas bags. They were used for fuel, and although she knew it was an unreasonable fear, it was a real one to her mind nonetheless, that the trailer might dislodge itself. How would the driver know what had happened if she wasn't there to call out?

So many strange sights had become the norm these past years, like seeing the little ones carrying their gas masks to school with the same nonchalance as if it were a lunch box. Off they'd trot of a morning, straps slung over their shoulder for convenience, to carry those hideous, alien masks housed inside the brown boxes. Or, the sight of the planes flying low overhead and the ships decorating the Solent. Then there was this evening, she thought, thanking the driver and stepping down onto the pavement; it was not the norm. In fact, it was decidedly, deliciously different because she was stepping out with Henry Johnson! It was as though Mother Nature had decided to wave her wand over the day too with it being gorgeous for this time of year. The unseasonal early spring heat promised to linger well into the evening.

Constance felt as if she'd been holding her breath since Monday night willing the days away for Friday. Then and only then would she be able to exhale. All week she'd felt as though one sharp prod and she'd combust with the pent-up nervous excitement fizzing around inside her like bubbles in lemonade. How she'd wished she could click her fingers to make time speed up but here, at last, it was Friday evening!

She clipped her way home from the bus stop nodding good evening to the familiar faces but having no wish to stop and chat. She was in a hurry, and she picked up her pace as she neared Pier View. As she ran up the stairs, she heard her mother and Ginny chatting in the kitchen, and she paused popping her head around the door. They were sitting with a cup of tea each between them and once she'd said hello, she raced on up to her room. The whiff of boiling cabbage nipped at her heels, and she hoped she wouldn't smell of it when Henry called.

Constance clambered out of her overalls and threw her slip on over her head before whipping off her turban. To her relief, she saw the pin curls she'd set her hair in the night before had held up well. Her best dress was laid out on the bed. It had been Evelyn's, but she'd grown out of it and knowing how much Constance loved the rose pink colour, her mother had remodeled it for her birthday. Ginny had placed her white cardigan, the one she knew Constance coveted, next to it and she felt a surge of gratitude toward her mother and sister-in-law.

She slipped the dress over the top of her head and, as she smoothed her hair back into place, she wondered whether hers and Henry's conversation would be as easy as it had been on Monday. Perhaps it would it be stilted and awkward with the expectation of having made an arrangement? Oh stop it, Constance Downer, she said to herself in the mirror, wondering if she should risk a slick of the lipstick she'd pinched off Evelyn. She heard her mother's voice call for her. Best not, she decided venturing back downstairs.

'You look pretty as a picture, Connie,' her mother exclaimed, before gesturing to Ginny. 'Go on then.'

Constance looked from one to the other wondering why they both looked so pleased with themselves. Ginny looked up at her. 'I'm having Ted's baby—isn't that wonderful!'

Constance's eyes widened, she hadn't expected that. 'But how?' slipped out of her mouth and she flushed as the two women looked at one another and laughed. 'I mean—'

'It's all right. I know what you mean. I must have fallen just before Ted left. I thought it was grief making me sick and then it dawned on me my courses hadn't come on in ages either. I paid a visit to the doctor, and he confirmed it. The baby's due early August.' Ginny's eyes were bright for the first time since she'd opened that awful telegram.

'A summer baby,' Constance breathed, still stunned by the news but gathering herself enough to give her sister-in-law a hug and a kiss on the cheek. 'Ginny, that's wonderful. I'm so very happy for you. Mummy, you're going to be a grandmother!' She scooted around the table to where her mother was sitting looking as pleased as punch and squeezed her shoulder. 'It's wonderful!' she reiterated.

Arthur who'd shut the shop for the day appeared in the kitchen. He looked at his wife who was smiling but crying at the same time and at his daughter and daughter-in-law, both of whom had silly grins plastered to their faces, with bewilderment. Daddy, Constance thought a minute later seemed to stand a little straighter at the news he was to be a grandfather. A shiver coursed through her and she saw that her skin had gone goosy. She rubbed at the fair hairs on her arm that were standing on end beneath the soft wool of Ginny's cardigan, not liking the sudden sense of foreboding that had assailed her. She shook it away. This baby of Ginny and Ted's had offered them all a way to move forward toward a happier future.

'Well, I think this calls for a glass of something special, don't you, Mother?' Arthur rubbed his hands together, and Constance looked over at her mum who'd gotten up from the table and was already bent down retrieving the sherry bottle from the cabinet.

So it was when Henry rang the bell twenty minutes later, he was greeted at the top of the stairs by a very jolly Mr Downer who'd pushed the boat out by downing two tots in a short space of time. Not so jolly, however, that he forgot to remind Henry of Constance's nine o'clock curfew! Constance pushed past her father eager to be off and not wanting to give him the opportunity to invite Henry up to share in a celebratory tot. She wanted him all to herself.

Chapter 16

Henry complimented her on how pretty she looked in her dress and then they danced around each other on the street outside Pier View House, two birds of paradise performing a difficult ritual of courtship. It was as Constance had feared—the easy banter from Monday now felt forced. They were like strangers once more. Henry shifted his weight awkwardly from foot to foot, asking how her week had been. Of course, she couldn't tell him that she'd been like a duck out of water all week. So, instead, as they set off, she relayed Ginny's happy news. Henry, she saw glancing up at him, looked genuinely delighted.

'That's wonderful,' he said, stopping to smile down at her, and she liked the ways his eyes crinkled at the corners. The grand facade of the Royal Kent Hotel loomed large behind them as she smiled back.

'Isn't it just? Some happiness to come out of so much sadness.'

They walked a little further, and the silence was no longer awkward. The tension between them had dissipated and vanished like the last dregs of sea fog on a sunny day.

'Shall we cross and walk along the seawall?' Henry asked, pausing to roll and light a cigarette.

'That would be nice; low tide's my favourite. I like watching the sandpipers and geese look for their dinner in the wet sand.'

'I love to watch the great blue herons.' He exhaled a plume of smoke. 'Although they're more grey than blue. They're like streaks of silver catching their supper in the water.'

'At Stanley Park,' Constance said, recalling their conversation at the folly on Monday night.

'Yeah, at Stanley Park,' Henry echoed, pleased she'd remembered.

'When I was younger, I used to go crabbing and cockling with Ted and my sister, Evelyn—she's only a year older than me, but you'd think it was five years given the superior way she behaves. Evie's in the Land Army at Norris Castle Farm.' Henry looked amused as Constance chattered on. 'The three of us nearly got caught out by the tide once. We were so busy digging and filling our buckets that we never saw the water coming back in; it was so fast, like a giant arm sweeping up the beach. I got pulled under, but Ted picked me up and dragged me back up to the shore. We got a right telling off from Mum, for not keeping an eye out, when we got home, and I could taste sand in my mouth for days after.'

'That would have been frightening,' Henry said, grinding his cigarette out before holding out his arm. Constance linked hers through his and let him steer her across the road.

'It was, but the lure of Mummy's cockle fritters and crab meat pasties was too strong to stay away for long.'

Henry grinned. 'I can't say I've tried a cockle fritter, but my mom makes a mean crab chowder.' He glanced up at the sky; they had an hour or so before the light would fade by his reckoning. 'The days will be getting longer soon, which has to be a good thing. You're not cold, are you?'

'No, I'm fine thank you. It's been such a glorious day.' She wouldn't have cared if it was sub-zero temperatures Constance thought, feeling the friction of his coarse shirt sleeve rubbing against the wool of her cardigan, so long as she was with him. She talked on about her workday life, and as she told him about mouthy Myrtle's tussle for top dog in the world of riveting, he threw his head back and laughed. She felt inordinately proud that she was the one responsible for his mirth.

'I'm performing in a show at Darlinghurst House next Wednesday night,' she confided as the folly came into view. She explained how she'd been roped into it and was very nervous about the whole thing, especially given she was expected to sing a solo.

'I'd like to come and hear you.'

'That would make me more nervous, Henry! When do you think you'll be back at Puckpool?'

'I'm already there, I moved back to camp on Wednesday afternoon, and I've been put on light duties in the interim.'

She noticed him grimace. 'Is your leg still very painful?'

'It's not too bad, and the doc said exercise is good for it.'

'You will tell me, won't you, if it's hurting you?'

'I will.' His smile made her heart flutter in a manner she was not used to.

'So, I've learned something else about you, Constance Downer.'

'Oh?'

'You can sing.'

'You haven't heard me yet,' she muttered. 'I'm dreading it, getting up in front of all those soldiers and the nursing staff—it makes me feel ill just thinking about it.'

'That's not true you know.'

'What?'

'I have heard you sing.' He began humming the tune from the Wizard of Oz they'd sung on Monday night and Constance giggled.

'That doesn't count.'

'You'll be great, and I'll be there rooting for you.'

'Just so long as you don't catcall.'

Henry grinned at her, and she could see in his cheeky look what he would have looked like as a young boy getting up to childish mischief. She watched as he placed his thumb and middle finger in his mouth and gave a shrill wolf whistle. 'Like that you mean?'

She elbowed him. 'You wouldn't dare! The matron would have you out on your ear!'

'You're not wrong there.'

As they reached the folly, the rocky outcrop they'd been following gave way to an uninterrupted stretch of sand. Constance had a sudden yearning to feel the sand between her toes. 'Shall we walk along the foreshore?' she asked, indicating the steps leading down to the beach. The water was a long way off and would be so for a good bit yet.

'Sure.'

Constance sat down on the same bench where she'd been sitting when she first laid eyes on Henry and slipped her shoes off. The air was biting on her bare feet, and she twiddled her toes while she waited for Henry to ball his socks. He stuffed them inside his boots, and placed his boots under the bench saying, 'They'll be all right there for a bit.' Constance did the same with hers and followed him down the steps to the beach. She looked at his straight back and broad shoulders, and as he turned to hold his arm out for her once more she felt a shock, almost electrical in its intensity somewhere deep down in her belly at the thought of those strong arms wrapped around her.

They left their footprints in the soft sand as they strolled along. She pointed out the different birds, and they watched a tussle between a seagull and a gannet over a dead fish lying in a shallow pool. The seagull won, winging its way off into the deepening sky victoriously.

'Tell me more about your family, Henry.'

'Well, my sister Nancy's not long turned twelve, and she's quite the tomboy. She won't be seen dead in a dress unless she's going to church, and only then because she has to. Mom shakes her head over her, especially when she comes home with rips in her pants from climbing trees or riding her bike too fast. I think Mom worries she runs a little wild what with Dad not being around anymore to keep her in check. I mean I do my best, but I think she should enjoy being a kid while she can.'

Constance nodded her agreement, thinking of all the fun she'd had clambering around the folly as a child, and she had the scars to prove it! 'What was your father like? Do you take after him or your mother?'

'My dad, that's where I get my red hair. My mom's a blue-eyed blonde and lucky for Nancy she got Mom's looks.' He lifted his hat and dipped his head to show her his crop.

'It's more gold than red,' Constance said, resisting the urge to run her fingers over his head. She knew from doing the same to Ted when he got his first buzz cut that it would feel like velvet.

'He dropped dead when I was fifteen; his heart just stopped one day when he was at work.'

'Gosh, that must have been awful.'

'It was. My mom fell apart for a while, and I had to step up, you know, help take care of Nancy. She was only seven and a real daddy's girl. It hit her hard—it hit us all hard, but we muddled through. It's true you know, and you might not believe me now, but where your brother's concerned time does heal. You never stop missing the person, but one day you wake up and realise them not being here anymore wasn't the first thing you thought about when you opened your eyes. It stops being so raw and becomes this throbbing pain that slowly turns into a dull ache and then it stops hurting physically, but the scar's always there to remind you.'

'I hope so,' Constance said, her eyes smarting as she thought of her brother. It was hard to believe and sad to think that one day Ted's death wouldn't sting like an open wound.

'I think my mom may have a beau.'

Constance blinked the tears back where they belonged. 'Really?'

'Yeah, I'm kinda reading between the lines, but in her letters, it sounds like Mr De Rosa, who owns this Italian deli not far from where we live, is sweet on her.'

Constance frowned. 'What's a deli?'

Henry looked at her, his eyes widening. 'You've never heard of a deli?'

She shook her head.

'Ah, you don't know what you're missing, Connie. A deli sells fine foods; you know, cured meats, cheeses, and olives. There's this smell when you step inside Mr De Rosa's shop, and it's how I'd imagine walking down a street in Rome would smell. It's kinda garlicky and peppery and cheesy all at the same time.'

'You're making me hungry!'

'Well, I did promise you a fish supper.'

'And I'll hold you to that, but let's walk a little further. If your leg's not hurting you?'

'I'm fine.'

'Would you like your mum to remarry?'

'Do you know what? I would. I'd like her to be happy, and Mr De Rosa is a good man. And I'm all for it if it means I get a lifetime's supply of his pastrami.' He read her expression and grinned. 'Pastrami is a cured meat that's mixed with spices and then smoked, and you can't beat a pastrami sandwich from De Rosa's Deli. Although pancakes from the Sweet Jam café come close, they just drip with maple syrup.'

'What's maple syrup?'

'What's maple syrup?'

She nodded, giggling at his incredulous expression.

'Connie, you haven't lived until you've tasted maple syrup. It's the liquid from inside a maple tree, and when it's boiled up, it becomes this gooey sweet syrup. It is the best.'

Constance closed her eyes and imagined she could taste it. She opened them deciding it was time she gave him a run for his money. 'You can't beat a piece of fresh-from-the-sea fried haddock, chips and mushy peas from Mrs Hennings' Fish Shop either.' It was one of the few treats the war hadn't managed to snaffle.

'Mushy peas?' Henry raised an eyebrow.

'Halt! Who goes there?' A voice shouted across the sand from the Esplanade and Constance glanced anxiously up at the seawall. A sailor manning the old Victorian gun emplacement shouted from the beachside entrance to Puckpool Camp. She hadn't paid attention to how far they'd walked.

'Wing Commander Henry Johnson, Royal Canadian Air Force, and Constance Downer of Ryde.'

Constance felt in her pocket for her identity card which she handed to the sailor to examine. He glanced at it and, satisfied, passed it back.

'As you were,' the voice said, and Constance flushed seeing him wink at Henry.

'All this talk about food's made me hungry.'

'Me too,' Constance agreed, and as they turned back retracing their footsteps in the sand, the sun dipped low and the tide began its stealthy ascent up the beach. By the time they barrelled into Mrs Hennings' Fish Shop, it was dark.

'Good evening, Mrs Hennings. Could we have two fried fillets of haddock please and chips for two with a serving of mushy peas, please?'

'Hey,' Henry laughed. 'I never agreed to the mushy peas!'

Chapter 17

'Okay, I'm still on the fence about the mushy peas, but I will hold my hand up to that being the best piece of fish I've ever had,' Henry said, as they strolled toward Pier View House. He was mindful of making sure Constance was home by curfew.

Constance groaned. 'I ate too much, my tummy hurts.'

Henry laughed. 'There were rather a lot of chips.'

'Mrs Hennings is not normally that generous. I think she rather took a shine to you.' Constance had thought the woman, who at times looked like she would rather be anywhere than in her fish shop with her swollen ankles and red work-worn hands, had seemed to prance from fryer to till at the sight of Henry. She wasn't the only one either. The two girls who'd been huddled over a shared plate of chips in the corner began giggling and stealing surreptitious glances at him. Henry seemed oblivious to the effect his tall, handsome presence was having. Constance eyed the girls, recognising one of them as Flo Brown from the factory. She was a terrible flirt, or so the factory gossips said. She held onto Henry's arm just a little tighter.

It had been a wonderful evening, she thought with a happy sigh, as they passed by the edifice of the Royal Kent Hotel once more, deliberately slowing her pace because she didn't want it to end. The only sour note had been the two lads who'd brushed past them, deliberately knocking into Henry as they left the fish shop.

'Hey watch it, mate!' Henry called, as they laughed and carried on their way but Constance had pulled him inside to the warm glow of the shop. She knew some of the local lads were envious of the foreign boys and the almost exotic appeal they held for the girls on the island. 'Ignore them, Henry, I know Willy Parker's mother and believe me he doesn't know any better.'

It was ten minutes to nine when they reached the little side gate beside A Stitch in Time.

'It's not that I want to cut our night short, Connie, it's just that I want to be sure your father is happy for me to call on you again.'

Constance felt a thrill run through her at his words; he wanted to see her again! It was just as well because she'd die if he didn't feel the same way as she did. 'Thank you for a lovely evening.' She smiled up at him. The evening had been more magical than she'd imagined it would be as she'd tossed and turned each night from Monday through to the wee hours of Friday morning. Although in her dream date she hadn't gotten a green smudge from the pea she'd dropped down her front on Ginny's cardigan. How she was going to get it out, she didn't know!

Her hand reluctantly reached out for the latch, but her gaze never left Henry's. She didn't want the evening to finish. It was far too early she thought, mentally poking her tongue out at her father. All the other girls didn't have to be home until ten thirty. It wasn't fair. But all thoughts of her father and anyone else for that matter vanished as Henry gently cupped her face in his hands and his eyes seemed to darken as he looked at her with an expression she couldn't read. Instinctively she tilted her chin raising her mouth toward his. She tasted salt as their lips connected and a jolt, almost electrical in its intensity, coursed through her. As she pressed herself against Henry, she sank deeper into her first kiss. Her body seemed to no longer belong to her and she fell further into the realm of a foreign desire not knowing and not caring where it took her.

The jarring sound of tin hitting tin caused them both to jump apart as it shattered the still night air. Constance was breathless, and she took a few seconds to regain her equilibrium, unable to look at Henry for fear of falling off that abyss she'd been teetering on. Her father never put the rubbish out this late at night. It was his way, she knew, of making sure there was no funny business going on out the front of A Stitch in Time!

'You'd best go in.' Henry's voice was ragged around the edges.

Constance nodded but made no move to do so.

'I'm not sure when I'll be able to get away from the camp next but when I do can I come and see you?'

The bin lid rattled once more. 'Yes, of course.' She gazed up at him taking a photograph of his face to pull out between times. When she was sure every detail of his features from the glint of stubble determined to make an appearance to the line of freckles marching across his nose was firmly imprinted in her mind's eye, she stood on her tippy toes and kissed him hard on his lips. 'Goodnight, Henry,' she whispered, unlatching the gate. She didn't dare look behind her as she disappeared down the path for fear that she would be unable to leave him.

Later she lay restlessly on her bed, her blankets in a heap on the floor where she'd kicked them off. It was an unseasonably warm night, but even if it had been the kind of night when she donned a woolly hat and slippers for bed, she knew she wouldn't have been able to nod off. Her thoughts were too full of Henry and the way her body had taken on a life of its own responding to his kiss. Her legs had seemed to liquefy and there had been an ache inside her that needed filling. Constance knew as she stared up at the ceiling that when she met Henry at the folly last Monday, she'd been a girl but as she'd tripped up the stairs tonight, pausing only out of politeness to tell her parents and Ginny that she'd had a lovely evening, that she wasn't that girl anymore. She, Constance Mary Downer, now knew what it was to be a woman with all the promises of something wonderful waiting just around the corner.

A familiar drone began to grow louder and she knew not even a trip down to the Anderson shelter would dampen her ardour. She might have only known Henry a short while, but she was in love. She knew this with the same certainty she knew the bombs would rain down on the island that night.

~

Wednesday night arrived despite Constance's best efforts at willing it away. She was wide-eyed thanks to a mix of terror at the evening ahead and awe at the room in which she was standing. In its heyday, this had been Darlinghurst House's formal dining room. The only clues to the room's glamorous past now, however, lay in the crystal chandelier dangling from the ornate ceiling rose. It didn't sparkle as it once had thanks to the film of dust coating the teardrop crystals. There was no one left with the time or inclination to look after it now. The upstairs and downstairs staff of yesteryear were long gone. The ornate, gilt-framed portraits of disapproving relatives in old-fashioned dress frowning down at whoever stepped across the threshold were a reminder too, of the wealthy and somewhat ostentatious Bournemouth set who'd opted to vacate the home and head back to the south coast beach town whence they'd come. They'd no wish to limit themselves to the two rooms allocated them after the house was commandeered for the war effort.

The atmosphere in the room was oppressive despite the large windows letting in the last of the days light, their square panes framed by heavy, velvet drapes. The low hum of voices bounced off the rich, dark, oak-panelled walls as the voices of the soldiers well enough to attend this evening's show rose and fell. Some had robes on, some were in their pyjamas; all were in varying states of bandaged repair. The nurses too milled about making sure their charges were comfortable. Tonight was a break from the ho-hum routine of the soldier's respite and making her presence known lest any of her boys get too excited was the matron. She reminded Constance of a bird of prey, but the woman's hawkish gaze was forgotten as she spied Henry.

Her heart soared—he'd come! He was standing at the back of the room near the wide entrance, framed by a sturdy set of intricately carved double doors, his wedge cap clasped in his hands. She forgot to be coy as she'd heard Myrtle and her worldly posse at the factory say one should be when it came to dealing with boyfriends. Her face broke into a wide smile of its own accord, and she waved, leaving the huddle of animated, overexcited girls all dressed in their very best she'd arrived with and weaving her way through the crowded room to where Henry stood.

'I couldn't get away from the camp before now, but I was determined not to miss out on hearing you sing tonight.' He smiled down at her, and it was evident to Constance in the way his eyes softened as he looked at her that he was as pleased to see her as she was him. In that instance, she forgot her roiling nerves as her emotions swung between elation and relief at the sight of him. In the days that had passed since she'd fallen for her handsome Canadian Air Force man, she'd replayed their evening together over and over in her mind. As time ticked over with no word from him, however, she'd begun to wonder if she was, as Evelyn had said on Saturday afternoon, naïve.

Her sister had called home with an offering of early spring carrots and a pat of butter. As their mother busied herself rustling up a plate of cheese sandwiches, Ginny had shared her happy news with her sister-in-law. Evelyn had been just as thrilled at the thought of a baby coming into the family as the rest of them and the atmosphere as they fell upon the sandwiches, agreeing they tasted that much better thanks to the smearing of real butter, was jovial. Constance was helping herself to another triangle when Ginny elbowed her. 'Connie has a bit of news too, Evie.' As Ginny had predicted, Evelyn turned a pale green on hearing the news. Her little sister had a good-looking beau and a Canadian one no less. Their mother had clucked her tongue at her elder daughter, telling her to be nice before heading down the stairs to relieve her husband from the shop for half an hour while he had his lunch.

Ginny, who'd been feeling tired of late, went for a lie down and it was left to the sisters to make a fresh pot of tea for their dad, and to clear up.

'I'm sorry I was a bite, Connie,' Evelyn said breaking the silence as she measured the tea. 'You're a little trusting when it comes to the real world that's all, and I don't want you to get hurt. It doesn't pay to fall too hard for any of the soldiers gadding about town.'

Constance was reminded of an actress's line she'd once heard in a film. She was also irked by her sister's condescending tone. *Trusting indeed!*

Evelyn, however, wasn't finished. 'There are a lot of smooth operators in uniform around. Soldiers who know how to woo and sweet talk a girl and how to break her heart good and proper.'

It was only when Evelyn had left to catch the bus back to Norris Castle Farm that Constance forgot her irritation with her sister as the penny dropped. Evie had been talking about herself. Some cad had given her the runaround. Her heart went out to her sister then, and she wished she could catch her up and give her a hug, but the bus would be halfway to the farm now. The seeds had been sown though, and as each day tumbled into the next, she'd begun to wonder if she was just one of many girls Henry took a turn-about with. Was she as Evelyn had suggested a silly, and naïve girl who fell head over heels the first time a man showed interest in her? Now, at the sight of him, all those traitorous thoughts picked up their hems and marched out the sturdy oak doors. He was here, and that was all she needed in the way of reassurance.

She spied Doris Cosby arranging herself at the piano and her stomach lurched as she was reminded of why she was here. 'I feel sick, Henry. I don't think I can do this.' Constance's voice came out in a broken rasp. How she was supposed to sing when she could hardly speak was beyond her.

Henry took her hand. 'Hey, of course, you can, Connie. Look around you. These poor guys deserve a little cheering up, doncha think?'

Constance's eyes settled on a soldier with a bandaged head His arm was in a sling and his leg, in a cast, was stretched out in front of him. She felt a tug at her heart.

'Take it from someone who knows, you girls singing tonight will be the only bright spot in these fella's lives at the moment. They're missing their sweethearts, their families, and you can help take their minds off all that for an hour or so. Is it so hard?'

He was right, she thought. It was such a small thing she had to do compared to what these boys had had to do and had gone through in the name of the war.

'When you sing, pretend it's just you and me.' He gave her hand a gentle squeeze.

'Connie, come on!' Lil tugged at her arm. There was no time for introductions so Constance gave Henry one last smile before following her friend through the crowded space to where the cluster of girls from the shipyard were gathered in front of the tiled open fireplace, the mantle providing a frame behind where they stood. It was down to Sybil MacKay, as the eldest of the group, to step forward and say a few words before Doris began to play the opening notes of "Boogie Woogie Bugle Boy" with gusto.

While they weren't The Andrews Sisters, the girls held their own and, hats off to Doris, the songs she'd insisted they play were going down a treat. They were foot-tapping and fun, and Constance smiled spying two of the nurses jitterbugging together down the back of the room. Even the po-faced matron was swaying along to the rhythm. The fast-paced set finished, and it was Constance's turn to step forward. She took a deep breath and looked around the room at all the poor battered men, determined to do them proud, before her eyes sought Henry. His gaze never faltered from hers, and her voice seemed to take on a life of its own, dipping and soaring over the notes of the Vera Lyn melody. She felt like she *was* soaring over the white cliffs of Dover and when the song came to a close, she saw one or two of the nurses wipe their eyes. The applause was thunderous and she grinned as Henry gave her a thumbs up before returning to her spot next to Lil. 'You were fantastic,'

Lil managed to whisper before Doris began pummelling the piano keys once more.

The show was over far too soon, and that it had been a success was evident in the whistles and shouts for more that had seen them perform one last number. They'd opened on The Andrews Sisters, and they closed with the trio's "Rum and Cola". Constance looked at her workmates' faces; they were flushed with the success of the evening. She too was on a high. It was true she thought, turning her attention to the audience, that music had the power to move people. The atmosphere had been heavy and spoke of pain and suffering when they'd first arrived. Now, she thought, listening to the buzz of conversation as memories of bygone dances were relived, the mood had lifted.

'Are you coming with us?' Lil asked, elbowing Constance out of her reverie.

'I'm not sure,' she replied as Henry crossed the room toward her.

'Constance Downer, you've gone and got yourself a fella, haven't you?' Lil laughed. 'And a fine looking one at that.'

Chapter 18

It was nearly a month since Constance and Henry had met, and there weren't many moments in Constance's day when he didn't occupy her thoughts. She'd wonder what he was doing, and as she toiled at her mundane task in the factory, her mind would drift replaying their last outing. As though using a fine-tooth comb she'd scour each detail of their time together, unaware of the lovelorn look on her face until one of the girls would elbow her as they passed by telling her to stop daydreaming. She couldn't help herself though; it was the only way she could get through the minutes, hours, or days until the next time she saw him.

Today as she left the factory, boarding the bus for home and taking her customary seat down the back, she was filled with a sense of desperation. It was Thursday, five whole days since she'd last seen him and she'd exhausted the memories of that last encounter during that time. They'd gone to the Saturday night dance at the Shanklin Theatre; it had been Henry's idea as he reckoned his leg was strong enough for a few turns on the dance floor. 'I want to show my girl off,' he'd said, and she'd thrilled at the way he'd called her 'my girl'. Henry had proved he was trustworthy when it came to looking after his daughter, and so Arthur Downer had agreed that yes, Constance could go to the dance in Shanklin with him.

It was the first dance of that scale Constance had been to, and she'd been a little in awe as Henry led her past the milling animated crowd up the theatre's grand, classical staircase and in through the main doors. She couldn't wait until she saw Norma next so she could tell her all about it and she'd memorised the lively scene for her friend's benefit. She and Henry had fun jitterbugging and doing the Lindy hop under the domed ceiling with its bright lights, their feet skidding over the polished floors. Constance had felt a surge of gratitude to Evelyn as she whirled and twirled, for teaching her the dances and hoped her sister had forgiven her for the number of times she'd trodden on her toes! She'd been surprised too that Henry, despite his stature, was light on his feet and, as her dress spun out around her thighs, she'd felt as though she was starring in a Hollywood film.

They left before the dance finished, beating the throngs to catch the bus back to Ryde. Constance flopped down in her seat and leaned her head on Henry's shoulder. The lights, the noise, the dancing, and the late supper had worn her out. She closed her eyes and must have drifted despite the bus's juddering motion, but she was startled awake by Henry's voice.

'I've got something for you,' he said.

Constance rubbed her eyes and swiveled in her seat so she was facing him. He reached into his pocket and retrieved a small bag with drawstring ties, like the one Ted used to keep his marbles in she thought, watching as he opened it.

'Hold your hands out, palms up.' He smiled, and Constance cupped her hands curious to see what would spill out onto her upturned palms.

It was an assortment of pretty shells of all different shapes and sizes, and she gave a delighted cry, 'Oh, they're such lovely colours.' Her fingers sifted through them feeling their smooth sea-worn exterior beneath their tips. The colours were the same soft oranges and pinks of a setting summer sun. She already knew what she held in her hands were much more than just shells; they were treasures.

'You can hear the sea with this one,' he said, holding it to her ear, and Constance smiled as he covered her other ear and she heard the tide.

He grinned. 'Sometimes when I can't sleep, I do that, and it always sends me off.' He sorted through the little pile. 'That one there was such a pretty colour I couldn't resist it.' He indicated toward a vibrant pink and purple scallop shell.

'It's gorgeous,' Constance breathed, as if he'd just pointed out a precious gem.

'I've been collecting them since I arrived here on the island. I've quite a stash back at my lodgings, but those there are my favourites. There's seven of them, one there for each day of the week.'

He didn't say the words, but Constance knew, the sentiment behind the gesture was so she'd know he was thinking about her each time she held them.

Now as the bus shuddered to a halt, she shoved her hand into her overalls pocket and her fingers closed over the shell she'd chosen to carry with her today. It was no good, she thought, bidding the driver goodnight; she couldn't face another night sitting by the wireless with Daddy while Mum and Ginny clacked away with their needles. She needed to put her mind at rest. Constance looked down the long stretch of waterfront ahead of her; there was nothing else for it—she'd go to Puckpool. She had to see him.

So it was twenty minutes later she found herself being barked at as to what her business was. She retrieved her identification card and handed it to the police officer on duty at the entrance to the camp, explaining she'd come to see Wing Commander Henry Johnson. Satisfied the officer nodded and handed her card back which she duly tucked away once more in her front pocket where there was no risk of it falling out.

She moved away from the front gates and stepped further into the grounds of the former holiday camp. She hadn't a clue where she'd find him, she realised looking around at the unfamiliar scene. Gone were the days when shouts of laughter would ring out from the camp, the sound of families enjoying the summer weather on their annual hols; now the grounds were a hive of naval activity. The main building was to her right, and she supposed that would be as good a place as any to start.

It had been given over to offices she saw, poking her head around the door to where a handful of Wrens were busy at their desks or industriously engaged in filing. 'Hello,' Constance called tentatively. 'Er, excuse me.'

One of the girls, with glasses perched on the end of her nose making her look older than she probably was, had a manila file in her hand. She was standing in front of an open filing cabinet and, stopping what she was doing, turned her attention to Constance. 'Yes?' Her tone was impatient.

'I'm sorry to bother you, but I was wondering if you'd know where I might find Wing Commander Henry Johnson.'

'Henry?' Her face smiled at his name which was said with such familiarity that Constance felt her stomach twist. She was aware she must seem like a silly little girl next to this glamorous lot. This was his world, and it was one she knew nothing of. 'He's probably heading over to the dining hall about now I should think.' She turned away, silently dismissing her as she retrieved a sheaf of papers from the file she held. Constance thanked her before taking her hint and leaving her to get on with her task.

She had no idea where the dining hall was she realised, looking around the busy camp and receiving a curious gaze from a passing officer. She felt foolish standing there, conspicuous and out of place in her factory overalls with her hair hidden away beneath its turban. She shouldn't have come. Constance made her mind up to go home; Henry would call when his duties allowed him the time to do so. She was about to turn and head back toward the gate when she saw him, and her heart plummeted.

His tall, rangy figure was unmistakable as he appeared from between a cluster of cottage buildings. At his side and with her arm linked firmly through his was a pretty WRN, her blonde curls escaping from her peaked navy hat. The girl was looking up at him in a way that made Constance feel very strange; her face grew hot as she watched the young woman's face light up with laughter at whatever he was saying. She'd seen enough and turning she walked from the camp as swiftly as she could manage without drawing attention to herself. Her eyes burned with threatened tears and she thought she heard him call out to her, but she might just as easily have imagined it.

Evelyn's words ran through her mind. She *was* too trusting, and she *was* stupid, but most of all she was heartbroken.

~

'I always said she should be on the stage, that one,' Eleanor muttered to Ginny as though Constance weren't sitting at the table and perfectly able to hear her mother. It had been nearly a week since her fateful visit to Puckpool Camp. Henry had called twice at Pier View House, but she'd refused to come downstairs to see him much to her parent's bewilderment. A girl had to have some pride she'd told herself, biting her nails in her bedroom as she fought the temptation to hear what he had to say. Their puzzling over what had transpired between the pair of them filled many an evening, but bafflement soon turned to chagrin when Constance refused to tell them what the matter was. She hadn't told anybody about seeing Henry with the pretty WRN who was hanging off his every word and his arm. It was mortifying enough, without her parents and Ginny feeling sorry for her as well. They'd be sure to tell Evelyn too, and Constance couldn't bear the thought of hearing her say, 'I told you so.'

As the days wound on, they grew tired of their daughter's endless sighing and hangdog expression. Constance scowled at her mother's back as she carried on unpicking the hem of the dress Mrs Drury had brought in for altering. Ginny was sitting opposite her shelling peas. They were early peas, and a bag of the sweet pods had been dropped in by Arthur Downer's old mate, Terry, who was a keen gardener and often shared his excess with the Downers in exchange for the odd bit of mending. Constance was pretending not to notice how many peas Ginny was popping in her mouth and not the bowl—she was eating for two after all.

Eleanor glanced over at her daughter from where she was scraping potatoes and waved the knife at her. 'You need to get down off that high horse, young lady, and patch it up with your Henry. I'm fed up with looking at the face on you.'

Ginny took a more gentle tack. 'It's a lover's tiff, Connie. It's a rite of passage in a romance, but you do need to make it up with him. Look at you, old thing—you're miserable!'

It was true, Constance thought, finishing the last of the unpicking, she was miserable. She got up from the table and carried the dress downstairs. Her mother would re-hem it to a shorter more fashionable length by machine later. She whiled away half an hour in the shop, glad of the peace away from her mother and Ginny as she tidied the shelves. Her father, knowing better than to chat with her given her current mood, carried on with his mending work and they toiled in an easy silence. She glanced out across the road to the sea. The activity on the Solent seemed to have intensified, and the sense that something was brewing was growing stronger too. People were waiting with bated breath to see what would happen next and everybody was praying whatever tactics were planned would see an end to this interminable war.

It was the next evening, as Constance stepped down from the bus, that she saw Henry. He was leaning against the rails of the pier waiting for her. She hesitated. It was all well and good saying she didn't want to see him when she was tucked away upstairs at home, but she could hardly avoid him now. Besides, he'd already seen her. Despite this, she turned as though to cross the road to Pier View House and heard him call her name. He reached her before she could make her mind up what she should do.

'Connie, please talk to me.'

Constance risked a look up at him and saw hurt and confusion etched into the face she knew by heart. 'You played me for a fool, Henry Johnson,' she managed to say, and as she moved away, he grabbed hold of her arm.

'I don't know what you're talking about. Please just talk to me, explain why you're so mad.'

'I saw you at Puckpool last Thursday night with that WRN, and you can let go of my arm, thank you very much.'

He dropped his hand. 'I'm sorry. I just... I, well... I just don't understand,' he said, shaking his head.

It was evident he was telling the truth, about that at least, Constance thought. 'Blonde, pretty, arm linked through yours,' she spat, wanting him to own up.

To her amazement, he threw his head back and laughed.

'It's not funny, Henry, I trusted you.' Anger replaced the hurt of the last week.

'I know, but it kinda is funny, Connie. That WRN is Helen Kent. She's married to my pal, Don, and believe me she is mad about him. Connie, I've only got eyes for you, and it's driven me mad this week not seeing you.'

Constance swallowed hard. Perhaps she'd seen what she wanted to see that evening at the camp, her imagination running wild thanks to Evelyn's words of advice and not having seen Henry. 'I hadn't seen you in days and when I saw you with her, I thought—'

'Something is happening. I can't talk about it, Connie. I couldn't get away.'

Constance sniffled. She'd got herself into a terrible state over nothing. 'I'm so sorry, Henry.'

'Hey, come here.' He opened his arms, and she fell into them.

He stroked her hair and she breathed in the smell of him; she felt the roughness of his shirt against her cheek. She didn't want him ever to let her go.

'I love you, Constance Downer.'

'I love you too.' She had from the first moment she'd seen him.

Chapter 19

'Henry, I can't keep up!' Constance laughed, feeling the wind whip her hair back. She'd lose her scarf at this rate, she thought. The skirt of her dress ballooned out as she pedalled as fast as she could down the empty lane to catch him up. They were nearly at their destination, the ruins of Quarr Abbey. The spiky blackthorn hedgerows with their smattering of dainty white blossoms loomed up on either side of them. They were just high enough to hide the patchwork of green fields she knew lay on the other side. Above her head, the blue sky was clear, save for the puffballs of white skimming their way across it.

'I gave you an advantage. I've got a dodgy leg,' Henry called back over his shoulder, kicking his leg out to demonstrate. It wasn't quite true, time was a great healer and the passing month had seen his limp become virtually imperceptible. The warm weather May had brought helped the dull ache he had been plagued with while it healed too. He slowed his bicycle to a stop and Constance puffing now, caught up to him. She pushed her hair back as she turned her face to the sun and caught her breath.

It was a glorious Sunday afternoon, but then again, every day had been glorious since she'd met Henry. It was three whole months since she'd first laid eyes on him at the folly. Since that evening the war had faded into the background for Constance, her mind preoccupied with the business of falling properly in love.

Today, he'd swung a couple of hours off duty and Constance had arranged to meet him at Puckpool. They'd bypassed the marching that was in progress on the quarterdeck and crept past the café area to the back of the office building where she'd encountered the Wrens when she'd been looking for Henry. The thought of how she'd misread the situation still made her feel ashamed, and she'd made a silent vow from that point on to always have faith in him. She never wanted to feel as miserable as she'd felt in those days when she'd refused to see him, ever again.

The reason for their subterfuge was that behind the building was where the women who were beavering away in the office inside left their bicycles. The bikes had been borrowed, without permission, with Henry reasoning the girls wouldn't miss them until their shift was finished at six o'clock that evening. Where was the harm? He'd said the same thing for the past six Sundays.

Now, in the middle of the lane, Henry cupped her face in his hands and kissed her firmly on the mouth. She didn't want him to pull away; she wanted to stay there locked in that instant forever. He did, however, pull away and he gazed down at her, a solemn expression on his face. 'I love you, Constance Downer, and I can't wait to marry you.' It was said with just as much conviction as it had been the first time he had announced that one day when the war was finished, he wanted to marry her. There was nothing Constance wanted more than to be Henry's wife.

The words had initially been uttered under the shadows of the looming rocks with their creeping vines denoting the passing of time at Quarr. He'd made her a daisy chain ring and as he slid it on her finger, promised that one day he'd buy her a proper one. Those ruins had become their place. They were quiet and secret with the only sounds the shushing Solent tide intermingled with the birds flying overhead, and behind them the soft chanting of the Benedictine Monks in the Abbey proper.

It was in the ruins where they'd sit and talk. On those bright and sunny Sunday afternoons, the perilousness of the times was forgotten, and the future stretched ahead of them like a never-ending road, full of twists and turns.

Constance had been whiling away the hours when she wasn't with Henry imagining what life would be like in Vancouver. Through their conversations, she felt as though she knew his family already. His mum, he had assured her would welcome her as another daughter, and her family could visit whenever they wanted. She would picture her parents, with Evelyn bossing them along, embarking on an epic journey to what they thought of as a frontier land, her sister determined to meet a handsome young Canadian of her own. As for Ginny and the baby she liked to think they'd visit too. She would take them to all the wondrous places Henry talked about. The baby would love to see all the birdlife, and she'd like to see a bald eagle at Stanley Park and, of course, the great blue herons.

'My mom bakes the best cookies, and she's real house proud,' Henry would say, before talking about tomboy Nancy's prowess and lack of fear on the sled he'd made for her. His sister was the apple of his eye. He missed her and his mother terribly and he couldn't wait for the trio to meet, calling them his three best girls.

Constance would spend her working week lost in her imagination. Instead of sitting at her tedious task in a hot and dirty factory, she was in a land full of beautiful snowy mountains and lakes with Henry at her side. It was the likes of which she'd only ever seen in picture books. And, if it were nearing dinnertime, she'd always find her mouth watering at the thought of a visit to Mr De Rosa's Deli.

'I love you too,' Constance murmured now, and she looked up at his handsome features determined to memorise those flecks of gold in his eyes. That strong nose with its slight bend, broken he'd told her during a robust game of ice hockey as a kid. The freckles that mapped a path across the bridge of it. She reached up and traced her finger over the crescent moon scar on his jaw. It was as a result of landing on a stone when he fell out of his tree hut shortly before his tenth birthday. She felt the prickle of red-gold stubble, which didn't quite cover the scar, beneath her fingertips. Constance was filled with such an immense feeling of joy she wished she could bottle it and bring it out to inhale for the times they were apart.

It was then the sky began to reverberate, and her eyes widened. She knew exactly what that sound meant. Henry snatched hold of her arm. 'Quick!' They clambered off the bikes and dragged them to the side of the lane, pushing them under the hedgerow. Constance wriggled under a gap in the shrubbery feeling the brambles rake her skin as she forced her body deeper into the undergrowth. There was no time for Henry to follow suit and he hunched flat against the brush.

Constance felt cold despite the heat of the day. She was aware of a mosquito whining past her ear, and then all hell let loose; the awful ack-ack of bullets raining down from the drone above them, hitting lord only knew what in the fields either side of the hedgerow. One stray bullet and she would die, Henry would die. She clasped hold of the hand he thrust down to reassure her and told herself that so long as neither of them let go of one another, they'd survive this. Her thoughts tumbled over and over as the smell of burning hit her nostrils.

Constance could taste the smoke in the back of her throat now and her body convulsed in terror as she heard a whistling, frighteningly close, followed by a deafening boom. She squeezed her eyes shut and sent up one final prayer and then just like that, there was silence.

They stayed where they were until it was clear the danger was over and the plane had flown on, its bloody job done. Henry got up and pulled her out from under the hedge helping her to her feet before checking her over for injuries. Apart from the scratches which had begun stinging, neither of them was harmed. Henry's pallor was deathly Constance saw, grabbing onto him and holding him tight. Her legs trembled with the knowledge of how close they'd come to being killed; she'd forgotten for a while on that perfect late spring afternoon that it was always there, beckoning, just around the corner under the guise of war.

'Wait here. I'm going to check the field.' He disentangled himself and walked a short way up the lane to where there was a gate and disappeared from her view.

Constance's breath came in shallow bursts while she waited, feeling as though the green belt on either side was pressing in on her.

Henry reappeared, and her breathing steadied at the sight of him. 'There's no sign of anyone in the field, but there's smoke beyond it where the bomb must have hit, and I could hear the sirens coming. I'll see you home. It was wrong of me to bring you out here. I've been putting you in danger with these outings, Connie. It won't happen again.'

'No,' Constance said, her forcefulness surprising even her. 'I don't want to go home. They've gone. It's over, and we're alive. I want to feel alive, Henry. Properly alive. Please, let's carry on to the ruins.'

Henry looked at her for the longest while before retrieving their bikes.

The Quarr Abbey ruins were their secret; they'd sat many times, hidden from view, and been sent on their way once too by a strolling monk who'd stumbled across them. As they embraced in the shadows cast by the old stones, Henry kissed Constance with an urgency she hadn't felt before. She disentangled herself from his arms and took a step back, lifting her dress over her head, so she was standing before him in her slip.

'Ah, God, but you're beautiful, Connie,' Henry's voice cracked, as she removed her slip and stepped back into his arms, pressing her naked body against him.

'I won't be able to stop, Connie,' he warned, his voice husky.

'I don't want you to.'

Chapter 20

Constance sat in the sitting room with her mum and Ginny, who was looking like a barrel fit to burst. It was Arthur Downer's evening for patrol duty. The two women's conversation floated over her head as she relived what she and Henry had done at the ruins these last three Sundays. A delicious shiver coursed through her at the memory of how only yesterday she'd lain down on the grass and closing her eyes felt his fingers stroking her bare flesh. He'd been tentative at first, and it had been her that had urged him on wanting more. His mouth grazed her neck and then travelled further settling over a nipple and sending an exquisite sensation rocketing through her. She'd moaned and arched her back raising herself to him as she turned her body feeling his hardness pressing against her. He'd paused only to take his own clothes off before she'd given herself completely to him, and for a brief moment in time, they were one.

'Constance!' Eleanor Downer said, impatience in her voice.

'Sorry, Mummy. What did you say?'

'You're away with the fairies these days, my girl. I was just telling Ginny that your Grandma June used to make the most delicious jam roly-poly pudding and that the secret, she always said, was in letting the pudding sit before unwrapping it.'

'Yes, that's what she used to say, and it was gorgeous, Ginny.' Constance smiled, hoping her eyes weren't too bright or her cheeks flushed. Her mother had eagle eyes at the best of times and Constance didn't want her guessing what had transpired at the abbey ruins. She might not be married in the eyes of God but she *felt* married. She was Henry's wife in all ways now except for the piece of paper legally saying it was so. Her mother would not understand any of that though.

All three jumped as the air raid siren sounded and needles and wool were abandoned as they made their way downstairs. There was a sense of urgency among the trio as they filed outside to the Anderson shelter. As Constance bent her head and clambered inside the tin hut after Ginny, she wondered, as she always did, how having nothing but a mound of earth above their heads was supposed to keep them safe.

Inside the shelter, it was cold, dark, and dank. It was a nightmare in itself, but the alternative was worse. Constance clutched her sister-in-law and mum's hands as they crouched down. She had no right to complain; their present circumstances must have been intolerable for Ginny given the mound protruding from her middle. She knew too that Mum would be fretting. She always did when the siren sounded, and Daddy was on patrol. 'Mummy, tell us a story about when Teddy was little,' Constance said to distract her. Ginny liked to hear Teddy spoken of. She said it made her feel he was still there with her. It was therapeutic for them all, Constance thought. There was no sadness in the life lived, only in the life lost.

Eleanor Downer relayed the story they'd heard ten times before about Teddy having always tended to independence from the moment he'd grabbed hold of his mummy's skirt and hauled himself upright. On this particular occasion, he had been returned home—his parents thinking him napping in his cot—having been found helping himself to an orange from the greengrocers, at the age of two. A smile played at the corners of Constance's mouth, despite their circumstances, as she listened to the familiar tale. The state of limbo waiting for the raining bombs to subside was interminable, and while Eleanor's voice threatened to give out, her well of stories, however, would never run dry.

Constance was convinced the Jerrys would not be satisfied until the island was nothing more than an echo of its former self. It was always the worst bit, she thought shivering, not knowing when the siren sounded to signal it was safe for them to venture outside whether there'd be a home for them to return to. It did stop eventually like it always did, and the weary trio trooped back inside Pier View House and up the stairs to their beds.

~

In the comforting light of a new day, with bricks and mortar cocooning her, Constance looked around their small kitchen perturbed. 'Where's Daddy?' It was strange not to see him seated in his usual position at the breakfast table especially after all the activity last night. She knew he'd returned safe and sound from duty in the wee hours because, hearing his familiar tread up the stairs, she'd gotten up to see for herself that he was unscathed. He was weary but not physically wounded, and he brought the news home with him that Darlinghurst House had taken a bad hit. A Nazi Luftwaffe Dornier Do 217 on a mine laying mission, had veered off course and dropped a mine that had torn a hole in the manor's roof. By some miracle, the fatalities were few, the injured, however, many.

Constance had felt a chill course through her at this news and had sent up a silent thank you that Henry was no longer recuperating there. She'd left her parents sitting in the kitchen with a pot of tea between them and had taken herself off back to bed to try to grab a few more hours sleep.

It felt like only minutes had passed since she'd closed her eyes and sent up a prayer for all those suffering, before Eleanor Downer was sweeping open her curtains. She was reluctant to get out of bed, wanting nothing more than to burrow under the covers and sleep all day long. She knew she wouldn't be the only one feeling like that this morning after the night they'd all passed. Then, thinking of all those poor men and the nurses at Darlinghurst House she tossed the covers aside and got up.

The cold water she splashed on her face helped penetrate the brain fog, and she patted her face dry before tidying her hair and finishing her morning ablutions. She checked her appearance to see she looked as wan as she felt, but she'd have to do, and so she headed for the kitchen. It was Tuesday, which meant it was an egg in a nest day. Father was a man who lived by his routines and his breakfast would be made with real egg this week thanks to Evelyn having dropped six fresh eggs in at the weekend. It was a rare treat which was why it didn't bode well to find he was nowhere in sight now.

Constance's stomach churned ominously at the thought of eggs; she couldn't abide them of late, powdered or fresh. She picked up her bag from where she'd slung it the day before on the back of the door.

'He went back down to Darlinghurst House at first light to help move the patients. They've set up temporary accommodation for the poor loves at St Catherine's Home in Ventnor.' Her mum abandoned the sink wiping her wet hands on her pinny. She spied Constance's bag. 'You've not had breakfast, my girl, and I've not made your sandwiches yet. You can't go to work on an empty stomach, Connie.'

'I'm not hungry, Mum. I feel a bit peaky, to be honest.' She should've known better than to mention she wasn't feeling too bright. It was exhaustion, that was all, from the broken night's sleep. They were all in the same boat. Eleanor wasn't letting her off that lightly though.

'You've not been right for over a week, Constance. Perhaps you'd be best to stay home today?'

'Stop fussing, Mummy. I'm fine. I've just not much of an appetite that's all. It's a good thing with what Ginny's managing to put away! Besides, when I think of those poor men and women at Darlinghurst House,' she shook her head, 'well, getting myself off to work is the least I can do.'

At the thought of what had happened overnight, Eleanor sighed heavily. 'I suppose you're right. I'm going to finish up here and go down to help your dad. Ginny's still in bed; poor love is tired out. She's all baby. The sooner the little mite makes itself known to us all the better. You be sure to put something in that stomach of yours before the morning's out though, Connie. We don't need you fainting on the job.' She patted her daughter on the cheek. Calling after her, as she heard her daughter thundering down the stairs, 'Remember to eat something!'

'I will!'

She didn't. Constance's queasy stomach intensified throughout the morning, but she kept her fingers and mind occupied with her work and tried to ignore the horrid tang of metal that had settled in her mouth. It was as if she could taste last night's shelling. She was swallowing down the acidic bile that kept rising up in her throat when she started at a tap on her shoulder. It was Myrtle and the expression she wore on her over-made face made Constance's blood run cold.

She allowed the older girl to take her arm and escort her to the factory entrance where an aircraftman she recognised as one of Henry's chums waited. The grip with which he held his hat was white-knuckled. She knew the look on his face; her mind flew back to the awful day the news of Teddy's death had arrived. She'd seen that same look back then too. He delivered the news, as was his duty, that Henry had been caught up in the bombing at Darlinghurst House and had not survived. Constance's knees buckled, and the world went black.

Her father was fetched to bring her home, and her mother wrung her hands and cried before putting her to bed. Ginny watched on from the sidelines, her bright blue eyes enormous orbs in a pale face. It was she who curled up next to Constance on the bed and held her through that long night despite her girth.

Days later when she took herself down to Puckpool Camp seeking answers, this time not caring in the slightest whether she fit in or not, she would find out that Henry had gone to the old manor house to visit a young officer cadet from Vancouver who'd lost his leg and was not recovering emotionally. One of the nurses had sent word to him, remembering he too hailed from the same city, and it was hoped a visit from someone from the cadet's hometown might improve his wellbeing. The young man survived because Henry had thrown himself on top of him protecting him from the falling debris.

His name was Robbie, and Constance went to see him, the journey to St Catherine's passing in a fog of detachment from the world around her. The young man reached out and squeezed her hand trying to convey how grateful and how sorry he was for her loss in that simple, human gesture. She'd hoped that going to see him would help. Perhaps she would feel Henry's death had not been in vain. He had, after all, died a hero's death, but Constance could find no comfort in the visit—death was death. It meant she would never set her eyes on him again. She would never feel his gentle touch on her or laugh so hard, at something he'd said, she couldn't breathe, ever again. She'd never more hear him say I love you. She was a widow who'd never been wed.

Her heart shattered into pieces knowing all this. It was broken into a mosaic so tiny that she knew it would never be put back together again.

The weeks passed in wave after wave of grief, her exhaustion was all-encompassing, and the nausea had only grown stronger. She blamed having all that sorrow tucked away inside her for her sickness; it had to come out somehow. It was only when her waistband grew tight, despite her lack of appetite, that it dawned on her, with an understanding as terrifying as any bomb that could fall, that she was pregnant.

Chapter 21

Constance waited in the hallway as she'd been instructed and pulled her cardigan tightly around herself as she listened to poor Ginny's howls emanating from her room. The guttural agony in her screams was plain to hear. It was like nothing she'd heard before and she was terrified both for Ginny and herself. She hadn't come on in three months and had taken to rising before anybody else in the house to hide away in the bathroom each morning. The sickness arrived like clockwork as soon as she swung her legs over the side of her bed and sat up although it had eased a little these last few mornings. It was a reminder of what was happening inside her and listening now to Ginny's distress it was as though the fug that had clouded her thoughts since Henry's death cleared. She knew she had to take action and soon.

Her mum was helping the midwife, and her dad unaware of the drama unfolding in his home, was out on patrol. Ginny's pains had begun in earnest, with no gradual build-up or warning, as the three women had tidied away the dinner things earlier that evening. She'd dropped the plate she'd been drying, and as it smashed to the ground, she bent double. Constance's mother at the sink, her hands immersed in hot water, had remained calm, galvanising Constance, who was frozen to the spot, to go and fetch the midwife while she settled Ginny upstairs.

Ginny's panic at the sudden onset of the pain was evident and Constance was grateful to escape it into the fresh air outside. That the air-raid siren remained silent was a blessing, she thought, as she ran through the empty streets, her breath coming in short puffs of white, to the cottage where Bessie Parker lived. Bessie had grabbed the bag she kept at the ready and called out to her oldest that she was in charge of getting the littlies to bed before setting off. The pace the midwife set was a swift clip and Constance, tired from her run, struggled to keep up. It was a relief when they arrived back at Pier View

House and Bessie disappeared up the stairs, a calm and efficient arrival in a house that felt anything but. Ginny was in safe hands.

Now as the seconds, minutes, and hours ticked by at a slower pace than any had ever passed in the Anderson shelter, Constance began to pace the hallway. She was like an expectant father, useless and unable to do anything except wear the hall runner with the constant retracing of her steps. She could see Ginny in her mind's eye writhing and, pausing in her pacing, she clasped her hands in prayer. She raised her eyes to the ceiling, willing God to let Ginny's misery be over, and for the baby's safe arrival.

The night was interminable. Her father arrived home and sat next to her on the floor outside the bedroom where she was slumped with her back against the wall, worn out from worry. By the time her mother opened the door, the sun was beginning to peep through the cracks in the curtains at the top of the stairwell. Constance frowned, suddenly alert, unaware her father was gripping her hand; she hadn't heard any lusty cry. Her mum's face in the dim light of the hallway was ashen. She shook her head, and as she got to her feet, she heard her father's breath catch and felt him stagger beside her; ignoring the wave of nausea that washed over her she fell into her mother's arms. Ginny's baby, a boy, who she'd have called Edward in his father's memory, was born with the umbilical cord wrapped around his neck; he never drew breath. Tragedy had again come knocking at the Downers' door.

~

A malaise settled over the family at Pier View House; it was such a heavy veil that not even the news of D–Day's success could lift it. Ginny, once a wife, now a widow, and a woman who should have been diving headfirst into motherhood, no longer knew who or what she was supposed to be. All the while Constance's secret kept growing stronger and stronger. The days rolled over on top of one another and morale on the island grew scratchy. The war effort was wearing thin like the elbows of an old jumper, the end always just out of sight, just out of reach. For Constance, her mind was too full of loss, and fear for her situation, to muster up the energy to care about anything more than just getting through each day.

She'd overheard Myrtle, in that braying knowing voice of hers, talking about her cousin who'd been caught out by a good-looking corporal from

London, or at least that's what he'd told her. For all her cousin knew he could have been a deserter! Either way, he was long gone, and the cousin finding herself in the family way had resorted to gin and a hot bath. Whether it had solved Myrtle's poor cousin's predicament Constance didn't know; the older girl had moved out of earshot. The idea had been planted though and her mind was already mentally scanning the meagre contents of her parents' liquor cabinet. She'd seized hold of a possible solution because here was a chance to escape the devastation she would otherwise wreak on her family; she'd try anything.

It didn't work. For her efforts, Constance wound up in bed with a spinning head and red raw skin, her stomach still gently swelling. The idea that perhaps the answer might be tucked away in the pages of Molly's journal came to her in the dead of night. Indeed, in those yellowing pages were the suggestions of a soothsayer, and desperate, Constance who felt so very alone, ripped the page from the book. She folded it carefully and tucked it away in her bag, knowing that once she'd sourced what she needed, she would burn it. She'd want no tangible reminder of what she'd done.

When it came to it, she could not do it. Slippery elm and a leech, she could not let that leech do its worst. Instead, she took a deep breath and cornered her mother one morning as she cleared her father's breakfast dishes. For the rest of her days, Constance would not forget the way her mother's face had crumpled in shock as she grasped hold of the bench to steady herself. She learned too, when her mother whispered the situation their youngest daughter found herself in to her father, that there is a far worse emotion than anger. It was called disappointment.

PART THREE
Dandelion–'Taraxacum'

The common dandelion is used as a digestive/detox solution–it provides a cleansing effect with laxative and diuretic properties. Dandelion can also aid anemia, diabetes, liver disease, or simply liver cleansing.

Prevents urinary tract infections.
Treatment for inflammation of tonsils.
Aids appetite loss.
Aids an upset stomach, intestinal gas, gallstones, muscle aches.
Root infusion encourages the steady elimination of toxins from the body.

As a tea, find a source of dandelion that hasn't been exposed to insecticides. Harvest the dandelion both root and bulb. Slice or crush the bulb and spread over a baking tray. Dry in an oven heated to 200 to 220 degrees Farenheit until evenly dried. Allow the root to cool and use one tablespoon as a loose-leaf tea in boiled water and brew for five minutes.

Constance & Isabel
Chapter 22

'Um, excuse me. I wondered if you could help me. I'm trying to find my great aunt, Constance.'

The receptionist, whose name badge said she was called Kristen, stopped twirling her hair and eyed Isabel curiously as she burbled on.

'What it is you see is, she had a falling out with my nana years ago, and when nan passed away a month back, she asked me to find her sister, Constance, and tell her she was sorry. The only clue as to her whereabouts that she gave me was that at the time of their argument she was living in Ryde, here on the island.' Isabel shoved her hands into her jeans pockets and fidgeted from foot to foot hoping she didn't look shifty as she carried on. 'I've just moved over here myself for a bit and my landlord mentioned he'd bought his property from a woman called Constance Downer who resides here. My nan's maiden name was Downer, so I'm fairly certain she's my great aunt.' She stopped talking and drew breath. The expression of the young girl, whose layer of foundation was so thick she'd give Charity a run for her money, gave nothing away. She did, however, step out from behind the reception desk telling Isabel to follow her.

'I think Jill's probably in the Oceania Lounge. She'll be able to help you.'

'Oh, thanks.' Isabel's heart leaped. This was positive, she thought, keeping pace with the younger woman as she strode importantly down the plush carpeted corridor, the off-white walls broken by splashes of colour from the tasteful artworks hung on them. They passed by a hair salon and a family meeting room where a motley group was clustered around a frail looking woman. Isabel was busy hoping they weren't coercing the poor dear into changing her will when she nearly smacked into Kristen. She had come to a halt in the doorway of a large, airy room. Groups of people were sitting at tables engaged in craft work, card games or just enjoying the view of the water outside the picture window over a cup of tea.

Kristen scanned the room. 'There she is.' She led Isabel over to where a nurse was tending to a lady with a halo of wispy white hair. Isabel thought she looked as though she'd snap in half in a strong breeze as she watched the nurse settle her into an armchair.

She didn't look right sitting in such a big chair; it was as though the plump cushions were about to swallow her up whole, a bit like Little Red Riding Hood visiting grandmother. Isabel's fanciful musings weren't helped by the little lady's red pullover either.

The nurse turned her attention to Kristen and Isabel with a smile. She was clad in a crisp white blouse with a navy stripe running through it and navy pants. The name badge pinned to her chest declared her to be Jill Davies. The nurse looked both kindly and efficient, with her smiley brown eyes and bobbed grey hair, thought Isabel, taking in the sprightly figure. She got the tick at the end of her appraisal. Jill, she decided, was the kind of woman one wanted to look after one's loved ones in their twilight years.

'Hello.'

'Hi.' Isabel smiled back waiting for Kristen to elaborate.

'Jill, this is—sorry, I didn't get your name?'

'Isabel, Isabel Stark.'

'Isabel's nana passed away recently and asked her to find her sister, Constance, who Isabel has never met due to a family feud, to pass on her nana's regrets over it all.' Kristen looked to Isabel for approval.

Isabel nodded. She'd worded it well, much better than her rambling tale at the reception desk.

'Her mother's maiden name was Downer, so she is pretty sure, our Constance is the great-aunt she's looking for.'

Jill nodded. 'Thanks, Kristen.' It was said in a, *I can handle this from here*, tone.

'I'll leave you to it then.'

'Thank you,' Isabel said to the younger girl, who looked reluctant to leave them but who finally marched off with a flick of her hair. Isabel had the distinct impression her showing up asking for Constance with hints at family feuds was the most exciting thing that had happened to her so far that morning.

'Isabel, why don't you have a seat over there and I'll be with you in a jiffy?' Jill gestured across the room.

'Oh, okay, thanks.' She took herself off in the direction she'd been pointed in.

She smiled as she passed a group of silver-tops playing cards, wondering if Constance was in their midst. The Oceania Lounge was true to its name following a coastal theme with its palette of blue, light grey, and cream. The furnishings were new obviously but were still sympathetic to the era of the house, she thought, sitting down and feeling at home on the squishy settee. A coffee table with a newspaper open to the sports pages was in front of her, and she flicked through a couple of pages, feigning interest in the local news until Jill came and sat down across from her.

'So, you think you might be related to Constance.' She smoothed the creases in her pants.

Isabel tried not to squirm in her seat at the fib. There was no going back on her story now though, not when she was so close. She nodded. 'I wondered if it would be possible to meet her.'

'It will be all over Ryde, you know. Constance's long-lost great-niece having come to make peace.'

Isabel looked at Jill surprised.

'Kristen.'

'Ah, I see.'

'Our Constance is a well-known personality in these parts. Some would call her an eccentric who has led a colourful life.'

'My landlord told me a little about her. She ran a herbal shop, didn't she?'

'She did, yes, and it was before its time, but that's Constance all over, and she was successful, nonetheless. That was due in part, I think, to her family name. The Downers, you see, were related to Molly Downer, the last witch on the Isle of Wight. But then you'd know that, wouldn't you?'

Isabel had not known that, but she played along. 'Of course, yes. Erm, Nan only mentioned the connection in passing and she never told me what happened to Molly. She wasn't burnt at the stake or anything like that, was she?'

'No, those days had long since passed when Molly was around, but she was viewed with superstition and a little bit of fear by the locals, nonetheless. Her cottage was burned to the ground after she died, you know.'

'Oh!' Images of flaming torch-wielding locals marching up to an empty stone cottage flashed before Isabel's eyes.

'So, when Constance opened her own herbal remedies shop you can imagine how the stories swirled amongst the Islanders as to her link with Molly.'

'Oh yes, I can see they would.' Isabel was intrigued.

'She played her part well too, she was very flamboyant in her day, our Constance. Was your nan?'

'Um, I suppose so, yes.'

'I'm not surprised,' Jill said, eyeing Isabel's hair. 'You take after her, do you?'

'A little.' Isabel was vague.

'She's a lovely lady, our Constance, but she's also lonely. She's no family left here now, and I would hate for her to be—'

Isabel twigged as to the purpose of this conversation. The nurse was protective of her charge and didn't want her hurt. She was unsure whether Isabel was telling the truth or not.

'Nurse Jill—'

'Just Jill's fine, dear.'

'I just want to relay that my nan was sorry about the way things transpired between them that's all. Make peace between them.' It was a rather big white lie.

Jill eyed Isabel for a moment and then nodded before getting to her feet. 'Come on then. I'll take you upstairs to her room. Constance likes to have her morning cuppa in the armchair by her window so she can smell the sea air.'

~

'Knock, knock, Mrs D.' Jill opened the door a crack and turned to Isabel. 'Just give me half a minute while I tell her she has a visitor.'

Isabel nodded, and as she stood outside in the corridor, she was reminded of a cruise ship with its rows of cabins. A geriatric apparition in a blue quilted dressing gown and matching slippers appeared from one of the rooms a few doors down, and as she spied Isabel her eyes lit up. 'Psst,' she said, beckoning to her. Isabel was unsure as to what she should do, but the woman was not going away. 'Psst. Have you got the macaroons?'

Jill reappeared and pulled the door to before waving to the woman. 'No, Phyllis. She's not here for a midnight feast, she's here to see Constance.' She turned her attention to Isabel. 'You go on in. I'll leave you to it. I didn't go into anything. I just told her a young lady who said she's related to her was here to say hello. She looked surprised at the news of a relative, I must say.' Jill shot her a sceptical look and then, as Phyllis asked where the eclairs were hidden, she stepped aside. 'I better see to Phyllis. She thinks she's back at boarding school. She challenged me to a running race to the end of the hall and back yesterday!'

Chapter 23

A few hours had ticked by since Constance had been swept back to her youth with such clarity that she'd not heard Jill knocking at her customary time. The poor woman had been most concerned when she'd burst through the door, unsure of what she would find. Constance had waved her nurse's concern away, her irritation at being rudely startled back to the here and now leaving her unwilling to explain herself. So it was that this morning having woken far too early, Constance was feeling out of sorts. She was sitting by her window, a cup of tea on the tray table beside her and an untouched biscuit nestled beside it on the saucer, when the past came knocking.

Isabel stepped into the room feeling as though jelly had been piped through her veins. The window was open just a crack; it was enough for her to be able to smell the salted tang drifting in and made her think of fish and chips which took her mind off her jangling nerves. She made a mental note to treat herself to a scoop for lunch today.

She didn't know what she'd expected. From the stories she'd heard, a colourful character certainly, but this woman had a touch of the dowager duchess about her. There was something about her though. It was almost familiar, yet Isabel knew they'd never met. She was looking at Isabel expectantly and the thick rose pink drapes, held back by cream tiebacks, framed her like a portrait. All that was missing was a string of pearls around her neck. Where was the flamboyant woman she'd heard spoken of?

'Erm, hello, Miss Downer. I'm Isabel Stark.' Now she was here, Isabel was unsure how to proceed, and she stood awkwardly in the doorway. The room she was gazing into was rather lovely with its warm pinkish tones but now was not the time to be admiring Sea Vistas' plush furnishings she thought, as the realisation that she didn't know what sort of impact her message would have on Constance hit her. Was she foolhardy? What if the shock of Ginny's passing proved too much especially given her age? She had no idea who Ginny had been to Constance, and now she wished she'd been completely honest with Nurse Jill as to the purpose of her visit.

'It's Constance, and come in, I can't abide a hoverer.' It wasn't pearls draped from her neck but rather glasses on a cord, and she lifted them to her startlingly green eyes to better inspect her visitor. 'My, my, what an unusual choice of hair colour. Is that the new fashion then, is it?' There was something, a twinkle dancing in those bright eyes that belied her years and reassured Isabel that she was made of stern stuff. 'Why don't you sit down there?' She directed Isabel to the chair on the other side of the window. It was angled just so, to enable the visitor to talk directly to Constance and afford a glimpse of the beautiful backdrop the Solent provided. 'No, no. Don't sit on them!'

Isabel, her bottom about to touch base, froze mid-landing and, patting beneath her, produced a half-eaten bag of Maltesers. How she'd missed those with their bright red packaging, she didn't know.

'Put them on the bedside table,' Constance tsked, not offering her one of the chocolate balls.

Isabel did as she was told. She was relieved she hadn't sat on the bag of sweets, unlike the time she *had* managed to sit on something untoward at the bus stop in Southampton. On that occasion she'd proceeded to walk around town in her white jeggings looking like she'd been hitting the prune juice too hard for the best part of the morning. It was only when she'd gotten a tap on the shoulder from a concerned pensioner asking if she was alright that she'd realised the looks coming her way were not because she was looking particularly hot to trot in her skin-tight trousers.

'Now then. I think we both know you're not a long-lost relative. So, is the reason you've conned your way in here because you're going to try to sell me something?'

Isabel shook her head, taken aback by Constance's directness. 'No.'

'Good. I was never one for Tupperware and the like. So then, come on. What is it that has brought you here to see me today? You're not one of those God botherers come to convert me before I meet my maker, are you?'

There was nothing frail about Constance at all, Isabel thought, unnerved by her barrage of questions. She clasped her hands tightly and was embarrassed by the tight-lipped disapproval the sight of her bitten fingernails garnered.

'Nasty habit that. Are you a nervous Nellie then?'

God, she was a right bite. 'Not particularly.' *Or at least I wasn't until I met you.* She rearranged her hands hiding them away and pretended to be interested in the strip of blue she could see from the window. 'It's a lovely day today, isn't it? I can see why you like to sit here; with that view it's gorgeous.'

'Young people never know what to say when they're in the presence of the older generation. I was your age once, you know, and I couldn't have given a fig as to the view. I'm quite sure you're not here to talk to me about the weather or my sea view.' Constance was not a woman who could be doing with trite pleasantries; life was too short.

Isabel bit back the retort that she hadn't had a chance to tell her why she was here and decided just to say what she'd come to say and leave the old grump to it. 'I have a message to pass on to a woman called Constance, who I am fairly sure after making enquiries around town, is you. That's why I'm here.'

'I'm intrigued, dear. Do go on.'

'Well, I was in New Zealand a few weeks ago at the end of a year tripping around Australia when my friend and I happened across a car accident. There was no one else at the scene and, while my friend rang the emergency services, I went over to the car to see if I could help. The driver was an elderly woman, and I held her hand until she passed away.'

Constance tutted. 'That must've been difficult, but I don't understand the relevance of your being here. I don't know anyone in the Antipodes.'

'Well, the woman's name was Virginia Havelock, she went by the name of Ginny.'

Constance paled beneath her rouge as she leaned forward gripping the arms of her chair. 'Ginny? Go on.'

Isabel was emboldened; she was on the right track! 'She found the strength to ask me, in the moments before she went, to tell Constance that she'd wanted to go back to the Isle of Wight to say that she was sorry, she should never have left. She made me promise I'd do this and well, a promise is a promise. So there you go, I have kept my word and passed her message on.'

Constance was leaning back in her chair once more, silent, her pallor ghostly white.

'I'm sorry. I didn't even know for certain you'd be the right Constance. It's all been a bit of guesswork but you can see can't you, given the circumstances, why I felt I needed to try to find you? Erm, are you all right? Should I call for Nurse Jill?'

Constance turned her attention to Isabel, her voice sharp. 'It will take more than a voice from the past to see me off, young lady. I lived through the war and worse.'

'Yes, of course. Well, I've said what I came to say.' Isabel got up from her seat feeling disgruntled and deflated at the same time. There would be no cosy chat about who Ginny was to Constance or why she felt she shouldn't have left the island. She would never know, but at least she'd done her part—she'd kept her promise. Isabel made to leave, but Constance spoke.

'What I don't understand is, if all you had to go on was a name and the Isle of Wight how you found me?'

Isabel explained her conversation with Father Joyce at the funeral and how she'd felt compelled to come to Ryde and at least try to fulfill her promise. She told her about finding work at the Rum Den and how she'd trooped around the various rest homes to no avail, finishing by telling her how she'd come to be renting a room in Constance's old house. 'So you see it was as though clues were being dropped my way wherever I went, but it was enquiring as to the room to let that led me to you in the end.'

'I see.'

Isabel had said what she'd come to say, and she hadn't been made to feel welcome. In fact, she felt like she'd already outstayed it. 'Well, it was nice to meet you, Miss, er, Constance.'

'Is that eczema on your neck?'

Isabel paused mid-step startled by the question, and her hand flew to her scarf. She thought she'd hidden the patch successfully, but this woman was hawk eyed.

'Let me have a look.' Constance beckoned her closer, putting her glasses on once more.

Given Isabel had always been taught to respect her elders she dutifully undid her scarf and bent down to show Constance the irritated skin.

'Hmm, a chamomile bath, using the dried flowers tied off in a cheesecloth or piece of muslin would help with that. Or, and listen carefully, because I think given the rawness of your skin this will be more effective. Boil two cups of horsetail herbs in four cups of water for ten minutes and add it to a tepid bath. That should do the trick. You can follow the treatment up by dabbing honey, raw honey mind, on the areas affected. The inclusion of bone broth in your diet is helpful too as is a regular dose of cod liver oil. A daily dip in the sea or application of seawater to the affected area will help relieve the itching.'

Isabel's gaze flitted to the window. A dip in the sea could induce hypothermia. She was acclimatised to warmer waters than the English Channel, but the rest sounded interesting and the day was stretching long ahead of her. She had nothing to lose by trying something different, and this woman by all accounts knew her herbs.

'Where would I find horsetail herbs?' Isabel envisaged herself trudging over fields with a basket slung over her arm foraging for herbs.

'There's a new shop opened on Union Street. It's not hard to find, and there's not much the young lady who owns it doesn't stock.'

'Oh.' The romantic image vanished. 'You must miss your shop. It was very popular I've been told.'

Constance gave a little nod.

There was something in her expression, a hint perhaps of the loneliness of old age that made Isabel ask, 'Shall I come back and tell you how I get on?'

'I'd like that,' Constance replied, to Isabel's surprise, and she was pleased she'd suggested a return visit as she caught a glimpse beneath the woman's hardened shell to the softer centre inside. As she turned to leave, Constance called out to her, 'Would you like a Malteser before you go, dear?'

Chapter 24

The Solent's water journeyed in with gentle lapping and covered Isabel's bare feet. She couldn't help but squeal at the coldness of it, hopping from foot to foot as it whooshed away again leaving rivulets of water running down the sand. Her jeans were rolled up to her calves but were still damp thanks to the odd rogue wave. She wasn't the only hardy paddler on the bluish-grey horizon. Two women a short distance from her were laughing, their skirts held up in bunches, as they ventured deeper into the water where it formed white tips. They'd get wet knickers if they carried on, she thought sagely. There were even a few brazen enough to go for a dip she saw, as one man reared up out of the water. He shook his head, sending droplets of water flying. He looked like a seal in his wetsuit, she thought. A seal who was auditioning for a shampoo advert.

The next time the water swished in, she was ready and, bending down, she filled the empty medicine bottle she'd picked up at Boots, her second port of call after the herbal health store. The store, she'd seen from the twirling sign as she walked up Union Street, was called The Natural Way. Inside, it was light and modern and, just as Constance had said she would, she'd found everything she'd needed for what she was now thinking of as her war on eczema.

The shopkeeper, a woman around her age, had looked up from the box she was unpacking as Isabel entered. For someone working in a magic potions shop, she looked rather normal, as did the shop Isabel decided, taking in her faded khaki cargo pants and yellow T-shirt with a white dove pictured on it. She was pretty, she noticed absently, her pixie cut framing a roundish, friendly face. There was no nutcracker nose, chin with warts, or pointy black hat to be seen.

'Hi, I'm Delwyn—how're you today?'

'Good thanks.' Isabel's eyes scanned the shelves.

'Is there anything in particular you were looking for?'

'There is, yes. Raw honey for starters, please.' Isabel followed Delwyn's lead and stood staring at the array of jars. 'It's for my skin.'

'I've just the thing.' She picked a jar filled with golden liquid off the shelf and handed it to Isabel. 'This is fresh from a local hive as of yesterday.'

Isabel swallowed hard upon seeing the price. *It better be worth it.* 'Thanks. I also need some dried chamomile please.'

The shelves of the shop Isabel saw scanning them were full, but not cluttered, with packets of every kind of dried herb imaginable. There were specialty teas, and aromatherapy oils, and her eyes scanned the 'raw materials', shelf with curiosity. Distilled witch hazel, neroli oil, organic beeswax, myrrh gum—it really was a shop full of ingredients for a witch's brew.

'Believe it or not, I'm out of dried chamomile, sorry. I'll have it back in stock by the end of the week. I could give you a call as soon as it arrives if you like?'

Isabel didn't want to wait that long. 'Oh, bugger. Well, what about dried horsetail herbs then?' She hadn't fancied the sound of that, but Constance had said she thought it would be more effective. In for a penny, in for a pound and all that, as her mother would say!

'Yes, that's not *quite* such a big seller.' Delwyn smiled, scanning the shelf. 'Ah, here it is. Horsetail likes the banks of streams and boggy ground. It's rampant in these parts. If you don't mind my asking, what are you using it for?' She handed the packet to Isabel for her to inspect.

'I don't mind. I get a bit of eczema. It's not severe enough for a visit to the doctor, but it's enough to be annoying, and Constance Downer recommended it, I think you might know her?'

'Oh yes. She's an amazing lady. Quite the legend around these parts and very knowledgeable. I've only met her the once when she called in and introduced herself. I could chat with her for hours; there's not many self-trained herbalists left.'

Amazing and grumpy, Isabel thought unkindly. 'Well, I had a chat with her this morning about my eczema, and she recommended bathing in chamomile or a brew of horsetail tea.' She showed Delwyn her neck, seeing her wince at the sight of the weepy, red patch.

'Is she still doing consultations then? I thought she'd retired when she moved into Sea Vistas. That is where she's living, isn't it?'

'Yes, and I don't think so. I had a message to pass on to her from a relative and she spotted the patch on my neck. That was how the conversation came about.'

'Ah, I see, well, Constance would know. I've thought about calling on her. Like I said, I'd love to talk to her about some of the old remedies.'

'You should. I got the feeling she's lonely.'

'Really? I thought she'd have a steady stream of visitors. I will go and see her then.'

'Be warned, she can be a bit—'

'Acerbic?'

'Good word.'

'My granny was like that; loneliness can do that to a person. Whole days could pass after my granddad died without her seeing anyone. It won't faze me. Good luck with the horsetail and honey. I'd love to hear how you get on. If it makes a difference, it means I can recommend it to other customers with confidence.'

'I will,' Isabel said, following Delwyn to the counter. She handed her the honey and herbs and waited while she rang them up before handing over a decent wedge of the previous night's earnings. She thanked her and took the bag from her before heading down to the water.

Now, satisfied she had enough water in her bottle for the eczema assault, she headed back up the beach. She sidestepped a woman who'd draped a striped beach towel over her lap to keep the brusque wind at bay and was sitting in a fold-out chair, her nose in a book. Isabel paused to admire the sandcastle her two girls were building nearby before carrying on. Her feet were coated in gritty sand by the time she reached the spot where she'd left her shoes.

'It's good for the garden that, isn't it? Seaweed's even better, though.' A gent walking his dog nodded toward the bottle in her hand while the Labrador pulled at its lead eager to be on its way.

He must have watched her scooping it up out of the sea, Isabel realised.

'Brings my carrots along a proper treat does seaweed.'

She smiled at him. 'Oh, I'm not using it for my garden. I'm going to try it on my eczema.'

He rubbed his chin, with his free hand. 'Eczema, you say? Stop pulling, Riley, old boy.'

Isabel nodded brushing the sand off her feet.

'My wee granddaughter has a bit of bother with that. She's only nine, poor love, and it drives her mad, not being able to scratch it. Her mother's even resorted to putting socks on her hands at times. I'd like to know how you get on with that.' He nodded toward the bottle. 'Can I give you my mobile number?'

Isabel was a little taken aback but couldn't see any harm in giving him a quick call as to whether her remedies were successful or not. 'I'm using it in conjunction with a few other bits and pieces I picked up from the herbal shop up the road there.' She gestured vaguely in the direction from which she'd walked down to the water before putting the bottle down. She dug her phone out of her pocket while he chatted away.

'My name's Don, and this impatient mutt is Riley. Say hello, Riley.'

Isabel gave the panting Riley a wary pat—one canine admirer was quite enough thank you very much—before entering the number Don relayed into her contacts. 'Okay then, I'd best be on my way, but I'll be sure and give you a call, Don, to let you know if any of this stuff helps.'

'That'd be great, thank you, lass. Come on now, Riley.'

~

'Ow, ow, ow,' Isabel moaned into the bathroom mirror, as she spritzed the seawater onto her neck. The salty bite stung but was bearable, only just. She'd put a pot stuffed with horsetail herbs on to boil as soon as she'd raced up the stairs, grateful Rhodri was busy downstairs. He'd been talking to a customer when she'd breezed past and had given her a passing wave. She hadn't wanted to hang around explaining what she was about to do, eager just to get on with the task at hand. She wanted to tell someone about her visit with Constance though, and so as soon as she'd hung her damp jeans over the clothes rack, she rang her mum.

'You're doing what?' Babs asked.

'I am boiling horsetail herbs up in a big pot to pour into my bath.'

'Why? And what are you doing having a bath in the middle of the day? You're not royalty you know. Oh dear, Prince Charles has just had an accident. Outside now! It's the second time since you left. Shoo, off you go.'

Isabel heard the door shut and then her mum came back on the line.

'I think it's anxiety from you leaving again. Give me a sec to mop this up, will you?'

'Hey, don't blame me for your incontinent corgi,' Isabel said knowing it had fallen on deaf ears. She trawled through the drawers until she found what she was looking for, a wooden spoon.

'Right, that's sorted. So come on then tell me what on earth it is you're up to and more importantly how you got on visiting the woman in the retirement home. Was she your Constance?'

'She was.' Isabel relayed the story of the cantankerous Constance and how she'd given nothing away where Ginny was concerned. She also told her how she'd spotted the flare-up on her neck and had suggested a remedy for it. 'Remember I told you she used to run a herbal remedies shop in the gallery part of Pier View House?'

'Yes, and you've nothing to lose I suppose. I tried rinsing my hair with beer once to give it extra shine, but your dad wasn't too happy. Said it was a waste of good ale. It worked a treat though. It sounds to me like her snarkiness is because she's lonely. Your nan was the same, but then she was the one who opted to go to a care facility in flipping Dorset. There was nothing whatsoever wrong with Sunny Days around the corner here.'

Her words echoed Delwyn's and Jill's. 'Jill, one of the nurses who works at Sea Vistas, said the same thing, Mum. I'm going to go back and see her, tell how I get on with this brew.'

'Let me know and all. One of the ladies at work; her son suffers from it something awful too. She'd be interested to hear of an alternative remedy.'

'Alright, Mum, love to Dad. I've got to go.'

'Bye, Isabel, and remember to scrub the bath out afterward. You don't want to mark your card with your chap this early in the piece.'

'Landlord, not chap, Mum,' Isabel said, before hanging up.

She'd turned the element on the stove off. The herbs were giving off a slightly sweetish smell, almost like wet grass, but nothing noxious enough to send Rhodri flying up the stairs to see what she was up to. It felt rather decadent running a bath in the middle of the day, she thought, putting the plug in. It was only going to be tepid so it shouldn't send the heating bill through the roof. Leaving the bath to fill, she padded back into the kitchen to strain the herbs before carefully carrying the full pot back through to the bathroom. She upended it into the water and watched the steeped brown mixture slosh in with a grimace. It didn't look very appealing but needs must.

Chapter 25

The stinging on her neck from the salt water was easing now, and it felt pretty good, Isabel thought, clambering into the bath, trying not to shiver at the cool temperature. She took a deep breath and submerged herself up to her chin in the water, glad she'd had the foresight to put a shower cap on. She didn't want her hair getting wet; it would be her luck the herbs would set off some strange reaction with the colour. As her body adjusted to the temperature, she relaxed, beginning to drift.

In her mind's eye, she conjured up a symphony. They were waiting for her to come on stage; Isabel cast around, where was she? Oh, there she was stepping out from the wings, draped in a fabulous silver gown. The dress shimmered beneath a moonlit sky and moved to the rhythm of her steps. The fabric rippling like cascading water as she glided confidently across the stage bearing an uncanny resemblance to Celine Dion but with green hair. Andrea Bocelli stood spotlighted in his white tuxedo, looking impossibly handsome and Isabel took his outstretched hand before whispering in his ear.

A cheer went up from the crowd, who were reclining on picnic blankets, the sweet scent of the Tuscan grass tickling their senses as bottles of wine were drunk, and cheese platters indulged in. The eager audience had been waiting all night for this moment, her and Andrea's duet.

The cheering grew to a jungle-like roar in its power as Andrea leaned down to kiss her on the cheek. They waited for an age for the sound to die down and then as it ebbed, Isabel opened her mouth and, submerged in a bath full of horsetail tea, she began to sing.

Her voice rose carrying itself up and over the notes of the hauntingly, beautiful, "The Prayer". She could hear her favourite Italian singer's wonderfully rich voice as clearly as if he was there singing alongside her—not soaking with her in the bath *obviously*. She hadn't taken complete leave of her senses. Besides, he was a happily married man and she would never do that to another woman. Isabel enjoyed the sensation of effortlessly climbing to the highest pitch. It was an otherworldly feeling of her voice almost not belonging to her as the purity of a note soared free. It was why she loved to sing.

The acoustics in the bathroom were pretty good, she thought, launching into "Time to Say Goodbye", the shampoo bottle an improvised microphone. By the time she climbed out of the bath, despite the water being stone cold, she felt amazing. Euphoric, almost. Singing did that for her. It lifted her to a higher plane, if only for a little while. She gave a little bow to the empty bathroom before pulling the plug and wrapping herself in a towel.

Her neck looked better already she decided, wiping a patch of condensation off the mirror and peering at it. She scooped a blob of honey from the pot and plastered it onto the patch. Next, she daubed it on the pesky area inside the crook of her arm. Isabel twisted this way and that, but, so far as she could see, she hadn't come out in any hideous spots.

Yes, it had been worth all the palaver, she decided, straightening up the bathroom before swishing out the bath until she was satisfied there would be no telltale brown rim left behind. Her clothes lay in a pile where she'd stepped out of them and scooping them up a sprinkle of sand fell like fine drizzle to the floor. She'd sweep up the remains of her walk on the beach in a bit but first things first, she needed some fresh clothes to change into. Her jeans, she remembered, were on the clothes rack in the sitting room drying out.

'Oh, you startled me.' Isabel jumped at the sight of Rhodri who was standing in the kitchen. He was pouring boiling water into his teacup and, remembering her state of undress, she clutched at the towel with her spare hand.

'Sorry about that, I called out, but you can't have heard me. I popped upstairs to make a brew and I wanted to know how you got on with Constance today.' He turned away fishing the teabag out of the cup, but not before she saw the amused look on his face.

She took the opportunity to scoop her jeans up off the rack. 'It was her, but she didn't give anything away,' Isabel said, before hot-footing it back up the stairs to her bedroom.

'You've got a great voice, by the way,' he called after her.

Isabel closed her bedroom door and leaned her head against it, realising, as she did so, that she still had the shower cap on. Oh well, if she was going to make a complete prat of herself, she might as well do a proper job it. There was a lot to be said for living alone, she decided, pushing away from the door and digging out a clean T-shirt to wear with her jeans. She debated hiding out in her room until Rhodri had returned to the gallery but decided she'd better face the music.

'I meant it, you know. You do have a lovely voice,' Rhodri said, as she reappeared fully clothed and minus the shower cap this time. He frowned, putting down the packet of digestive biscuits he'd just opened and tapped the side of his neck. 'You've something there.'

Her hand inadvertently flew up to her neck and connected with the honey she'd slathered on after her bath. She looked at the sticky mess on her fingers deciding an explanation was required. 'It's honey. I get a bit of eczema now and then, and just before I left her, Constance, who was the same Constance I was looking for, shared a natural remedy with me for it. I thought I'd give it a try,' she offered up before adding, 'I don't make a habit of running baths in the middle of the day either, but she also recommended bathing in horsetail tea, and I wanted to see if it would work.'

'Horsetail tea?' He raised his teacup. 'I think I'll stick with good old Earl Grey thanks. And, hey, it's fine by me if you want to have a bath in the middle of the day.' Rhodri took a sip of his tea before asking, 'Did it work?'

'Yes, actually, it did.' She held her arm out and inspected the crook where the angry red patch had been only an hour ago. Now, the patch had faded to a muted pink and didn't feel in the least bit irritable. She felt inordinately pleased that her efforts had been worthwhile and made a note to telephone Don, the man she'd met on the pier, to pass on her results.

'Do you always like a bit of a sing-song when you're in the bath then? I suppose the bathroom has good acoustics,' Rhodri said, interrupting her train of thought.

This time, it wasn't eczema that caused her skin to flame. She'd been so caught up in her wee operatic world she hadn't given a thought to how bloody loud she was. The whole of Ryde Pier had probably heard her imaginary concert with Andrea.

'Personally, I always like to belt out a bit of Tom when I'm in the shower.'

'Tom?'

'Jones, of course. I'm Welsh, and we come from the same town, Pontypridd.'

'Ah right.' The name rang a bell; she'd Google him later she decided raising a small smile.

A silence stretched between them as Isabel set about making herself a drink. Rhodri lingered a fraction longer than was necessary before saying, 'Well, I'd best be getting back downstairs to deal with the hordes of art connoisseurs waiting patiently for me to finish my tea break. And I'm glad you found Constance. Do you feel any different having passed the message to her?'

'No, if anything I'm even more curious to know the story behind what Ginny said now. She didn't give anything away. I'm going to go back and see her in a couple of days, even if she was a right Oscar the Grouch and tell her how I got on with her recommendations. Who knows, maybe she'll tell me how they were connected once she's had a chance to mull it over. I think hearing Ginny's name came as a shock to her.' Isabel helped herself to a digestive biscuit and bit into it. She'd have to sweep those crumbs up along with the sand, she thought, looking at the kitchen floor. 'I'm happy to mind the shop for you from time to time, you know.'

'Thanks, I might take you up on that. It'd save hanging my 'back in five minutes' sign up and maybe missing that crucial sale.'

She smiled, and mumbled through a crumbly mouthful, 'It's the least I can do.'

. . ❧ . .

ISABEL WHILED AWAY what was left of her afternoon off with a stroll along the pier, and as she ascended the stairs to the flat, her nostrils twitched. She could smell something cooking and whatever it was promised to be divine. Rhodri had his back to her as he stood at the stove, and he jumped as she appeared alongside him curious as to the contents of the pot he was stirring on the stove.

'Sorry, that smells gorgeous, what's for dinner?'

'My mum's stew; it never lets me down,' he offered by way of explanation. 'Glass of red?'

'Ooh, lovely, yes please.' Isabel pulled a chair out at the table while Rhodri poured her a glass from the open bottle on the bench next to him. He put it down in front of her. 'I'm quite enjoying my stay at Pier View Guest House so far. Cheers,' she said, the cheeky twinkle in her eye as she raised her glass not escaping him.

'You'll leave a good review on Trip Advisor then?'

'Five stars.' A conversation ensued about a documentary Isabel had seen on people who take reviewing on the popular site a step too far. She finished telling Rhodri that she thought it was a rather sad way to live your life, going around picking holes in people's livelihoods. 'The Internet has made everybody an armchair critic,' she announced, as Rhodri popped a breadboard and knife down in front of her and handed her a baguette in a brown paper bag.

'Butter's in the fridge; you can do the honours if you like.'

Isabel retrieved the butter and began to slice the fresh bread, slathering a piece in butter. She popped it in her mouth while Rhodri's back was turned. He turned from the stove to see her looking rather chipmunk-like.

'Caught you!'

She cut him a piece and buttered it before handing it over. 'Now we're even.'

Isabel tucked into the plate Rhodri popped down on the table a short while later. The meat melted in her mouth and she made short shrift of her dinner, mopping the sauce up with the bread.

He looked at her with amusement. 'You've got gravy on your chin.'

Isabel wiped it away with the back of her hand, embarrassed at how she'd hoovered her meal down, but she'd been starved. 'That was delicious; you're a really good cook. Thanks.'

'You're welcome.' He glanced at his watch. 'I better get a move on; I've been invited round to a friend's for coffee and dessert.'

Isabel's antennae quivered. Coffee and dessert, eh? That sounded rather posh. She didn't know many fellas who would lay on coffee and dessert for their mates. Come to think of it she didn't know any girls who'd do that either. She wondered who he was off to see. He hadn't alluded to a girlfriend as yet.

He got up from the table, 'Sorry to leave you with all this.' He gestured at the bench.

He was even a tidy cook, Isabel thought, looking at the neatly stacked pots and pans. 'Don't be silly, that's our arrangement, remember. You cook, and I'll clean, and having just sampled your culinary skills I think I got the winning end of the deal.'

He grinned and shrugged into his jacket. 'It's nice to have someone to cook for.' As he reached the top of the stairs, he paused and called over to her, 'You know, Isabel, this is your flat too, so feel free to have your friend over.'

Isabel, still sitting at the dinner table rather too full to move just yet, looked over at him blankly. She didn't have any friends on the island except Brenda. She wasn't sure she could count her as a friend though, given she was her boss and she'd only known her for two days.

'Er, the friend you were meeting after you left here yesterday.'

Her face felt as though someone had turned the oven dial to high heat.

'Oh, I see,' Rhodri said. 'Very sensible.'

'You can't be too careful,' Isabel said. 'You know stranger danger and all that.'

Chapter 26

'Penny for them?' Rhodri said appearing in the kitchen with an empty mug in hand. It was Friday morning, and they'd settled into a companionable routine of sorts over the course of the week. His day began well before hers. He liked to squeeze in a few early morning hours painting downstairs in the gallery before opening up for the day. Rhodri would usually appear in the kitchen in search of a hot beverage and to exchange morning pleasantries while Isabel was still in her pyjamas reading the latest island news over coffee and toast, much to his amusement. It wasn't that she liked to keep up with the island's current affairs so much, it was more that it made her feel like a proper Islander when she sat reading the paper and she liked that feeling.

The days panned out with Isabel heading off to the Rum Den at midday and reappearing back at Pier View House when her dinner break rolled around. Her waistband was already feeling a tad tighter thanks to her second helpings each night.

At the sound of his voice this morning, however, she recalled their conversation over dinner last night and hoped by confiding in him as much as she had he didn't think she was a total loser. It had begun with her breaking her mum's golden rule of talking with her mouth full as she told him, 'You should have been a chef you know. You missed your calling.'

Rhodri had put down the spoon upon which he was using his fork to twirl his pasta up. 'You've bolognaise sauce on your nose.' He grinned before adding, 'And thank you for the compliment, but sometimes when a hobby becomes a job, the joy can disappear from it.'

'What do you mean?' Isabel had asked, picking up the napkin next to her glass of wine and using it to wipe off the offending sauce.

'I love to cook, it relaxes me but *having* to cook and under pressure too would be a completely different thing. I'd turn into Gordon Ramsay effing and blinding. It's the same with my painting. If I were to paint full time and try to earn a living from it, then it would become forced, and a lot of the pleasure I get from the process would disappear. I like the freedom of being able to paint what I want, not what someone else wants me to. It's the same with cooking. Not a great attitude to have if you want to make a living at something. Hence I run a gallery selling other people's work.' He'd popped the pasta laden fork in his mouth.

'I'd like to see some of your work,' Isabel said. The easel upon which he was currently working was always hidden away under a sheet by the time she ventured downstairs for the day. Rhodri didn't reply, and she'd pondered over what he'd said while running a finger around the edge of her bowl to mop up the last of the tomato sauce. It was another dinnertime misdemeanour that would have got a slap on the hand from Babs Stark. *Yes*, she'd thought, savouring the sauce, she could understand what he was saying.

'And, Isabel, I could say the same thing to you about your singing you know. You have a beautiful voice so why aren't you doing something with it? How come you're presently pulling pints in a pub and not a YouTube sensation? Not that there is anything wrong with pulling pints. I'm curious that's all.'

That had taken her aback. It reminded her of a game of 'I'll show you mine if you show me yours' she'd played as a youngster with Steven Flintoff who'd lived across the way. She'd thought for a second, unsure how far she wanted to go with this conversation, and then decided to tell Rhodri the truth. There was something open and honest about him that invited her to confide. 'When I was a kid, all I ever wanted to be when I grew up was a singer. The thing is though it's not enough just to sing, you have to be the full package, and I'm not.' She'd shrugged. 'I never had the confidence to put myself out the front of anything really and to just go for it. And, I'm okay with that. I have come to the conclusion I'm a bit of an introvert.'

Rhodri looked incredulous. 'With that hair? And what about the way you barrelled on up to my American customer the other day? That sale wouldn't have happened without you. No, an introvert you're not,' he said, shaking his head.

Isabel toyed with her glass. 'It's hard to explain, but when it comes to some things I can push myself out of my comfort zone, but when it comes to singing, that's strictly relegated to the privacy of the bathroom.'

The smile Rhodri had given her across the table reassured her he wasn't judging her, so she'd carried on. 'I never found anything else I was passionate about other than singing, and after I left school, I worked here and there and went out with my friends and had fun.' She paused before blurting, 'Then I met Connor. I thought he might be 'the one' until I surprised him one night and found him shagging Ashley, one of my best friends. I took off for Australia after that.'

'I don't blame you. That's awful. But you know, shit happens, and you move on.'

'It does, and I did, or I thought I'd put it all behind me while I was away. I mean I'm over Connor; he was an arse and Ashley, well, she was never really my friend. Not if she could do that to me. The thing is I ran into another friend a couple of days after I arrived home. To cut a long story short, she's getting married, and Ashley is one of her bridesmaids. She asked me if I'd try to patch things up with her so I could be in the bridal party too.' This time it had been Isabel who shook her head. 'There's just no way. I can't forgive either Connor or Ashley for what they did. If I'm honest, it was a relief to get on the ferry away from all of them, so here I am pulling pints on the Isle of Wight. Speaking of which,' she said, getting up from the table and carrying her empty bowl over to the sink. 'Now you know my life story, I'd better wash this lot up and get back to work.'

Now, with the smell of toast and coffee hovering in the air, Rhodri nodded toward the paper Isabel had spread across the table. 'It's not that scintillating, surely?'

Isabel realised she'd been staring at a headline emblazoned with the news that a Green Party MP was due to visit the island.

'No it's not. I'm away with the fairies, sorry.' The week had whizzed by thanks to her busy shifts at the Rum Den, and she was just about used to the long hours and late finishes. Her mind, before Rhodri's appearance, had been on Constance. She'd decided she'd call in at the shop where she'd bought her herbs and honey and pop in on Constance before she was due at the Rum

Den at lunchtime—let Delwyn and Constance know how she'd gotten on with her concoctions.

Rhodri moved toward the kettle, but the bell at the top of the stairs that was connected to the front door rang, signalling somebody had just walked into the gallery. 'Bugger, I was going to make a cup of tea.'

'Go. I'll bring you one down on my way out.' Isabel raised a smile.

By the time she'd finished getting ready and had taken the tea down to the gallery, it was empty save for Rhodri.

'It was just a courier.' He pointed at a box by his feet before taking the mug from her. 'Thanks for this, just what the doctor ordered. How was last night's shift?'

Isabel was about to fill him in on her rather uneventful evening at the Rum Den when the door jangling interrupted her. A woman appeared, looking impossibly ethereal as she called out hello to them both before gliding toward the counter. She was clutching a Grecian blue bowl, and Isabel couldn't help but think she looked as though she would kneel down when she got to the counter and make an offering to the gods. She was blonde and beautiful, and Isabel was instantly reminded of Ashley.

The woman didn't kneel but rather placed the misshapen bowl on the counter. 'You left this in the studio, Rhodri. I meant to give it to you the other night but forgot. I was passing, so I thought I'd drop it in. It's a bit of a masterpiece.' She smiled, and her accent made Isabel think of posh parts of southern England. 'I'm Nico, Rhodri's pottery tutor.'

The famous love scene in a movie her mum loved, *Ghost,* flashed before her eyes except instead of Demi and Patrick in the lead roles it was this Ashley impersonator and Rhodri. It took her a second before she saw that the woman was staring at her expectantly.

'Oh sorry, I'm—'

'She's away with the fairies thanks to a late-night shift at the Rum Den,' Rhodri interjected with a laugh. 'Nico this is my new flatmate, Isabel.'

'Hi, Nico. Nice to meet you.'

Nico smiled back at her.

'Thanks for dropping this in. This was my very first attempt,' he said to Isabel. 'Pottery is not easy. The wheel has a mind of its own.'

'It's cute,' Isabel said, picking up the bowl and pretending not to notice its odd shape. 'I love the colour.'

'It's rubbish, but I can only get better. Right, Nico?'

'Right.'

Isabel laughed. 'I remember having a go on a potter's wheel in art at high school. It was fun getting all messy, but I don't think I came home with anything worth shouting about.' Isabel inhaled reminding herself that this woman was not Ashley and to be nice. 'Where are your classes held, Nico?'

'I have a little studio at the bottom of my garden, and I'm pretty flexible with whatever works with my students, time wise. You're welcome to pop along sometime with Rhodri and have a turn. I love your hair by the way.'

'Oh, thanks, and thanks for the offer. I might just do that.' She had no intention of doing that; there was something a little intense about Nico's gaze. 'Right, well nice meeting you, but I'd best be on my way. I have a few jobs to do before my shift.'

'Bye, nice meeting you too.' Nico gave her a slow smile.

'Okay. Catch you later,' Rhodri replied, still inspecting his bowl.

~

Isabel pushed open the door to the herbal shop five minutes later.

'Hello again,' Delwyn said hearing the bell jangle. She put the brochure she'd been flicking through down and came out from behind the counter. 'I hope you've come to tell me how you got on with your horsetail tea and honey?'

'I have.' Isabel grinned. Today she noticed, Delwyn was wearing jeans teamed with a white peasant blouse which along with her pixie haircut, gave her a bohemian look. She liked her style and made a mental note to ask where she'd gotten her blouse; it was gorgeous. 'Look,' she said, tilting her head. She pulled her hair back with both hands before angling her neck.

Delwyn leaned in to look, smelling of Irish moss.

Isabel sniffed; she loved the stuff. Her mum always bought it for her when she had a cough. She'd tell her not to eat the whole bag of soothing black jubes like they were sweets. The thing was they were covered with a sugary coating and reminded her of black jelly beans, so eat them like sweets was precisely what she used to do. Isabel let her hair swing free as Delwyn took a step back, inspection done.

'What a difference. It's only been, what?'

'Four days,' Isabel announced proudly. 'I spritzed with sea water which did sting but took the itch away, and I bathed daily in the horsetail tea brew just like Constance suggested before applying the honey to the affected spots. It's worked wonders. Well worth all the sticky messiness although the tide marks around the bath are a sod to get off.'

Delwyn laughed. 'A rub down with baking soda should do the trick. I'll make a note of all that if you don't mind?' She grabbed a pad from beside the till before scribbling the information down. 'Thanks for the recommendation. It's always good to hear back from customers first hand as to the success of a product.'

'No problem.' Isabel liked Delwyn; there was something unaffected and genuine about her. She was in need of a friend too she realised. A proper one. She decided to find out more about her. 'How long have you had the shop?'

Delwyn looked up from the notepad. 'Oh, just over a year. It was a scary step going into business for myself, but so far so good. I moved over from Dorset which was lovely, but my heart is here on the island. It's a special place and the people are very open-minded.'

'Did you have to train in herbs then?' Isabel frowned. 'Sorry, that didn't sound right. I don't know what the correct terminology for knowing about all this stuff would be.' She waved her hand toward the shelves.

'You're not the only one! And some would say and have said, I studied for a degree in pottiness, but I am a qualified naturopath. I have an honor's degree in herbal medicine from Westminster University. It took three years and, I have to say, in some ways it was easier being a poor student than being a grown up with her own business. There's nothing else I'd rather be doing though, and nowhere else I'd rather be.'

That was something Isabel could relate to. Being a grown-up was bloody hard work sometimes. She envied Delwyn her conviction that she was on the right path. 'But how did you decide you wanted to learn about all this stuff?' She gestured around the shop.

'That was easy. I always loved pottering in the garden when I was little, and my mum was a keen cook who kept a fabulous herb garden. I was fascinated by the way the different herbs added so much flavour to food, and I loved the different smells. I used to mess with making my own natural body lotions when I was a teenager for myself and my friends and to take it further was a natural progression. It's funny really,' Delwyn continued, 'because in another era the locals would have pointed the finger at me for being a witch. My shop would have been burned to the ground.' Her eyes twinkled. 'Your friend Constance knows all about that.'

'Oh yes. One of the nurses at Sea Vistas told me the story of how she was related to the last witch on the Isle of Wight. And she's not my friend; I don't know her. Well, not really. I'm hoping to get to know her a bit better. I didn't tell you the whole truth about why I went to see her the other day.' Isabel found herself relaying the tale of her encounter with the dying Ginny, and how she'd come to meet Constance. Delwyn was fascinated.

'Gosh, that's some story. I wonder who they were to each other.'

'You and me both. Constance didn't give anything away when I went to see her. I'm going to call in on her before I start work today to thank her for sharing her remedies with me.'

'Well, would you mind seeing how the land lies if I were to visit her on my day off, Sunday? Look, you've given me goosebumps.' Delwyn held her arm out. 'Don't you think it's uncanny how you've wound up living in her old house above her old shop?'

'Yes, I suppose it is strange how things all fell into place once I arrived here on the island. It was like I was given clues along the way as to how to find her.' Isabel explained how she'd found work at the pub and gotten her first inkling as to where Constance might be, but it was only when she'd ventured into A Leap of Faith to ask about the accommodation on offer that she'd found out for sure where she was.

'It's like somebody was guiding you, Ginny perhaps?'

Now the hairs on Isabel's arms were standing on end. 'I hadn't thought of it like that.'

'Ah, don't mind me. I have an overactive imagination. I'm sure it's all just coincidence,' Delwyn said noticing how pale Isabel had gone. 'I've popped into A Leap of Faith a few times; I bought a gorgeous print for my cottage from Rhodri not long after I moved to the island. He's rather gorgeous too. I've seen him out and about a bit with a pretty blonde woman. Is that his girlfriend?'

Nico, Isabel thought shrugging. What was it about blondes? 'I'm not sure. If it's who I think it is then her name's Nico, and she teaches him pottery, but he didn't introduce her to me as his girlfriend.'

'He's a lovely guy, but you get the sense there's a lot of stuff going on beneath the surface. Do you know what I mean?'

Isabel looked at Delwyn. That overactive imagination of hers was obviously in overdrive. 'Let me guess. You watch Poldark, right?'

'Guilty, well, one or two episodes anyway.'

Both women laughed.

'I've meant to pop into the Rum Den for a drink; it looks lovely and quaint. I don't know many people here yet though, and I've been so busy with this,' she gestured around her shop, 'it's not left me much time to socialise.'

'Well, you've met me now, so call in anytime, and I'll reserve a stool at the bar for you.'

'Thanks, I'll take you up on that.' The two women grinned at each other. 'And I'm pleased Constance suggested you try her recipes and that the products worked for you. Otherwise you might not have come back in to say hi.'

'It's the first time I haven't had to resort to getting a script from the doctor's for a flare-up when it's been that bad. It felt good knowing everything I was putting on my skin was natural for a change too.'

Delwyn was nodding. 'That's what I'm all about. I want to give people an alternative option. I'd never advocate not going to see a GP, but it's not the only route available for minor ailments.'

'That's another reason why I've called in again; I'd like to buy more of the same ingredients please.'

'Stocking up?'

'No, I still have plenty to be going on with and hopefully I won't need it for a while. I met this lovely chap near the pier the other day when I was bottling the seawater, and we got chatting. His granddaughter suffers from eczema too, and he asked me to let him know how I got on too. I thought I'd bottle a brew of the horsetail tea and buy some more of the honey for him to pass on to her to see if it's of any help.'

'That's kind of you.'

Isabel shrugged. 'I know what it's like to be in her shoes. It's even worse when you're a kid, and everyone's on at you to stop scratching because you'll only make it worse.' Her mum's face flitted before her; it was her favourite catchphrase. 'It's like constantly telling a smoker, smoking is bad for them. You know it, but you can't help it. The urge is far too strong for words to stop you doing it. So, if I can help ease someone else's urge to scratch, then that's great.'

Delwyn grinned at her turn of phrase and went to the shelf where the bags of horsetail herbs needed for the tea were.

Chapter 27

Isabel found Constance, as Nurse Jill said she would, in the library. She loitered in the hallway outside, momentarily unsure of the reception she would receive. A woman of great years such as Constance was entitled to be disagreeable if she so desired, she supposed. The library, she saw, was a large airy room lined with wall-to-wall books. A lady with a salt and pepper crop, decked out in smart leisurewear, was holding a fat novel in her hand and inspecting the back cover with a frown on her face. A picture window dominated the far end of the room. Its purpose was to let the natural light flood in and to beckon to the expansive back lawn and surrounding gardens beyond. The window was framed with thick velvety russet drapes, which added to the overall inviting warmth of the room.

Constance, with her glasses sliding down her nose, was seated at the antique oak table decorated with a scattered array of newspapers. She was, however, reading a book and must have sensed Isabel's presence as she looked up and spied her hovering in the hall. 'I've always loved to read,' she said, peering over the top of her glasses 'C. S. Lewis once said, "You can never get a cup of tea large enough or a book long enough to suit me." It's large print only or talking books for me these days, and the selection's not so good. This one's a load of old twaddle. I might give it away.' True to her words she closed it with a snap.

'Hello again, Constance,' Isabel said, entering the room. Her exterior might be that of a frail old woman but she was sharp as a tack, she thought, sitting down opposite her. The woman with the salt and pepper crop who'd been appraising the novel, tucked it under her arm and left the room leaving them alone. 'I said I'd come back and tell you how I got on. I followed your remedies to the letter, and it's worked a treat, thank you.'

Constance pushed her glasses back up her nose and peered across the table eyeing Isabel's neck before taking her hand and turning it so she could inspect the crook of Isabel's arm. Where there'd been an angry red patch the other day, the skin was now smooth. She finished her inventory with a look of satisfaction and released Isabel's hand.

'I've made up another brew of the horsetail tea too and bought more honey off Delwyn to give to a gentleman I met when I was collecting seawater to spritz. We got chatting, and his granddaughter suffers from eczema too. I'm going to give it to him for her to try to see if it's as successful as it was for me. Delwyn wondered if she could visit you on Sunday? Oh, and I brought you these.' Isabel produced a packet of Maltesers from her tote bag and passed them to Constance whose hand was already outstretched.

'They're my favourite.'

Isabel smiled. 'I guessed.'

Constance met her gaze and held it then her expression changed as she seemingly made her mind up. 'Ginny was my sister-in-law.'

'Oh!' Isabel was startled by the abrupt change of subject.

'Yes. She married my older brother, Teddy, during the war. They were only married a short while before he was killed in battle. She was pregnant when he died and we lost touch after the baby was born. I assumed she would have remarried being such a young widow, but I didn't know she'd gone to live in New Zealand.'

Isabel was unsure of what she should say. It explained their relationship to one another, but it didn't explain why Ginny was sorry. Perhaps she was simply referring to the fact they'd lost touch.

'It's Isabel, isn't it?'

'Yes, that's right.'

'Tell Delwyn I will be in all day Sunday. There's something I'd like to show you in my room, Isabel. You might be interested in it.'

Isabel checked her phone; she had just over an hour until she had to be at work. 'Okay.' She was curious as to what it might be, and she stood up waiting for Constance, who struggled to her feet.

'I'll need to hold your arm, I am eighty-nine you know.' The tone was admonishing.

'Oh right, of course. Sorry.' Isabel flushed and held her arm out for Constance who leaned heavily on it; she let her set the pace as they stepped forth. As they passed the dining room, Isabel glanced in and saw a sea of heads bent over their closely held cards; bridge seemed to be the order of the day. Together, she and Constance made their way down the plush, thickly carpeted hallway toward the lift, with Constance nodding greetings to passing residents. There were no echoing hospital style corridors to be found at Sea Vistas, Isabel thought, guessing it cost a pretty penny to see out your days here.

The lift took an age, and when the doors slid open, they moved aside to allow the sweet-faced lady, who was clutching a Zimmer frame with a death-like grip, room to shuffle forth. She paused in her efforts. 'You'd never believe I was once the school cross country champion, would you?'

'Were you? Good for you, I was hopeless at it.' Isabel smiled back, watching the woman for a second as she carried on her cumbersome way. She regretted her first impression of an old dear struggling to walk. She was a person who'd no doubt led an interesting life as would have most of the residents housed within these walls. She probably had some wonderful stories to tell if people, including herself, took the time to listen. Just like Constance here would too. She shot a sideways glance at Constance as they stood in the lift taking them to the second floor, her curiosity as to what she had to show her mounting.

'My neighbour Ronald, he's in number ten across the way from me,' Constance said, as they exited the lift and began the slow shuffle toward her room, 'is driving me demented.'

'Oh dear, that's no good,' Isabel tutted.

'No, it's not. He gives me daily breakfast updates on his gout, and I don't mind telling you Isabel, he picks his moments. His medical monologues are timed for the precise instant I dip my toast into my egg. It's most off-putting, and I do so enjoy my breakfast. I told him his gout would undoubtedly improve were he to knock his nightly tipple on the head, but he got rather snippy with me and said that I couldn't possibly know what it was like to suffer as he did. A nightly tipple, he said was the only thing that eased his discomfort.' She opened the door to her room.

Isabel, bemused by the monologue, followed her inside with absolutely no idea as to where Constance was heading with the gout story.

'Close the door behind you, Isabel, and help me to the chair over there.'

Isabel did as she was told. She was beginning to get used to the lack of pleasantries.

'I wondered if we might look up a remedy in a book I have and if you'd be so kind, you might be able to pick up what's needed to help fix Ronald's problem.' She didn't wait for Isabel to reply; the assumption was evident that she would do as she was asked. 'Now then, go into the top drawer over there by my bed and bring me the box that's in there and we'll find a solution to this little conundrum.'

Isabel did as she was told, retrieving the box. It was such a pretty shade of blue, she thought. Very shabby chic. It was the sort of box that should be on display and filled with jewelry in some French boudoir, not tucked away in a bedside drawer in a retirement home. She passed it to Constance.

'Sit down, dear, and stop hovering over me; it's most unnerving.'

Isabel sat down in the same seat she had earlier in the week.

Constance sat with her hand resting on the lid of the box. 'When I turned seventeen my parents bought me the most beautiful pair of pink satin dancing shoes.' She sighed, and her gaze slipped toward her feet, housed in those hated flat, black monstrosities. 'Age, my dear is a bugger.'

Isabel looked at the shoes on Constance's feet. They were what she would call old lady shoes, and it was hard to imagine her ever having worn pink satin dancing shoes. She said nothing, waiting patiently while Constance lifted the lid of the box and began sifting through. 'This was our ration book.' She held it aloft before putting it back and this time showing her a ticket stub. 'My father took me to the circus in Portsmouth before the war. It was magical.' Next, she produced a photograph, and held it out to Isabel. It had the creases of time and, of course, it was in the black and white tones of the era.

Isabel took it and gazed at it for a brief moment. 'Is that you on the left?'

'The smallest one, yes, that's me and Evelyn, my elder sister, although there was only a year between us, is next to me. She's no longer with us. Evelyn left the island not long after the war ended; she married a chap from Cornwall. They were only married a year, and she got sick with cancer, the ovaries it was, and that was that.' It still made her eyes smart all these years later. Evelyn had been so full of life, and she too had it snatched away before she had a chance to live. And here she was in her ninth decade, no rhyme nor reason other than that was Evelyn's lot, and this was hers. 'We were a well turned out bunch, the Downers, but then you'd expect us to be given Mum and Dad's line of work. They owned A Stitch in Time, a haberdashery shop where your Welsh friend's gallery is now. My father was a tailor.'

They were indeed a smart lot, Isabel agreed, looking at the picture of the young Constance and her family. Constance was very pretty, and looked to be around fifteen or sixteen, with her hair falling to her shoulder in soft waves. It was held back by a ribbon, which she'd fashioned into a side bow. She wore a polo style top and culottes, white bobby socks and flat loafers. A scarf was knotted at an angle around her neck, a hint of the young teenager's mischievous personality. Evelyn had styled her hair into a victory roll, making her look much older than her sister despite there only being a year between them. A year could be a gulf in your teenage years though, Isabel mused, noting Evelyn's figure-skimming dress. She wondered as to what colour it might have been. Isabel fancied both sisters would have had a sense of fun about them.

'My brother Teddy is in uniform, and that's Ginny next to him.'

Isabel stared at the image, greedily eager to wipe away the image of the dying old woman whose hand she had held in her last moments and replace her with this vibrant soul looking back at her. 'She was very pretty.'

'Yes, she was. Her eyes were the colour of cornflowers. Teddy was absolutely besotted. They were besotted with each other.'

'How sad.' Isabel looked at the handsome soldier and back to Ginny. They'd have had so much hope for their future when that photograph was taken. It was a good job, she mused, that none of us knew what fate had waiting around the corner for us.

'All of it was so very sad.'

Isabel sensed there was much more to her words, but Constance held her hand out and took the photograph, placing it in the box and this time producing a leather-bound journal.

'I can't see the text anymore so I wonder if I might borrow your young eyes to glance through and see what, if anything, there is for gout.'

Isabel took the book from her. It must have been where Constance recorded her remedies, she thought, the leather rough beneath her fingers with the ripples of time. It was not much bigger than a notebook, and she looked at it a heartbeat or two longer before, sensing Constance's impatience, she opened it. Her eyes settled on the tea coloured page inside, and she frowned. This was old, very old. It was filled with swirly, generous, and almost illegible handwritten notes.

She focused on the writing, taking her time to get used to the different style, and slowly the words began to make sense, despite being the prim language of yesteryear.

'Chamomile, boil the flowers in a posset. Drink to produce sweat and to help expel all colds and aches and pains. It is also excellent for the bringing down of women's courses,' she read out loud before turning the page. It felt brittle to the touch as though it could crumble away to dust if she said the magic word. The script on the next page revealed a cure for boils using a bread poultice and the next, a remedy for hay fever involving the brewing of butterbur tea.

The wording was too old-fashioned to have been Constance's, she decided and looked over at her wondering if she'd tell her where this book had come from.

'The journal came to me when I was a young girl. I believe it once belonged to Molly Downer. We were related she and I, you know—much to my mother's shame.'

Isabel's mouth fell open. 'This was Molly Downer's? As in the last witch on the Isle of Wight?' The words came out in a whispered gasp, and she had no idea why she felt the sudden need to lower her voice. The days of witch hunts were long gone.

Constance looked amused, and the light dancing in her eyes told Isabel she'd enjoyed Isabel's reaction. 'Yes.' She tapped the side of her nose. 'It's our secret, Isabel. Now I believe you were looking for something to ease gout.'

Chapter 28

'Are you getting dinner ready?' Isabel asked upon hearing her mum's harried tone answer after a few rings. She'd not long come home, on her dinner break and was stretched out on her bed, wrestling with her shoes trying to kick them off one foot at a time. Her nose twitched at the delicious aroma of garlic, onion, and spices sizzling in the pan as it made its way up the stairs and wafted under her door. The soft rhythm of a tune she didn't recognise was playing beneath her, and her shoe fell to the floor with a satisfying thunk. She wriggled her toes to ease the aching of having been on her feet for the last five hours. She had just about an hour and then she'd be back at the Rum Den for her shift through to closing.

She'd been pleased to see Rhodri wielding a knife and humming his way through dicing an onion when she'd popped her head into the kitchen five minutes earlier. She'd needed reassurance that sustenance wasn't far away and, satisfied things were underway, she'd called out a quick greeting before tripping up the stairs, quite literally.

'Watch your step!' Rhodri called out to her, as she picked herself up and carried on up to her room.

'Mmm, I'm making steak and kidney pudding,' her mum said, her voice nearly drowned out by a whining in the background. 'Shoo! Out you go; Daddy's going to take you for a walk when he gets home.'

Isabel waited until all was quiet. 'So, how's Prince Charles getting on? Has his little, er, problem settled down?'

'It has actually. Your dad's been taking him around the block, despite his strained this or pulled that, when he gets home from work, and he manages a piddle on every gatepost. Prince Charles that is, not your dad. We think he's smitten with the cocker spaniel at number eighty-two and we're encouraging the relationship. It's healthier than him mooning around after you.'

'Much healthier,' Isabel agreed, pleased to hear the corgi was moving on in his affections.

'Now then what about you? How're you getting on, love?'

Isabel brought her mum up to date with everything she'd been up to, leaving out the part about Constance having shown her Molly's journal. The journal was their secret; she wouldn't breathe so much as a word about it.

'So we now know that Ginny was Constance's sister-in-law and that she was widowed when she was pregnant, but that's it right?'

'That's it. I don't think there is much more of a mystery to solve, Mum. I reckon Ginny felt bad about emigrating and not keeping in touch that was all.'

'Perhaps. I'm not convinced though. Something in my waters is telling me there's more to it. Will you go and visit Constance again? She might open up a bit more as she gets to know you.'

'Yes. She's asked me to pick a few things up for her neighbour who suffers from gout. I shall call in tomorrow. I was a bit scared of her when I first met her, Mum. She was very sharp, but I'm beginning to think that's a reaction to her circumstances. I like her, and I don't suppose you get to her age without having a certain amount of spirit about you.'

'I'd think not. So now, tell me was it worth sloshing around in all that horse poo tea, then?'

'Horsetail, thank you very much, and yes it was.'

'Now that I think about it, Isabel, you couldn't ask Constance whether she knows of a natural remedy for jock itch next time you see her? I don't like the thought of your father putting chemicals down his pants.'

Isabel grimaced. 'Eeew! Please don't say anymore, my dinner's nearly ready. I'll check it out online and get back to you all right?' She had no intention of mentioning her dad's little problem to Constance. She was beginning to side with her mum when it came to her dad's burgeoning mid-life football career. From what she could gather, he seemed to limp off the field with one medical complaint after another and, they'd yet to win a match!

'Okay, sweetheart, but I'm telling you it's not a good look. Your father has a bad case of it, his hand's permanently—'

'Mum, I am hanging up now!'

Isabel kept her word and Googled 'jock itch'. She'd just finished tapping out a text back to her mum when Rhodri called from the bottom of the stairs that he was about to serve up. She pushed send on the information that her dad needed to stop wearing tight underwear, sweating excessively, and that he could do with losing a few pounds. On top of that, washing the area concerned with diluted apple cider vinegar was advisable.

As it happened, nothing would have put Isabel off her dinner, not even jock itch and she barely said a word other than to give her compliments to the chef before she began wolfing it down. It was chicken curry but not as she'd had it before and if she closed her eyes, she could've been dining in a street café in Malaysia. Rhodri had made the sauce from scratch, hence the delicious smells emanating throughout Pier View. She was also conscious of the spicy smells that would be emanating from her; all over her punters at the Rum Den tonight if she had the second helping Rhodri was presently offering.

It was a tough call, and she stared at the pot on the stove for a couple of seconds, teetering on the edge of another dolloping until Rhodri shrugged and dipped the spoon into it, ladling the fragrant sauce over the remains of his rice. Nope, Isabel reaffirmed to herself with a rueful glance at her middle. A skipped lunch and a regular person sized portion of dinner would not do her any harm.

'That was ridiculously yummy, Rhodri,' she said, pushing her chair back. She made no move to get up and rested her hands on her belly like a satisfied statue of Buddha. 'Thank you. What are you up to tonight then?' It was a Friday night after all; she guessed he'd have plans.

Rhodri sat back down at the table. 'I'm off to the cinema to see the new *Blade Runner* movie.'

It didn't escape Isabel's attention that he hadn't mentioned who he was going with. She debated picking up her plate and licking it but decided that would be going too far. Instead, she did her usual trick of tracing her finger around the rim of her plate to scoop up the remains of the yellow sauce. He'd make some lucky lady a fantastic husband, she mused. I mean he was good looking, house trained, and he could cook. What more could a girl want? So why was he single? If indeed he was single. Nico flashed to mind once more. 'So, Rhodri,' she angled, slyly seeing confirmation of her suspicions. 'You're off to the movies. Are you going with anyone special, like Nico for instance? Feel free to tell me to mind my own business, by the way.'

He looked amused. 'I wouldn't say "special" with an inference of romance. If that's what you're getting at.' He carried on eating for a minute before taking a serviette from the container he'd placed on the table. He wiped his mouth before speaking, 'There was someone before I moved to here, but it didn't work out. I suppose you could say I ran away, like you did.'

Something in his tone told Isabel he'd said all he was going to say on the subject. 'Ah well, her loss,' she murmured, getting up from the table to fill the sink. It took her a moment to figure out why she felt disgruntled, and as she squeezed the detergent into the hot water, it dawned on her. She'd poured her heart out to him as to what had happened with Ashley and Connor the other night, but he didn't feel he could confide in her. It irked her and turning off the hot water tap she set about washing up with more gusto than usual. With her back to the table, she missed seeing Rhodri's bewildered look as she banged a pot upside down on the bench to drain.

~

'You wouldn't happen to have anything for relieving bunion pain, would you?' Brenda hopped from one stilettoed hoof to the other. She'd hobbled around calling last orders twenty minutes ago and the pub was slowly emptying out. Isabel had been giving her daily updates on her eczema treatment. She'd just finished telling Brenda she'd phoned Don and had arranged to meet him in the morning to pass on the same ingredients she'd tried to his granddaughter. 'And don't tell me to get a pair of sensible shoes because it ain't happening.'

'I wouldn't dream of it.' The thought of Brenda in flats was absurd, but a boss with bunions was not an ideal scenario. They were bound to affect her mood, and not for the better. She'd have loved to have a look through Molly's journal to see what she suggested, but for now, Google would have to do. She fished out her mobile and keyed in the search. 'Well, Brenda, according to Google, castor oil is a good idea as it contains anti-inflammatory properties.'

'Gordon Bennett. I remember me old mum shoving that stuff down my throat as a kid.' Brenda raised an expertly filed fingernail to her mouth and tapped it as she frowned, thinking. 'Hang on a minute, maybe it was cod liver oil. Either way, it was horrible.'

'It says here that if you heat half a cup of castor oil in a pan and soak a thin cloth in it before wrapping it around the bunion, it will help. Oh and put a towel over the oily cloth to keep the heat in. It should reduce the swelling, and you can do it up to three times a day to relieve the pain.'

'It's worth a try, I suppose.' Brenda rearranged her face and turned her attention to the stocky chap who'd placed his empty glass on the bar top. 'Ta, love, mind how you go now.' He nodded his goodnight before shoving his hands into his jacket pockets and shuffling forth into the dark outside.

It wasn't long until it was just the two of them and Brenda and Isabel settled into what had become their end of night routine, whipping through the cashing up and clearing up in next to no time.

'While I think of it, I've hired a karaoke machine for the last Friday night of the month. If it goes over well, we might make it a regular thing. What do you think?' She moved toward the door to let Isabel out.

'Sounds like a good idea. It should get a few more punters in the door.'

'I'm glad you think so because I'd like you to kick it all off with an introductory song. You know, get them queuing up to request a number themselves.'

'Ah, no way, Brenda. I'm not getting up on stage.'

Brenda flapped her hand, holding the door open to the cool night outside. 'You'll be fine, the star of the show. I'll see you tomorrow night.'

Isabel knew her boss would not let her off the hook. There was no point standing here arguing and besides she was bushed. She shook her head signalling defeat before saying goodnight. Brenda reiterated the sentiment and shut the door, and Isabel heard the bolt slide into place behind her. She was about to stride off when a man materialised from the mist, seeming to emerge from the stonework of the shop frontage he must have been leaning up against. Isabel faltered mid-step, and her breath caught in her throat, her heart skipping a beat.

'I thought I'd walk you home.' A voice with an accent as thick as homemade soup sounded loudly on the still air.

Oh, thank God for that. Her heart restarted. 'Rhodri! You frightened me!'

'Sorry, I didn't mean to,' he said, taking a step toward her. 'The film's not long come out, and I was walking right past.'

'Oh well, thanks. Good movie?'

'Not as good as the original but then they never are. The popcorn was good though, extra butter.'

'Yum.'

'How was your night?'

Isabel told Rhodri about Brenda's bunions and had him laughing over her depiction of her hobbling around ringing her bell for last orders. 'I found a natural remedy on Google that might help her poor feet although I should have let her suffer like she's going to make me suffer.' She sighed heavily as she thought of Brenda's karaoke plan.

Rhodri glanced at her. 'That sounded like the weight of the world is on your shoulders. What's up?'

She told him in glum tones what Brenda expected of her as they rounded the street corner and Pier View House came into sight. The Esplanade echoed of another era, the street lights sluicing through the wet mist. She could hear the gentle shushing of the waves as they lapped beneath the pier. Somewhere tucked away in the buildings behind them the thudding music of a late-license venue along with sporadic shouts of revelry broke the night. Rhodri was silent for a step or two and then turned to Isabel and said, 'Would it help if I got up on stage with you? We could do a duet?' Isabel looked at Rhodri, her eyes wide in the dark. At that moment in time, she could have kissed him.

Chapter 29

It was Saturday morning, and the town of Ryde was bustling as Isabel made her way up Union Street to The Natural Way. This morning, she planned on being a Good Samaritan. Delwyn was in deep conversation with a customer, she saw upon pushing the door open, and so she took the opportunity to browse the Aladdin's cave. There were so many weird and wonderful packets and jars, lotions and potions. She'd love to know what their different purposes were but for now, she was on the hunt for some apple cider vinegar. Molly would have made her own she guessed as her eyes settled on a bottle of the organic vinegar she was after. It was locally brewed with apples grown on the island and picking it up she read the label. Delwyn, came over to say hi leaving her customer to weigh up the anti-inflammatory benefits of turmeric.

'Apple cider vinegar's brilliant stuff. It helps with all sorts of things from diabetes and weight loss through to sinus congestion. It's nature's tonic.'

'Really? I'm getting it for gout.'

'Gout? Well, that's one ailment I haven't heard of it being used for.' She looked at Isabel in surprise, her eyes dropping down to her legs, which were hidden beneath denim.

'Not for me, thank goodness. That on top of eczema would not be a good look. No, it's for one of the resident's at Sea Vistas. That and some cherry juice if you have it?'

'We do. It's even on offer this week.'

Delwyn retrieved a bottle and handed it to her. 'Well, I have to say. I'm learning all sorts from you, Isabel. I ought to put you on the payroll. Did Constance suggest it?' Delwyn looked at her curiously, head cocked to one side, making her look like an inquisitive pretty little robin redbreast.

'Yes, her neighbour is driving her potty by giving her daily updates on his gout and Constance reckons this will fix him. Oh, and she told me to tell you she will be in all day tomorrow. It might pay to take her in a packet of Maltesers; she loves them.' She turned the bottle over, and her eyes doubled in size, and she tried not to balk as she spied the price stuck firmly to the back.

'Great, I'll definitely call on her, and yes, it's a bit pricey I know, but it's the real deal and one hundred percent organic. You can take about two pounds off that price too,' Delwyn offered up.

It was still an eye-watering price for squeezed cherries, two pounds off or not, Isabel silently huffed. Constance had better bloody well enjoy her egg tomorrow or gout would be the least of the old boy's problems. Today's haul was going to set her back to what amounted close enough to a night's wages. It was an expensive business helping others, she thought, as Delwyn rang her purchases up and gave her the total. In for a penny in for a pound, she thought, spying the bags of Irish moss in a basket beside the till. 'I'll take one of those too, thanks, Delwyn, and don't forget to call in and say hi at the Rum Den one night soon.'

Isabel had arranged to meet Don in the same spot where they'd first encountered each other. He was on time and greeted her jovially before sitting down next to her on the bench seat where she'd been waiting. She felt like a spy meeting with her foreign contact as she handed him the bag. He was peering inside it now exclaiming with the same enthusiasm she imagined a small child might ripping open a lucky dip. It might have cost her most of her pay, but it was worth every penny she concluded, watching his face light up.

Riley who had flopped at his master's feet was feeding off his excitement by emitting little woofs; his tail thumped against the pavement with the rhythm of windscreen wipers in heavy rain. Isabel leaned over and patted him. 'Hello, boy.' She shivered a little as Don retrieved his glasses out of his top pocket and wished she'd had the foresight to put a jacket on. You'd think she'd know by now it was always a degree or two colder on the waterfront. Don looked rather like a wise old owl as he peered over the top of his glasses, she thought with amusement, watching him pull the contents out of the bag for inspection one at a time.

'Thank you, Isabel, it was very kind of you to organise this,' he said his inspection finished, closing the bag with a rustle. 'It's definitely worth our

Chloe giving it a try. Is the receipt inside the bag too? I can pop over to the cash machine and fix you up now if you like. I'll be back in a jiffy.'

'No thanks.' Isabel held her hand up. 'I don't want anything for it, Don, but I would like to know whether it's successful. You will let me know how Chloe gets on, won't you? I've popped my number in the bag.'

'Of course, I will. I have to pay you though.'

'No, please take it, I've been there. I know what it's like and I just hope it helps your Chloe.'

Don looked momentarily taken aback before he beamed. 'Well, thank you very much, my dear. It's most kind. Now, what do we do with it all?'

'The instructions are in the bag.' Isabel had written the steps out carefully before enclosing them in the bag, along with a spritzer bottle of seawater she'd collected while she waited for the hour to tick over until it was time to meet Don. She'd brewed up the horsetail tea back at the flat after she left The Natural Way, much to Rhodri's amusement, and poured it into an empty two-litre milk bottle salvaged for that purpose. The jar of organic honey was inside the bag too. She'd removed the Irish moss though, having eaten most of it while waiting for the horsetail herbs to steep, secretly pleased Rhodri wasn't a fan—all the more for her! It was a good job she'd checked her smile in the mirror before leaving the flat, as her lips were liquorice green.

The cold was seeping into her bones. Isabel got up from the bench; she was keen to get moving to warm up. She patted Don's shoulder. 'I've got to go. It was lovely to see you and Riley again. Promise you'll call and let me know about Chloe?'

'I will indeed. You're an angel, Isabel. I'll be sure to ring.'

Isabel didn't think she'd ever been called an angel before and the expression gave her a much-needed warm glow. She gave Riley one last pat before striding off down the Esplanade toward Sea Vistas. She had a lady to see about gout.

~

Constance was sitting with a cup of tea in the dining room when Isabel located her. She deposited the cherry juice and apple cider vinegar on the table. A stream of sunshine poured in through the bay window puddling on the floor beside her. It was a lovely spot, and on a clear day like today, the view to the Solent was unimpeded by grey skies. A piece of shortbread sprinkled with icing sugar sat untouched on a plate next to the cup and saucer. Afternoon tea, Isabel surmised. Her tummy rumbled, but she ignored it stating, 'Job done, Constance. Your gout worries are over because this little lot here should fix your man good and proper.'

'He's not my man,' Constance replied, her face a picture at the very thought of it.

'A phrase, that's all.' Isabel pulled the chair out opposite and sat down; she hadn't expected a thank you. She eyed the shortbread thinking it was a waste for it not to be eaten but not liking to help herself. Constance saved her the trouble by sliding the plate toward her and, not needing to be asked twice, she took the biscuit. All this charging around had made her peckish. Constance slid a ten-pound note across the table which Isabel slid back. 'It's on me because I'm glad to help.'

Constance looked at her for a second, her expression thoughtful before tucking the money away. 'Tell me a bit about yourself, Isabel.'

Isabel had a wee while yet before she was due at the pub and so she settled back into the chair and told Constance, the basic facts. 'Well, I'm twenty-six, and an only child if you don't count our neurotic corgi, Prince Charles—I did not name him by the way, my mum did. I grew up in Southampton. My mum works at Asda and is a royalist of the highest order and Dad's going through a belated mid-life crisis but in a good way, not a cheating on Mum with a blonde half her age sort of way. They're both a bit nuts, but I love them to bits, especially from a distance.'

Constance's mouth was twitching at Isabel's eloquent description of her family. 'But what about you, Isabel?'

'Me?'

Constance nodded.

Isabel gazed at the strip of blue outside for a minute before she found herself telling the same tale she'd told Rhodri. Constance had tutted sympathetically and muttered, 'Good riddance to the pair of them,' when she told her what happened with Connor and Ashley.

'And so you ran away. All the way to Australia. The other side of the world. That was very brave of you, Isabel.'

It was the first time anybody had said that to Isabel. She'd always felt that perhaps it had been the coward's way out. She hadn't thought of taking off the way she had as being a bold thing to do before. She found herself sitting a little straighter in her seat as she relayed some of her travel stories and told Constance how different Australia was to here. How she'd loved the carefree freedom of travelling and would like to do more, but first she needed to figure out what she wanted to do with her life. 'I think I need some direction, Constance. The problem is I don't know which way I want to go.'

'You modern young women have so much choice; you can be anything you want.'

'That's just it, Constance; it's overwhelming. I remember talking to the careers advisor at school, and for me, it was kind of like when you fancy something sweet, you know like a packet of biscuits. So off you go to the biscuit aisle, but you can't decide what you want because there are just far too many options on the shelf and you can't afford the ones you want the most. So you wind up buying chocolate.'

This time Constance did smile. 'Perhaps you're overthinking things.'

'Hmm, maybe. Did you ever travel?' Isabel knew she'd stayed here on the island, taking over the family business before changing tack and opening Constance's Cure-alls but that didn't mean she hadn't had trips abroad.

'I wanted to go to Canada when I was young, but it wasn't meant to be. I couldn't leave my parents after Evelyn died, and then it got so that I didn't want to be anywhere other than here.'

'But you still wound up following your passion by opening your shop, right?' Isabel was surprised to find she was seeking reassurance. It had taken Constance a long time to find what she loved doing; perhaps the same would be true for her.

'Ah, but, Isabel, I wanted more; so very much more.'

Isabel didn't want to go, she wanted to find out what Constance meant, but she did not want to incur the wrath of Brenda by being late either. 'It's nearly twelve, Constance. I've got to get to work.' She got up from her seat pushing her chair in. 'Monday's my day off. Do you fancy a trip into town? We could call in on Rhodri and have a wander around The Natural Way too, if you like?'

Constance nodded. She would like that very much indeed.

Chapter 30

The weekend was a blur of pint pulling and Monday morning rolled around with clear, blue skies. A perfect day for an outing, Isabel thought with a spring in her step as she arrived at Sea Vistas. Kristen was at her reception post and was engaged in flicking her hair back as she smiled up at a young man at the counter. Someone's grandson or a young doctor, perhaps? Isabel wondered but didn't have time to ponder further as she spied Jill emerging from the dining room. She hurried down the hallway to catch up to her. 'Morning, Jill, I wondered if I might be able to borrow a wheelchair today. I'd like to take Constance out you see, and I don't think she'd last too long walking around Ryde.'

Jill clapped her hands and smiled. 'How lovely. Constance did mention something about that this morning. She's been ever so bright of late, you've been a breath a fresh air for her, and the young lady who runs The Natural Way was in to see her yesterday. It's a beautiful day for an outing too. I'm sure we can arrange a chair for you. A wander around her old stomping ground will do Constance a world of good, Isabel. I'm forever trying to get her to go on one of our shopping excursions. We go all over the island, and she'd enjoy herself, but she always cries off. Between you and me I think she feels she's far too young to gad about with the rest of our ladies! Now, if you just give me a few minutes, I'll go and see what I can do about organising a chair for you to use.'

True to her word, Jill reappeared pushing a wheelchair and she gave Isabel a crash course in operating it. After Isabel had given her a demo on applying the brake, she was satisfied Constance would be in safe hands, and she continued on her rounds. Isabel went in search of Constance, finding her in her room. She was sitting in her chair by the window with her handbag perched on her lap.

'All set, Constance?'

'Well, I'm ready for the off if that's what you mean, but I won't be able to walk far, Isabel. I am eighty–nine, you know.' She took Isabel's outstretched hand and allowed her to help her to her feet.

'I do know, Constance, and it's all sorted. Your chariot awaits you downstairs.'

Constance's expression when she saw the wheelchair waiting by the front desk was similar to her dads when fish pie was on the menu, Isabel thought. It was like watching a young child weigh up the odds of stamping their foot or not. If she did refuse to get in it, then that would be that, no outing. Constance came to the same conclusion as she reluctantly thrust her handbag at Isabel before easing herself down into the chair.

Isabel did not hang about, not wanting to give her a chance to change her mind and so, with a 'cheerio' and a promise to return both the chair and Constance in one piece tossed in Kristen's direction, she pushed forth.

The folly had a few curious tourists milling around it, Constance spied from her seated viewpoint as Isabel wheeled her past a few minutes later.

'Every time I walk past that I always think of the fairy story, Rapunzel,' Isabel said, leaning over the chair for her charge's benefit. The breeze along the Esplanade was strong enough to carry her words away. She'd worn a dress today, one of the few she owned. It was a pretty yellow swing dress, and she'd felt pleased when Rhodri had called out that she looked nice as she sailed out of the gallery earlier. Now though she wondered if she might have been better in jeans and jersey.

Constance had thought the folly the stuff of fairytales as a child too. Her story had begun there, but she never got her happy ending. Further along, she saw the hovercraft coming in. Its whirring as it flew across the Solent, in its ten-minute journey from the mainland always made her shudder. The incessant reverberation reminded her of the Luftwaffe fighter planes as they flew low over the island readying themselves to offload their bombs. There was a resonance to it that once heard was never forgotten. It was uncanny the way certain sounds could carry you back to flashes in time as quickly as changing the channel on the television. The images popped up before her of the carnage those planes left in their wake, and she shook her head to shoo them away. Her mind was living more and more in those dark days of late, and it was not where she wanted to be now.

'Are you cold, Constance?' Isabel asked, leaning over the chair once more, having just seen her shiver.

'No, I'm fine.' Constance turned away from the craft. It was nearly to the beach now. The hovercraft's first-time passengers would be keen to tell their friends they'd "flown" to the Isle of Wight as was the correct terminology for crossing the Solent in the amphibious machine. Her hands tightened around the handbag perched on her lap as she focussed her attention determinedly on the bustling pavement ahead of them.

It was a powerful tool, a wheelchair, she decided, beginning to enjoy how it gave them the automatic right of way. People sidestepped apologetically to let them through. She felt like Moses parting the red sea. Even the traffic came to a standstill to let them cross as Isabel pushed her across the road to the line of shops on the other side of the Esplanade.

It was either the chair or Isabel's hair that was stopping traffic, she thought, upon catching sight of them both in a shop window. It always startled her to be confronted by this new self, a woman with candy floss hair whiter than the cliffs at Freshwater.

Now, as Isabel pushed her around the bend and Pier View House came into sight, Constance felt a tightening in her chest. It never got easier seeing her home and knowing she'd never live in it again. Still, there was some comfort to be found in the fact such a nice young man had bought it from her.

'I told Rhodri we'd call in, Constance. Then I thought we'd have a wander up Union Street and say hello to Delwyn at The Natural Way. How does that sound?'

'Good,' Constance said, with a regal bow of her head. 'I enjoyed my conversation with her yesterday.'

Rhodri had just finished hanging a new canvas on the wall when Isabel tapped on the door. She'd given up on trying to figure out how to open the door and hold on to the wheelchair at the same time. He opened the door and seeing her predicament held the door open wide for her to come in.

'Thanks, Rhodri. Constance and I are having a girls' day out,' Isabel said, wheeling the chair over his foot as she entered the shop. 'Ooh, sorry, I probably should have a license to drive this thing.'

Rhodri flexed his foot and grinned. 'I don't think it's broken.' Then, shutting the door behind them to ward off the keen sea breeze he focussed his attention on Constance.

'Hello there. It's lovely to see you again. Do you know, Constance, not a day passes that someone doesn't pop their head in and ask me where you and your shop have gone.'

It took Constance a second or two to decipher what he'd said. 'I'd forgotten how thick your accent is.'

Rhodri laughed. 'Well now, a Welsh accent never leaves you, no matter how many years you might leave Wales.'

Constance smiled then and allowed herself a moment to look around her. She liked what he'd done with the old place. It was light and airy with no hint of the dust that had once haunted it. The artworks on the walls were in contrast to the plainness of the room; their bold colours showcased like a rainbow against a grey sky. Constance had always preferred modernist art; she liked the brashness of it. She wasn't one for the fiddly brushwork of fine art or the wishy-washiness of a watercolor, and the print that had caught her eye was right up her alley.

'That's stunning,' Isabel said, following her gaze and beginning to push Constance in the direction of the canvas Rhodri had just hung on the wall.

'I can walk Isabel; I'm not an invalid.'

Duly chastened but not in the least offended, Isabel helped her out of the chair. Constance allowed her to take her arm and lead her over for a closer look. She wasn't aware she'd clutched Isabel's arm tighter as she gazed up at it. Art spoke to you, she'd heard said, and this big, bold painting, had shouted out to her.

Isabel peered at the white card on the wall beneath it. 'It's called *Quarr*, Constance, but the artist's name's not printed below. That's a bit strange. Isn't Quarr the name of the big abbey where all those monks still live near Fishbourne? I think I went there once with Mum and Dad.'

Constance nodded. The name of the artwork had not surprised her. She'd known at once that the painting depicted the ruins on the road between Ryde and Newport in the grounds of Quarr Abbey. She closed her eyes seeing the main abbey building with its imposing towers and expanse of orange and red, sometimes pink bricks, which made her think of a mellow sunset. The light at certain times of the day seemed to dance across those bricks. For her, when she was a girl, the abbey had symbolised peace at a time when the rest of the world seemed to have gone mad. She'd liked to observe from a distance the order and routine of the day-to-day life of the Benedictine monks who lived there. There was comfort in all that sameness.

The Quarr ruins were dear to her heart, hidden away from the road that she'd cycled down as a girl with Henry. Oh, she knew they were considered a place of great historical significance these days, but back then it had been her and Henry's secret place. She'd fallen in love for the first and only time in her life against the backdrop of those crumbling ruins covered in creeping vine. She recalled the time one of the brothers had reared up at them from behind the stones. He'd looked a bit like a soaring kestrel, with his wings stretched wide as he flapped his arms about shooing them on their way. She and Henry had climbed on their respective bicycles, giggling and flushed at being caught, although they'd been doing no more than holding hands. Now, she could almost feel the wind on her cheeks as she'd pedaled furiously away, with Henry keeping pace alongside her. Of course, as time went on, they'd done much more than just hold hands.

Constance opened her eyes, surprised to find herself leaning heavily on her new young friend and not perched on a bicycle. She knew she had to have this painting. She didn't care what it cost, she wanted to wake up for the rest of her days with this painting on her wall, and she asserted this to Rhodri.

Rhodri looked startled as did Isabel, not just by Constance's obvious agitation but because she'd also spied the hefty price tag.

'We need to go to the bank, Isabel,' Constance announced imperiously. She'd have to withdraw the money to purchase it. She had a debit card, but it had a daily limit on it and her days of operating a Visa card were long gone. She wanted to make haste, to seal the deal before somebody else came into the gallery and fell in love with it, just as she had.

Rhodri put his hand on hers. 'No, Constance, really there's no need. It's yours. I'd like you to have it.'

Constance shook her head. Was the dear boy mad, giving away expensive art pieces? Surely he worked on a sale and commission basis? She heard Isabel gasp.

'Rhodri, it's yours!' Isabel pointed to the black swirl in the corner of the painting. 'Your signature is as illegible as your accent is indecipherable,' she declared, her eyes wide. 'You told me you dabbled in painting but this, well this is not dabbling, this is amazing.'

Constance tried to follow the conversation.

Rhodri smiled at her guilelessness. 'I told you, it's a hobby really and occasionally if I'm pleased with a piece, I try my luck, pop a preposterous price tag on it and hang it here in the gallery.'

'You're bloody brilliant,' Isabel said, watching him take it back down from the wall.

Constance made protesting noises about paying for the work, but Rhodri paid no attention.

'No, I want you to have it.' He was insistent as he promised her he'd deliver it personally after he shut the gallery for the day.

Constance was taken aback, but there was a serendipity to it all. That this painting, by the man who'd bought Pier View House from her, should be of somewhere so dear to her heart and would hang in her room, well it just seemed right somehow. She settled herself back down in her chair and thanked him.

He patted her hand. 'You're welcome. Thank you for Pier View House. It came along at the right time.'

Isabel gazed at him curiously as Constance made noises about getting on their way.

'I'll just nip up to the loo. Back in a sec and we'll get on our way.' Isabel reappeared a minute later, 'Ooh, that's better, right, forward march.' She took hold of the handles of the wheelchair and pushed Constance forward. Rhodri held the door open for them. As she passed by him, he tapped her on the shoulder.

'Mmm?'

'Your dress is a bit caught up there; you might want to adjust it before you hit the street.'

Isabel felt around her back and pulled her dress out from where it was firmly tucked up in her knickers. Rhodri, she realised scowling, was grinning, and with a face the colour of port wine, she made her exit.

Chapter 31

Isabel paused as they passed a shoe shop on Union Street to admire a sparkly pair of summer sandals. They'd go lovely with her dress, she thought. She caught the wistful look on Constance's face and thought of the pink satin shoes she'd mentioned her parents had bought for her eighteenth birthday. She recalled too her disparaging remarks about the shoes she was currently wearing. Perhaps new shoes were the order of the day. 'Shall we have a look inside?' She didn't wait for Constance to reply as she turned the chair and went into the shop backward.

She helped Constance up, and together they went to browse the shelves.

'Isabel, these are pretty.' Constance announced holding a pair of sapphire blue ballet flats aloft. They had a diamante butterfly sitting on the soft, ruched fabric near the toes.

Her eyes had lit up like a magpie spying shiny things, Isabel saw, as she held the shoes closely and stroked the smooth leather upper with the pads of her fingertips before turning them this way and that. Her examination of the shoes was as thorough as a doctor giving his patient their annual physical.

'They're very pretty, Constance, and flat, so they're practical—sort of.'

'And the leather is very soft.'

Both women's gazes went toward the counter to where a young girl was frantically texting having given them a token hello as they entered the store. 'Excuse me do you have these in a—what size are you, Constance?'

Constance shook her head, she wasn't sure, and she directed Isabel to help her sit down holding her foot out for the unimpressed shop assistant to measure.

Five minutes later having tried three different sizes, she'd found her Cinderella slipper. The young lass, whose facial expression could have curdled milk, completed the sale and then settled back to her texting as Constance was wheeled out of the shop. A bulging bag hung from the wheelchair, contained her precious new shoes. She'd bought the blue pair, and a white pair with a pink bow, and was already vowing to say sayonara to the black ones when she got back to Sea Vistas. Constance sat up straight in the chair. She felt all tingly, in a good way. It was with a sudden clarity she understood that the woman who'd been disappearing bit by bit these latter years was shaking off the cobwebs and re-emerging. It was as simple as having bought a pretty pair of shoes.

Isabel was enjoying herself. It had been lovely seeing Constance so animated and spying the Royal Victoria Arcade she suggested they have a look around.

~

'It's gorgeous in here. It's like stepping back in time,' Isabel enthused wheeling Constance over the tiled floor. 'How about we wander right down to the end?'

Constance nodded. She too was enjoying herself and looking at the eclectic businesses on either side of her, she spied a colourful clothes shop she wanted to peruse. She was pleased the arcade had been restored to its former glory. The building was a survivor having been threatened with demolition more than once. The same could be applied to her, she thought ruefully.

They passed a sign for the Donald McGill Museum with its collection of saucy seaside postcards tucked away in the basement. Those postcards used to make Constance's mother blush and tut when she spied them for sale along the Esplanade, and she'd thought it just desserts when five shops daring to stock his lurid cards were raided in Ryde. That was back in 1953; the date sprang to mind the way certain events do, forever cemented in the recesses of memory. There were over five thousand cards seized in that raid Constance recalled. As she spied a couple of young lads mooching along, peering into the taller of the two's mobile, she wondered how the times had changed so. These days youngsters could access all manner of unspeakable things with a push of a button on their phone before their hormones had even had time to produce so much as a pimple!

Isabel distracted her train of thought by coming to a halt outside a coffee shop. 'I think it's cup of tea time.'

'Yes,' Constance agreed, eyeing the narrow doorway. She didn't fancy her chances of getting the chair through it, and she didn't fancy the palaver of collapsing it for the sake of a cup of tea either; 'Just park me there, Isabel.' She waved towards the nearby tables dotted about. She was content to be parked up by the arcade's pièce de résistance, the rotunda, with its lead-painted glass domed ceiling and frescoes, happy just to sit for a while and watch the world go by. Isabel manoeuvered the chair up to one of the empty tables.

'I'll surprise you shall I, Constance?' she said, receiving a nod before she pushed open the café door. Constance had barely had time to frown over the noise a toddler, unhappy about something or other, was making nearby when Isabel reappeared with a number. She placed a plate with two Wagon Wheels on it down on the table and gave the mother dealing with the tantrum-throwing tot a sympathetic smile.

Constance sighed with relief as he was picked up and marched out of the arcade. All that ruckus would have given her indigestion.

'I hope you can get your teeth through one of these.' Isabel giggled, pulling a chair out and sitting down.

Constance had already snatched up one of the marshmallow filled, chocolate biscuits from the plate, not having had a Wagon Wheel in years. Her narrowed eyes said Isabel was a cheeky mare as she began nibbling around the edges. Their tea appeared, and with a sip from the pretty china cup, she realised she'd been gasping.

The two women sat in companionable silence watching the world go by until, fed and watered, Isabel suggested it might be time to mosey off. Constance, still buoyed by the success of the shoe shopping expedition, conveyed that she'd like to have a little look in the clothes shop she'd seen near the entrance. Perhaps this peahen might get to don some beautiful plumage! She'd liked the look of the brightly coloured rack of sale clothes that had caught her eye earlier.

For her part, Isabel was excited by the glimpses of this different Constance, and she pushed her through the arcade toward the entrance at a rate of knots. Constance found herself clutching her handbag with one hand and holding onto the armrest for dear life with the other. Their mutual excitement waned, however, after a desultory search through the half price items on the rack outside the shop yielded nothing worthy of a try-on.

There was nothing that was *her* in the slightest, Constance thought, disappointed. She'd look ridiculous in a red velvet jacket, like a female

Liberace, and as for those nautical stripes, what was she supposed to do? Greet people with a cheery, 'Ahoy there, me hearties?'

'Come on. We'll have a look inside.' Isabel bumped her over the lip into the shop, putting the brakes on beside a mannequin with a lopsided wig in an unnatural shade of red.

'Right, Constance. Give me your hands,' Isabel bossed. 'I can't hold anything up against you when you're sitting in there.' She took both her hands in her own and pulled her to her feet. Satisfied Constance was perfectly able to stand for a bit, she flicked through a rack and produced a dress. She inspected it briefly before holding it aloft. Much to Constance's relief she shook her head and put it back. It had not been her sort of thing at all. As Isabel neared the end of the rail, she gave a sharp intake of breath. 'Oh now, Constance, look at this, it's gorgeous!'

Ah now, this was more like it, Constance thought, greedily eyeing the dress Isabel was holding up.

'Do you like the colour and the pattern? It's what's called a batik print, and it's all the rage. I think you'd look lovely in pink. A little cardigan over the top and you could wear leggings under it. It'd be just perfect for now and when the weather gets warmer.'

'What are leggings?'

'They're like tights, Constance, only with no feet in them. They're ever so comfy.'

Tights with no feet sounded rather absurd to Constance's mind but Isabel's enthusiasm amused her as did the word batik, the young always thought they'd invented everything. She'd lived through the seventies for heaven's sake and had worn more batik prints than Isabel had probably had hot dinners. Still, she was trying so hard to muster enthusiasm in her that the least she could do was oblige.

She'd mustered plenty in the young sales girl who didn't look old enough to have left school in Constance's opinion. She was busy disentangling a chunky beaded necklace off the stand by the counter. The beads, Constance saw as she carried them over were of a polished rosy hue, and the girl looked pleased with herself as she held them up against the dress. 'I thought they'd work. It goes a treat with that dress, doesn't it? Go on try it on; I'll keep an eye on your chair for you.' The girl whose name badge said Tara, had already kicked the brake off as though well used to dealing with parked wheelchairs and began pushing it towards the back of the shop.

With nothing else for it, Constance linked arms with Isabel, and they followed Tara's lead to the fitting room. Isabel hesitated, and Constance huffed, 'You'll need to help me, Isabel.' She turned toward young Tara, 'I'm eighty-nine, you know.' There was no room for embarrassment when you got to her age, Constance thought, as Isabel squeezed into the cubicle alongside her. Jill regularly had to help her do up her bra on those days when her fingers wouldn't quite work properly.

'Well, you don't look it.' Tara gushed, holding the curtain so Isabel and Constance could squeeze into the cubicle.

Constance fiddled with her blouse and let Isabel help her shrug out of it, leaving her skirt on before sliding the floaty tunic styled dress over her head. It felt comfortable, fitting nicely across her bust, and draping loosely over what once upon a time had been her waist but what was now most definitely her middle. She liked the sleeves too, elbow length, and the hemline stretched to below her knees. No woman should wear a mini dress past forty in her opinion, and there was nothing at all titillating about the knees of a woman who was flirting with ninety years.

Isabel opened the curtain and stepped out of the cubicle allowing them both room to breathe. She gave Constance the once-over, her expression that of the self-satisfied. 'I knew that was the right dress, I knew it. Constance, you look fabulous! Come and have a look in the big mirror out here.'

Constance wasn't sure she wanted to look. Would she see a batik print beach ball and one with a slow puncture at that gazing out at her from the mirror? Nevertheless, she bravely took Isabel's outstretched hand and allowed her to position her in front of the mirror. She blinked at the reflection staring back at her. Gone was the little old lady she barely recognised and wholeheartedly disliked and in her place was Constance Downer. She'd forgotten the power colour had to perk her up and the bright pink background of the dress had just given her an instant lift. Her new shoes, the white ones with the pink bow would go perfectly too, she thought before Tara appeared and draped the beads around her neck.

She hadn't had this much fuss since the day her mind had wandered off, and she'd failed to stop when the lights went red on the East Hill Road into

Ryde. Her beloved Morris Minor went up the back of the post van, and that had been that. It was all the excuse the powers that be needed to slap her in the face with her septuagenarian digits and revoke her license. This was, of course, a much nicer sort of fuss, and although she'd never have admitted it, she was enjoying being the centre of attention.

'Oh that's lovely on you,' Tara declared, standing back to admire her handy work. 'Almost perfect but just give me a minute—' she disappeared into the shop and began rifling through a pile of folded knitwear on a stand in the middle of the shop.

A twinkling later, she was back with a few items draped over her arms. 'Here,' she said, handing a white cardigan to Constance, 'with this you can wear the dress now and when it gets warmer. Oh, and I found the same size dress in this gorgeous yellow here.' She held it aloft for them both to yay or nay with her spare hand. 'You look like you'd suit yellow to me. What do you think?'

'Your blue shoes would go lovely with it, Constance,' Isabel interjected before Constance could say a word. 'Do you happen to have leggings?' she carried on.

'I've got them right here.' Tara looked pleased with herself as she hung the yellow dress on the handle of the fitting room door. She produced a pair of white leggings hidden beneath the cardigan draped over her arm.

'Right well, I think we're sorted don't you, Constance?'

Constance was too overwhelmed by it all to do anything but nod.

Chapter 32

Constance felt like a film star in her new clothes, which she'd refused to get out of as Isabel wheeled her out of the shop. She gave a final wave to Tara who, having snipped off the tags, promised to drop a brochure of the latest season's fashions in at Sea Vistas.

'Isabel, do you think we could call in at the hairdressers?' Constance asked as they left the arcade. She was eager to complete her makeover before she was deposited back at Sea Vistas. There was no point in doing half a job. 'Why don't you freshen up your colour, dear, or try something new. I think you'd look lovely with a nice bright blue; it will be my treat.'

Isabel laughed. 'You're the first person older than me that hasn't asked me to let my hair go back to its natural colour. Come on, there's a salon, over there. Let's see if they can squeeze us in and then we can go and show off our new looks to Delwyn.'

So it was, both women wound up sitting next to each other trying to keep straight faces while Jackie, with the odour of a freshly smoked cigarette enveloping her, fussed around them. Constance's hair was woven around perming rods, and Isabel's was covered in tinfoil.

'We look like visitors from another planet,' Isabel whispered to Constance while Jackie busied herself squeezing some noxious smelling solution all over Constance's head.

'Cup of tea ladies?' Jackie beamed, checking under Isabel's tin foil to reassure herself that nothing untoward was happening.

'Oh, lovely, yes please. Constance?'

Constance nodded and blinked, her eyes watering from the solution.

'We both have milk and no sugar. Thanks, Jackie.'

'Right, two teas it is then. You two behave yourselves.' She wagged a pink talon at them before clacking out the back.

Isabel rifled in her bag for her mobile. She swiveled her chair over to Constance's and held the phone aloft. 'Say cheese.' Constance mumbled something close enough, and she clicked. 'I've got to send this through to Mum; it will make her day.' She grinned as she uploaded the photo texting an explanation before hitting send.

Constance nodded off in the hair salon and Isabel hoped she hadn't been knocked out by the perming solution fumes. She flicked nervous glances over at her now and then between leafing through a magazine. Jackie had woken her gently when it was time for her hair to be rinsed and Constance was quick to tell her she was entitled to forty winks given she was eighty-nine, you know! When it was Isabel's turn, Constance clapped her hand in delight as her new colour was revealed. She'd felt herself flagging earlier but was bright as a button once more, thanks to her little nap.

'You look like a fairy from a picture book,' she said, and argued with Isabel for two solid minutes over it being her treat. Jackie had settled the matter in the end by taking Constance's debit card from her and telling them both she didn't have all day.

Constance was sitting a little straighter in her chair desperately hoping the breeze wouldn't get up and trifle with her hair. As for Isabel, she kept slowing her pace to catch glimpses of her new blue do in the shop windows as they made their way up to The Natural Way a couple of hours later. She loved it—they made a good team, her and Constance, she thought.

~

'This is a lovely surprise. The pair of you look fabulous. I love the hair, Isabel, and, Constance, your outfit is just gorgeous!' Delwyn exclaimed as Isabel filled her in on what they'd been up to. The shop was empty, and Delwyn had been in the midst of unpacking an order when the two women called.

Constance was eager to be out of her chair; there was so much to look at in Delwyn's shop. The days of gathering herbs down by the riverbanks were long gone she thought, glancing around at the laden shelves.

'You picked the right day to call in. It's always quiet on a Monday afternoon,' Delwyn informed them. 'I use the time to unpack my orders.'

Isabel wandered around the shop picking up different bottles and reading the labels, Delwyn and Constance were chattering nineteen to the dozen about the herbs that grew wild on the island and their different uses.

'You still haven't popped into the Rum Den,' Isabel interrupted, inspecting a bottle of vitamins. 'What do you use hawthorn for?'

'It's useful for high blood pressure,' Delwyn said. 'And I promise I'll pop in for a drink later in the week.'

'Good. Gosh, I love this place. The fact that stuff that grows wild can potentially help people is amazing.' It was a different language, Isabel realised. The language of plants and herbs and all their different healing purposes was fascinating.

Delwyn and Constance smiled at each other. Isabel was a kindred spirit; she just didn't know it yet.

~

Constance arrived back at Sea Vistas worn out. It had been a wonderful day, she thought, as Isabel fussed about returning the chair. She saw her up to her room before throwing her arms around her in a spontaneous goodbye hug. Constance patted her back awkwardly, realising it had been a long time since someone had hugged her. She let Isabel settle her into her chair, and as the door shut behind her, she closed her eyes enjoying the warmth of the afternoon sun streaming in through the window—a little siesta was in order before dinner.

Later, when the evening meal was done and the day was well and truly catching up on her, Jill had come to help her get ready for bed. She'd been taken aback at how well Constance looked and told her so. 'A day out suits you. That great-niece of yours is a tonic.' She'd winked and smiled, as she unhooked the beaded necklace from around Constance's neck before carefully laying it down on her dressing table.

Now, as she rested her head on her pillows, Constance allowed herself a moment to reflect on the evening. She'd so enjoyed the looks on the other residents' faces as she'd staged her grand entrance at dinner time. In her batik print finery, she'd glided—glided might be a stretch—made her way across the parquet floor in her beautiful ballet flats with her head held high knowing the ball of floss atop her head was now tamed into smooth rippling waves. She'd even been accosted over her bowl of summer pudding by Jean and Iris. They were desperate to know where she'd gotten her dress and who'd done her hair.

Jackie had done a marvelous job with Isabel too. She looked so pretty when she left the salon; she was a beautiful, bright butterfly that one. She wondered what Rhodri thought of her new look; she'd put money on romance being afoot there, not that either of them knew it yet. At the thought of the handsome young Rhodri, her eyes flitted over to the armchair against which the canvas *Quarr* rested. He'd kept his word and dropped it in. Constance was smitten with both Rhodri and his artwork and tomorrow she'd arrange for Bill, Sea Vistas' jack of all trades, to hang the canvas for her. It had been so very generous of him, she thought as her eyes began to droop.

Ginny, inadvertently sending Isabel to her, had brought some colour back into a world that had become rather beige, she thought, pulling the covers until they rested under her chin. Her last thought as she drifted off was that she could rest easy now she'd found the right person to pass Molly's journal on to.

Chapter 33

Isabel strode down the Esplanade. She'd just had a cup of tea with Constance and checking her phone she saw she still had plenty of time until she was due at the Rum Den. It was such a lovely day; she'd sit down by the pier and soak up a bit of sun while she could she decided, spying a spare bench seat. She glanced down at it with a frown and wondered if an albatross was responsible for the monstrosity deposited in the middle of it. She perched to the right to avoid getting the mess on her pants and leaned back enjoying the soft breeze. It was almost balmy today, and the water was twinkling, there were far worst places to while away half an hour, she thought.

The apple cider vinegar and cherry juice had been a resounding success, Constance had informed her cheerily that morning. She'd enjoyed her breakfast for the first time in a long while. The gout was no more, and Ronald had a new lease of life by the sounds of things. Isabel crossed her fingers upon hearing this; she hoped she wasn't going to be asked to find a herbal equivalent for the little blue pill as Constance filled her in on how he'd taken to having a morning dip before breakfast. She was certain he timed it to cop a look at Nancy from three doors down, a sprightly figure in a one-piece swimsuit at a mere seventy years of age.

Isabel jumped as her mobile rang and with a glance at the caller display, she saw it was from Don.

Five minutes later she shoved her mobile back into her jeans pocket and got up from the seat. It seemed Molly's remedies had procured another success, with young Chloe having experienced pleasing results. Don had rung on his daughter's behalf to place another order for more of the same, insisting, however, that this time she must let him pay for it. It amused Isabel as she made her way toward Union Street that he saw her as his herb broker. Nothing was stopping him going to The Natural Way himself, but she was pleased he'd left it up to her. It gave her a reason to pop in on Delwyn and ask her how she'd enjoyed her night at the Rum Den.

Delwyn had called in for a drink as she'd said she would, and the timing had been perfect with Rhodri propping up the bar deep in conversation with Nico. Isabel had introduced her to them, and they'd chatted for ages, all seeming to hit it off.

'Hi,' Isabel called out, stepping inside The Natural Way. The shop was empty except for Delwyn who was standing, with a perplexed expression marring her pretty features, over a stack of boxes. They were piled in the middle of the shop, and she looked up from them with her hands on her hips to smile a greeting.

'Hey, Isabel, good timing. I was just wondering where to start with this little lot the courier's not long since dropped in. I wasn't expecting a delivery today, and you are the perfect excuse to ignore it for a bit longer.'

Isabel grinned back. 'Glad to be of help.'

'Are you here as a friend or customer?'

'Both. I've been asked to pick up more horsetail tea and honey, and I wanted to see if you enjoyed your night at the Rum Den. Oh, and before I forget, the apple cider vinegar and cherry juice have worked wonders on Ronald's, from Sea Vistas, gout.'

'That's good to know, and I had a great time. Thank you for introducing me properly to Rhodri and Nico. They're a nice couple. I'm going to try my hand at a spot of pottery too. And what about you? You've got the beginnings of a cottage industry on the go with all your potions.'

'I wouldn't go that far, but it's nice to know they were successful and that I've helped a little girl feel better and an old man for that matter too.'

'It does make you feel good when your suggestions help someone. It's why I love what I do. Listen, since you're here you couldn't hold the fort for a few minutes, could you? I just want to nip out and get a bite to eat. I'm starving, and it would save putting the "Back in five minutes" sign up.'

'Of course. Take a proper break. I'm not due at the Rum Den for an hour yet. I could make a start on those for you, if you like?' Isabel pointed to the boxes.

'Really?'

'Really.' Isabel grinned. She'd enjoy reading the backs of all the different products, to see what they were for.

'Ah, thanks, Isabel, my stomach appreciates you. If you can just unpack everything on to the trolley; it's out the back in the storeroom and tick it off on the invoice inside the box as you go that would be brilliant.'

'I think I can manage. Go. Enjoy.'

'Cheers. I'll be back in a jiffy.' Delwyn grabbed her tote from behind the counter and disappeared out the door.

Isabel shoved her bag under the counter and looking up saw a face had appeared in the storefront window. She mouthed, 'I'll be fine' and waved Delwyn on her way before popping out to the storeroom to retrieve the trolley. As she pushed the door open with her backside and reversed into the shop, she heard the door jangle. She let go of the trolley and turned around expecting to see Delwyn once more, having forgotten her purse or some such. Instead, a woman who looked a little like a French Resistance spy in her trench coat and beret was perusing the shelves nearest the door.

'Hello, how're you today?' Isabel called out with a smile.

'Hello, I'm good thanks, pet,' a northern accent intoned as she turned her attention to Isabel.

A holidaymaker then Isabel surmised.

'I'm after something for my daughter's skin. She's had an outbreak of spots, and I want something natural to clear it up. She's only thirteen, and I don't like the idea of her slathering her face in chemicals.'

'Fair enough too,' Isabel said wishing she had Molly's book to hand. She cast her mind back trying to visualise the pages. She knew her holy grail, apple cider vinegar was good; she'd been reading up on all its different uses. She was sure too she'd read something in there about dandelion tea being used to treat skin complaints. She headed over to the teas and ran her finger along the shelf until she found what she was looking for, Dandelion Tea. She glanced at the back of the box and was pleased to see she was on the right track. 'Here we are,' she said reading the instructions. 'If your daughter drinks one to two teaspoons of the dandelion tea leaves steeped in hot water three times a day, it will help clear her skin up. If you've got a sec, I'd like to look something up for you?'

The woman smiled and nodded that she was happy to wait, so Isabel took herself out the back to the storeroom and using her phone Googled her apple cider query. She reappeared. 'I just wanted to check the administration of it. Apple cider vinegar one part, to two parts water dabbed on the affected areas with cotton wool will help too,' she said, retrieving what was becoming her go-to remedy of choice, a bottle of the organic vinegar.

'Thank you.' The woman took both items, turning them over to glance at their respective prices before passing them back to Isabel. 'We'll give them a go, ta very much.'

Isabel glanced at the counter hoping the till would be user-friendly. She rang the purchases up without any problem and even managed to navigate the card machine, passing it over to the woman to swipe her card without any bother, thanks to having had practice at the Rum Den. As she called out a cheery goodbye and left the shop holding her The Natural Way bag, Isabel felt inordinately pleased with herself. She'd completed a successful sales transaction. Then, seeing the boxes she reminded herself she had a job to do.

~

By the time Delwyn breezed back in Isabel had served two more customers, unpacked both boxes, and was familiarising herself with the different products as she put the stock away.

'I hope I wasn't too long? I did rather make the most of you being here.' She gave a sheepish grin.

'I was fine. I sold a box of dandelion tea, a bottle of organic apple cider vinegar, some vitamin E tablets and a chamomile body wash.'

'And you've unpacked and put away most of that order. Wow, well done you! It was a treat to sit down and eat and not shove something down behind the counter like I normally would. You can guarantee the shop will be dead until I have a mouthful of sarnie. Nothing like a gob full of egg sandwich to win a customer over. Thanks heaps, Isabel; you're a star.'

Isabel flushed at the praise and slid the bottle of maca liquid onto the gap on the shelf. 'What's maca liquid?'

'Maca root is a super food of the Andes, and it's used to build up a weakened immune system. The ancient Incas were big fans—Isabel, have you ever thought about studying herbalism or naturopathy?' The latter was blurted out.

Isabel's hand remained in mid-air, floating beside the tub of vitamins she'd been about to pick up. 'Pardon?'

'It's just, you have an obvious interest in natural remedies.'

Isabel looked around the shop filled with so many weird and wonderful lotions and potions and then back at Delwyn. A seed had been planted. 'I didn't know I had until I met Constance.'

Chapter 34

Constance wanted to go back to Quarr; it had been hers and Henry's special place, and she needed to go there. Why? She wasn't sure other than there, she knew she would feel close to him. She would broach it with Isabel, she told herself, twisting her necklace of beads. Perhaps she would take her to the Abbey ruins on the bus or failing that they could share a taxi. Oh, how she missed her trusty old Morris Minor and the freedom that vehicle had given her. One didn't appreciate one's independence, taking it for a daily given and then suddenly poof! It was gone, just like a puff of smoke, a distant memory. She took a sip of her tea, placing the bone china cup back in the saucer.

The thing about reaching her age, Constance mused was that she'd never really imagined what it would be like. She'd never bothered to think about the business of getting older; she was too busy getting on with the business of living. The war had made one think about life differently. It was fragile, fleeting, and so very precious. It was one's duty to get through each day as best one could. She'd survived those fraught times when so many others hadn't, and she had no idea why. She was nearing the final march now, but she did not intend popping off just yet.

Death held no fear for her. In a way, it would be like going home given the plot where she'd be buried was next to her parents and Evelyn at Brading Cemetery. Molly too was there somewhere, although as the site was unmarked, no one knew where exactly. Teddy was a name on a memorial. Perhaps she would get to see her family again, now that *would* be nice.

She looked around the bustling dining room and knew that if her fellow residents were privy to her thoughts, they'd accuse her of being maudlin. Constance didn't think dwelling on the inevitable was maudlin though. Wasn't dying the only guarantee in life?

'Constance, are you all right?'

She turned toward the voice, blinking up at Isabel with the languidness of someone who'd just woken from a peaceful doze in the sun.

'I asked if you were okay.' She held out a serviette picked up from the table.

Constance looked at it blankly.

Isabel touched the serviette to her cheek and dabbed gently. 'You're crying,' she said, showing her the sodden tissue before crumpling it and putting it down on the table. 'I just popped in for a cuppa and a chat. I'll get us a fresh pot. Tea fixes everything, or so my mum always says. That and a piece of her fruit loaf but I can't offer you that I'm afraid.'

Constance smiled her thanks and watched her young friend walk toward the tea tray. Her hair was the colour of the Solent today, she thought randomly. It wasn't true; tea could not fix everything. She knew a cup of Earl Grey couldn't change the way it had all worked out so long ago. Nothing would; it was simply far too late.

· · ❧ · ·

AS SHE SAT AT THE TABLE, her meal in front of her, Isabel fidgeted in her seat. She was out of sorts as she thought back on her visit with Constance, who hadn't been herself. That's not what had her knickers in a knot so to speak. She stared at the piece of schnitzel she'd speared onto her fork. She should eat; she loved Weiner schnitzel, and chips were her weakness. Rhodri had put his usual time and effort into preparing their evening meal, and it all looked delicious, cooked to perfection, but her insides were agitating like a washing machine. It was only an hour until she was due at the Rum Den. She'd already popped her head in just before lunch because Brenda had wanted her there when the karaoke machine was delivered. The bald man with the ring in his ear, whose tattooed arms bulged from his T-shirt, had set it up on the stage before giving her the rundown on how to operate the blasted machine.

Brenda had decided to give it a whirl and Isabel had found Rod Stewart's "Sailing" on the playlist for her. She'd done her best at doing a proper introduction, channelling her inner Ant and Dec to make her boss feel special. It'd been hard not to laugh as Brenda had stepped up onto the stage in the empty pub, shook her hair back and grabbed the mic. Her rendition of the old hit, however, had reminded Isabel of the cat fight that had gone on below her window the night before. A vicious ear-splitting, caterwauling. She pitied the punters if Brenda decided to grace them with her version of "Da Ya Think I'm Sexy" that evening.

Still, it wasn't playing a few songs for people to sing along to that had her in such a stew she knew, taking a desultory bite of her meat. Being the karaoke DJ would be a bit of fun. A break from her normal bar duties. Nope, it was standing up in front of a pub full of people, feeling all eyes on her as they waited for her to open her mouth and sing that had her tummy in knots.

Brenda had been busy spreading the word about town all week too. Hear ye, hear ye, Friday's Karaoke Night at the Rum Den. Well, that was a bit of an exaggeration, Isabel thought, but still, she regretted Googling how to soothe bunions for her boss now. If she hadn't been feeling so sprightly, she wouldn't have been strutting about telling all and sundry in Ryde about tonight's happening at the pub.

'Are you okay?' Rhodri asked, slicing into his crumbed meat. 'You look a little peaky.'

'I don't feel too good.' She put her fork down. It was no good. She couldn't stomach anything, not with the night that loomed ahead of her. 'It's not the meal, I promise. You know I normally tuck on in.'

'That's true.'

Isabel glanced sharply at him unsure what he meant by that.

'You enjoy your food; that's a good thing,' he elaborated swiftly.

Was he saying she was a bit of a pig? she wondered. Not that she cared because truth be told she did have a healthy appetite—just not this evening.

'I think perhaps you're suffering from a touch of karaoke-itis.' He popped a piece of schnitzel in his mouth.

He'd remembered tonight was the night then, and she wondered if he remembered what he'd said when he'd walked her home from the pub a fortnight ago too. She hadn't wanted to bring it up in case he'd regretted opening his mouth. 'I think you're right,' she said. Her mobile bleeped from over on the bench, but she ignored it, feeling rude enough for not having touched her meal without getting up and messing about with that as well.

'I meant what I said, you know, about singing a duet together.' He shrugged. 'It's no skin off my nose, and if it makes things easier, I'll get up and belt out a song with you. I'm bound to make you look marvellous by comparison, and if anything it'll be a bit of a laugh.'

Isabel felt a flicker of hope flare, she could pretend he was Andrea, and she was Celine and that they were on stage in Andrea's hometown not singing karaoke at the Rum Den. That way she might just be able to get her nerves under control and pull tonight off after all. 'Are you sure?' She sounded pathetically eager, even to her ears.

'Of course. I wouldn't have mentioned it if I wasn't. I'm no Andrea Bocelli, but I reckon I could stretch to doing my best Tom Jones.'

That crushed her Tuscan fantasy. Perhaps she'd just have to pretend she was in the bath then, Isabel thought, flushing as she recalled him overhearing her bathroom performance.

'So how about we do that number he sang with the pretty blonde girl back in the late nineties?'

'You're showing your age, Rhodri; I was still in the infants then. What song?'

'"Burning own the House." I loved that one. I remember breaking out my moves at the school disco with Myfanwy Davies, my first love.'

Ha! Isabel had known a Myfanwy would pop up sometime. The song rang some vague bells, she thought. She'd Google it in a mo.

'I can still swivel my hips with the best of them, and I've got a black polo neck in my drawer begging for an outing. We'll be a hit!'

Isabel giggled. His enthusiasm was infectious. She was warming to the idea and to her amazement her appetite returned with a vengeance. She missed Rhodri's grin as she sawed into her schnitzel with relish and demolished what was left on her plate in record time.

She pushed her chair back from the table. 'That was delish, thank you. I'm going to have a listen to that song, "Burning Down the House".'

He nodded.

She carried the plates over to the sink before retrieving her mobile. The bleeping earlier had been courtesy of her mum. She and her dad had been over for a visit the previous weekend; Prince Charles thankfully had stayed at home. Mum said she'd left his favourite CD on for him in the hope he wouldn't shred the furniture in protest at being excluded.

They'd met Rhodri, Constance, Delwyn, and Brenda, who'd all made a fuss of them. Constance had told them their daughter was a credit to them; Mum had forgiven her for being the instigator of the blue hair at those words of praise. Her dad was on the fence where Rhodri was concerned, given he was a rugby man, but her mum had thought him a dreamboat; that had been her exact terminology. Isabel had primly replied that she didn't look at him in that way, what with him being her landlord, because it would be inappropriate. Her mum had raised an eyebrow but hadn't said anything more on the subject. She was texting now to wish her luck and request a video link of her only child's moment in the spotlight.

'It was a band called The Cardigans he sang the duet with,' Isabel said clicking on the arrow. She had heard the song before, she realised, and it was catchy.

'Ah yeah, that's right.' Rhodri said, peering over her shoulder at the images on the phone. 'You know you look a little like her, except for the hair of course.'

Isabel felt herself stand a little taller; she was secretly pleased because the woman was gorgeous. As she watched Tom, the Welsh crooner she'd discovered thanks to Rhodri, do his thing she said, 'Rhodri, do you promise there'll be no hip-swivelling or thrusting on stage?'

He grinned and winked naughtily. 'I can't promise a thing.'

Chapter 35

It was standing room only in the Rum Den; it was the busiest Isabel had seen it in the month or so that she'd worked there. Brenda, she saw with a glance toward the bar was revelling in it. She was in her element prancing around and bantering with the punters. The people of Ryde were obviously partial to the sound of their own voices, she thought wryly. Her eyes swept over the pub from where she stood on the stage, partially hidden behind the karaoke machine—it was a full house.

A few minutes earlier, Brenda had promised her a cash bonus for her efforts tonight. It was a moment of generosity brought on by the heaving tavern and the scowl on Isabel's face at having to be the first act on stage. The thought of the extra spends didn't quell the butterflies in her stomach though, despite knowing Rhodri would be right there next to her. She just wanted to get on with things now; it was the anticipation that was the worst of it. She checked her phone. Ten minutes until showtime, which meant she'd better do a sound check.

'Testing, testing, one, two, three,' she breathed into the microphone, wincing as it screeched into life garnering a few catcalls from the waiting crowd. Her face flamed as she thought she heard someone call her Smurfette. This was going to be worse than she'd imagined.

But then she caught a glimpse of Rhodri. He was leaning up against the bar nursing a pint and catching her eye he raised his pint glass to her and grinned before mouthing, 'We'll be great.' She couldn't help but grin back as he winked and did a cheeky hip swivel. He'd worn his black polo neck she noticed, giving him a quick once over. But thank goodness his jeans were a loose fit. She was the only one who needed to hit the high notes, thank you very much.

She gave him a thumbs up and was about to carry on with the task at hand when she saw a familiar blonde turning heads with each step as she weaved her way toward the bar. It was Nico making a typically grand entrance with no effort on her part whatsoever. Ashley had always had that effect on people too. It was the first time she'd thought about her ex-friend in ages, Isabel realised, seeing Delwyn bringing up the rear. Oh, that was just terrific, she thought, kicking a wire out of the way so nobody would trip as they ascended the stage, more witnesses to her humiliation. Ah well, now Delwyn was here, she could ask her to record their performance for her parents. They deserved to see it having listened to her bedroom performances for so many years. She waved over and managed to attract Delwyn's attention.

Isabel watched as she began to elbow her way through. She hadn't been able to stop thinking about Delwyn's suggestion that she look into taking her obvious interest in natural healing further. She'd gone so far as to check out the courses online and the seed was beginning to sprout, but she wasn't ready to tell anyone about it just yet. Not until it had properly taken root.

'Hi, Isabel. Gosh, it's a packed house,' Delwyn said, reaching the stage at last.

'Tell me about it.'

'I heard you and Rhodri are doing a number.' She grinned. 'Is that what the lemon balm tea and lavender oil you bought this morning was for? That rude man interrupted before I got a chance to ask you.'

'Uh-huh. I hoped they'd get rid of my headache. This,' she gestured at the karaoke machine, 'was an order from the boss. She reckons someone has to kick things off and encourage others to get up and have a go. I drew the short straw and Rhodri gallantly offered to perform with me as moral support.'

'Well, don't look at me. You know that saying—I'm a lover, not a fighter?'

Isabel nodded.

'Well, I'm a herbalist, not a singer.'

'Fair enough.' Isabel laughed. 'Hey, can you do me a favour and record Rhodri and me? I promised my folks I'd forward a video of it to them.'

'Sure, no problem. I liked your parents; they were a laugh.'

Isabel passed her her mobile. 'Yep, they're hilarious, and thanks.'

'Um, Isabel?'

'Yeah?'

'Would you be able to do me a huge favour tomorrow and man the fort at the shop for an hour from eleven? It's short notice, sorry and I know you start at the Rum Den at twelve. You'd be cutting it super fine so if you can't it's no—'

Isabel knew Brenda wouldn't like her being late but it would only be a matter of minutes, especially if she ran all the way there and there was something rather magical about The Natural Way. She didn't want to turn Delwyn down. 'I'll be there on the dot.'

'You're a life saver, thanks.'

'No probs.' Isabel smiled. She'd relish the time on her own in the shop.

'Okay, well, break a leg.'

'Cheers, with my luck that could well happen.' She almost wished it would remembering how as a kid sometimes she'd wish she could be sick so she wouldn't have to sit her maths test or take part in the cross country. She'd feigned an upset tummy once or twice but had never managed to pull it off. Her mum had always seen through her.

Now, she thought, it was incredible how slowly five minutes could pass when you were looking forward to something and how it could be swallowed up in the blink of an eye when you weren't. She was relieved when at last Brenda caught her eye and tapped her watch to signal it was time to get the entertainment underway. She pressed her lips together and closed her eyes for a half a second. Channel your inner Celine, and breathe, Isabel, just breathe. One, two, three and it's showtime! She stretched her mouth into what she hoped was a welcoming smile and stumbled over the wires as she stepped up to the microphone. She desperately tried to ignore the sniggers and, as she began to speak, she felt as if she were having an out-of-body experience.

'Good evening, everyone and welcome to the Rum Den's Karaoke Night!'

A cheer went up along with a mass raising of glasses and Isabel's nerves dissipated a little. So far so good. She'd sounded enthusiastic, and her voice hadn't betrayed her with so much as a wobble.

'My name's Isabel, and I'm your hostess tonight.'

'With the mostest, eh, love!' Some ruddy-nosed fellow, who should have been at home with his wife and kids on a Friday night, yelled out. He received a smattering of titters for his effort. Isabel ignored him as she launched into the rundown as to how the night would work. This was nowhere near as scary as she'd imagined it was going to be.

'Okay, so now everyone knows what they have to do. I'm going to get this party started with a little help from a friend of mine, Rhodri. You might know him from his fabulous gallery on the Esplanade, A Leap of Faith. Come on up, Rhodri!'

Rhodri put his pint down on the bar top before pushing through the sea of people. He stepped up on the stage to clapping and a few whistles. Isabel pushed "play" on the machine and then came to stand alongside him to share the microphone. She wondered if his accent would be as broad when he sang as it was when he spoke as he launched into the first line.

It wasn't, and he sounded great, she thought taken aback but quickly gathering herself in time to lean into the mic to sing her line. A feeling of euphoria at her pure pitch filled her. Rhodri was superb, she thought as he minced it up and she played the cool blonde, er blue, to his Sir Tom. By the time the song finished she'd relaxed into the rhythm enough to let her body move to the beat. Their performance had gone over well; she could tell by the audience's faces, and she grinned up at Rhodri who put his arm around her shoulder and squeezed it. They'd done well!

'More, more!' A group near the stage began to chant, and the rest of the crowd joined in. Rhodri inclined his head and whispered in her ear, and she nodded; great idea. She was surprised to find she was as eager to do another song as the audience was to hear one and she disappeared back behind the karaoke machine to locate the track Rhodri had suggested, "Mustang Sally."

He was brilliant, and a group of young girls began to dance near the stage as he growled his lines. Isabel did her bit, even incorporating a bit of a twirl, as she harmonised alongside him. She'd forgotten she was channelling Celine and pretending Rhodri was Andrea. She was happy just being themselves, doing their thing at the Rum Den on a Friday night. And most of all she was enjoying herself. By the time the music wound down, Isabel was buzzing and was reluctant to let Rhodri leave the stage or give up the microphone. Brenda's plan had worked though, and people were lining up to request songs.

'Thanks for joining me, Rhodri,' she said into the microphone. 'Give him a round of applause, everybody!' He took her hand, and they took a bow to the cacophonous applause before he jumped down and headed back to the bar getting his back slapped on the way. Isabel checked her playlist before introducing Joy, an older lady with a steel coloured helmet of hair, who wanted to treat them all to Gloria Gaynor's "I Will Survive". Next, it was a young fellow who decided to crucify "Livin' on a Prayer", and the Island's answer to Cher, Freddy Mercury, and Ed Sheeran kept the night humming along.

By nine o'clock Isabel was ready to take a short break. This karaoke business was hard work, she thought searching out Rhodri. He was easy to spot with his height and was flanked either side by Delwyn and gorgeous Nico. That the two women looked like groupies flitted across her mind, and she dismissed the thought as quickly as it had come. It wasn't nice, and Rhodri *was* nice; look what he'd done for her tonight. It was his inherent niceness which made beautiful women like Delwyn and Nico hang off his every word. She couldn't blame them.

She made her way over to the trio, gratefully accepting the orange juice Brenda slid her way. She had a strict no drinking policy when on duty, which was fine by Isabel. She'd enough trouble remembering who'd ordered what and how much change she was handing over without being tipsy on the job too.

'I've already told Rhodri—you guys rocked,' Delwyn gushed, passing Isabel her mobile. 'Your parents are going to love it.'

Isabel grinned. She was still floating on a high.

'Hey, Isabel,' Nico said appraisingly. 'You looked great up there.'

'Thanks. Have you put your name down to have a go?'

'No way. I can't sing to save myself. I have to say, you're a woman of hidden talents, though. Your voice is fabulous. Have you ever sung professionally?'

'Oh.' Isabel was taken aback by the genuine comment. 'No, and you, by the way, are a dark horse.' She turned her attention to her flatmate. 'You've got a fantastic voice. You gave Sir Tom a right old run for his money.'

Rhodri raised his pint glass. 'Strictly for in the shower,' he winked at Isabel, 'or the bath, and for karaoke. Here's to us nailing it.'

'To us.' She clinked her glass against his and was filled with a warm sense of pleasure at the way the evening was progressing. She felt a tap on her shoulder and turned to see a woman around her own age. Her dark curls framed a round face with endearing dimples and warm brown eyes. She reminded Isabel of a currant bun, and she liked currant buns. She couldn't help but smile back at her. 'Hi.'

'Hi, I'm Alice. I'm with that lot over there.' She gestured over to a nearby cluster of women who varied in age. They waved, and Isabel raised her hand back at them.

They were probably out on a work do, she guessed, given they were behaving far too civilly to be on a hen's night, and she was betting Alice was about to ask whether Beyonce's "Bootylicious" was on the playlist.

'We're the Angels of Wight Acapella Group.'

'Oh right. I didn't know there was an acapella group here on the island.' It was a silly thing for her to say given there was no reason she should have known. She wondered where the conversation was going.

'Acapella singing's barber shop style, is that right?' Delwyn interrupted, having overheard.

'Sort of, but basically it's singing without musical accompaniment,' Isabel explained. She'd seen *Pitch Perfect*. 'So, are you going to get up tonight and do a number?'

'Of course. A bit of Little Mix never goes amiss, but we'll do it with the music tonight!' Alice laughed.

Isabel smiled. 'Good for you. I'd love to hear what you sound like together.'

'The reason I came over is because of why we're here tonight. Can you see the tall girl with the chin length, blonde hair?'

'Yes.' Isabel wasn't sure where this was headed.

'Well tonight's her farewell drink, and we thought it'd be a bit of fun to pop in here and have a go at the karaoke. Linda's moving to the mainland with her husband, Rob, for work reasons.'

Isabel nodded wishing Alice would get to the point.

'Well, having heard you sing, we wondered whether you might like to audition for our group. We liked your voice and thought you'd be a great fit.'

Isabel hadn't expected that and she stared blankly back at Alice.

'Look, there's no pressure, but we meet at seven o'clock every Monday night to rehearse at Melton Hall on Dover Street. If you're interested why don't you pop down this Monday and check us out, see what you think?'

'Okay well, I'm—' Isabel cast around for an excuse as she processed what Alice had said.

'She'd love to,' Rhodri interjected.

'Great. Well, we'll see you Monday night then.' Alice gave her one last grin and made her way back to her fellow singers.

Isabel closed her mouth and swung around to look at Rhodri, intending to tell him off for speaking on her behalf, but he cut her off.

'Well, that voice of yours is too lovely to do nothing with it except give private bathtub performances,' Rhodri said, his breath whispering on her neck as he leaned down to be heard.

A tingling ricocheted up her spine and she chewed her bottom lip. It had been a long time since she'd felt a sensation like that and it unnerved her. She told herself he was her landlord and to stop being silly, but the feeling persisted.

'Did you ever think you might be a team player and not a diva? What have you got to lose?'

Isabel looked up at him and took a steadying breath, deciding to focus on being annoyed with him, but it was no good. She couldn't be mad not after the way he'd helped her out tonight. Besides, he was right; what did she have to lose? Monday was her night off and just because she popped along to check the group out didn't mean she was making a lifetime commitment to sing with them. A jostling nearby caught her attention, and she looked around. The crowd was getting restless. It was time to get on with the show. Isabel pushed her conflicting thoughts aside and drained her juice.

~

The Angels of Wight were bringing the house down with their rendition of "Bootylicious". Isabel was standing to one side of the stage, grooving along and mouthing the words, watching them do their thing. They were good. They were better than good—they were bloody great, she thought watching them.

A bubbling feeling she recognised as excitement, surged. These girls, up dancing and singing, were having a fantastic time together. It was fun, pure and simple, and they wanted her to be part of all that. She let herself get pulled up on stage to shake her backside with the best of them for the last few lines of the Destiny's Child hit.

Chapter 36

'Last orders!' Brenda shouted, posturing about the pub as she rang the bell. She was in great form after the runaway success of the karaoke night, Isabel noted. She watched her in amusement from behind the bar where she'd begun clearing up. She was obviously feeling magnanimous having asked Rhodri, Delwyn, and Nico if they'd like to stay for an after-hours tipple seeing as they were friends with Isabel and all. Delwyn and Nico had demurred. Rhodri had accepted though, and she was pleased. She fancied a celebratory drink and who better to clink glasses with than her singing partner in crime.

Brenda, who'd broken her no drinking when on duty rule in the excitement of having a full house, had also asked another chap if he'd like to stay behind for an on the house tot. Isabel was guessing, given the way his headful of shaggy blond hair had shaken with enthusiasm at her invitation, that a drink wasn't the only thing Brenda was offering. It hadn't escaped her notice that Brenda had been draping herself over the bar to take his orders throughout the night. She'd let him cop an eyeful of Wonderbra each time he'd asked for a pint. Ah well, she thought, beginning to load the dishwasher, each to their own. If you ignored the missing tooth and if you were three sheets to the wind as she was beginning to suspect Brenda was then he did have a vague look of Rockin' Rod about him.

'Night!' she called over the top of a few die-hard drinkers' heads to where Delwyn was waving out. 'See you tomorrow at eleven.'

Delwyn gave her a thumbs up and then followed Nico's lead toward the door. Who'd have thought those two would be thick as thieves? Isabel thought, picking up an empty glass and wondering if it bothered Nico that her boyfriend was staying on at the pub for a drink with her. Probably not, she decided, Nico was far too bohemian to be jealous.

Half an hour later, the pub was empty except for the four of them. The tables had been wiped, and the dishwasher was grinding away. Brenda had kept her promise, and Isabel had stuffed the additional rumpled notes she'd produced from the till into her jeans pocket. Rhodri was sitting on a stool at the bar with a tumbler of whisky, courtesy of Brenda, in front of him and Isabel perched next to him, glad to take the weight off her feet.

She was shattered; it had been a huge night, and her drink of choice was a vodka lemonade. She hadn't let the spirit mix pass her lips in a long time, not since a particularly big night in Sydney. One minute she'd been dancing on the bar top with Helena, egged on by a cheering crowd, and the next she'd woken up back at the hostel feeling as though she'd been poisoned. She shuddered at the memory and took a tentative sip of the drink. The very smell of it might make her gag at the overindulgent memories conjured, but to her surprise, it went down rather well. A few sips later she felt it ease away the fatigue that was hovering over her.

Her eyes flitted in Brenda's direction. She wondered if she should invest in a Wonderbra. Brenda was sporting a most impressive cleavage that was once more getting an airing as she hung off her Rod lookalike's every word. It was lucky for Terry that he was away again because theirs was most definitely a private party for two, she decided. Now would not be the moment to present her with the packet of turmeric powder she had in her bag. Delwyn had recommended it, saying that when mixed with water to make a paste, it worked wonders on bunions.

Now, however, *would* be the perfect time to get to know Rhodri a bit better. She snuck a surreptitious glance up at him over the rim of her glass. All she knew about his past was that he'd grown up in the same Welsh town as Tom Jones and had gone on to be a mover and shaker in London's art world. The alcohol made her bold, and she decided to get the ball rolling.

'I'll tell you a random fact about myself that you don't already know and then you do the same, okay?'

Rhodri looked bemused. 'Okaay,' he drawled, unsure what would come next.

'Well, I'm an only child.'

'I knew that.'

'I haven't finished,' Isabel admonished. 'I'm also adopted. Mum had some complicated women's problem, which meant she had to have a hysterectomy not long after she and Dad were married. Mum always says I was meant to be theirs because when I was born in 1992, there weren't a lot of babies being put up for adoption, but they got me.'

Rhodri smiled but stayed silent, waiting for her to continue.

'They didn't meet my birth mother, but the staff at the agency they went through said she was a lovely, young woman who wanted the best for me but who needed to move forward with her life. She felt she couldn't do that if the adoption were to be an open one, you know, where she could've visited me or received regular updates as to how I was getting on.'

'Would you have liked it to be open?' Rhodri asked, leaning forward on his stool.

'No, I don't think I would have, it would have scared me. I mean what if she changed her mind and decided she did want to keep me after all and tried to take me away? That happened in the States you know? I read about it online. I mean, I know it was highly unlikely, but that's how I would have felt as a child. I needed the security of knowing Mum and Dad were my mum and dad. Kids are black and white.'

Rhodri nodded. 'Yeah, I can see that. Have you met her, your biological mother?'

'No, I haven't felt the need to. If I'm honest, like I said, *my* mum and dad are my parents and besides which, she will have moved on with her life.' Isabel eyed her drink. 'I suppose I sometimes wonder if I have any brothers or sisters. I mean I probably do, and it's a strange thought that I could walk past my birth mother or siblings in the street and not even know it. It scares me a little, the thought of this whole other life I could've had. I don't do change well.'

'Oh, I don't know about that. You put yourself down too much, Isabel. You've lived on the other side of the world and look where you are right now. I think you do change pretty good.' He swirled the ice in the bottom of his glass. 'Do you think that's possible though when a child is involved? To move on with your life, I mean.' His tone was sharp, and Isabel looked at him over the top of her glass, startled.

'I don't know, but I have to think that it is otherwise it's rather sad.'

'Yes, I suppose you do.' His eyes were hooded, and Isabel was puzzled. 'What is it?'

'I have a child, or I think I might do. It sounds crazy, but I know nothing about him or her, not even their sex. I told you I ran away too?'

Isabel nodded; she was all ears.

'Yeah. Well, Sal, my ex and I were engaged. We'd been together nearly four years, and marriage seemed like the natural next step. I thought life was moseying along pretty well. We both had careers we loved—she's a lawyer and a good one. We had a great social circle, a smart flat, and I thought we were happy. When I think back on it now and believe me, I've thought back over it.' His laugh was ironic and unfamiliar to Isabel's ears, 'I was caught up in myself, work was my focus, living the London lifestyle to the hilt and that included Sal. She fitted the bill for what I saw as a successful life for this small-town boy from Wales. You know a great job, beautiful girl, but I suppose she was also pretty shallow and so was I. Anyway enough of the retrospection. The wedding plans were almost finalised. We'd booked a country house in Shropshire. She'd been going for dress fittings, the whole shebang. It was a done deal, or so I thought. Then one evening I came home to an empty flat. All her stuff was gone; it was like she'd never lived there. She left me a note, you know, how sorry she was blah, blah, she never meant to hurt me, it just happened.' He paused and took a sip of his drink.

'What just happened?'

'I was so caught up in myself and living what I thought was my dream that without me noticing she fell out of love with me and in love with my so-called best mate, Darian. It fell to me to cancel all the wedding arrangements. And when I stopped being angry enough to want to see them both, to get some sort of explanation as to how it happened, I couldn't find them. They'd deliberately disappeared. Then one of our friends let slip that they thought perhaps this crazy out of character behaviour of hers was down to her hormones. When I pressed, her she told me Sal was pregnant when she left.'

'Oh God, Rhodri! That's awful!' Isabel reached over and placed her hand on top of his. She'd struggled with what Ashley and Connor had done to her, but this was worse. He'd almost made it to the altar. She could only imagine what it would have been like having to cancel all those arrangements and explain to everyone that the wedding wasn't going ahead. 'Did you try to find them?'

'Yeah, it wasn't hard. We had the same social circle, remember, although when you split with somebody, you soon find out where people's loyalties lie.'

'I know,' Isabel breathed. That had been the worst of it when she and Connor had broken up, realising people you'd counted on weren't there anymore. You didn't just lose your partner you lost your way of life too. It explained Rhodri's casualness where Nico was concerned too, she realised. He would be wary about diving in again after what he'd been through. It was the same for her. She hadn't been interested in taking anything further than a bit of a snog on the dance floor while she'd been in Australia.

'Yes, you do.' Their gazes locked. Rhodri was the first to look away. 'They're living in Manchester, and that's as far as I took it. I didn't want to go any further. They wanted a new life, that much was obvious, and it made me stop and take stock of my own. It was a pretty empty existence and,' he shrugged, 'you know the rest.'

'Oh, Rhodri, I'm so sorry that's—' Isabel couldn't find the right words—awful or terrible didn't quite cut it.

'History, that's what it is, and I think a lucky escape too.'

'What about the baby though, I mean, what if it was yours?'

'You just summed it up. The baby might be Darian's, it might be mine, but either way Darian is his or her father and my busting in on their suburban existence demanding a paternity test, I just don't see what it would achieve.'

'Relationships and friends can be total shit.'

'Yes, they can.'

They drifted into silence, and the only sound in the near empty pub was the low murmur of a private conversation broken by Brenda's throaty laugh at the other end of the bar.

'I think we'd better be on our way,' Rhodri said, scraping his stool back.

Isabel wondered if he regretted having told her what he had. She swung her bag onto her shoulder. 'Goodnight, Brenda, and er—'

'Al.' Rod filled in the blanks for her.

'Al.' She nodded. 'Thanks for the drinks, Brenda. Oh, and before I forget I might be a minute or two later tomorrow. I'm doing a favour for a friend.' Her look challenged Brenda who was three sheets to the wind to argue with her especially after what she'd done for her tonight. Singing and manning the karaoke machine had not been on the cards when she'd gratefully accepted her offer to pull pints. To her surprise Brenda waved her hand and slurred, 'Day off, my treat just be here for six.' She went back to her whispering in Al's ear.

Rhodri thanked their hostess before saying goodnight to her paramour, and the two of them stepped out into the cool night air.

Chapter 37

It was a quiet walk home for Rhodri and Isabel if you didn't count the chap on the corner of Union and Castle Streets. He was leaning against the wall, his hands clutching onto a grease-soaked bag of chips for grim life. He recognised the duo walking toward him from the Rum Den and decided to burst into song with "Delilah". His plaintive, '*Why, Why, Why,*' breaking the silence of the night as he tried to engage them in the song.

Isabel half expected a head to pop out the window of one of the flats above the row of shops to tell him to shut up. They'd be well within their rights to do so, she thought, coming over all holier than thou. He was silenced when he dropped his chips; she paused to help him. He needed them to soak up all the booze. Rhodri, however, was in no mood to hang about. He kept walking and she scurried to catch him up.

'Chips with curry sauce. I'm sorry to say they couldn't be saved.'

'Well, I pity the poor sod who stands in that treat tomorrow morning on their way to work,' he growled as they rounded the corner onto the Esplanade. They reached Pier View a few short steps later. Isabel stood alongside Rhodri in the doorway waiting for him to unlock it. Her key would be buried at the bottom of her bag somewhere, and she couldn't be bothered rummaging for it in the dark.

'Rhodri,' she said tentatively. 'Our conversation tonight won't go any further.'

He turned toward her, his dark eyes searching her face for a second before he turned the key in the lock and pushed the door open. He felt around on the side of the wall for the switch and flicked the lights on. Isabel followed him inside eager to be out of the cold.

'I know it won't.' He headed over to where the canvas he was working on was covered with a sheet. 'I might sit up for a bit and work on this.' He hovered by the sheet waiting for her to pass by before taking it off. She took the hint.

'Well, goodnight then, and thanks again for this evening.' Isabel disappeared out the back to take the steps two at a time up to her room.

~

Isabel was tired but not sleepy. She could not stop thinking about what Rhodri had confided to her at the bar. What kind of woman was this Sal—to have behaved like that? He'd had a lucky escape in her opinion, and his so-called mate was just as bad. To go behind his back the way they had. And they'd left him to clear up the mess they'd left behind while they sneaked off and lived their happy homemaker existence elsewhere. It was incomprehensible and it made her blood boil.

She pulled the bed covers up with her spare hand, her other was holding her mobile, and it shook as her hand trembled with indignation at it all. It had stirred up all her emotions where Connor and Ashley were concerned. She wondered how he could just shelve the idea that he might be a dad too. I mean, she'd heard what he'd said, but not to know one way or the other? She frowned. She was going around in circles, and she'd be awake all night at this rate. To distract herself, she replayed the video Delwyn had recorded of her and Rhodri in action.

It did take her mind off it as their onstage antics made her mouth curve. Watching it now as an observer, she could see they had sounded good, and they'd had stage presence too. It dawned on her that it was the most fun she'd had since the car accident where she'd encountered Ginny. Actually, that wasn't strictly true; she'd thoroughly enjoyed her makeover day with Constance too. Her mind flicked to her invitation from Alice to the Acapella Group's practice. They'd seemed like such a great group of girls. There was a real sense of camaraderie about them, and she'd loved the way they'd harmonised together. It would be nice to be part of something where everyone pulled together. She was looking forward to seeing them in action rehearsing on Monday night.

Her promise to cover for Delwyn in the morning sprang to mind, and she wondered where she was off to. It was none of her business but thinking back on their earlier conversation at the Rum Den, she'd looked quite desperate for Isabel to say that yes, she'd man the fort. Isabel had been far too nervous about her and Rhodri's performance to pay much heed at the time; now she hoped everything was okay. She'd check in with her friend tomorrow. Delwyn had asked her to be at The Natural Way for eleven so if she got up at a reasonable clip in the morning, she'd have plenty of time to call in on Constance beforehand. The afternoon would be hers to do whatever she wanted with. Isabel frowned. Something was going on with Constance too, she was sure of it.

It had been a few days since she'd last caught up with her, but she'd noticed then how preoccupied she seemed. She'd listened to Isabel's chatter, nodding and commenting in all the right places, but it was as if part of her hadn't been there in the room. Something wasn't right, and tomorrow, Isabel decided, she'd delve into it. A problem shared was a problem halved after all or however the saying went. Her finger remained in limbo over the video. She'd promised Mum she'd send it through and so she sent it off not expecting to hear back from her until the morning.

She lay there propped up on her pillows for a minute or two holding her mobile and debating putting her bedside light out. She knew she should, but she still felt wired. Instead, she reached over and put her phone down on the drawers that served as her bedside table, and her eyes stared blankly at the wall wondering what Molly would have recommended for sleeplessness. That morning had seen her wake up with a dull throb in her temples; it was anxiety about the evening ahead at the Rum Den that had brought it on.

The subconscious was a powerful thing, and it had been needling away that she was going to have to get over her fear of standing up in front of a crowd and singing because it was a done deal. She'd called in to see Constance and asked if she could have a look at Molly's journal to see if there were any suggestions. She'd found what she was looking for under a heading of hysteria. Borderline hysterical was exactly how she was feeling! It was followed by the suggestion of lemon balm steeped in boiling water. Lavender oil too was helpful for calming the nerves.

She'd picked up both from The Natural Way and had come home to make herself a brew of the lemon balm tea. The fragrant tea had been sipped slowly while soaking in a bath with a few drops of lavender oil. It had taken the edge off her aching head.

Isabel felt an affinity with Molly, thinking that if they'd been born in the same era, the pair of them would have been friends. She'd been misunderstood, she decided, and if she were alive now she'd more than likely be into homeopathy or be a herbalist like Delwyn. Who knew? Maybe she would have even become a doctor. Either way, Molly had been different, and Isabel guessed if she were around now, she'd have blue hair too.

It was the superstition of the times Molly lived in that had labelled her a witch. Isabel had looked her up on Wikipedia and knew she'd had her issues; living in squalor and canting a curse on a local woman that had come to fruition. Neither were good looks in the 1800s. Still, she'd been guilty of the same thing too. Not the squalor bit; you couldn't be messy in a hostel dorm room—Lidija from Latvia with whom she'd bunked down in Cairns proving the exception to the rule.

She could recall, however, directing a silent curse at Charlotte Hervey-Moorcraft more than once during her high school years. The golden girl who had confidently taken the lead in every school production. She hadn't *really* wanted her to break her ankle so that she could step in and save the day because she wouldn't have had the courage to do so, anyway. Well, maybe she had just a little. It just hadn't seemed fair that Charlotte had gotten the whole package, but it hadn't worked anyway; as for Ashley and Connor the ill thoughts she'd wished upon them didn't bear thinking about. It had probably been the same for Molly. She hadn't *actually* meant to do the girl she'd cursed real harm.

The tide had turned against her with the village folk because people were quick to believe the worst. Poor Molly had been wronged because, in Isabel's opinion, it was just a sorry coincidence. She rolled onto her side and contemplated flicking the light off spying the unopened paperback lying next to it.

Perhaps reading would help her unwind. The book had been lying on top of a pile of others on a cluttered shelf in the flat's sitting room, and the cover had grabbed her attention. Rhodri had spotted her scanning the blurb and said it was a good read; she was welcome to borrow it. So, she'd taken it and put it on her bedside table for moments like this, when she couldn't sleep. She opened it to the first page and snuggled down turning the pages faster as she got into the story. She was completely engrossed in other people's dramas when she was startled by a message pinging its arrival. Isabel snaked an arm over to retrieve her phone, and she squinted at the screen. It was from her mum.

'Loved it! You up?' she read out loud, her voice seeming noisy in the empty room.

'Yep.' She punched in her reply.

A moment later her phone rang. 'Hi,' Isabel said, surprised. 'Is everything okay? What are you doing awake?'

'I couldn't sleep,' Babs Stark replied. 'And I was fed up with listening to your father snore. It's like lying next to Thomas the flipping Tank Engine listening to him huffing and puffing away all night. So I made myself a warm milk, and that's when your video arrived.'

Isabel sniggered. 'Rather, Thomas than the Fat Controller, Mum.'

'I heard that!'

'I thought you said Dad was in bed?'

'He is, we are, but I woke him up to watch you and your Rhodri fella in action. Oh, Izzy, you were fantastic. Dad thinks so too, don't you?'

There was a grumbled consent followed by a high-pitched whine.

'Prince Charles knows it's you on the line. Don't ask me how; it must be a doggy sixth sense. Look you'll have to have a word, or he'll never settle down again. You're a naughty boy, yes you are.'

Isabel sighed. She'd heard her mum use a far sterner tone on her over the years, but it was no use protesting. 'Go on then, put him on.' The fact that she was about to have a heart to heart with a lovesick corgi at one in the morning did not escape her. 'Hello, boy. How are you?' The reply was a pant.

'Now listen to me, Prince Charles. You need to be a good boy for Mummy and do what she says, all right?' The panting got heavier. Isabel took it as a yes. 'Now then did you see your girlfriend when you went for your walkies with Daddy today? She might get jealous if she knows you're chatting to me, you know.' Oh, my God, this was getting ridiculous, she thought as the panting reached a crescendo. 'Mum, I'm tired I'm going to hang up now.'

'All right. Night night, sleep tight. I'm going to sleep in your room, this is ridiculous.' A snore erupted in the background.

Isabel smiled. 'Night, Mum, Dad, Prince Charles. Love you guys.'

Isabel abandoned her book, flicking the light switch off. It was late, or early however you wanted to look at it. She needed to try to get some sleep.

~

Isabel was just on the verge of slipping into a solid slumber when her mobile shrilled the arrival of the morning like an annoying cockerel. She dragged herself out of bed and stumbled bleary-eyed into the bathroom.

A glance in the mirror revealed mussed hair and dark shadows under her eyes making them look too big for her face. Hopefully a shower would sort her out and turning the handle she waited for the water to heat up. She stood under the hot needles for a length of time that would have had Dad banging on the door when she was younger. There was nobody around to tell her off now though. Rhodri, she knew, was downstairs in the gallery. The only reason she got out of the shower was that she was beginning to resemble a prune. And thankfully, by the time she'd had coffee and toast, and managed to cover those raccoon-like rings under her eyes with concealer, she felt part of the human race once more.

It was nine am already, and if she wanted to stick to her plan of seeing Constance before she was due at The Natural Way, then she'd best get a move on. Now, where had she left her boots? She decided a room search was in order although it was getting too warm for boots. She'd have to splurge on some summer sandals. Maybe she should use the extra pounds Brenda had flicked her way, she debated with herself, getting down on all fours and locating the errant boots hiding under her bed. She shoved her feet into them and slung her holdall over her shoulder before taking the stairs two at a time.

Rhodri, she saw, upon entering the gallery, was in deep conversation with a customer over a bold painting she hadn't noticed on display before. She hung around behind the counter for a second until she caught his eye and sent him a tentative smile to see how the land lay this morning. She was relieved to see him grin. It was a new day, and she swept through the gallery to the bustling Esplanade outside with a lighter step.

A brisk walk later she arrived at Sea Vistas and Nurse Jill, who she commandeered as she stepped out of the lift, informed her she'd find Constance outside enjoying the morning sunshine. Isabel exited through the doors the nurse gestured her toward, and she followed the path that wound its way down into the garden.

The day was a stunner, she thought, spying the bench seat up ahead where Constance was sitting. Isabel smiled upon seeing she was dressed in her yellow outfit. Her snowy halo was dipped slightly as though she might have nodded off. There was no sound as she approached apart from that of her feet crunching on the loose gravel path and two speckle-chested song thrushes having a noisy dispute over a worm beneath the rose bushes. The expansive shrubbery on either side of the path gave up the heady scent of flowers just beginning to burst into bloom. There were far worse places to while away a morning.

'Constance, it's me,' she called, not wanting to frighten her by suddenly looming up beside her. Constance turned her head slowly in acknowledgment of her approach, and Isabel picked up her pace for her last few steps. 'Well, you've found the spot. It's a glorious morning,' she announced with all the gusto of a Butlins' Redcoat.

Before Constance could get a word in, Isabel produced her phone. 'This will make you smile.' She held it aloft, shading it from the sunlight as she played the video back.

When it had finished Constance demanded she play it again, but this time pulled her glasses out of her pocket before taking the mobile from Isabel. Isabel watched on amused as her eyes lit up and her mouth quivered with amusement; she patted her free hand on her lap along to the music.

'Well done. You and Rhodri make a good team. I used to sing once.'

'Did you?' Isabel was only half listening. She was thinking about Rhodri. They did make a good team. They understood one another she thought, her mind flitting back to the conversation they'd had last night. She would have loved to talk to Constance about it, but she'd promised it would go no further and a promise was a promise. 'I wouldn't have had the nerve to get up there if he wasn't standing alongside me.' She carried on chatting telling her about Alice, and the Acapella Group she'd been invited to join, but by the look on Constance's face, she knew she was only half listening.

'Are you all right, Constance?' To her alarm, as she looked at Constance in the hope she'd confide, she saw her eyes were shiny with unshed tears. She thrust her hand into her bag and hurriedly felt about for the packet of tissues she knew was in there somewhere. Her hand closed over the pack, and she pulled one free, passing it to Constance who dabbed at her eyes before speaking.

'I'm a silly old woman.'

'No you're not. You're far from silly, and I've decided you're not the type to be old.'

That raised a glimmer of a smile. Constance took Isabel's hand in hers and held it tightly. 'I need you to take me somewhere, Isabel. I have a story I need to tell.'

Chapter 38

Isabel strode up Union Street at a clip that had her puffing. She didn't want to be late. She'd stayed with Constance longer than she'd planned that morning. It was the second time she'd seen her upset, and it had unsettled her, and she'd not wanted to leave until she was sure she was all right. She was frustrated too by Constance's refusal to elaborate further on the story she wanted to share with her. Although, she was guessing she would finally learn the truth behind what Ginny's last words meant. It was very much a dangling carrot, but Constance would not be swayed further on the matter. The most she'd said was that this was something she needed to do as soon as possible.

In the end, Isabel had guided her back up the garden path and settled her in her easy chair over by the window in her room. She'd gone back downstairs and made her a cup of tea, doing her best not to spill a drop as she rode the lift back to her room. 'I'll sort it out, Constance, all right? We'll get to wherever it is you want to go,' she'd promised before leaving.

It would have to be tomorrow because she'd ask Delwyn, who had a car, first and that was the only day the shop was closed. If she wasn't free then she could ask Rhodri; he closed the gallery mid-afternoon on a Sunday. He and Delwyn were the only two people with transport that she knew well enough on the island to ask. She didn't fancy all the effort involved with getting Constance on a bus, but a bus to where? A taxi perhaps then? That could be pricey given she had no idea of the destination Constance had in mind. She'd cross that bridge when she came to it. First things first, she'd see how the land lay with Delwyn. Brenda sprang to mind. She'd have to ask her for a few hours off in the afternoon which wouldn't go over well. Unless she went in to work earlier this afternoon to make up for it, that might swing it. Her brain buzzed with the planning of it all.

The sign for The Natural Way came into sight, and she burst through the door a few seconds later. Delwyn looked up, startled, from the counter where she was in the middle of ringing up a customer's purchase. Isabel smiled a greeting at both Delwyn and the young man she was serving before disappearing out the back to deposit her bag and give herself a quick tidy up. She was glad she'd shoved her brush into her bag as she peered into the small mirror on the wall. She tugged it through her tangled hair and once she was satisfied she wouldn't frighten any customers away, she ventured out into the now empty shop.

'Thanks so much for coming in, Isabel; I appreciate it.'

'It's no problem. Is everything okay?' She hoped she wasn't being nosy.

Delwyn's smile was wide. 'Everything is great—better than great, actually. Nico's holding an exhibition of her pottery work in her studio from eleven and I promised her I'd be there for an hour at least to show moral support. It's very early days for us, so I didn't want to let her down. To be honest, Isabel, I can't believe she's interested in me, she's so talented and super gorgeous. I think she comes across as super confident, but she's a bit of a marshmallow once you scratch the surface. I've got you to thank, you know, for introducing us.'

Isabel gazed at Delwyn's daft expression and the penny dropped with a resounding clunk. Delwyn and Nico were an item! How could she have been so blind? Her mind raced and she wondered if Rhodri knew. So much for her thinking those two were an item of sorts, she thought, still gobsmacked as Delwyn continued talking.

'You can close your mouth, Isabel. I take it you didn't know I was gay?' Delwyn looked amused, and Isabel guessed her reaction was one she was used to.

'No, and I don't have a problem with it, really I don't, you just took me by surprise. I thought Nico and Rhodri had a thing.'

'Rhodri?' She snorted. 'Sorry, he's lovely looking and all but definitely not Nico's type. I rather thought he was more yours.' Her eyes twinkled.

Isabel flushed. 'He's a friend and my landlord that's all.' She realised he had become her friend over the weeks since she'd been living with him at Pier View.

'Then why've you gone red? Ah, don't worry about it I'm teasing you. And you're not the first to be surprised by my sexuality; it's something I don't broadcast. I don't see why I should. It makes no difference to who I am as a person.'

'You're right, you shouldn't have to.' Isabel was feeling embarrassed by her decidedly uncool response to Delwyn's news and was keen to move away from the subject of her Welsh landlord.

Delwyn, however, smiled. 'It's no big deal. Anyway, I'd better get a move on; I promise I won't be late back and thanks for this.' She held her hand up in a wave and strode to the door.

'I'll be fine.' Isabel managed to call after her, watching her walk out the door, with a flummoxed look on her face. It was then she remembered she'd meant to ask her about taking her and Constance on her mystery outing. *Bugger;* it would have to wait until she got back now.

~

The time sped by as, in between the steady flow of customers, she familiarised herself further with the different products displayed around the shop. She read the labels explaining what they were for, her mind soaking up all their different uses like a sponge. She was almost disappointed when Delwyn reappeared a little after midday. She was glowing, and Isabel doubted it was down to any potion she stocked in the shop.

'Hiya. How did it go?' She put the bottle of rose water, which she had just learned was one of nature's skincare superheroes, back on the shelf.

'It was great, thanks. That woman is so talented. She took two commissions and sold four pieces.'

'Brilliant,' Isabel enthused. She felt a surge of pleasure at seeing her friend looking so happy.

'Has it been busy?' Delwyn threw her bag into the back room.

'It's been steady.'

'Saturday customers are the best; they're never in a rush and always in a good mood.'

'You're right,' Isabel said thinking back to the lady she'd had a lovely chat with about the benefits of aloe vera juice.

'Well, don't hang about talking to me you'd better get to work.' Delwyn opened the till and fished out a handful of notes holding them out to Isabel. 'Here, take this.'

'Oh, I didn't expect you to pay me! It was just a friend doing a favour.'

'No way—that's not fair, go and treat yourself.' Delwyn was insistent. 'If you don't take it then I won't feel as though I can ask you again now, will I?'

Isabel took the money, albeit reluctantly. It was all well and good to be magnanimous when one was rolling in it but she was not, and she needed a pair of summer sandals. This would go toward them. 'Thanks. Oh, before I forget. I promised Constance I'd try to arrange a lift for us on a bit of a magical mystery tour. She won't tell me where she wants to go, and I know tomorrow is your day off. So, I wondered how you were placed?'

'Oh, Isabel any other time I'd say yes. I'd love an outing with you both, but I already promised Nico a trip over to Yarmouth for lunch tomorrow.'

'No problem,' Isabel said quickly, seeing Delwyn felt bad. 'I've got a backup plan. I'll check in with Rhodri and see if he'd mind doing the honours. His car must be due for a run, or the battery will go flat.'

'Well, good luck and if he can't, I'd love to go next Sunday.'

Isabel did not think she could wait an entire week to hear whatever it was Constance was going to say. 'Cheers, Delwyn. Enjoy Yarmouth.'

'Will do, and say hi to Rhodri and Constance for me.'

Isabel gave her friend a final wave and raced off down the bustling street. Her mind was whirring over Nico and Delwyn having gotten together and even though the money was burning a hole in her pocket, she decided to head straight to A Leap of Faith and then she'd best get to the Rum Den. It might pay to get in quick with Rhodri to see if he was free after the gallery shut tomorrow. The longer she left it, the more likely he'd be to have made other plans, she thought, hot-footing it back there.

Rhodri was rolling a poster print for a customer, and when the coast was clear Isabel, fit to combust, burst out with, 'Did you know Nico and Delwyn were an item?'

Rhodri laughed. 'I don't think they've made it official, but yeah, I had a pretty good idea they were smitten.'

'Well, I had no idea.' Isabel was almost indignant. 'I felt like a right plonker when she told me.'

'I'll admit I was surprised they got together because it was you Nico had the hots for initially.'

'Pardon?' Isabel spluttered, certain she'd heard wrong.

'Why else do you think she was in and out of the gallery? It wasn't to discuss my potting attempts; it was to catch a glimpse of you.' He looked bemused.

Isabel was dumbfounded. How'd she managed to miss that? 'I thought she was always showing up because you two were an item.'

Rhodri roared with laughter this time. 'Er no, I'm the wrong sex I'm afraid, besides Nico isn't my type.'

'What, you don't do blonde and beautiful? And I'm glad my naivety so amuses you.'

'It is pretty funny. Anyway, it doesn't matter now that Nico's moved on and I think her and Delwyn make a much better match, don't you?'

'Yeah.' The memory of Delwyn's shining, happy face flitted to mind. 'I think so too. Um, Rhodri is there any chance of you doing me and Constance a teensy favour tomorrow? I wouldn't ask, only it's rather important.'

Chapter 39

Constance was waiting in the foyer of Sea Vistas when Isabel and Rhodri arrived at the arranged time on Sunday afternoon. Brenda, while not being what you could call graceful, that wasn't her style, hadn't kicked off about Isabel's rejigging of her shifts. She'd managed before Isabel had happened along, she'd manage now, so long as she didn't make a habit of it, was all she'd muttered. She was a bit of a lion with a teddy bear's heart, Isabel had decided.

Constance was ensconced in the wheelchair Jill had organised for her once more, and Rhodri who had been more than graceful in agreeing to escort them out this afternoon greeted her effusively. Constance preened, pretty in pink, when he bent down and planted a kiss on her cheek. She made to get up from the chair, perfectly capable of walking the short distance out to the carpark, and he helped her to her feet before linking his arm through hers.

He turned his attention to Nurse Jill affording her a grin as he gestured to the wheelchair. 'Do we need a crash course in operating this piece of equipment?'

Jill had been filling in paperwork at the front desk, something she'd confided to Isabel drove her potty about nursing these days. Isabel watched on amused at the way the sensible nurse, glad of the distraction, flushed under the handsome Welshman's gaze and fiddled with her hair. 'No, Isabel has had the run down; she holds a full license.' Her giggle was positively girlish. 'Enjoy your outing, Constance.'

'Are you off somewhere nice then?' A baritone voice called over.

Isabel turned in its direction and saw that the rich, rumbling tones belonged to a dapper gentleman. He'd have done well on the radio with a voice like that she thought, idly taking in his well-cut suit. His generation didn't do casual and there was something rather romantic about that bygone era of smooth-talking, black and white movie heartthrobs. A newspaper was rolled up under his arm, and he'd obviously just come from the dining room. He would be around the same age as Constance, but his posture was still admirably ramrod straight. 'Actually, I'm not sure where we're off to yet. Constance's got us heading out on a bit of a mystery tour,' she said, smiling at him.

'Does she now? She was always a theatrical one. Well, mind how you go and look after her.'

Constance, however, announced she was not in the least bit prone to dramatics in a loud enough voice for them to get the message before she put her best ballet flat forward, eager for the off.

'We will.' Isabel smiled at the elderly gent, touched by the genuine concern she'd heard in his voice.

'Right, let's get this show on the road.' She took the handles of the wheelchair and followed Constance and Rhodri's lead out into the fresh air.

'Who was that?' she whispered loudly in Constance's ear as she caught up with them, even though they were a safe distance away not to be overheard.

'Who?'

'Don't be all coy with me, Constance; the dreamboat in the suit.' She used her mum's turn of phrase for Rhodri.

'Dreamboat? That's rather a stretch, Isabel. *That* was Walter. I've known him forever. He used to run an antique store a few doors down from my little shop.'

'Ah, I see.'

'There is absolutely nothing to see, young lady, so you can get that daft look off your face.'

Rhodri's mud-splattered and somewhat battered Land Rover was parked nearby, ready and waiting. Isabel had been bemused by how someone who hardly ventured out in his vehicle had managed to get it so dirty. He'd laughed and told her he liked to get off-road sometimes to scout for painting locations. His smile dried up though as they pondered how they'd get Constance into it.

The pair of them supported her weight while she made indignant murmurings but, ignoring her, they managed to hoist her up into the passenger seat. Isabel helped her with the seatbelt before tackling the wheelchair which was also a two-man job as they tried to figure out how to fold it. 'So much for you having a license,' Rhodri muttered, but they got there in the end. Once it was stowed in the boot, Isabel clambered into the back seat and buckled in. Rhodri slid behind the wheel, and she leaned into the space between the front seats and said, 'Right, Constance, *now* are you going to tell us where we are going?'

'Quarr Abbey ruins,' Constance directed, turning her head toward Rhodri who gave her a salute by way of reply. She batted his hand.

'Okay, Quarr Abbey ruins it is. I'm glad I brought my painting gear, It's a great spot to while away a few hours.' Rhodri turned the ignition key; the engine roared to life.

'But you already painted the ruins,' Isabel said.

'I have a work in progress that I'm painting from memory. It'll be nice just to sit somewhere peaceful to paint. I always work better outdoors than in the gallery. I think it's the light.'

'Oh well, that's all good then.' Isabel bounced along in the back watching the green and gold of the countryside speed by as they wound their way in toward Quarr. She glanced toward Rhodri, catching his face in profile as he chatted to Constance about an artwork he'd sold yesterday. She was touched by his sensitivity in not enquiring as to why all the cloak and dagger carry on, on Constance's part. He was happy just taking the afternoon in his stride.

The drive to the abbey didn't take long and Rhodri soon crunched onto the graveled car park, sliding the Land Rover into a space. As Isabel got out of the car, she paused to admire the beauty and sheer scale of the looming monastery's brickwork. It was a visual treat in its woodland shrouded grounds. Despite the other cars filling the parking lot signifying fellow day trippers, there was a feeling of tranquil solitude about the place.

Rhodri set about hauling the wheelchair out of the boot and unfolded it deftly. 'Easy when you know how,' he said, before signalling to Isabel that he needed a hand. Together, they helped Constance down from the four-wheel drive, the queen alighting from her carriage, and saw her seated comfortably in the chair. 'Right, ladies. It's my treat in the abbey tea rooms at say,' Rhodri glanced at his watch, 'four o'clock. It's just on two now. Constance, will that be enough time?'

Constance nodded folding her hands in her lap. She'd never get used to being pushed around in a wheelchair, but needs must if she wanted to get to the ruins before nightfall. She knew her limitations! She mumbled her thanks to Rhodri for bringing them, which Isabel reiterated, and then they left him unloading his art gear. Isabel had no clue where it was Constance wanted to head as she pushed her forth. She'd follow her lead, but for now, she figured she couldn't go wrong by heading to the main grounds.

Constance waved her this way and that until they reached the sign for the Woodland Walk. Isabel hoped she wasn't expecting her to push her along the looping track, but apparently she was, given the way she turned to ask what they were waiting for.

'Are you sure you want to follow that trail, Constance? It might get a bit rugged. I don't think the monks laid it out with wheelchair access in mind.' Or flimsy but oh-so-pretty new summer sandals either, she thought, with a rueful glance at her footwear. Constance wouldn't be able to walk it, Isabel thought as she contemplated their choices; one false step, and she could break a hip. That was an incident she did not want to have to explain to Nurse Jill, or Walter, with his obvious soft spot for Constance, upon their return to Sea Vistas.

'Yes, yes. To the ruins, Isabel,' Constance demanded. She was straining forward in her chair in an agitated manner and Isabel, knowing how stubborn she could be, took the hint and ventured on to the track. It was against her better judgment, and she ignored the strange looks they received from a wholesome family of walkers, the two young children clutching a bug pot each. It was a shame, she thought, that the chair didn't come with a lap belt as they ventured deeper into the woods. It would not be a good look were she to hit a rogue tree root and send Constance airborne.

The ground at least was dry—Isabel was grateful for small mercies—and the terrain was manageable. She'd be like flipping Popeye with bulging muscles though, from pushing this tank of a chair by the time she got them both to the ruins. Despite her shortness of breath, Isabel still found the small talk flowing from her like a babbling brook. She chattered on about how well the monks maintained the grounds of the abbey, and what it must be like to live virtually self-sufficient in the same way the Benedictine monks resident at Quarr had done for hundreds of years.

She was nervously excited as to what Constance would divulge that afternoon and why she was so insistent on waiting until they got to the ruins. Constance was muttering something, and she paused, grateful to stop for a second. 'What was that, sorry?'

Constance shook her head not wanting to repeat herself and impatient to get to where she wanted to be.

Isabel frowned, spying a red squirrel who'd heard them coming dart up a tree. She could have sworn Constance had said that perhaps Isabel should think about taking a vow of silence!

It wasn't long before they veered off the trail and bumped their way over to the clearing where the remains of the old abbey stood. Isabel could see there were a handful of tourists milling around the ancient stone walls, which were strewn with threads of green creeper trying to lay claim to the ancient rocks. Just beyond the ruins was a slash of blue where the Solent waters lapped. It was an atmospheric sight, Isabel thought, conjuring up images of the brown-robed monks of old setting about their daily tasks, a white-sailed ship idling in the harbour beyond. She flapped away the random image of a swashbuckling pirate straight from the cover of a romance novel, who bore an uncanny resemblance to Rhodri, and bumped Constance across the grass.

She wheeled her up to one of the remaining great stone arches and watched as Constance leaned forward in the chair, resting her hand on the fine stone masonry for a moment. Her lips were moving as though she were speaking to someone, and Isabel thought she heard her say she was sorry but she couldn't be sure. They certainly didn't build 'em like that anymore, she mused, marvelling at how the walls of the abbey had stood the test of time. She stood silently alongside Constance. This was her afternoon, and she'd reveal why they were here when she was good and ready. There was no point rushing her, Isabel knew, watching out the corner of her eye as Constance closed hers briefly, continuing to press her hand to the wall as though it were communicating with her.

The seconds ticked by and a middle-aged man in outdoor wear with a camera slung around his neck gave them a wary smile. They must make an odd sight, Isabel thought. She tried to convey in the smile she sent his way that they were perfectly normal. At last Constance let her arm fall back to her lap and opened her eyes blinking against the sunshine as she came back from wherever it was she'd been. She pointed Isabel over to a sun-stippled patch of grass a short distance from the other visitors milling about and Isabel's stomach lurched. The time had come to learn the truth of what had transpired between Ginny and Constance all those years ago. She steered them over to the spot in the sun.

Chapter 40

Isabel sat down on the grass, stretching her legs out in front of her. She was too distracted to admire the beautiful setting, and for want of something to do with her hands she plucked a few daisies. Her fingers were thumbs as she tried to make a chain from the dainty flowers waiting for Constance to talk. Constance watched her for a moment. It was an echo from the past, she thought, thinking of the daisy chain and promise Henry had made her.

'I used to come here on a Sunday with Henry, my beau, when I was a young girl. He was in the Canadian Air Force, and we were engaged, well, unofficially,' Constance said after a while, gazing into the distance as though she could see him standing just beyond the ruins, waiting for her. 'We'd borrow bicycles from the girls at Puckpool Camp where he was stationed and cycle here. It was the folly where we first met, but it was these ruins that became our place. It was here I fell properly in love with him.'

Isabel pulled her knees to her chest and wrapped her arms around them as she sat with her head tilted to hear better as Constance's sad love story began to unfold. She felt as though she were an observer to their romance, hovering on the periphery of their intimate conversations as she listened to Constance. She wasn't to know that it was the first time in over seventy years that Constance had spoken of Henry and how he'd died. It was only when her nose began to run as she heard how he'd been killed protecting one of his countrymen by a bomb dropped on what was now Sea Vistas, that Isabel realised she was crying. It was so much sadness for someone so young to go through, she thought wiping the tears away with the back of her hand.

Constance finished talking and reached into the pocket of her tunic. Isabel thought she was fetching her a tissue to blow her nose on, but instead, she produced a folded piece of paper. That it was old was evident in the discolouration of the paper, and Isabel took her hand away watching as she held it to her chest for a moment, her lips moving silently before passing it to Isabel.

She blinked against the afternoon's bright sunshine wishing she'd thought to bring her sunglasses as she read the typed words in front of her. It took her a few seconds to digest that the paper Constance had handed her was a birth certificate for Ginny's son—Edward Henry Downer, born on the twenty-second of October 1944 in Salisbury. The space next to where his father's name should be was blank, but it was what was typed next to 'Mother' that Isabel couldn't make sense of. It was Constance Mary Downer.

'Why's your name on Ginny's son's birth certificate?' She looked up at Constance puzzled.

'Teddy wasn't her son; he was mine.'

Isabel's eyes widened, 'What do you mean?'

'Ginny's baby was stillborn, and I was pregnant when Henry died. It was deemed that her adopting my baby was the perfect solution to the mess I found myself in.' Constance looked away before her tears could brim over and turned her gaze to the shimmering waters in the distance. Her verdant surrounds seemed to tilt on their axis as the mist descended and she found herself back in another time.

1944

It didn't matter that Constance loved Henry, the words sounded hollow to her parents despite their fondness for him. By dying, he'd left it up to them to pick up the pieces he'd left behind and make things right.

She felt the tiny fluttering of life growing inside her for the first time the day her mother told her the local vicar would be consulted, on the quiet, of course, as to what their options were. The tremulous leap she felt in her belly took her by surprise as did the realisation that this baby was part of her, not what had been done to her. It was a shock to understand that there was a very real chance she would love this child with a fierceness she'd never imagined possible.

Her mother was true to her word, and so it was two days later tea was served at the carefully laid table at precisely three o'clock as had been arranged with the vicar's housekeeper, the formidable Mrs Chubb. 'Reverend Hayles is a busy man you know,' Mrs Downer had said earlier as she set out the china, as though he were bestowing them with the greatest of gifts with his visit. Constance had nodded meekly as she carried on with the dusting task she'd been set. She knew she was not in a position to comment.

Throughout the reverend's visit, Constance sat with her eyes cast downward seemingly entranced by the intricate lace flowers of her mum's best tablecloth brought out for the occasion. She was willing this nightmare to end. The reverend, with his perfect shiny dome for a head surrounded by its shock of white that looked as though pieces of unspun wool had been pasted on, cut a portly almost comical figure across the table from her. He reminded Constance of the Friar Tuck painted on the pages of a Robin Hood picture book she'd loved as a child. The idea of robbing the rich to give to the poor had caught her fancy. It was still tucked away upstairs on her bookshelf, but its pages would be gathering dust these days.

Ginny was seated to her left, and she held her hand under the table, giving it a reassuring squeeze now and again as Mother, Father and Reverend Hayles talked over the top of their heads. Their agenda: to decide what to do about the problem that was Constance.

She listened, feeling as if she were floating slightly above them all, to the reverend as he told her parents of a Mother and Baby Home he had connections with through the church. It was a reputable home and was run by the good people of The Salvation Army. He'd manage to secure a place for Constance there. The words bounced back and forth across the table with it transpiring the home was near where a cousin of Ginny's lived in Salisbury, and a plan was hatched over a generous slice of Mum's cake.

It was as if she was on a train which would not stop, Constance thought as the voices bounced back and forth around the table. Ginny compliant in the conspiracy, would go and stay with her cousin; the poor girl was recently widowed. She would be glad of the company and people would understand Ginny's decision to leave the island; she needed a fresh start. Constance inclined her head to look at her sister-in-law, and for the first time since her baby's stillbirth, she saw hope flicker on her pretty features. She wondered why.

It was decided that the tale to be told to anyone forthright enough to enquire, was that Ginny had gone to Salisbury to stay with her cousin, also a war widow. They could be of comfort to one another. It was too painful for her to stay here in Ryde, so it was the obvious solution for them both.

Now that it was deemed safer for the girls to travel with the Allies gaining strongholds and keeping the Jerrys at bay, Constance would go with her to help settle her in for as long as it took given her fragile state.

It was her mother who wondered out loud as to Constance's baby being handed to a stranger after it was born and wouldn't it be lovely if the wee one could somehow stay in the family? Ginny's intake of breath was sharp as the hope Constance had seen flickering suddenly flared. 'I'd love the baby as my own,' she whispered, squeezing Constance's hand so tightly that Constance would have cried out had she not been numb. 'Perhaps we could say my cousin was pregnant, but she died in childbirth and there was no one else but me to care for the baby?'

The air itself seemed to sigh with Ginny's sentiment. It was then that Constance understood that this had been the plan all along. They were all acting out their parts in an elaborate charade. She looked to each parent and saw their faces unknot. She read their expressions. They'd have their grandchild after all, and young Ginny would get to be the mother she deserved to be. It was a white lie they would all tell for the greater good. As for Constance, well, she'd return home, and it would be as it was before. All their lives would carry on without the blight of scandal marring the future because nobody except the five people seated at the table need ever know of the circumstances that had befallen Constance.

A solution amenable to all had been found, and the reverend coughed before glancing at his watch. Mrs Chubb would have his sherry poured by the time he got home to the vicarage. Mother nudged Constance with her foot under the table.

'Thank you, Reverend,' she said quietly.

His smile was kindly as he assured her that God still loved her and that she was not the first to slip but that she should learn from the error of her ways.

Constance nodded, then dropped her gaze to the lacy cloth once more as her parents left the room with him, their hushed voices floating up the stairs as they finalised the arrangement. They were good people, Mum and Dad but their lifeblood was the shop, and its business had already suffered from the effects of the war. The shame of an unwed pregnant daughter would destroy their standing in the community. They'd had so much to cope with already.

This, she knew was the right thing to do. There was a part of her too that was relieved to have matters taken out of her hands. She felt Ginny's questioning gaze seeking reassurance.

'It's for the best, Ginny, it's the right thing to do,' she said, verbalising her thoughts, 'and you'll be a wonderful mother. There's nobody else I'd rather—' her voice threatened to crack, 'Thank you,' she managed to whisper before her throat closed over with unshed tears.

Ginny let out a sob and pushed her chair back. She leaned over and pulled Constance to her, kissing the top of her head. Constance couldn't stop the tears from spilling over, and as they traced their way down her cheeks, she felt a part of herself close down.

~

Constance was dragging her heels, her brown suitcase banging against her thigh as Ginny urged her on. They were making their way up the long driveway to Saint Augustine House. 'We're expected at eleven, Constance so do come on we don't want to be late. That would get things off to a bad start.'

The Mother and Baby Home was set well back from the road and hidden away from prying eyes as the driveway curved around it loomed in front of them. It was a sprawling manor house shrouded by trees with a curtain of ivy clinging to the bricks around the front entrance. Its abundance of chimney stacks gave a clue as to the many rooms tucked away inside. It would have been rather grand in its day, but now it looked as though it were sagging under the weight of time. Tiles were missing from the roof, and the paint on the gables had all but flaked off. Its myriad windows made Constance feel as though they were being watched and she was assailed with an urge to turn on her heel and run. But where would she go? She couldn't go home not until after the baby was born. Her hand rested protectively against her belly as she reluctantly followed Ginny's lead up the stairs to the imposing entrance.

The front door swung open before Ginny had a chance to rap the lion's head knocker. A woman of indeterminable age whose austerity was not softened by her drab grey matron's uniform stood before them and taking in her pinched features, Constance felt her knees beginning to tremble.

'Constance Downer?' she asked, in an accent Constance couldn't pinpoint other than it was northern. She gave Constance and Ginny a tight-lipped smile, which did nothing to lessen her severity, as Constance managed a nod. 'I'm Matron Holt; I've been expecting you. Reverend Hayles' church has been a generous benefactor of ours in the past which is why I've made room for you. We have twelve girls here at any given time, but we found an extra bed when he wrote and informed me of the situation you find yourself in. And you must be Mrs Virginia Downer?' She looked down her long nose at Ginny.

'Yes, good morning, Matron Holt. Thank you for being here to greet us. It's very good of you.' Ginny was bright and breezy, determined not to be intimidated lest Constance pick up on it.

'Very good. Right well, don't just stand on the doorstep girls, come in. We have some paperwork to do, and then I shall give you a tour of Saint Augustine's.'

The door shut behind them and Constance felt trapped as she stood in the gloom of the foyer. Her sense of foreboding intensified as she followed Matron's clicking shoes. Matron Holt bypassed the sweeping staircase with a nod in its direction. 'The front staircase is for our nursing staff and visitors only. There is a back entrance and staircase the girls use. I shall show you where it is once the necessary forms have been filled in.' She ushered them into her office. 'Have a seat please.'

Ginny and Constance quickly sat down in the empty seats in front of Matron's desk while she took herself around to the other side and settled herself before opening her desk drawer. She produced a pair of glasses, which she slid on to the end of her nose before opening the file that sat on the top of a pile of identical ones stacked on the desk. She took a sheet of paper from it and handed it and a pen to Constance. 'I need you to sign this please. And you too, Mrs Downer, in your capacity as Constance's guardian while she is staying with us here at Saint Augustine's.'

Constance wasn't sure what it was she was signing, but she obliged by putting her signature to the form. She had no wish to experience the sharp end of Matron's tongue by questioning her as to what it was for. Ginny took the time to read over the document before doing the same and sliding it back across the table. Matron Holt gave it a cursory glance. 'That's all in order,' she said, placing the form back in the file and closing it. 'If you'd like to follow me, please.' She got to her feet and smoothed the creases in her skirt before marching forth.

Constance's eyes were wide as she looked around at what would be her home for the next four months as Matron led them further down the hallway to where what once would have been the servants' entrance and staircase were located. There was a sense of sadness about the house, she decided, and the weary furnishings and peeling wallpaper did not help.

'We're very fortunate to have a maternity wing here at Saint Augustine's for when baby arrives, Constance. It's on the south side, for the sunshine.'

Constance wasn't sure if a reply was expected from her or not, but before she could decide whether she should voice her agreement that yes they were fortunate, when she felt anything but, Matron spoke again.

'We're all about routines here at St Augustine's; we find it makes the time pass quickly for our girls if they know what is expected of them each day. The girls rise at seven o'clock and then we have prayers at seven fifteen followed by breakfast, after which the girls commence their daily chores. There's no substitute for hard work, don't you agree, Mrs Downer?'

'Quite right, Matron Holt,' Ginny replied, and Constance glimpsed the matron's mean little smile once more as she came to a halt outside a room. The door was shut, but the sounds of laughter drifted under the gap beneath it. That was heartening, Constance thought, her eyes meeting Ginny's reassuring gaze as she wondered who was on the other side of the door.

'This is the recreation room. The girls are having their morning break, so it's a good time to introduce you to them, Constance.' She opened the door into a high-ceilinged room flooded with light, which was a relief after the gloom of the stairwell and hallway. The room was scantily furnished with a trestle table in the centre around which were seated several girls who weren't much older than Constance. A few of them were engaged in a game of cards while others were just sitting talking, cigarettes dangling from their fingers. A haze of smoke was trapped in the rays of sunlight streaming in through the windows; it had settled over the top of their heads. The chatter died as Matron Holt appeared. One of the girls reminded Constance of Myrtle from the factory and she looked away as she met her gaze with a hardened, and defiant stare. She would not fit in here, Constance thought. These girls might be of a similar age to her, but she could tell they had a toughness about them that she lacked.

'Girls, this is Constance. She's from the Isle of Wight.'

One or two of the girls smiled over, but most just eyed her warily.

'Five minutes and back to your posts, please. The laundry won't wash itself, and the sandwiches won't get cut on their own.' She turned away and Constance spotted several of the girls rolling their eyes.

'Constance, I'll show you up to your room in order for you to settle yourself in before lunch.'

Ginny and Constance dutifully followed behind her.

Her room had an iron bedstead in each corner. All the beds were neatly made, and there was a wardrobe at either end.

'I'll leave you now to unpack your things, Constance. Mrs Downer, perhaps you'd like to say your goodbyes and let young Constance unpack her things. Now, now, no tears.'

Constance gulped and swiped at her cheeks. Ginny pulled her into a hug. 'You'll be all right, Constance. I'll be back to visit you on Wednesday. The time will whizz by, and you'll make friends of the girls you'll see.' The girls were allowed visitors on a Wednesday and Saturday afternoon.

'Quite right,' Matron said. 'Mrs Downer?' She waited for Ginny to follow her lead and as they left the room, Constance heard Matron say, 'I find drawn out goodbyes don't do anyone any good.'

Constance perched on the edge of her bed with her little brown case beside her and sobbed.

Chapter 41

'Saint Augustine's was a horrible place, Isabel. It was damp and draughty, and the nurses weren't kind,' Constance lamented, her voice etched with tiredness, as the shadows from the ruins began to stretch long. 'I did make friends though, despite my initial misgivings. That you should never judge a book by its cover is one thing I learned during my time there. Those girls who'd seemed so worldly compared to me were nothing more than heartbroken children once you cracked their hardened veneers. We were all in the same boat, and we were all terrified of what was to come with our babies' birth. Nobody told us anything, and the only knowledge I had was from listening to Ginny's labour. Oh yes, we were scared all right. Funnily enough, it was the girl who'd reminded me of Myrtle from the factory where I worked in Cowes that I grew closest to.'

Isabel picked another daisy to add to her lengthening chain and stayed silent, not wishing to interrupt until Constance's story had reached its conclusion.

'Her name was Frances, and she had a baby girl a month or two before I had Teddy. The bonniest little thing she was too and born with a full head of hair. Frances called her Mary, and then one day, a few weeks later, Matron Holt came to the nursery and said it was time for baby to go. That was that; she took Mary away, and we watched from the nursery window as a smartly dressed couple arrived in a shiny Rover and drove off with her. It broke Frances's heart. Teddy arrived with a roar and a lot of bother on my behalf a few days after that, but by then Frances was gone too.

'We didn't keep in touch after we left the home. Neither of us wanted to be reminded of our time there. Sometimes, I can still hear the girls I shared my room with crying when I close my eyes because not a single night passed at Saint Augustine's without one of us crying ourselves to sleep.' Constance shook her head still lost in another time. 'Come Sunday we'd be marched in an alligator line to church, so as all and sundry knew us as the girls from the local home. They worked us to the bone too. One of the girls said it helped keep us flexible, made the birth easier, but I think that place would have fallen down around our ears if it weren't for us girls keeping things running.'

Constance's body trembled even now with indignation at the memory of it, and her words faltered while she regained a modicum of equilibrium. 'I made Teddy a baby-box when I was waiting for him to arrive. I covered the box with the prettiest of yellow wrapping paper and put a blanket I made for him along with a little white cardigan and booties I knitted for him in it. He wouldn't have wanted for much in the way of a layette, not with all the work Mum and Ginny had put into preparing for her poor little babe, but I wanted to give him something from me. The other girls stayed on at Saint Augustine's for six weeks after their babies were born, but given my circumstances, Teddy only stayed with me a week before I handed him to Ginny. I was to go home, and I thought she would come with me, but she said she wanted to stay on at her cousin's for a few days longer and get him settled into a routine. She'd follow before the week was out, she assured me.

'The story would be put about that Ginny's cousin had died in childbirth and that she had been named as his guardian. She'd raise my boy at Pier View House as her own but she never came back to the island, and when Mum and Dad tried to find her, she and Teddy had vanished. I wanted them to go to the police and report them missing, but they wouldn't because that would have meant telling them the truth behind Teddy's birth. I went to the station once. I sat outside for an hour trying to find the courage to go inside, but in the end, I couldn't do it. There were times I thought I saw them, but they always turned out to be strangers, and for a long time I'd think I could see Teddy's face every time I spied a child who looked to be of a similar age.

'I light a candle for him on his birthday; I've never missed, not once in all these years.' She paused, exhausted from all those emotions and watched a seagull as it dipped and soared over the Solent. 'All those years we never knew where they went or even if they were still alive. The first news I've had of her and what happened to my boy since I said goodbye to her at Saint Augustine's was when you came, Isabel. I left Pier View House with a little brown case, and I returned to it with that same brown case, and it was as though the whole thing had been a dream. It was as if Henry, my getting pregnant, Teddy's birth, none of it ever happened. Then, when I turned seventeen Mum and Dad gave me a pair of pink satin dancing shoes and told me that whenever I wore them, I was to look to my future, not my past. And that's what I did.'

Isabel gasped. 'Oh, Constance, I'm so, so sorry. How could Ginny do that to you and your parents?'

Constance looked at her, her eyes weary with the telling of her tale. 'Ah, looking back now there were signs that she wasn't well after her baby died. There's a name for it now, post-natal depression, but back then there were no labels for things like that. I think she was frightened that I wouldn't be able to let go of Teddy if she brought him back here, that I'd always be hovering in the background trying to take him off her. She was probably right. In some ways, it would have been worse to have him close and not be his mother. Perhaps she convinced herself initially that Teddy was her biological child, and then with the passing of time as her mind cleared, she felt it was too late to go back. I'll never know, but at least I know she was sorry for what she did.'

Isabel pushed her daisy chain from her lap and got to her feet. There were times, she thought, that a gesture could mean as much as any words and sometimes there simply were no words, and so she'd embraced Constance as tightly as she could without hurting her. Beneath her words, buried deep in the subtext, she'd caught the lingering shame instilled in Constance all those years ago, and she tried to vanquish it in that hug.

A burst of laughter sounded behind them, and to her ears, it sounded obscene. She turned her head to see who the culprits were. Two women, giggling over something or other, had appeared at the edge of the woodland path. She shot them daggers willing them to shut up, but Constance was unperturbed, her mind still foggy with the past. Before they set off Constance took hold of Isabel's hand and patted it. 'Thank you for listening, Isabel.'

Isabel fought back the tears. This lady whom she'd thought so formidable initially had become a special person in her life. She rested her other hand on top of Constance's as though they were about to engage in a game of paper, scissors, rock, feeling humbled that she had confided in her.

'I'm so sorry for all that you've been through, Constance. It was all so very unfair.'

'It was a very long time ago, but it never got easier losing Teddy. There's not a single day that's gone by since I put him in Ginny's arms that I haven't thought of him, but I've done what I came here to do. I wanted to tell Henry I was sorry I couldn't keep our boy. I forgive Ginny for what she did too, you know, Isabel, because you can't look back in life, that's something you learn with each year that passes by. You have to keep putting one pink satin shoe in front of the other, and that's what I did.' She sighed, and the larger-than-life Constance Downer suddenly looked frail as she said, 'I think it's time we went home now, Isabel. I'm eighty-nine, you know.'

~

Rhodri was waiting at a table, seats saved for them in the packed courtyard of the abbey proper's tea garden when Isabel pushed Constance back over the lawn toward the outdoor dining area. It was a perfect afternoon for tea and cake in the sun, and it looked as though half of Ryde had agreed with the sentiment, Isabel thought. She and Constance hadn't spoken on the way back from the ruins. They were both spent with the emotion of what had been revealed.

There was no sign of his painting gear, Isabel noted now as Rhodri got up from his seat to greet them. She hoped he hadn't been waiting long; it was only just after four pm though, the time they'd agreed to meet.

'I've ordered a pot of tea and a scone each with jam on the side. I hope that's all right? The monks make their own jam. I poked my head in the farm shop and bought a couple of jars of their raspberry preserve as well as some relish. You can't beat homemade.' He smiled at them both.

'Lovely, I'm parched,' Constance said nodding, her earlier sentiment about it being time to go home forgotten at the thought of tea and a scone.

'Me too,' Isabel reiterated with a smile. 'Did you do some painting?'

'I did thanks, and then I packed up so as I could mooch around the abbey. There's all sorts to see here, you know. I spotted one of Nico's works on display in the art gallery, and the brothers keep pigs and rescued hens as well as maintain an impressive vegetable patch. They're pretty much self-sufficient.'

'It's not changed since I was a girl,' Constance said.

'No, I'd imagine not,' Rhodri replied. 'It's a special place.'

Constance and Isabel looked at each other upon hearing that sentiment not long since uttered by Constance. Isabel reached across the table and patted her hand, and Rhodri's gaze swung between the two of them unsure as to what had transpired that afternoon but too polite to ask. The arrival of their tea and plump scones with a pottle of homemade jam provided a diversion, and the trio tucked in. A few bites later and with crumbs all down her front, Isabel declared the scones and jam, 'Delicious.'

It was a silent ride back to Sea Vistas and sensing no one was in the mood for chatting Rhodri let the radio play softly. From the dip of Constance's head, Isabel was guessing she'd nodded off. She gazed out the window but didn't see the countryside this time; her mind was too full of what Constance had told her. Rhodri had stilled the engine before Isabel caught up with the fact they were back at Sea Vistas. The car park was nearly deserted save for the staff members with most of the Sunday visitors having headed off to let the residents have their dinner.

Rhodri got out and unloaded the wheelchair not bothering to mess about with unfolding it; it had taken them long enough to collapse it once more in the first place. He leaned it against the Land Rover before giving Isabel a hand to help Constance down. Isabel linked her arm through Constance's and followed Rhodri's lead as he carted the chair inside to the foyer ahead of them. It was a different girl on reception, there for the evening shift, and she introduced herself as Courtenay with a 'C'. Isabel hadn't seen her before, and she returned her greeting cheerily.

'Did you have a nice outing?' Courtney directed her question to Constance who told her she was Constance with a 'C' before giving her a curt, 'yes thank you'. The girl's manner was that of someone fresh from school and to whom anyone over the age of thirty-five was ancient. Isabel bit her lip to stop herself from smiling at the exchange. It didn't pay to talk to Constance as though she'd been put out to pasture. Rhodri, she saw too had a gleam in his eye.

He jangled his keys. 'I've got a pottery class tonight, Isabel, do you want a lift to the pub?'

'Yes please, Thanks so much for taking us today Rhodri.' She made a mental note to purchase some petrol vouchers, not that he was likely to accept them.

'It was my pleasure. Right then, Constance, I'll be on my way. I'll meet you in the carpark, Isabel.' He leaned down and kissed Constance on the cheek, ending the day as it had begun.

'Thank you for today.'

'You're very welcome.'

The two women stood and watched him go.

A clatter from the direction of the dining room reminded Isabel of the time. 'Would you like to pop through to the dining room and see what's on offer?' Isabel didn't want to rush Constance, Brenda could wait.

Constance shook her head. 'No, I'm not hungry. Are you?'

'No, that scone did the trick. Shall I see you up to your room then?'

'Yes. I'm quite done in.'

Isabel wasn't surprised; it had been a huge few hours. They made their way to the lift that was standing open waiting for them. The corridor outside Constance's room was deserted, Isabel saw as the doors slid open. She took Constance's arm and matched her pace, waiting patiently as they reached her room. She opened her purse asking Isabel to retrieve her room key and a moment later Isabel followed her inside and paused to admire the pink glow the room was cast in as the last of the day's sunshine bounced off the soft furnishings. It was such a warm and welcoming space, she thought. The significance of Sea Vistas to Constance's past suddenly struck her. It was where she met Henry and lost him too. Henry Johnson, the great love of her life, had played out the final scenes of his life in this building.

Her eyes flitted toward Rhodri's painting; she understood now why Constance had wanted it the moment she saw it. Quarr was hers and Henry's place; it was where Teddy had been conceived.

She led Constance over to her chair by the window and watched her sag into it.

'Would you like me to stay for a bit, Constance?' She would if she wanted her to. It was going to be such a struggle to concentrate on pulling pints after the story she'd listened to this afternoon.

'No, dear. I think I'd like to be alone.'

'You're all right?'

'I'm perfectly fine; just tired, which is only to be expected because I am eighty-nine years old, you know, so don't fuss, Isabel.'

That was the Constance she knew and loved. 'Okay, well, I'll come and see you tomorrow morning.' Isabel turned to leave, pausing in the doorway and turning around. 'Constance?'

'Hmm.'

'I'm so very glad I met you.'

'And I you, Isabel. Isn't it strange that I have Ginny to thank for my having met you?'

Chapter 42

Somehow Isabel got through her shift at the Rum Den that evening despite her head humming with all that Constance told her that afternoon. She managed to give the wrong change out twice, receiving a sharp look from Brenda, whose patience with her tardy employee had already been tested. It took a supreme effort on her part but somehow she managed to focus on the pint pulling at hand. The pub was bustling and the hours flew by until last orders, by which time Isabel's feet were throbbing. She'd been run off them all night, and she took the notes Brenda scooped from the till gratefully forty minutes later when they'd finished clearing up for the evening.

'I'll see you Tuesday, thanks, Brenda, unless you'd like me to come in tomorrow. You know, to make up for all the messing about this weekend?'

'No, it would be silly having both of us twiddling our thumbs behind the bar.'

Isabel nodded, she wasn't going to argue and she slung her bag over her shoulder making for the door. She was eager to be off.

''Ere 'ang on a minute. Can you pick me up some more of that turmeric powders? It's worked wonders with me bunions. And what do you reckon we can do for my varicose veins? It's all the standing behind the bar that aggravates them.'

'I'll call in on Delwyn tomorrow and see what I can find.'

'Sandshoe, because they ain't half giving me grief.'

'Pardon?'

'Sandshoe. Its cockney rhyming slang ain't it, for thank you. What 'ave you got planned tomorrow?'

'I'll pop in on Constance in the morning, and my mum was making noises about getting the ferry over for the afternoon if she could swing the morning off work.' Isabel hoped she didn't bring Prince Charles with her.

The last time she'd brought him with her, reluctant to leave him at home on account of his separation anxiety, he'd been so excited to see Isabel he'd cocked his leg on the gallery floor.

'Well, be sure and bring Babs in for an on-the-'ouse drink if she does, she'll have to leave that pooch outside though.'

Isabel didn't raise a smile.

Brenda frowned, and Isabel noticed one eyebrow had been painted-in higher than the other. 'You all right, luv?' she asked.

'Yes, I'm fine, thanks.'

Brenda moved over to the entrance and unlocked the door. 'It's just you seemed like you were somewhere else tonight.'

'I was a bit. I'll have my mind on the job come Tuesday, I promise.'

Seeing that was as much as she was going to get out of her, Brenda opened the door and stood, hand on hip waiting for her to pass, 'If you say so, me girl.' As Isabel walked past her, she reached out and touched her arm. 'If you need someone to talk to—'

'Thanks, Brenda, I'll remember that.'

To her surprise, her boss gave her a smile that was almost maternal. 'Night now and mind how you go.'

Isabel was touched and returning the sentiment she stepped outside eager to get home and be alone with her thoughts. She jumped as a man stepped forward from a darkened doorway and her hand flew to her chest. 'Bloody hell, Rhodri! You have got to stop doing that.'

'Sorry, I didn't mean to frighten you. I've not long finished my pottery class with Nico so I thought I'd walk you home.'

'Thanks.' Isabel knew his pottery class had finished ages ago. She heard the lock turning in the door behind her, pleased Brenda hadn't seen him. Her boss, she knew would be all too quick to read things into the situation that weren't there. 'Did you finish your masterpiece?' She knew he was working on a salad bowl.

'No, the glaze is done, and it's back in the kiln. Hopefully, I can bring it home next week and make—'

'A Caesar salad?' It was Isabel's favourite. 'With croutons and a poached egg that's not too runny?'

'A Caesar salad with croutons and a poached egg with a set white it is then.' He grinned, his teeth white against the inky night.

They walked along in silence for a bit, illuminated by the thick yellow street light. 'Rhodri, thanks again for today,' Isabel said, as they passed by the Cancer Research Shop. The headless mannequin dressed in a pretty summer frock looked almost spooky in the muted light.

'It was no bother; it was a nice afternoon. I enjoyed myself.'

'You're a very kind man.'

'Ah, no more so than anyone else.'

'No, that's not true. The way you are with Constance it's lovely, and gifting her that painting, well, I think that was the highlight of her year.' She didn't add that the way he waited around outside the pub late at night to walk her home was sweet too.

'She reminds me of my nan; she was a proud lady too. I miss her. It's a funny thing when someone you've been close to all your life is suddenly just not there anymore.'

Isabel didn't have much experience of that and so she stayed silent.

He nodded before saying, 'I can see her in you too.'

'Your gran or Constance?' Isabel wasn't sure she liked the direction this conversation was going in.

'Constance,' he shrugged, 'How can I word it? You're both like these colourful, vibrant butterflies.'

'Oh.' Isabel didn't know what to say, it was such a lovely sentiment. As they rounded the bend onto the Esplanade, she looked up and saw a carpet of stars over the Solent. 'Do you fancy walking for a bit? It's so quiet, and I love the sound of the water when the tide is in. My brain's been whirring away at a hundred miles a minute this evening and I find the sound of the sea relaxing. I once fell asleep at the end of a yoga class my friend, Helena, dragged me along to in Melbourne when they played beach music at the end.'

Rhodri laughed. 'I hope you didn't snore, and why not, it's a nice night for a walk, almost tropical.'

'That's taking things a tad too far.'

They walked in silence for a bit with no noise other than their footsteps and the shushing waves below them.

'Rhodri, Constance told me she had a son today.'

'Really? I didn't know she had a child.'

'I didn't either, and it's rather a sad, long and complicated tale which isn't mine to share, but her son was adopted when he was barely a week old. That's the last time she saw him. She said not a day goes by even now that she doesn't think about him and each year on his birthday, she lights a candle for him.'

'I'd imagine giving up your baby is something you'd learn to live with but would never get over.'

Isabel mulled his words over; they were an echo of what had been on her mind since hearing Constance's story. 'The thing is, Rhodri, as I listened to her talk about what it was like for her to adopt her baby out it dawned on me that maybe I've been selfish.'

'What do you mean?'

'Well, I've only ever thought about being adopted from my perspective. I never considered how my birth mother might have felt all these years. I mean, I felt grateful to her for having me and that I got such great parents but I never went any deeper than that. I suppose I thought she would have just moved on with her life. But now, after listening to Constance and seeing how giving her baby up has shaped her life, I can't stop wondering about her.'

'Maybe you weren't ready to try to find her before.'

'I don't know if I am now. I'd have to ask Mum for my records and think about it—how would she and Dad feel about me suddenly announcing I'd like to try to find my birth mother. It just feels so disloyal.'

Rhodri stopped walking and sat down on the seawall. 'Isabel, do you love your parents?'

'Yes, of course, I do. They're my mum and dad, and if I'm honest, I even love that bloody corgi.'

'Well, then that's all you need to say to them.'

'How so?'

'Don't overthink it. Just because you're expressing an interest in finding your biological mother does not mean you are going to stop loving your parents suddenly. We human beings have a great capacity for love. Even if they do feel a bit unnerved initially, they'll get their heads around the idea and understand it's natural for you to have a curiosity to find out more about where you come from.'

'I could have a brother or a sister or both.'

'Yeah, you could.'

Isabel began chewing on her nail. 'She might not want me to contact her. For all I know she could have a life that I won't fit into, and my file might be permanently closed.'

'And she might have spent the last twenty-six years wondering how your life is turning out.'

'What if she's dead?'

'Then at least you'll know.'

'Oh God, Rhodri, what if she's awful? She could be a criminal or, oh, and this would be worse, on some reality TV show, anything—for all I know.'

'Isabel, stop it. She won't be.'

'How do you know?' Isabel paused in her pacing.

'Because she had you.'

Isabel looked at him, and for a moment she thought he might lean forward and pull her toward him, but he didn't. Instead, he stood up and said, 'Come on. Let's head back. It's getting late, and I want to get up early. The end is in sight for the painting I've been working on.'

Isabel felt vaguely disappointed as she followed his lead back to Pier View House.

Chapter 43

'Morning, Constance, how are you today?'

'I'm perfectly fine, Isabel.'

'I bought you a Wagon Wheel and a packet of Maltesers.' Isabel handed her the paper bag and sat down opposite her at her table in the tranquil Oceania lounge. 'You don't happen to know off hand of something that's helpful for varicose veins, do you? Brenda's bunions are better, but her veins are playing up now.'

'Two teaspoons of apple cider vinegar diluted in water sipped twice a day will help. As will soaking a cloth in witch hazel. If she applies the cloth to the affected veins several times a day, it will help ease them so long as she keeps it up. It can take a month or two to feel the benefits from it. How's your little skin complaint these days? I haven't noticed you scratching of late.'

She was a marvel, Isabel thought, storing the information away. 'I shall pass it on, thanks, and my eczema has cleared up with the horsetail tea and honey treatment. Touch wood—' she tapped the table. 'I haven't had a flare-up since.' The scene outside today was a moody mix of greys, Isabel saw, turning her gaze to the picture window and watching what looked like fine rain beginning to drift in from the sea. 'I hope that wind doesn't get up. Mum's coming over this afternoon, and she can go a bit green around the gills on boats at the best of times. I'll bring her to see you, shall I?'

'That would be nice. Is she bringing my little friend?'

'I bloody hope not.'

'Oh, Isabel, he's a lovely little chap.'

'You wouldn't say that if it was your leg he took a shine to on a regular basis.'

Constance's mouth twitched, and she took a bite of her biscuit eyeing Isabel speculatively for a moment. 'I have a proposition of sorts for you.'

'Oh, yes.' Isabel raised an eyebrow.

'Pour yourself a cup of tea first.'

That Walter fellow was right, Isabel thought, spying him across the room. He was reclining on a two-seater with a book, looking like an old-time movie star and she gave him a wave. Constance *was* dramatic. She'd have done well in the theatre biz.

'Don't encourage him.'

'Why not? I think he's very dashing.'

Constance flushed beneath her powdered cheeks. 'Just pour your tea and stop fraternising with the menfolk young lady.'

Isabel grinned and did as she was told. Stirring the milk in she said, 'Right, what's this proposition of yours then?'

'I want you to have Molly's journal.'

Isabel gasped and nearly dropped her teacup. She hadn't expected that.

'I want you to cherish it as I have, Isabel, and to look after it—keep it safe. When the time comes as it has for me, I want you to find the right person to pass it on to. You'll know who, just like I do.'

'Wow, thank you, Constance, I'm honoured,' Isabel breathed, but Constance held her hand up.

'My passing on her journal to you comes with a condition. There's something I want you to do.'

'What's that then?'

'Isabel Stark, you have a gift, and it's time you acknowledged it. You need to stop being frightened of trying to become the best you can be. Life, my dear is too short for procrastination. Take that from someone who has reached the other end and knows. With that said, I want you to look into taking your interest in natural healing further—get a qualification. The days of being self-taught like I was, with a little help from Molly, of course, are long since gone.'

Isabel put her teacup back on the saucer. 'Have you been talking to Delwyn?'

Constance had the grace to look a little sheepish. 'I have, and we both agree. You're one of us, Isabel, that rare breed of woman who has been put on this earth to help heal others.'

Isabel thought about it; she liked that analogy. She was a healer. Yes, she liked it a lot. She couldn't stop the grin that had spread across her face.

'Constance, I haven't told anyone else yet. I was waiting until my place was confirmed, but I've put my name down to begin studying for a diploma in naturopathy through the College of Natural Medicine in London.'

Constance looked delighted as she took a bite of her biscuit. 'Good for you, Isabel, good for you. That calls for a Malteser, my dear. Go on. Open the bag and help yourself.'

Isabel did so, and when she'd finished munching on the chocolate ball, she said, 'And now, Constance Downer, it's my turn. I have a proposition for you.'

Constance raised an eyebrow.

'I want us to sit down together and write to Teddy.'

She put the serviette down with more force than was necessary and one or two of the residents glanced over curiously. 'No.'

'But Constance—'

'Isabel, think about it, for goodness sake.' Her tone was clipped. 'He might have no idea he is adopted; the shock would be terrible. And I would never burden him with the knowledge of what Ginny did.'

Isabel would not be beaten. 'Yours and Henry's love story deserves to be told and what if he does know he's adopted? What if Ginny told him, or what if he's always known? You don't know—you have no idea what his situation is. Ginny wanted to come back to the island. She was obviously trying to right her wrongs, and perhaps that involved telling Teddy the truth. Or at least a version of the truth. He might have no inkling of where to find you or even how to go about it. Or, worse he may think you don't want to meet him.'

Constance pursed her lips with an expression Isabel had come to recognise as meaning she was mulling over what she'd just said.

'We could broach it with Father Christopher; you know the priest who took Ginny's funeral service. He was good friends with her. He might act as an intermediary and contact Teddy for you to see how the land lies. We can ask him not to mention that Ginny broke her word to you and your family.'

Constance remained silent.

Isabel leaned forward in her seat; she was not letting this go. 'Constance, you just sat there and told me I had to stop being frightened, and how short life is. Well, now it's my turn to say the same thing to you.'

Constance eyed her speculatively for a minute longer before dipping her head. It was as close as Isabel was going to get to a go ahead and having come prepared, she retrieved her laptop from her bag.

Father Christopher's email wasn't hard to find and half an hour later, having laid out all that had happened since she had met him at the funeral, Isabel clicked send. 'It will be about ten pm in New Zealand, Constance, so we may not hear back from him until tomorrow.' She leaned back in her chair, hoping for both their sakes that Father Christopher would not leave them hanging.

~

Isabel whiled away a pleasant afternoon with her mum who had brought Prince Charles with her; he was ecstatic to see Isabel. Once she'd got him off her leg, it had been on the tip of her tongue to ask her mum about her birth records. The words had dried in her throat though as her mum waffled on about the latest outfit the Duchess of Cambridge had worn to some function or other. What if it spoiled a lovely afternoon? She decided she'd wait until she had both parents together. Instead, mother, daughter, and dog did the rounds calling in on Rhodri first. As they left him to tend to a customer, Isabel hissed in her mum's ear, 'If you call him a dreamboat one more time, Mother, I will not be responsible for my actions.'

Babs was not in the least bit contrite, 'I tell you what, Izzy, if I were thirty years younger, I wouldn't be messing about the way you are.'

'Don't be disgusting, Mum,' Isabel shot back before suggesting that as the weather seemed to have decided to turn it on, they should pick up a spot of lunch and picnic in the lovely gardens at Sea Vistas with Constance.

Constance, Isabel could see as her mum admired the fresh blooms on display in Sea Vistas gardens, was glad of the distraction they provided. She couldn't blame her; time always crawled by when you were waiting for news. Especially news the like of which Constance was waiting for. She'd been waiting over seventy years for it! Once their picnic was finished, Isabel decided to commandeer the wheelchair, and so it was a foursome who made their way up Union Street to see Delwyn.

Isabel left her mum and Constance chatting with Delwyn while Prince Charles, for once sat obediently at Babs' feet. She scanned the shelves for witch hazel, grabbed a packet of turmeric, and picked up another bottle of her trusty apple cider vinegar. Delwyn suggested it might be time they got going when Prince Charles tethered, outside the shop, lifted his head and began to howl like some wolf-come-corgi-beast scaring several potential customers away.

Their last port of call for the afternoon was Brenda who took the items Isabel had purchased from her gratefully before hobbling off to sort them out with a jug of lemonade to enjoy in the sunshine.

The reply from Father Christopher came through not long after Isabel and Constance waved Babs and Prince Charles off on the ferry. They'd begun making their way back to Sea Vistas when Isabel heard her phone ping the arrival of an email. She veered out of the way of the foot traffic, parking herself and Constance on a bench seat near the folly. 'It's from him, Constance,' she said, and Constance promptly squeezed her eyes shut as though to soften any blows his message might contain.

Chapter 44

Dear Isabel and Constance,

I have to admit I have been left somewhat stunned by your message and I don't know where to begin. In which case I shall just get on with it. I mentioned when we met, Isabel, that it had been obvious to me that Ginny had something on her mind before she died. Well, now we know what that something was and her reasons for wanting to return to the Isle of Wight.

She never confided in me that Teddy was adopted by both his parents and I am so sorry the circumstances of his initial adoption by Ginny played out so very differently than they were supposed to. There are no words for the years you must have spent wondering about your son and what happened to him, Constance. I can only hope that you take a little comfort from my telling you that when I met Teddy at Ginny's funeral, I was struck by what a fine man he was. He dotes on his family, which I also previously mentioned to Isabel was a source of consternation to Ginny given the considerable age gap between Teddy and his wife. But I say good for him!

I have written to Teddy broaching the subject of his having been adopted by his mother as well as his father as delicately as I could as I can shine no light on whether he is aware of this or not. I have, of course, not breathed a word about Ginny not keeping her word to you and your family. I agree that there are some truths one need never know. Accordingly, I have given him your email address, Isabel, and I have left the proverbial ball in his court as to whether he wishes to make contact.

I would dearly love to hear if things work out the way you would like them to, Constance, and if they don't, then God will forgive Ginny as you have. You are, I sense, a very special woman who your son would be proud of; I hope he grasps this opportunity to get to know you with both hands and then some!

I wish you only the best for the future. God bless.

Yours faithfully

Father Christopher Joyce

Isabel looked at Constance, and she saw hope written across her face. Two days later an email arrived from Teddy.

Dear Constance

My name is Edward Havelock or Teddy as I am known, and I believe you are my birth mother. The news from Father Christopher that I am adopted did not come as a total bolt from the blue. I was always inquisitive as a child, and it was while searching for my birthday present the year I was turning ten and thus hoping to find my parents had indeed bought me a bike that I came across a box. It was tucked away on a shelf in the garage, and I knew it was something special because it had been covered in beautiful yellow wrapping paper. Inside the box was a knitted blanket, baby jacket, and booties. As you already know that's not all that was in the box; there was a letter from you to me, which I took and have carried with me ever since.

I don't know if Mum knew I'd found the box, but if she did, we never spoke of it. I thought about broaching my adoption with her many times over the years, but there was something in the way Mum was that shut down that conversation. It was a neediness that didn't allow for me to rock the boat. She had a tough veneer, but there was a fragility about her too like she'd break if I pushed her too far. I have thought about you often too over the years and concluded that you would have moved on in your life and again there was that fear of rocking the boat and the unknown. What if you had another family, what if they didn't know about me? Far too many what ifs I fear.

Constance, I'm so very pleased you've reached out, and I would like nothing more than to come and see you. I think we have waited long enough, and I hope this is not presumptuous of me, but I have booked my flight to London for the end of the month. I shall be in touch before then with the date and time of my arrival on the island.

Love

Teddy

'Love Teddy,' Constance murmured wondrously. 'Imagine that.'

~

Later that night, Isabel lay in bed staring at the ceiling. Her mind was buzzing with the news that Teddy was to come to the island to meet Constance and that she'd been instrumental in it. Outside she could hear the wind whistling across the rooftops, and her tummy grumbled sounding obscenely loud in the darkened room. She sighed and rolled on to her side to check the time. It was nearly midnight, perhaps a bit of a midnight feast was in order. She happened to know there was leftover lasagne in the fridge. With the thought of mince and cheesy loveliness firmly on her mind, she knew there was going to be no getting to sleep, and she got up.

The stairs creaked as she descended them, despite her attempt to be as quiet as a mouse, making her wince with each step. She paused for a moment, but there were no sounds other than her own, and so she carried on to the landing, catching her toe on the doorframe and swearing softly under her breath. She did not want Rhodri to bust her with her head in the fridge at this hour of the night. It wouldn't be a good look. It was then she saw the light was on downstairs in the gallery. Surely he wasn't working this late? She'd pop her head around the door and see what he was up to.

She carried on down the stairs and pushing the door open wider she saw that the gallery was deserted. He must've been working on his painting until late, and left the light on by mistake, she decided. She was about to flick it off when she spied Rhodri's easel. He'd covered his work in progress with a sheet. He'd been very secretive about what it was he was working on, and the temptation to take a peek was strong. Her fingers were twitching, and she couldn't help herself, so carefully lifting a corner of the sheet and holding it aloft she stood back prepared to admire his work in progress.

She stared at the canvas not quite sure what she was seeing. The precise brush strokes depicted a bustling pier scene with a woman gazing out to the Solent at the fore. The background activity seemed to fade so that it was the woman who held your attention. She wore a rather dreamy, faraway expression, her blue hair whipping about her face, and there was something about the lines of her body that gave the illusion of a bedraggled mermaid. Isabel inhaled and chewed her bottom lip as the realisation sunk in. The painting was of her. An inscription in the corner of the artwork read, *The Mermaid*.

She stood for an age staring at the canvas, and slowly her mouth curved into a smile.

Chapter 45

One Month Later

Isabel's voice soared alongside the rest of the Angels of Wight Acapella. The All Saints Church hall was almost standing room only, and her eyes took in all the people who'd crowded in to see them perform. She saw the enraptured looks on the audience's faces and felt proud, not just of herself but the rest of the group too. They were brilliant, these girls, and she was so enjoying their regular Monday night get together as she got to know them all.

She scanned the rows of seats down the middle of the hall until she found who she sought, her mum and dad. Her dad, bless him, was on crutches, having sprained his ankle at football practice. Mum had informed her they were in serious talks about salsa. The dance lessons would be better for his health, and she thought that he might be coming around to her way of thinking given she'd added a bit of a sweetener. 'I told him if he comes with me to salsa classes, I'll forfeit my week in Benidorm so he can get himself a Premier League season pass.' Isabel shuddered at the thought of her parents getting hot and sweaty together as they attempted to learn the Latin American dance moves.

She'd finally mustered up the courage to tell them both that she'd like to try to find her birth mother on a visit home a couple of weeks ago. 'Mum, Dad, you know this doesn't change the way I feel about you. I'm curious that's all. I mean what if I have kids of my own one day and they want to know more about their biological background? Or, what if there's something medically I should know about?' They were all thoughts that had occurred to her since she'd made her mind up to try to find out more about where she came from.

Both parents had gone very quiet; this was so unusual that Isabel was assailed with guilt as she saw the flash of hurt and shock in her mum's eye. 'Mum, you'll always be my mother, nothing and no one will ever change that.'

Then, Babs and Gaz had begun talking quickly as though they'd practiced their reaction to this moment. Babs had opened the desk where she kept all their official bits and bobs to retrieve a manila folder. Inside it was a sheaf of documents including her original birth certificate. Isabel stared at the name on it feeling a sense of déja vu from her afternoon at Quarr with Constance.

Her birth mother's name was Veronica Kelly. It was a perfectly respectable name, she thought wondering what she looked like. Would she have the same slight bump that Isabel had in her nose? Maybe she'd gotten the dimple in her cheek from her. What was she like? Did she have a sense of humour? Was she overly sensitive or was she bold and brash? Questions flooded her brain, and she realised they'd always been there; she'd just chosen not to ask them until now.

It was later that her dad had taken her aside and with a rare show of insight explained to her that she needed to think about things from Babs' perspective. Of course she felt threatened. It was natural, but she'd get over it. It had come as a shock that was all, and she'd just need a bit of time. 'We never even think about you being adopted, Izzy,' he'd added. 'You've always been ours, and that's the end of it. But I can understand your curiosity. I'm surprised you've waited this long to be honest.' He gave her a clumsy hug. 'I hope you find what you are looking for.'

'I don't know what I'm looking for, Dad. I just know I need to look.'

She took the folder back to the island with her and put it in the drawer where she kept Molly's journal. She was almost ready to take the next step and contact the adoption agency, but not just yet.

Now, she almost lost her place in the song as she spied Edward sitting with his arm linked through Constance's. It warmed her heart to see them together. They fitted like the last two pieces of a jigsaw puzzle, and not just because he'd owned up to having an extensive collection of shoes and a love of flamboyant colour when it came to his choice of tie, today's being an unusual shade of lime green. Isabel was on the fence about that one; it made her think of the boxes of lolly ices her mum used to buy in summer.

The lime ones had always been the last ones left. It was interesting watching them together because certain mannerisms and expressions were the same. The look Isabel likened to a gin-soaked prune when they didn't approve of something being one of them! It was uncanny given they'd never met before. Mostly though, the similarity between them was in the certain glint they both had in their eyes—the glint that hinted at a propensity for naughtiness. It was that glint that had struck Isabel when she first met Constance and had been struck by the uncanny sensation of having met her somewhere before. She hadn't met Constance, but she had unknowingly met her son.

It was hard to catch up on a lifetime in a few short weeks, but they were doing their level best. Next time he came, he promised he would bring Olga and Tatiana with him.

The Angels of Wight voices ebbed away to silence at a mournful howling that drifted through the slightly ajar main doors and down the centre aisle. It was loud enough to ensure that all those in the pews either side were aware of the anguished corgi tethered to the railing at the entrance. His one true love so near and yet so far. Isabel shook her head; that bloody dog.

On Constance's other side, Walter was sitting with a proprietary expression on his debonair features. It was a wondrous thing, but it seemed he and Constance had begun courting. The last few times Isabel had called to Sea Vistas it had been hard to get a word in between the two of them! She was going to have to get used to sharing her friend.

The applause as their song reached its conclusion overwhelmed the sound of Prince Charles' whining, echoing and bouncing around the acoustically perfect hall. Isabel's gaze sought Rhodri and locating him three rows from the front, her smile was wide. He gave her the thumbs up and mouthed, 'You were great.'

They'd had their first official date three weeks ago; he'd taken her to the movies, and it was the strangest thing, but she couldn't tell you what they'd gone to see. She couldn't recall the plot either, but she could recall feeling giddy like a teenager when his arm had slid around the back of the chair and dropped down onto her shoulder. She'd nearly spilled her popcorn everywhere at the thrill of it all, and after that, she might as well have been sitting watching a blank screen. He kissed her on the way home as they strolled along the Esplanade listening to the song of the sea and it had been, well it was, perfect.

The only blip on the horizon was that she'd be leaving soon, heading to London to begin her course. She'd opted to study full-time, not wanting to waste any more time in getting to where she'd decided she wanted to be. There were weekends though; he would come to her, she would come to him. They'd work it out, baby steps built on trust, day by day.

They were meeting up with Delwyn and Nico at the Rum Den later for a birthday drink and she'd heard Brenda mention something about a cake. She had the night off because it wasn't every day one's new boyfriend turned thirty!

The audience rose and began to edge their way out through the doors to the waiting sunshine. Isabel stepped down from the podium and felt Alice nudge her as Rhodri angled his way toward the stage. She took his outstretched hand and directed him toward the door at the back of the stage. She pushed it open, and they stepped outside to the gravelly car parking area. It was deserted, the audience still milling about discussing the performance at the front of the church.

Isabel felt the late morning rays of sunlight warming her face as Rhodri, making the most of them being alone, turned her toward him. He placed his hands on her hips and drew her close. She raised her face, and as his lips settled on hers, she knew she was home.

Sometime in the not too distant future...

There was a blast of cool air from the street outside as the door to The Natural Way jangled open. Isabel's coursework lay scattered across the counter. It was a bank holiday weekend, and she was home from London making the most of the three-day break. Delwyn had asked her to mind the shop for a couple of hours while she went to an exhibition with Nico. She didn't mind manning the fort at The Natural Way; it was good experience, and besides, Rhodri would be busy in the gallery for the best part of the day. He'd suggested going out for a drink later, and it would have been nice to pop in on Brenda and her son, Russell, who'd moved back to the island to help out his 'old mum' as he called her. Isabel didn't want to go out tonight though, maybe tomorrow. Tonight she wanted Rhodri all to herself. She'd told him she wanted to do nothing more than devour his home cooking and snuggle up on the couch with him. 'Nothing more?' he'd asked with a gleam in his eye.

Now, she swept the papers into a tidy pile before looking up and smiling. 'Good morning.' She received a greeting by return from the tall, rangy customer who looked to be in his sixties; he was a George Clooney type or would be if George Clooney had sandy, reddish hair. Either way, he was one of those men who would continue to improve with the signs of age, she mused idly, like her Rhodri. She watched as he scanned the shelves.

'Is there anything, in particular, you're after, sir?'

'I need something to help with jet lag.'

'Oh, you're Canadian. Is that where you've flown from?'

'Yes, sure is and well done. Most people I've met so far assume I'm American.' He smiled broadly. 'I arrived in London a couple of days ago and pretty much headed straight here. I woke up this morning feeling like I'd been hit by a bus.'

Isabel walked over to the relevant shelf. 'Yes, it can take a few days to catch up on you. Valerian is good for helping you sleep while your body adjusts to the different time zone and we have a homeopathic option with wild chamomile, which will be helpful.'

He took the suggestions she was holding out from her.

'Are you enjoying your holiday so far apart from the jet lag?'

'I've only been on the island since yesterday, but from what I've seen so far it's a beautiful place. I'm not here on a holiday though, it's more a pilgrimage of sorts.'

'Oh?' Isabel was intrigued.

'My uncle died here in World War Two. I promised my grandmother before she died that I'd come here and see for myself where he spent his final days. Let him know we never stopped thinking about him.'

The hairs on Isabel's arms stood up. 'What was your uncle's name, if you don't mind my asking?'

He looked bemused, 'Henry, Henry Johnson. Why?'

Isabel's mouth dropped open.

'Are you all right?'

'I think so. It's a bit of a shock that's all. You see, you're not going to believe this but—'

The End

Isabel's story continues in The Dancer, read on for more information

If you enjoyed The Promise then taking the time to say so by leaving a review would be wonderful. A book review is the best present you can give an author. The sequel to The Promise, The Dancer which continues Isabel's story is available now through Amazon.

https://books2read.com/u/bOoBo0

. . ⚜ . .

Continue Isabel's story in The Dancer

A FATEFUL CHOICE. A staggering discovery. Is closure and healing finally within her grasp?

Former dancer Veronica Stanley feels trapped in a midlife crisis. Still mourning the baby given up for adoption, she struggles to forgive herself for that long-ago decision. But when her ill mother shares a shocking secret, the choices she made and the underlying reasons behind them become heartbreakingly clear.

Searching for answers to help ease the pain, Veronica uncovers family history that casts everything in a fresh light. But one more earth-shattering revelation is about to arrive in the post...

Can Veronica make peace with the past and embrace a fulfilling future?

The Dancer is a heartwarming women's fiction novel. If you like engaging characters, complex dynamics, and hopeful journeys, then you'll love Michelle Vernal's beautiful story.

Buy *The Dancer* to leap into new beginnings today!

If you'd like to hear about Michelle's new releases you can subscribe to her Newsletter via her website: www.michellevernalbooks.com[1]

• • ◦ఴ◦ • •

Come and Stay at O'Mara's
O'Mara's–The Guesthouse on the Green, Book 1

A JILTED BRIDE TO BE, a woman with a secret past and a pesky red fox...

Take a break you'll never forget at O'Mara's Manor House—the Georgian Guesthouse in the heart of Dublin's Fair City. Its cozy and elegant setting is where you'll fall in love with a cast of characters who'll stay with you long after you finish the book. Oh, and a full Irish breakfast is included.

If Aisling O'Mara hadn't winged her way home to the Emerald Isle to take over the running of the family guesthouse, she'd never have met Finn, and her heart wouldn't have been broken. She's been trying to put her life back together since he left, but now he's back and says he's sorry. Can she trust him again?

Una Brennan's booked into the guesthouse she used to walk past each morning when she was a girl full of hopes and dreams for her happy ever after. She left Dublin more than fifty years ago vowing she'd never set foot in the city again. Why did she leave and what's brought her back?

Meanwhile, the little red fox who raids the bins outside O'Mara's basement kitchen door at night would like to know why the woman in Room 1, cries herself to sleep each night.

Witty, sad, and insightful with a touch of romance. Come and stay at O'Mara's.

---

1.   http://www.michellevernalbooks.com

Made in the USA
Coppell, TX
14 September 2020

37727878R00173